# The German Messenger

## M. J. Hollows

ONE PLACE. MANY STORIES

HQ
An imprint of HarperCollins *Publishers* Ltd

M. J. Hollows asserts the moral right to be identified as the author of this work. A catalogue record for this book is available from the British Library.

PB ISBN: 9780008530419
TPB ISBN: 9780008537029

MIX
Paper | Supporting responsible forestry
FSC™ C007454

This book is produced from independently certified FSC™ paper to ensure responsible forest management.

For more information visit: www.harpercollins.co.uk/green

This book is set in 10.5/15.5 pt. Minion by Type-it AS, Norway

Printed and Bound in the UK using 100% Renewable Electricity at CPI Group (UK) Ltd, Croydon, CR0 4YY

'Absolutely heart breaking. Absolutely brilliant. Absolutely
… e by – you're going
… iewer. 5 stars

'Absolutely wonderful book, can't recommend
it enough!' Goodreads reviewer, 5 stars

'Absolutely fantastic.' Goodreads reviewer, 5 stars

'The further I got into the story, the more I wanted to read
and the quicker the pages turned. At one point, the pages
were turning that quickly that it was almost as if they
were turning themselves.' Goodreads reviewer, 5 stars

'A wonderful book… I really enjoyed this
story.' Goodreads reviewer, 5 stars

'Will make you cry (I did!)… Incredibly well crafted
with well-rounded characters. Heart wrenching and
thought-provoking, this is definitely not to be missed by
historical fiction fans.' Goodreads reviewer, 5 stars

**M. J. Hollows** was born in London in 1986, and moved to Liverpool in 2010 to lecture in Audio Engineering. With a keen interest in history, music, and science, he has told stories since he was little. *Goodbye for Now*, published in October 2018, was his first novel, which he started as part of his MA in Writing from Liverpool John Moores University, graduating in 2015. *The German Nurse*, his second historical novel, was a top ten Globe & Mail bestseller. He is currently researching towards a PhD in Creative Writing, working on his next novel.

🐦 @MikeHollows
www.michaelhollows.com

### Also by M. J. Hollows

*Goodbye For Now*
*The German Nurse*

*To all the friends who helped through lockdowns.*
*You know who you are.*

# Prologue

George almost tripped over an uneven cobblestone as he crossed Park Lane on his way home. His mum would say that he was always tripping over and his dad would scold him for being so clumsy, but at least this time he had managed to right himself. They would have had a laugh about it afterwards, smiling because his knobbly knees resembled the rough red brick of the house they lived in. At times his parents had to replace his trousers quicker than he grew out of them, which for a boy of his age was unusual. His friends had grown up faster and towered over him, which was strange because his dad was a tall man, and his mother was tall for a woman.

He jumped at the clattering of a tram as it passed on Church Street, shortly followed by another going the other way. He had almost forgotten how different it was to the countryside where he had been staying. Everything here was a lot tighter packed, the rows of terraced houses, the streets. He had missed it all.

He was looking forward to seeing his parents' smiles again. It had been far too long since he had seen them, although he had no idea whether his father was still out serving with the other sailors or not. The Cartwrights had told him that it was some kind of fake or phoney war and that the Germans weren't coming, but he didn't really understand what they meant. It had given him hope that his dad would be at home for once. He wanted to see his great-grandad, his friends. It put a spring in his step as he passed some dockers heading the other way. They ignored him, but a small group of women pushing prams eyed him warily as he passed. He had liked being out in the countryside, but he didn't want to live there. It was too quiet, and nothing ever happened. Not like here at home where there were always shop workers around to watch. And it was obvious that the Cartwrights didn't like him being there.

He hadn't thought he would be able to make it home, not when that platform guard had questioned what he was doing there, with his suitcase. There were no other children around and the Cartwrights had told him not to answer any questions or speak to strangers if they spoke to him. But the guard wouldn't let him board the train and held a meaty palm in front of George blocking his way. So he'd had to lie, his parents wouldn't be happy that he had told anything but the truth, but they didn't need to know. They would just be happy to see him. He had overheard Mr and Mrs Cartwright arguing about him one evening, and knew exactly what he had to do. He had told them he wanted to go home and that he had saved up his pocket money for the train fare. They agreed that he would be better with his family, rather than with them, but had said that the evacuation billeting committee wouldn't allow him to return home without permission from his parents.

'My mum and dad want me to be with them,' he had said and waved a letter under the guard's nose. The guard looked down at him and a frown crossed his brow as he perused the letter. The Cartwrights had written it, pretending that it was from his parents, and he had copied his father's signature for them.

'Hmmm,' the guard had mumbled, his eyes darting across the page. 'Haven't had anything like this before. You're better off here, son. And travelling on your own too.'

The guard's deep brown eyes had stared into George's, reminding him of his father when he was angry with him, and George's heart thumped in his chest.

'Very well then. Ticket please.'

George was so relieved that he had dropped his ticket on the platform. But after that the journey had been uneventful, apart from the enquiring glances towards where he sat on his own, his suitcase held tightly on his lap. He had never been happier to see Lime Street station, filled with steam from the engines. There was nothing like it in the countryside. Liverpool was darker than George remembered, but that was all right. He was going home, and that was all that mattered right now. He was glad to be back. He hadn't liked the other place; it was strange and smelt funny, like too much earth, a massive farmhouse in the middle of nowhere. A motorcar drove past and he relished the smell of the engine, its oil, its life. He had missed the smells of Liverpool and his home, his mother. He didn't know whether she would be glad to see him, or whether she would be angry that he had returned without asking her. The darkness and that thought made him tense. He had never walked from the station to his home in the evening before, but he wasn't far now, he was passing houses he had seen hundreds of times. Every one of them looked the same and it was comforting. He turned a corner and onto the main road that led to his home.

He heard the sound of other children playing, calling to each other in hushed voices. Before he could see them a palm pushed him firmly in the chest, and forced him back the way he had come. His suitcase landed where he dropped it and one of the clasps clattered loose. The boy who had pushed him was a head taller than George and broader, and the shove had winded him for a moment. George didn't have time to catch his breath before another shove, this time

3

from behind, propelled him forward and he fell to his knees. It wasn't the first time in his short life that he had ended up on the ground in a scuffle, but something about this hurt more than the last time. He had been excited about coming home, and he hadn't expected to be treated like this. It was not like any home he remembered, but at least he was no longer in the boring countryside.

He rolled over onto his bottom and looked at his knees. Bright red scrapes poked through the fabric of his trousers. The Cartwrights wouldn't be happy with him messing up the nice new trousers they had given him, but then he hoped never to see them again. They weren't his family, that was why he hadn't been able to stay there. No matter how much they tried to get him to fit their way of life, their ideals, he couldn't. They couldn't take him away from Liverpool, it was his home. He belonged here.

'Look at him,' they said, laughing. 'Sat on his arse like some kind of politician.'

'He looks like a politician,' one of the others joined in. 'With them fancy clothes.'

They pinned his arms down by his sides. He was trapped, and they were never going to let him go. Not until they had stripped all his clothing and belongings from him. Not that he had much, but that hadn't stopped them so far. They didn't know him, they didn't want to know him. Even if these boys had once been his neighbours, they no longer recognised each other.

'Where's his money? Share the wealth.' They all spoke over one another, describing what they would do to him if he didn't give up what he had to them. He didn't understand what some of the words meant, but he understood enough to know that they meant to do him harm.

'I'm one of you,' was all he could think to say. He didn't know what else would make them listen, make them leave him alone. Not for the first time he wished he was older than he was; then he would have the words to talk to them, make them understand, make them leave him alone. He pushed back the tears, that wouldn't help matters. 'Please. I don't have any money. You could have it if I did.'

'Ow!' one of the boys called out as a shadow grabbed his shoulder from behind and pulled him backwards. The others turned to shout at this newcomer, raising their fists, but the words died on their lips as they saw it was an adult.

'Get away, will you?!' The man pulled the biggest boy away from George and waved an arm at him as he took flight. The boy tripped over the edge of the paving and scowled back in their direction, before picking himself up and running as fast as he could. The other boys didn't stay long once their ringleader had fled. George knew that wouldn't be the last he saw of them, but for now he had been saved.

The man chased them a few steps, kicking out at one of them, but he didn't connect and let them go. He walked back to where George lay sprawled and bruised on the ground. Placing two big strong hands under George's armpits he forcibly pulled him up. George's feet touched the pavement and the man held him there for a moment to make sure that he didn't fall over again. George couldn't tell from the man's dark eyes whether he was concerned or annoyed. Up close the man had a distinct smell, but George didn't know what it was.

'There you are,' he said with an accent George didn't recognise. It wasn't like that of any of the people he knew in Liverpool, and it wasn't like the Cartwrights' either. Though it was closer to their Welsh lilt.

'Thank you,' George replied, remembering his manners as the

man brushed his clothes down for him, the force almost pushing him from his feet again. His hands lingered on the torn fabric and he tutted.

Ignoring his bruises, all George could think was who was this strange man and what did he want? George had never seen him before he had come to the rescue. And why had the boys turned on him, when he had just been minding his own business? Why was the man hanging around looking out for kids fighting? There were always kids playing and fighting around here, it was nothing new. He looked the man up and down. There was nothing unique about him, but at least he smiled a friendly smile. George wanted to say more, ask those questions, but his voice stuck in his throat.

'I should go home,' he muttered under his breath.

'Nice to meet you, George,' the man said, but George couldn't remember telling him his name. He must have said something in the middle of all the confusion, maybe one of the other boys had called him by his name. The stranger handed him his suitcase, the battered clip barely holding on, and George noticed the name label there, flapping in the wind. That must have been how the man had known, but still George was uncertain about something.

'Be seeing you,' the stranger said, touching his fingers to the brim of his hat before heading off in the direction he had come. George watched him go, wondering whether he would see the man again. He would have to tell his mum what had happened when he got home, but then he decided not to tell her about the strange man. That story would only worry her more. If he had been older he would have said he felt like he was being watched, but he just wanted to be home now, safe in his mother's embrace.

# 1940 – BEFORE THE FLAMES

## AUGUST

# Chapter 1

**Saturday, 17 August 1940**

Ruth moved a plate to the draining board. It slipped and clattered, falling to the side, too wet to sit neatly against another. She closed her eyes, leaning against the worktop, and took a deep breath. Picking up the plate she checked it for cracks, but the only marks were the faint black stains of wear that had been there since she'd inherited it. They were only just visible in the flickering candlelight. At least she hadn't broken something more expensive.

There may be less work for her to do around the house while she was on her own, but there was also less help. Still, she could always do the housework later. Who was around to even notice? Her family never came anymore, not since Peter had gone. She spun her wedding ring around her finger with her thumb while she thought. He had more family in the city than she did, and her own family thought that he was the best thing that had ever happened to her. Their behaviour showed exactly what they thought of her. *Deeds not words*. Principles were something a woman shouldn't have, according to her parents. If they could see her now they would simply tut and say, 'I told you so.' Oh well, she would show them.

She finished and dried her hands on a tatty towel that she then threw down on the worktop. Even with the sounds of her neighbours drifting through the adjoining wall, the house could be lonely at times. The faint murmur from next door made it feel as if it was haunted, the ghosts of past lives and stories lived permeating the very brick. Sometimes she wondered whether she was imagining it. Sometimes the echo seemed to come from all around her, even from the back of the house, which she now looked out onto. Their house was one of the usual terraced houses that lined the hills of the city. She had been told they were built around the turn of the century to house the influx of workers into Liverpool's growing docks. Those were the sorts of stories that were passed down the generations, the kind she was fascinated by but her family had no interest in.

She tried to fill her days with stories and noise, but it wasn't always easy. Her work gave her some opportunity, but she didn't have free rein over her time. Her editor had other ideas.

The kitchen door creaked open behind her and she froze. She was sure that she had shut it and no one else was in the house. She didn't dare turn around.

She grabbed a battered rolling pin from the worktop, her knuckles whitening as she gripped it tighter. After what felt like hours, she gave in, fearing what she might see behind her. Her gaze landed on the door, then dropped to where a small boy, about nine or ten, stood looking, frozen, up at her. At first, she didn't recognise him. He was wearing a smart little brown suit and waistcoat that were far too clean for the streets of Liverpool. They did not belong to him and he looked uncomfortable, far from the dishevelled scamp she had last seen boarding a train at Lime Street station. The fact that the knees of his trousers were torn was not unusual.

'George?' she breathed. His features flickered in the glow of the candles. He looked nothing like the child she remembered: he looked posh. It was the only way she could describe it. It wasn't that her family was poor, but the clothes he was wearing were a step above anything they could afford. Gone were his drab brown clothes. He had been close to growing out of them anyway. Where had they evacuated him to, exactly? Some country house? The address she had didn't give her that kind of information and his letters had only mentioned the countryside. She had thought that he was safe, he wasn't supposed to be in the city. What on earth was he doing home?

'Hi, Mum,' George said and grinned.

Realisation dawned that she had imagined that it was Peter, but there was no way that was possible. She would have known straight away if Peter had walked into the house, she would have been able to feel him, the warmth of him, rather than the uneasiness she felt now. He was still out somewhere with the navy, though she didn't know where. He wasn't allowed to say when he wrote to her, but he had left clues the censors hadn't spotted in his letters. Written in a code only the two of them would understand. They had developed it when they were first stepping out, from their mutual fondness for word games.

Her mouth hung open and he just stared back at her, smiling that sweet smile of his. It melted her heart, as it always did. Some things never changed. He didn't move, just stood as if he too couldn't believe what was happening was real. He had grown in a few months and there was something in his manner that hadn't been there before. She wondered whether, wherever they had sent him, he had been trained to stand to attention, and she longed for him to run to her so she could wrap him in her arms and keep him safe. She couldn't move herself, lest the illusion was broken and she realised she was imagining his presence.

For the time being she took two steps forward and pulled him into her arms. He had grown an inch or so in the intervening time and it made it easier to sniff his hair. That scent had been missing from her life and she closed her eyes to breathe it in as a tear rolled down her cheek. There was no need for any words. She had expected him to pull away, but he nestled into her embrace.

Ruth had been given no warning that he was coming home. As far as she knew all the children were still evacuated to the countryside. She wanted to go down to the local Ministry of Health offices and ask what they thought they were playing at. The city was nowhere for them to be, especially the younger ones.

'Sweetheart, what are you doing here?'

Had he run away? If so, how on earth had he had enough money to make his way back to Liverpool? The train alone would have cost a fortune.

'They sent us home, Mummy. The other children too.' He beamed at her again, clearly expecting a different response to the one she had given. There was an uneasiness there that belied his years, and he was trying to make up for it by smiling at her. The time they had spent apart had been difficult. She pulled him close, all her questions forgotten for a moment. He smelt different, fresh, nothing like the city.

'They said the danger was over.' The more he spoke, the more familiar his voice became, as if he was remembering himself and his surroundings, becoming her son again.

'They did?' she asked. How could they say such a thing? The French had just surrendered to the Germans, and now they were only just the other side of the Channel. If they wanted to invade Britain only the Royal Navy was stopping them, and who knew how long they would last if the entire French military had failed to keep the Germans at bay. They were either stupid, or they just simply didn't care. The bombs would come soon. For a moment of panic she feared they'd somehow discovered her secret. 'Who said such a thing?'

'The family we were staying with. The Cartwrights.' Ruth couldn't help but notice the 'we' again. From George's letters, Ruth knew there were two other children staying with him. They must have been sent home too. 'They said if the Germans were coming they would have come by now, and not to worry.'

She could see what they meant, but knew it was untrue. From the sound of what George was saying they were merely trying to reassure the children, take away the fear they surely had for what was about to happen. What could she say? Now that he was at home, back in harm's way.

'I didn't like it there,' he continued, filling the silence. It was matter of fact, as if it was perfectly understandable that he shouldn't like the place and that was that. 'But that's not why they sent me home.'

She found her voice finally, the catch in her throat gone and the initial shock starting to wear off. 'What do you mean, they sent you home?'

'Nothing, Mummy. I didn't do nothing.' He paused, his brow furrowing. 'I mean I didn't do *anything*.'

He wouldn't have corrected himself like that before. The writer in her was proud that he was learning and breaking out of the local vernacular, but the mother side of her was sad that her son was growing and changing and that she hadn't been around to see it. How much had she missed while he was in the countryside? She shook herself. That wasn't the point. He shouldn't have been back in Liverpool; who knew how long the war would last? Not that she was old enough to have lived through it, but the last one had lasted four years. They were barely a year into this one.

'They were saying that we should come home where our parents can look after us properly. That they can't keep paying for us. They argued.'

There it was then. The family that were supposed to be taking care of him had decided Liverpool was safe, as if because the Germans hadn't yet attacked the city they never would. Some instinct told her it was only a matter of time before the Luftwaffe came. Somehow she would now have to keep her son safe. She would have a word with the authorities, see if she could get them to change their minds. Maybe if she pleaded with her family they would finally come to her aid, but she wasn't sure she could deal with their knowing, smug looks.

To hide her tears she pulled away, took his bag and dropped it on the kitchen table with a thump. They could unpack it later together. He was about to close the door behind him, something else he wouldn't have done a few months ago, when there was a sound from outside. At first it was like a low hum, the burr of something getting closer, then it burst into life.

The shrill cry of an air raid siren pierced Liverpool's evening silence. Ruth was alert as her body tensed. She supposed it had that effect on everyone, but there was something about its scream that terrified her. What had once been tranquil evening air was now shattered by the oncoming darkness. The siren's steady rising and falling was a stark warning to everyone in the city, a sign that danger was on its way. It had become so familiar that many of the city's residents no longer reacted to its warning. There had not been any bombs to follow it yet. It was as if they were numb to the danger, paralysed by its constant attention, the indiscriminate destruction. It wasn't that they no longer cared, Ruth thought, but that they were now resigned to it.

It had become a kind of ritual, a tradition. They were all used to the raids, although some still acted as if they were invulnerable. They'd had drills and she had been trained for this moment when she volunteered, but that didn't make her any calmer. Especially now that George had come home. This time it felt different, the steady drone of aircraft could already be heard in the distance. George was still, too. The smile had dropped from his lips and he stared into the middle distance. Ruth didn't have time to wonder where he had gone and what he was thinking.

*He isn't supposed to be here*, she thought again, unable to push away the sentiment. It wasn't that she wasn't glad to see him, but that he was supposed to be safe somewhere else, anywhere else. The city wasn't safe for children. It was one of the reasons she had decided to volunteer. Some other parents had decided to keep their children at home despite the advice of the War Office. She had decided she needed to do something to help them.

George flinched as the siren started another cycle. What was she going to do about him? She couldn't take him with her, and she couldn't leave him here on his own. Her family were too far away in the middle of an air raid, and she wasn't sure she could rely on them anyway. One of her neighbours would have to help her.

She grabbed his hand, still small in her grip, and led him to the front door. Her mind raced, forgetting what she was supposed to be doing. The street outside was dark and she could make out the shapes of people leaving their homes, some in groups, others on their own. The front yards looked as if they were joined as one now that the metal fences had been removed for the war effort.

Harriet was already leaving her home when Ruth stepped out onto the street, and if not for a shout she would have disappeared around the corner of their lane. Thankfully Harriet stopped in her tracks, then turned. She was a short and stocky woman. Her deep black curls looked as if they required plenty of upkeep and she was dressed as if she was going to church. Ruth had no idea how the woman always managed to look so prim and proper, especially in an emergency.

'What's wrong, Ruth?' Her eyes widened as she noticed George. Her gaze flickered back to look straight at Ruth. There were questions in Harriet's eyes, but she didn't ask them.

'Right,' Harriet said, without missing a beat. 'You're back. Of course. Of course. Georgie, come with your aunt Harriet. Now. Your mother's got things to do, so why don't you tell me all about your trip?'

She held out a hand and he tottered over to take it as Ruth uttered a silent word of thanks to her neighbour. Harriet was one of the few women she could count on, having had a number of her own children and being a complete natural when it came to George. He had taken to her well when he was only a toddler, and Harriet had been effectively an aunt to him. Harriet was one of those habitual mothers, and at times it made Ruth feel inadequate.

Ruth watched the two of them go, seeing her son leave again. It pulled at her in a way she couldn't explain. She couldn't believe it was happening again. She longed to follow them, but knew she couldn't. Forcing herself to turn away from her son, from the safety of the shelter, she stepped back into the house.

Inside, she tried to compose herself, organise her thoughts into something coherent. The air raid siren still screamed at her, but now it was at the back of her mind. Even without bombs, she had realised after the first few drills that rushing and panicking through the blackout only resulted in other injuries. No, she took her time, getting her voluntary service overalls from the cupboard where she stored them, stepping into each leg one after the other and buttoning up the heavy plastic buttons. It denoted her authority and her right to be about the city during a raid. It would allow her to go where she needed to go. She grabbed her gas mask.

She almost left, then hesitated, turning back to grab the notepad she always kept in her handbag. She didn't know whether she would need it tonight, but she always kept it on her. She stepped over the threshold again, heading out into the angry night.

# Chapter 2

The door shuddered as Anthony hammered on it with his fist. It rocked in its frame, a sign that he could force it open with only a little more effort. He hadn't come south of the city to the Dingle to break in. He was there to make sure people were safe. But it was far from the first door he had banged on and it wouldn't be the last. He adjusted his glasses and sighed before knocking again. It was his job to patrol this part of the city and make sure that people were following the rules, but it was a more difficult task than anyone had anticipated. Even now, months into the war, people acted is if everything was normal. The French had surrendered, the Germans were just across the Channel. And yet some didn't even bother to obey the blackout.

The door didn't open, his knocking went unanswered, but there were people at home. The electric lights were a giveaway. Either that or they had left their lights on by accident when they went to the shelter. He had dealt with too many people during the drills to believe anything other than the fact that they were either too stupid to realise the danger, or simply didn't care.

Anthony looked side to side along the road, wondering whether he should try to find a way around the back. Apart from this house the street was almost pitch black. He had become used to navigating the dark streets by moonlight, from memory. It was like he had a map of the city in his mind. He had an affinity for maps and detail, and he often wondered whether he should have been a detective. Any light that shouldn't have been left on was like a beacon to him, hurting his eyes with its brightness. If it stood out like this on the ground, he could only imagine how much of a guiding light it would be for the Luftwaffe. Even if it wasn't their intended target, it was an indication of something they could bomb, some damage they could cause. The German bombers weren't simply looking for military targets, they were looking to spread fear and doubt. And so far, without having even dropped a bomb, they were succeeding.

He banged on the door again, this time hard enough to graze his knuckles. He wasn't sure whether it was the incessant burr of the air raid siren, or the ignorance of whoever owned this house, but he was growing more frustrated by the second.

'Come on, come on. Open up,' he said through gritted teeth. Then louder again for emphasis, as if the occupant couldn't hear him through the door. Anthony raised his fist again just as the door clicked open, revealing a man a few years younger than himself.

The man was hopping from one leg to the other, pulling up his trousers. He looped a tattered leather belt around his waist with one hand, while he held the door handle with the other. A scar ran from his broken nose down his right cheek, and cold blue eyes looked straight into Anthony's.

'Yes?' he said as if Anthony was some kind of salesman. 'I'm in the middle of something. Whadda ya want? Can't it wait?'

Anthony tapped the ARP logo on his blue overalls, thinking that his visit really didn't need any explanation. 'Didn't you hear the siren?'

'All right, lad. What about it?' The man had thankfully finished buttoning up his trousers and was now staring at Anthony. 'What difference does one light make? It's just scaremongering. There hasn't been a bomb round here since this all started.'

Anthony couldn't believe he was hearing this argument again. It was always the same, as if this man was somehow exceptional, special in some way that meant he didn't have to pay attention to the rules. Almost as if the rules weren't in place to protect them, but to oppress them. He knew he was frowning. It was a look he usually reserved for his pupils, but he couldn't help himself. He sighed and tried to calm himself. This man would need a different approach. It was no good having a shouting match, screaming that there was a war on. The man would only listen to a reasoned argument if he would listen at all.

'I just need you to turn your lights out, sir. And get to a shelter.' It sounded weak. Maybe he wasn't cut out for being a warden after all. He was a better teacher, but he had wanted to do his bit, do whatever he could for the war effort, the only thing they would let him do. The thing that truly frustrated Anthony was how long each of these situations took. He only had a short time to get everyone to safety. This time he was sure the bombers were on their way. He couldn't put his finger on it, but it didn't feel like a drill. There was something in the air that told him this time the Germans were actually coming. It was as if the air was thick, pregnant with malice.

'Listen, just fuck off, lad. You're not wanted here.' The man didn't speak angrily. It was if he was speaking to a friend. He had no appreciation of Anthony's authority.

'You need to turn your bloody lights out, sir.' He almost spat the last word. Years of training and decorum down the drain. Who knew adults could be more difficult to deal with than children? 'Otherwise you may be responsible for deaths in the area.'

'What makes you think they're gonna come now, if they haven't already?'

'Do you want any deaths on your conscience, sir?'

'What makes us so special, eh? We're just minding our own business.'

Anthony didn't pause to collect his thoughts. 'I was just wondering the very same.' This time he dropped the 'sir'. He pushed a little closer to the threshold, bunching his shoulders to make use of his full build. He was taller and broader in stature. He could see the red in the man's bloodshot eyes, and realised for the first time that he had probably been drinking.

'What makes you think you're so bloody special?' Anthony asked. 'That the rules apply to everyone else and not you? Even the King, God save him, has to put his bloody lights out when he's told. So what makes you different? That you can swear at me, when I'm out here trying to protect you?'

'Look, lad. Just leave us alone, yeah? They're not gonna bomb us now, are they?' He moved to close the door, but Anthony put his boot in it. The leather squeezed around his foot, but the door stayed open and he was determined to not show the wince of pain.

'I don't care whether they bomb you or not,' he said. 'Not the way you're behaving, but if your negligence puts other people in danger then that's my concern.'

'Negligence? Fuck off. What are you talking about, negligence? I'm just going about my day.' He still held the door handle and Anthony wondered whether he was going to try to shut it again. He kept his foot where it was; let him just try.

'Put your lights out, or I'll put your lights out.' The man's jaw hung open. He had no idea whether Anthony would follow through or not, but the look on Anthony's face was probably enough to concern him. 'Come on, sir. We all have to follow the blackout. You don't want to lead them right to your house. If I can find it then so can the Luftwaffe.'

Anthony edged the door open and this time the man didn't resist. He bunched his fists by his side.

'Don't be fucking coming in here. That's trespassing, and I'm within my rights to defend my home.'

Anthony didn't stop. He stepped into the hallway and realised that he was almost a head taller than the other man. He had never felt like intimidating someone before, but there was a first time for everything. He grabbed the man's shoulder, pinning him in place. 'You haven't given me much choice, *sir*.'

He could still be polite, even if he was angry. *Don't give the man any more fuel to burn you with.* At least he could always say that he had been polite, even if the police became involved. Anthony doubted that this man was going to run to the police. There was something about him that told Anthony he wasn't that kind of man, perhaps he had more to hide from the police than he did from Anthony. He decided to push his luck.

'Why don't we go and get the police involved?' he asked. 'I'm sure they would be happy to come to our aid. Though I'm not sure they would be on your side, sir.'

'Haven't the police got better things to do than come after someone just minding their own business?'

'Perhaps, but you're not minding your own business, are you? As I've said, that light could lead the bombers here and cause deaths. I think they might have something to say about that.'

'It's only one light. What difference does it make?'

'What's going on, Bill?' A woman appeared at the top of the stairs, thrown into silhouette by the incriminating light. 'That better not be your wife. You told me she were out!'

'Quiet, woman,' Bill shouted over his shoulder. 'This is nothing to do with you, I'll be back up in a minute, don't you worry.'

Anthony recognised her. She lived at the house on the end of his road, with her husband. When she caught him staring at her, her eyes widened and she ran back into the bedroom in a flurry of nightdress. Apparently infidelity was becoming more and more common as the war drew on. She had nothing to worry about, Anthony didn't know either of them that well, and it was no business of his.

Anthony pushed Bill against the wall, then walked into the living room. With a tug he pulled the blackout curtains closed and then turned the light out for good measure. The man had followed Anthony to the doorway, but he stood there dumbfounded as Anthony pushed past again.

'Next time,' he said as he was leaving, 'I'll get the bloody police.'

Suddenly the drone of aircraft was audible through the din, louder than Anthony had imagined in his nightmares.

'Shit,' the younger man said.

Anthony flicked a switch in the hallway, drowning them in darkness. As the whistle of the falling bombs hit him, Anthony realised that this time it was no drill. Their fears had been realised.

\*

Anthony walked as calmly as he could through the city. He hoped that Marc was safe, wherever he was with the army, having to deal with this every day. His son was all that he had left in the world, and he would do anything for him. His boy was smart, but he took too many risks. He was more like his mother in that. Anthony sighed and realised he had subconsciously increased his pace and was now close to a run.

Thankfully, he saw no more lights left on in houses, and for a few streets he didn't see another soul. He navigated from memory, accompanied by the drones of aircraft. The largest shelter was still a few roads away, and it was part of his duty to check on it. In the drills, he had felt like some kind of prison warden, keeping his inmates in place.

There was a loud squeal and as Anthony flinched, he heard a crash. So far the bombs had seemed far away, but they were falling thick and fast now, like cigars tumbling from a mishandled box. It was an inappropriate simile; the bombs were far more dangerous and he chastised himself for his flippant moment of fancy. It was the sort of thing one of his pupils might say.

He felt rather than heard a bang as one of the bombs fell nearby. The shockwave slowed down his run, but he pushed his way through. A building on the other side of the adjoining street had been hit. There would likely already be people on site, but he didn't know whether they would need his help. He could stop and telephone the fire brigade, but he imagined they were already on their way. His efforts were best placed seeing if there were any wounded and helping them to safety. As he turned the corner he could see the flames, bright orange topped with thick black smoke that rolled down the street and straight into his lungs. The air, thick with smoke, and the cacophony were nothing like the drills. He coughed, and pushed on. There were already other volunteers on site, fighting the fires. Civilians formed a perimeter around the building, and no one had yet told them to move away. Anthony tapped the nearest man on the shoulder and shouted at him to clear the area. Anthony forced his voice to be even and steady, but still the eyes that looked back at him were wide as the man wrung his flat cap in his grip. Anthony had to repeat himself several times before the man nodded, put his cap back on and pulled his friends away with him. None of them were used to this yet, but Anthony didn't doubt that they would be soon.

As the crowd started to disperse he looked around for whoever was in charge, but it was difficult in the gloom, even with the light provided by the fire. A woman pushed her way back through the crowd, coming face to face with Anthony. Her eyes flickered around as if she too was looking for something. She moved to push past him, but he put out an arm.

'Who on earth are you?' he asked.

Her red hair was tucked under a steel helmet emblazoned with the symbol of the Women's Voluntary Services. But he knew her. He had seen her around the school a few times.

She was one of those new journalists who had been poking their noses around, the socialist ones. It wasn't that he disagreed with their ideas, not exactly. It was that everywhere they went trouble soon followed. One of the volunteers helped someone out of the rubble, brushing grey dust from their suit as they helped them stand.

'Ruth,' the woman said as she stepped closer. Her voice was softer than he had been expecting. For some reason he had thought it would be harsh and aggressive. 'My name's Ruth. Ruth Holt. Who the hell are you?'

There was a faint glimmer of amusement on her lips. While he had expected her informality to anger him, for some reason it made him smile.

'Anthony.' His name escaped his lips before he could compose himself. He didn't know why he gave his first name either, it was most informal and direct. The tension of the raid must be getting to him.

'Pleased to meet you, Anthony. I think.'

There was something about her manner that reminded him of his Julie, but he pushed the thought away almost as soon as he had had it. For a start, Ruth was a good few years younger than Julie, and he would never have seen his wife dress like a man, even for the sake of being a volunteer.

'What are you doing here?' he asked.

She frowned at him, as if the answer to his question was obvious, expecting him to move out of the way and let her past. And yet he was still angry with her. Her volunteer's uniform was surely a ruse, a way of tricking them into letting her get closer to the bombings looking for things to write for that rag of hers.

'Shouldn't we be, you know, helping?' she said, nodding towards the bombed building and the other volunteers. They were now pumping water onto the flames, trying to push them back into the ruins.

What was she doing sticking her nose here in the middle of a bloody air raid? Anthony didn't care who she thought she was, it wasn't safe, and they were trying to make sure it was as safe as possible. It was bad enough without the press getting in the way, especially someone from one of those rags. They had absolutely no right, this was a bloody war zone. How stupid could they be? They were almost as bad as those who refused to fight. He had no time for them at all. This war belonged to them all, it was their duty to do their bit. Anthony would have happily donned khaki and picked up a rifle, if only they had allowed him to. Still, he would do what he could to keep people safe. He almost turned to escort her away, but hesitated.

'What are you really doing here?' he asked, his voice almost drowned out by another explosion nearby. He had to shout to be heard and he didn't know why he was giving her the benefit of the doubt. He should ignore her and stay well clear of it. Association with a woman like that would only end badly for him, but something about her intrigued him. 'You won't find any gossip here.'

A frown crossed her face. 'So you do know who I am then?'

Anthony nodded, unsure what else he could say. He hadn't really expected her to admit it.

'Yes, I'm a writer. People need to know what's happening to their city. Especially when they're not around to see it. Can you imagine what it's like in those shelters? Not knowing what's going on above your head, having no idea whether you'll see the morning light. Even before in the drills and the false alarms, when nothing really happened, I couldn't take it. That's why I have to be out here. I hate the uncertainty, the fear of the unknown.'

Anthony hadn't expected this level of honesty from the woman, and while part of him regretted the conversation for the simple fact of making it appear as if he was interested in what the woman was up to, he was intrigued by her sentiment.

'But that's not why I'm here.' She pointed at his chest with a long finger. 'I put on this uniform the same as you, because I want to help people. Now get out of my way, so I can do what I came here to do.'

Ruth pushed closer to him, trying to move his outstretched arm. But still he wouldn't budge and he almost embraced her. He knew he was being a fool, but some sixth sense was driving him. Maybe it was the raid, maybe it was something else, but he wouldn't let her near that building.

'Wait,' he said, but before she could respond there was a loud squeal and a whistle like a kettle going off but much louder. Anthony could feel movement behind him and Ruth's eyes widened as she looked over his shoulder.

'Look out!' a man shouted.

Anthony just had time to grab Ruth around her arms, pulling her towards him before the world turned upside down and his vision went dark.

# Chapter 3

Ruth's vision swam as she came to. Above her was the night sky, the moon and stars swallowed by the clouds. She was flat on her back against the cobbles of the street, which pressed into the small of her back like broken mattress springs. A weight pressed down on her and she couldn't move her legs. Had she been paralysed by the fall? She tried to move her arms but they were wrapped up in something heavy but soft. Her back protested the movement, sending shooting pain down her legs. She heard a groan as if it was coming from beside her ear. Was it her own voice? She couldn't understand what she was hearing, her ears were still recovering from the crash. Her head flopped to the side, apparently no longer under her control, and her vision resolved on a man's face.

'Anthony?' she croaked, her voice dry and uncomfortable. A cough only served to bring a pang of pain to her chest.

'Hmmm?' he replied, his accent becoming more Welsh, as if he wasn't thinking clearly. She hadn't noticed it before now. His deep brown eyes, magnified by his glasses, failed to focus on her, looking into the middle distance as if seeing something she couldn't. She could smell the scent of him, almost floral over the stench of cordite and fire wafting on the breeze. His moustache tickled the end of her nose and she almost sneezed.

Memory flooded back to her, and she remembered where she was. Anthony was pinned on top of her, after pulling her away from the blast. He must have been hit by the worst of it, and she wondered what his wounds were like, but he was a deadweight and she couldn't move him to have a look.

'Get off me, you great lout,' she said, hoping her anger would spur him even if he was injured. 'I can't breathe.'

As she pushed against him, he groaned again and his weight shifted as he rolled to his left. The pressure on her chest eased and she took a great lungful of breath, relishing the fresh air. There was a sharp pain and she wondered whether anything was broken there, but as she sat up the pain became less severe. Each lungful of air helped her to recover, and she rolled over onto her hands and knees. They were surrounded by a pile of red bricks, most of them broken in half, trailing back towards the house they had been standing next to. It was a ruin, but there was no fire, or signs of fresh bombing. She wasn't sure what had forced them over, but it couldn't be that. The other workers were moving around the wreckage, checking it for stability, while one or two stared at the two of them prone on the ground.

Anthony lay to her side, his eyes closed as if he was sleeping. His breaths came in ragged fits and starts, and a frown pulled at his brow. He was atop a pile of bricks that had tumbled from the house, and he resembled a marionette after having its strings cut. She reached a tentative hand out to his shoulder, letting him know she was there.

'Anthony?' she whispered. His eyelids snapped open and he stirred like he was coming around from a deep sleep. He tried to raise himself onto his elbows, but fell back. Another groan escaped his lips. 'Are you hurt? I can get help.'

'I'm fine, I'm fine.' He waved her away, then winced at the

movement. It was typical of a man to be in pain but claim that he wasn't. She didn't see any point in trying to convince him otherwise. If he wanted help, he would have to ask for it. She wasn't his mother.

'Are you all right?' he asked, to her surprise. He may have been in pain, but he was willing to ignore that to check on her. When he opened his brown eyes again, there was a genuine look of concern in them. She nodded; she was fine now that she was able to breathe again, and the pain in her legs was abating. They had been lucky this time. It hadn't been a bomb that came for them. Next time they might not be so lucky, if there was a next time.

'Good,' he said, nodding and pinching his nose. 'I thought the worst when I saw that shadow looming over you. I don't know what came over me. I'm sorry for my presumptuousness.'

'It's quite all right. I think you may have saved my life,' she replied, but he didn't seem to be listening. He hauled himself to his feet, then bent down to retrieve his hat and slung the box that contained his gas mask back over his shoulder, then smacked the dust from his trousers before turning back towards the house. He took a step and faltered. Ruth reached out to him, but he righted himself before she could lay a hand on him. She wondered whether she should get him to a medic to check over his wounds, but she didn't think she would win that argument. He was as stubborn as the rest of them, and if he was hurt he would have to deal with it himself. Anthony wasn't her responsibility, but even still she watched on, hoping that the colour would return to his cheeks.

'I hope that's the last time a house falls on me,' he said, kicking a brick into the distance. He then looked at her to gauge her reaction. She held a steady face for a second, before a laugh erupted from her lips. It was genuine too, and it felt good. The tension dropped from her shoulders as she let it go and took in a big lungful of air. She hadn't realised how much she had been holding in her breath.

'Me too, and I hope it's the last time you push me over. Although, I must say thank you.'

She expected that he really hoped it was the last time he saw her, but she knew that it would be unlikely for them not to cross paths again. If she wanted to write about the bombing raids then she would no doubt find herself in similar situations, and if he was the warden for this area, then they would see each other again. She knew that would only infuriate him more, but it wasn't her responsibility to prove to him that she was there to do her own job.

It was only now, standing up again, that she noticed how tall he was. He must have been six foot two or three, and even though she was tall for a woman, he still looked down at her. Peter had only been an inch or so taller than her, and often looked right into her eyes. At first it had been disconcerting, then she had become used to it. Anthony, on the other hand, had a way of never looking you in the eye when speaking to you, as if all the other things going on around him were far more interesting than the conversation. He was doing it now, but she thought it was more that he was struggling to focus.

'You're welcome. I suppose,' he said, finally settling his attention on her. 'Though I'm starting to think you're bad luck, Miss—'

'*Mrs* Holt.' He knew that she was married, so why was he being so awkward? Perhaps he had suffered concussion and didn't realise what was happening. He really should go to see a medic, but she couldn't make him. 'Are you quite all right, Anthony?'

'Hmmm? Yes.' He gingerly felt his side and gave a wince that he tried to hide. Then touched his hand to the brim of his hat. 'Quite. Quite. We should probably be getting on, no? Plenty of houses to check on. Goodbye and good luck, Mrs Holt.'

She realised for the first time that she could still hear the crack of anti-aircraft guns in the distance, and the faint murmur of planes. Every now and then there was a crump, which could have been the sound of an explosion, but it was difficult to tell amongst the cacophony of the guns and the ringing in her ears. It appeared the raid had moved on to another part of the city, but she had no way of knowing that she would be safe there. She looked back over her shoulder at the disappearing figure of Anthony.

He was a strange man, that was for sure, but for a brief time she had seen under the surface of his steely facade. It was all an act, she could tell. Much as she did in her own life, he presented a public persona that would keep others away, to prevent himself from getting hurt. She wondered what kind of sorrow lay behind those deep brown eyes. He might not want to see her again, but she knew with utmost certainty that they would cross paths again. And she felt like making it her duty to find out what troubled him and see if she could help. She wasn't the tricky journalist he thought she was, out to serve her own ends. Some of her colleagues were like that, but she had decided early on in her career that she would be different, that she would try to make a difference. She didn't need to prove it to the stranger, but she felt compelled to.

Unconcerned by her own cuts and bruises, she went to have a better look at the house. It was just like hers and the hundreds of others in this part of Liverpool, all built to the same design. It could quite easily have been her home, but thankfully she lived more than a few streets away. It was an end-of-terrace house, and the entire corner of the building had fallen down from the damage it had received, fallen on top of Ruth and Anthony. She could see straight into the house through the living room. It was a complete mess of blackened walls and furniture, as if some kind of demon had attacked and turned everything upside down. A coffee table was upturned, with two of its legs flung across the other side of the room, while the door hung limply in its frame. There appeared to be photos and other personal belongings scattered amongst the debris, but no sign that anyone had been in the house when it had been hit.

'Move back, lass.' One of the rescue men stepped in front of her, blocking her view. 'It's not safe around here.'

She took a last mental image of the ruined interior then moved away. She wished she had taken a handheld camera with her, and next time she was in the office she would have to see if she could borrow one for the raids. Just think of the kinds of photographs she could take, even as an amateur, of the bombings. If that was the damage that one bomb could cause, then they were going to see some sights. She had had her first glimpse of the war to come, and she was right to be wary. She would have to find some way to get George out of the city again. What would have happened if that had been their house?

She walked off to the WVS station, ready to do whatever duty they had assigned to her, even though she had already had a house fall on top of her. Such was the life of a volunteer, she supposed. She had known what she was getting herself into, it wasn't easy work, otherwise they wouldn't need volunteers. She reported to the station and was directed to the van.

The WVS had a van that had been converted as a mobile support centre. They had parked it on the corner of the road, out of the way of the trams and leaving enough space for other vehicles to get by if needed, but it was at a jaunty angle and no one could get along the pavement. They had perhaps hoped that no one would be outdoors in the middle of a raid, unless they were needed. A trestle table was set up by the side of the vehicle, like some kind of street party. A couple of the volunteers were arranging the items into wooden crates. They were at times disorganised, but doing the best they could with the resources they had.

'Where have you been?' one of them asked when she spotted Ruth. 'The bombers have been and gone, looks like they've moved across the water to Birkenhead. Looks like we're moving on too.'

The speaker was one of the older ladies in the team, and Ruth could easily imagine her as a matron, bossing everyone around in a hospital ward and acting like she owned the place. They had even taken to calling her the Matron, when she wasn't around. She had no training. She had just assumed her place in command by force of will alone. It would be fair to say that she scared Ruth a little. Her permed hair bobbed under her steel helmet as she talked, and her little eyes could cut like knives.

'See that those chaps have everything they need, will you, dear? Then when you're done join us in the van.'

Making tea was not exactly what she had in mind. She knew that a warm drink helped those working get through the night, but Ruth wanted to do more than that to help, be more than that. She could see her sister pouring out a lukewarm brew, but Ruth knew she should be helping with the rescue tasks themselves. They had been waiting for the bombers to arrive for months, and now that they were here she was certain this was only the beginning.

'Come on, what're you waiting for? The Luftwaffe won't wait for no woman.'

'I've got a driving licence,' Ruth replied, thinking quickly.

'So?'

'I can drive the van. How many others can say that? Let me be useful, anyone can make a cup of tea. The men could even do it themselves.'

'Nonsense, they've got important work to do; they can't waste time on making up a brew. What about the men that come out in shock after digging out some poor soul? Do you expect them to care for themselves?'

'All right, maybe so, but I would like to help more. Please. Let me drive the van.'

Ruth didn't know why it had taken until now to assert herself. It wasn't just that the Matron intimidated her, it was that until now the war had seemed so far away. They were all still trying to convince themselves that maybe it would pass them by, that Hitler and his Nazis would turn their attentions elsewhere, but now they had to face up to facts.

The Matron relented and turned to Trevor, who was usually borrowed from the rescue men to drive the van. 'They need some help shifting the rubble down the road,' the Matron said. 'Mrs Holt will take care of the van, for now.'

He eyed Ruth warily then rushed away. As she climbed up behind the wheel of the van she could see the orange flames on the horizon. The war had finally come to them, and by the look of things it wasn't going to be an easy one.

She gunned the engine, the motions coming back to her like getting back on a bike after a few years. The world lurched as she pulled away. Her father had driven during the war and when he came back he had taught her how. Ruth was only old enough to have vague memories of the last one, but she knew of communities nearby wiped out by fighting on the front. Her father had fought, and while she hadn't really known him beforehand, others in the family told her that he had been a changed man when he came back, quiet and sullen, and prone to fits of unjustified anger. Families seldom talked about what had happened to their loved ones in the last war, which gave Ruth enough clues to how bad it truly was. This war was going to be different. They hadn't had aircraft then, nor the bombers that descended on cities like Liverpool. If fighting had been terrible on the front last time, at least those at home had mostly been saved from attack; now it was going to be different.

Given the ease with which the Germans had invaded France only a few months ago, they were being told there was a good chance that they could invade Britain, and then what? There could be German boots marching down Bold Street, past Marks & Spencer in Compton House and on up to the Queen Victoria statue. At least Ruth could speak the language, but that didn't make her feel any better. For now she planned to keep that fact as secret as possible. Maybe that Anthony had been right about her. Even though she was no Nazi, nor Aryan, the people around her would become suspicious, and they would lock her up like her grandfather. No, she had to avoid that, show them all that she had been born here and was as British as the next woman.

By the time Ruth got home, George was already tucked up in bed. She had missed that moment once so precious to her, so before washing off the sweat and the grime she knelt next to the bed, brushed the fringe of his hair away and kissed his forehead.

He stirred in his sleep and his eyes blinked open, followed by a smile.

'I've missed you, Mummy,' he said.

'Me too, my love. Me too.'

# Chapter 4

**Monday, 19 August 1940**

Anthony had not slept well the previous night and his eyes stung every time he blinked. The all clear for the second night's raid had been called just after two o'clock in the morning, and when his head had finally hit the pillow, he had been too agitated to drift off. His side still ached and every time he rolled over in fitful sleep the pain had woken him up. Ruth and Anthony had been lucky, but some of their neighbours had had no such luck: they were the first casualties of the war at home, the home front.

Anthony's head had swum as he'd wandered away from the collapsed building and he'd felt strange, as if he had a headache. No amount of aspirin would get rid of it. He should have seen a medic before he left, but he couldn't stay with that woman there. On his way he had spoken to one of the rescue men, confirming that the residents of the house had not been inside when it had been hit, and so he had set off towards the shelter to inform them what had happened. This morning he was determined to do more.

He had been to the Ministry of Labour and National Service offices so many times that he suspected the receptionist even knew his name. He knew his way around its Victorian chambers almost as well as he knew the school building. As the staff attempted to direct him, he stalled them with a hand and walked past. There was a din filtering through the walls and along the corridors from the busy civil servants. Other men were already queuing up outside the National Service office. Most of them were younger than Anthony, barely out of their teens. One or two conscientious objectors queued outside a nearby office. They cast wary glances at the men waiting to enlist.

Having been refused before Anthony was an anomaly in age; most of the other men his age had already been called up. As they had extended the ages of national service, he had decided to try his luck again. Perhaps now the war had finally come to them they might turn a blind eye.

He didn't really want to leave Liverpool, but he had always wanted to do his bit, having been too young for the last war. He remembered his father, an officer, setting off, resplendent in his polished and well-tailored uniform. It had instilled a sense of heroic pride in Anthony as a boy, but his father had given him one piece of advice that had stuck with him ever since, 'If you ever find yourself fighting for King and Country, son, make sure you join the air corps. Those boys have all the fun.'

Of course it was the Royal Air Force now, but the point still stood. Anthony wanted to fly, to soar above the country fighting back the enemy bombers that were terrorising the people of his city. He had been fascinated by aeroplanes since he had first seen one as a little boy, and it had taken this fascination to university, but his life with Julie had led him to becoming a teacher instead. He didn't regret it for a moment, but if there was any chance he could fly now then he would take it.

Some of the other men talked amongst themselves as they waited, but Anthony kept his thoughts to himself. Already one or two more had queued up behind him. One by one the queue went down, closer to the door. It frustrated him how long the wait took, but not one of the conchies had been seen yet. Eventually he reached the front and was ushered in to give his details to the recruitment officer.

'Age?' the officer asked, without looking up from the paperwork. He had a bald patch on the top of his head, which was beginning to look like a tonsure, and he wrote like a left-handed man, the pad of his right palm smudging the ink before it could set.

'Thirty-five,' Anthony said, then gave his other details with practised efficiency. He remembered the last time. He'd practised all the way to the office. Anything to make the process go as smoothly as possible.

'Proceed through to the medical.' The officer waved the paperwork at Anthony and he took it on his way to the next room. Not once had he looked at Anthony.

The doctor was finishing up an examination and told Anthony to wait a moment. Anthony placed his coat on the back of a chair in the corner, making sure nothing fell from the pockets. The heat in the room was stifling and he could feel the sweat breaking out on his temples.

'Hello again, Mr Lloyd,' the doctor said when he spotted Anthony. 'Come on then, you know what to do by now.'

Anthony felt guilty that he had never bothered to learn the doctor's name and mumbled a hello. He stood on the scales and waited as the doctor adjusted the height measure to the top of his head before writing it all down on the form he had been given. From where Anthony stood he could barely read the handwriting, but he knew whoever ended up with that form would know everything they needed to know. Next, Anthony untucked his shirt from his trousers and undid the buttons. The stethoscope was cold against his chest as the doctor moved it around.

'Hmmm, hmmm,' the doctor said, closing his eyes to listen. 'Breathe in . . . and out. Nice and deep. There we go. Uh-huh.'

He let the stethoscope drop then flicked its tube over his neck before returning to his paperwork. Anthony buttoned up his shirt again and took care to tuck it into his trousers without getting caught up, knowing that the examination was over.

'Now, you know what I'm going to say, Mr Lloyd?'

'I suspect I do,' he replied. 'Same as last time?'

'Same as last time, I'm afraid. The heart murmur is still there. It doesn't need any further examination, but it's not going away. And with that, I can't possibly recommend you for national service.'

Anthony let out a sigh he didn't know he had been holding.

'I know you're keen and disappointed, but it's for the best.' The doctor scribbled notes across the paperwork. Anthony expected him to simply draw a big cross over the form. 'Besides, you're in a protected profession. The children still need teachers, don't they? You're doing your bit by giving them the education they need. So they can grow up and be doctors or teachers in their own right.'

Anthony had never met a more talkative doctor.

'I suppose,' he said. 'There aren't many children left in the city.'

'Come on now.' The doctor wasn't one to give up. Anthony had had the same speech every time he had tried to enlist. 'You're a warden too. We need men like you at home, just as much as on the front. And it's much better than being shot at constantly, wouldn't you say?'

'Is that much different to the bombing here?' Anthony moved towards the door, but it seemed that the doctor wasn't done.

'Well, yes. I would say so. The war may have come to us, but at least I get to sleep in my own bed at night.' The doctor went back to the notes on his desk.

'When there's not a raid on, at least.'

'Quite. Good day, Mr Lloyd.' He turned back to Anthony. 'Oh, and I wouldn't bother with the army or navy either, they'll only tell you the same thing. Carry on the good work on the home front. Chin up!'

Anthony had never felt like hitting someone before, but the doctor was trying his patience. Instead, he simply picked up his coat and left. Outside, the air was cool and it hit Anthony with a flush, like leaving a warm public bar after a few drinks. He swayed in his steps, and he wasn't sure whether it was the disappointment or simply the change in temperature. He felt like his entire life was unsteady, but at least he had a home and a job to go to.

*

He could have done with a week, no, a month off work, but even though there was a war on he had plenty to do. The school was quiet, the corridors filling with the click of Anthony's shoes on the tiled floor. It wasn't just the evacuation of the children; numbers had been dwindling. He passed empty classrooms, rows of wooden desks sitting patiently waiting for children to occupy them. Would the children miss out on too much schooling? He suspected they would be all right. Some had started to filter back to Liverpool, their parents recalling them from evacuation in what the press like that Ruth woman were calling the Phoney War.

He touched a hand to his side and winced. He hadn't realised at the time how much the brick fall had hurt him. In hindsight, he saw he had been more concerned about Ruth, than himself. Even if she was an underhanded journalist. Julie would have said that it was that kind of empathy that made him a good teacher, but he thought at times that it made him an idiot. He could be too trusting, that was why he was determined not to let that woman charm him. If he did, somehow it would come back to bite him. Next time he saw her hanging around in a raid he would ignore her. It was the only way.

Some families had refused to send their children away from the city. Anthony had had a number of conversations with them, advising them to reconsider. He wondered whether they would change their minds now that the first bombs had landed on the city and they had suffered the first loss of life. Some people would claim there was no danger. Some people didn't learn until it was too late. They believed bad things happened to other people, and they were privileged, but Anthony knew full well that disaster could strike at any time. The morning newspapers had reported that only a couple of people had lost their lives in an unnamed 'North West town', but rumours were already circulating that the true number had actually reached double figures, and Anthony knew it would only get worse.

The smell of school was all too familiar, like a second home. The dustiness of chalk and the sticky tang of varnished wood that despite its age never seemed to completely dry. Occasionally he would let his hand scrape along the wood, noticing the grain that rose and fell around knots. At least it had become a home as much as Liverpool had after he left his family in Wales. He had steadfastly refused to go back, and even though he and his family occasionally wrote letters to each other, it was a decision that suited them all. He had chosen a new life in a new city with Julie.

Most of the city's schools had now closed, but not St Thomas's. Whether the headmaster had just decided to carry on as if nothing had changed, or whether he really did have the children's interests at heart, Anthony could never be quite sure.

As he walked towards the staffroom the thick stench of cigarettes became the dominant smell. It was times like this that he regretted giving up smoking, but given the danger of a careless match during a raid he had thought it best to stop. His nerves had been on edge for weeks now, but he knew it was the right thing to do.

He pushed the door open, feeling the squeak of its hinges through the brass handle plate. It was a wonder the metal hadn't been taken for the war effort, but he supposed the school had certain privileges. The white plastered ceiling was stained yellow in patches. The room was about ten yards by five, and panelled in the same wood as the rest of the school. It was empty. Many of the other teachers had gone on to other work; had the others perished in the raid? Julie always said that he reached for the worst thought before thinking it through, and she had been right. That had become even more difficult after her death, but he had come to terms with it in time. He just wished he'd known it at the time.

The staffroom was the warmest room in the building, kept heated by two long radiators under the windows. The windows themselves were long wooden frames with large panes of glass, but heavy maroon curtains kept in the heat. At times it was too much for Anthony. Today was one such occasion, given the August sun. The headmaster, Robotham, revelled in the heat, as a man who had grown up in Africa.

The door squeaked open again and hit the wall with a dull thump. Anthony only opened his eyes a few seconds later, spotting that the headmaster had entered the room and now occupied the matching armchair opposite him, a newspaper clutched in his liver-spotted hands.

'Lloyd,' Robotham said, looking at Anthony over his pince-nez. 'You look as if you haven't slept in days, man. Burning the candle at both ends, are you?'

Anthony did not particularly enjoy his company, but they had at least been able to have civil conversations in the past. That was until the war had started. He stifled a yawn, lest it show his uninterest.

'Apologies, headmaster. We had the first raid the night before last and I'm afraid I didn't get much sleep. The bombing rather knocked it out of me.'

He winced at the unexpected and unintentional pun, but Robotham didn't appear to notice.

'Yes, indeed,' he replied. 'You really should consider which is most important to you, young man. Our school work is rather demanding, but it is all for the children after all. They do so need us in these trying times.'

Anthony didn't have the strength to argue. 'I understand, sir. The children are of course my top priority. It is a privilege to teach them.'

'Of course, of course, I know that. But what about all this other nonsense? Running around the city in the dead of night. What good does it do anyone? Least of all yourself.'

'I help to make sure that people are safe during the raids, sir.'

'Ahh yes, but really. As I say, it's all an old lot of nonsense. People will look after themselves, or they won't. It is a thankless task, is it not?'

There was some truth to what the old man was saying, but Anthony didn't agree. Robotham and he were a generation apart and their ideals were quite different.

'It's good work, sir,' he said, feeling a little rebellious for once. 'If men such as myself do not volunteer then I dare to think who would. As you said yourself, we are needed in times such as these.'

'Well, if you must insist on throwing my own words back at me, Lloyd. I must say that is quite unfair, I meant nothing of it. I simply wished to impart to you that you're trying to do too much and as a result I do fear that your teaching may suffer. It's just something to think about, that is all. I shan't make an issue of it, unless you wish to do so. Quite patriotic though it is.'

'I just want to do my bit, sir. As you and the others did in the last war.'

Robotham winced. Anthony had never seen the man give such an outward show of emotion, and he knew immediately that he had hit upon a raw nerve. The headmaster spoke quietly. 'If you had been through the last war, Lloyd, then you would not be saying that.'

Anthony kept his mouth shut. He had no wish to force the head-master to relive his experiences of the last war. Anthony had heard too many horrific stories to wish that upon anyone. However, he was curious as to Robotham's opinions on the current war effort. Having survived one, surely he would have something to say?

'What should one do, sir? The war has come to us this time, but we can't fight back. They won't let me sign up, so how do I protect people? How do we stop feeling so impotent, how do we take control?'

The headmaster thought for a long moment, and Anthony began to wonder whether he had not heard the question. A few other teachers had filtered into the room and were talking quietly amongst themselves. Anthony was relieved to see they hadn't fallen during the raid as he had feared. Robotham chewed on the end of his cigar and eventually turned to regard Anthony, once again looking over his glasses.

'What you do, son, is you look everyone you care about right in the eye and you do everything you can to remember their face, every line, every wrinkle, the colour of their eyes, the shape of their lips. Then you make sure you bloody well remember every little detail, because, and trust me on this, Lloyd, in war those faces will disappear before you have a chance to remember what they looked like, before you have a chance to say goodbye.'

He placed the cigar back between his lips, then let out a breath of smoke. Anthony felt it wrap itself around his nostrils, filtering through his mouth, enticing him with the taste of it.

'There is nothing else for it,' the headmaster continued. 'This is the hand we have been dealt. As for taking back control, well, there is always something you can do. There are many ways to win a war. We won the last one, even though all those poor young lads were dying on the front. We won that because we kept going. We did not let Germany win, and we will not let them this time.

'Fight in every way you can, Lloyd. Fight by not giving up, fight by supporting our boys in the sky, on the front, wherever they may be. Do your bit, we are all in this together. Teach their children so they can focus on the battle. Whatever it takes, just as the Prime Minister says. Now, if that's quite enough of that lecture, I must be getting on.'

Robotham stubbed out his cigar in a metal ashtray on the side table and hauled himself out of the chair by placing a hand on each arm. He left Anthony speechless. Anthony had expected the headmaster to compel him to sign up, to tell him that being a soldier was the only good, patriotic thing to do. Could it be that Anthony was doing the best he could after all? Only time would tell.

For the first time in months he was motivated, but even still, pulling himself out of that chair to go and teach was difficult. He would do it and he would do it well, but that night he would be out on patrol again, doing what he could to defend the city and the people he had come to love.

# Chapter 5

Victoria Street was up a slight hill from the city centre and Ruth was always surprised how out of breath she was by the top. Even with the aid of Peter's bicycle it was a struggle. Every time she took a moment to dismount and compose herself. She stood on the opposite pavement, looking over at the various offices. The *Liverpool Guardian* where she worked stood between her and the *Post* and *Echo* building at the far end. They were almost identical in their facades, the late Victorian architecture they had moved into at the end of the last century, but the *Post* and *Echo* building was topped with crenellations that made it look like a castle. They fancied themselves as superior newspapers. They had the highest readership in the city, but then her newspaper had a more niche appeal, those with more of a socialist view.

Unlike the General Post Office behind her, which was constructed entirely of stone, the buildings were red brick from the first floor up. The same red brick as her house and most of the others in the city. The upper three floors had many windows, some rectangular, others with an arch, designed to let as much light in as possible. Many were obscured with blinds and curtains. In the *Guardian* offices she could see people at work. On her very first day she had stood on almost exactly the same spot, not out of breath that time, but wondering if she truly appreciated what she was getting herself in to. Her family had almost disowned her when she had told them she was going to be a journalist. They had expected that as a woman she would end up making the tea and coffee for the male journalists, and she had stood there considering whether they were going to be right after all. It struck her now that in many ways they had been right, and when George had come along she had been determined to prove she could be a mother and still work. Harriet was looking after him again, but she would have to arrange something else for him soon, preferably out of the city.

After a lorry had clattered past, heading in the direction of the Mersey Tunnel, then a horse and cart in the other direction, she wheeled her bicycle across the road. On an island in the middle was the stairway to a gentlemen's public toilets, and the smell always caught her as she passed. Acidic and pungent, it stung her nostrils, and she winced every time. Maybe, she thought, she should write an article about the conditions of public toilets in the city, but she didn't expect her editor would think people would want to read about toilets. She suspected the smell had only got worse since they had taken the ornate metal railings away for the war effort. At least before it had looked pleasant.

The building had a central loading bay which went straight into the print room, where the lorries would be loaded with newspapers for distribution. When she had first started she had enjoyed looking around the print room, seeing how the machinery worked and chatting to the workers, but after being accused of slacking and distracting the workers she had not set foot in the room. Instead she edged around the corner and in through the staff entrance. Once inside the door there was a staircase which turned back on itself, leading up to the main floors of the offices.

The office she worked in was on the second floor, and when she entered she took her time to hang up her hat and place her coat on the coatstand by the door. The others in the office were prone to rushing about as if they were always working on a breaking story, but she could never bring herself to rush. Her grandfather had always told her that rushing made things worse, and he was the one member of her family other than Peter whom she trusted.

She perched herself at her desk, leaning forward on the edge of the seat and assessing the amount of paperwork that had built up there. Other desks in the office were tidy and ordered, but hers most definitely was not. No matter how hard she tried, she couldn't bring herself to work that way; it would only form a block in her mind until she could no longer function.

Right now the same thing was happening, she couldn't help but remember the times that Peter had come to visit her at work. He had often kept it as a surprise, even when he had come on leave. Ruth didn't usually like surprises, but he insisted that it was worth it to see the look on her face. She couldn't help but smile, recalling the memory of the first time. That had been before the war, when he was serving on his first posting. She had known that his ship was heading into dock at Liverpool. She kept herself apprised of shipping times through her work and her family, but she had not known that it had arrived two days earlier than expected. She had been quietly working away at some column or other, she couldn't remember which, it was that mundane, when she had heard a shuffling of feet in the doorway. Next thing she knew there was a bunch of flowers in front of her face. The pollen had almost made her sneeze, but instead she looked up at the grinning face of Peter, his green eyes shimmering with mirth in the candlelight. He was dressed in full uniform, lieutenant's stripes newly sewn onto his epaulettes.

'Hello, you,' he said simply, and as quick as that, every word she had ever known disappeared from her mind. It was just like the first time she had met him, at one of her parents' parties. There had been an awkward silence then too as her thoughts had stretched for anything to say to this resplendent man, anything that would sound intelligent and not pander to his obvious attractiveness. She allowed herself a sigh.

She wished he would walk through that door right now, sweep her up and take her away from all of this. But that felt like a betrayal of her beliefs. She didn't need him to save herself from boredom, she could save herself. She may be a woman, but she was in control of her own destiny, she had a job, and she could do what she wanted. Even still, she missed him. The smell of him on the bed next to her, the comfort of his arms wrapped around her despite their steel. Why couldn't she have both?

One of the office girls burst through the door, then looked around to see whether anyone had noticed her. Ruth may have thought of her as a girl, but Angie was only at most five years younger than her. Her straight black hair was plastered to her forehead with sweat and the buckle of one of her shoes had come loose. Her face was red, but not from rouge, and her chest rose and fell rapidly as she hunched over. Ruth stood up and went to her before any of the others caught sight of her.

'Angie, what's wrong?' she asked, almost in a whisper. Her body blocked the office's view of Angie.

'What's the time?' she replied, looking over each of Ruth's shoulders in turn in the hope of spotting a wall clock. Ruth repeated her question.

'I thought I was going to be late, but it turns out I'm early. Hah. Just my luck, ain't it? Never get an easy ride of it, eh? But me old mum always says we make our own luck. Didn't help me much this mornin', mind.'

Ruth hadn't had much call to talk to Angie previously. The girl was one of the typists, well trained in the use of a typewriter and by all accounts a hard worker, but Ruth seldom had need of her services. They had chatted at the occasional office party, but they were few and far between these days.

'But what happened?' she asked. 'You look like you've been running from a ghost. Let's get you cleaned up before any of the men see you like this.'

Ruth took Angie by the arm and led her back out of the office towards the shared toilets.

'I had to run part of the way.' Angie carried on talking as they walked, getting out words between deep breaths. 'It's quicker sometimes, you see, and, well, I can't afford the tram. It's a long way from Bootle without it, mind. All the way down Scottie Road. There are days where I long to be able to drive, or even better yet, have a horse. Wouldn't that be grand?'

'It would be quite nice,' Ruth had to admit, even though her family had owned horses when she was younger and she had never spent much time in the stables. The creatures had scared her as a child, towering over her, but as an adult she could appreciate how majestic they were. 'Why don't you ask for a little extra pay to cover the tram? You've been here long enough.'

Angie stopped dead in her tracks. 'I couldn't do that! Can you imagine, they'd sooner tell me where to go. No, no, I'll just have to make sure I leave home earlier, and then maybe on good days I can get back in time to spend the evening with the family. That'd be nice.'

'You're a good worker, Angie. They should take better care of you. You've earned it.'

'My, Ruth. What kind of world do you live in? It ain't the same as mine. I don't mean that rude like. You're kind, but things don't work like that, do they?'

Ruth let go of her arm. Angie's words had been more insightful than she had been expecting. She didn't talk about her background around the office, but at times it was horribly obvious that she had been given opportunities that the others hadn't. As much as she tried to hide that fact, blend in with the working classes, she couldn't keep it secret sometimes, and Angie had clearly seen right through her.

'I had to work hard to get here,' Angie continued. 'I wouldn't do anything that would jeopardise that, not when they could easily replace me. I'm not as valuable to them as you, Ruth. There's a million typists out there that would jump at this job soon as I opened my mouth to ask for a pay rise.'

'I'm sorry, Angie. I was only trying to help.' Angie smiled. 'If there's anything I can do at all, you just let me know, all right?'

'You're sweet. I'll be grand. Just got in a bit of a tizzy today, that's all. Thank you though.'

Angie locked herself into the toilet, leaving Ruth staring at the white-painted door. How many times had Ruth locked herself away in that cubicle to give herself time to think? Perhaps Angie was doing the same thing now, but it seemed that really she wanted to support herself. Ruth could empathise with that, she wanted the same in her own life.

*

Rupert came in and shuffled some papers on a desk, making a racket. The editor was looking for something but, already chastened once that morning, Ruth decided not to offer her assistance. She couldn't help but glance over. He switched a cigarette between hands as he searched amongst the papers, then he noticed her and took a pull while staring at her. His jade eyes were at times quite piercing as if he was trying to see your soul. A patina of sweat sat on his bald head. Ruth often thought that he must have been quite handsome as a young man, but the stress of the job had aged him.

'Good. You're here.' He interrupted her before she could bid him good morning. 'I had a chap here yesterday, from the Ministry of Information. He's asked me to make sure everyone's papers are in order, see. What with the war.'

Ruth's stomach sank and she swept a strand of hair away to cover her face.

'I remember you saying your parents are Austrian,' he continued. 'So if you could just show me your papers at some point, just a formality to prove you are indeed British-born, then we can all sleep at night. All right?'

She nodded, unwilling to speak. As he said, it was just a formality. There was no way he would scrutinise her papers, she knew he would barely look at them. She forced herself to breathe deeply before Rupert cursed.

'You seen the report about unemployment in the city?' He let the blue smoke drift around his face and up into the ceiling space, before taking another lungful. 'Can't find the bloody thing anywhere and I was sure it was out here.'

She resumed her work as if in the line of fire and he was about to blame her for the missing report.

'I thought we handed that to you weeks ago?'

'Hmmm,' he replied. 'You did, but there hasn't been any space to run it until now. I put it aside so that I could think about how best to publish the information. Blast!'

Ruth had worked on the report, one of a number of reporters who had been tasked by Rupert with getting information on the unemployment situation in the city. This had been before the war, but the details had been updated in the last month or so. As far as Ruth was aware, the level of employment had remained relatively the same. But that hadn't told the whole story.

Where others had spoken to Corporation officials and got the official numbers, Ruth had taken it upon herself, much to Rupert's annoyance, to speak to the city's unemployed. Many had had no wish to talk to her, but those who did had told her exactly what their lives were like. Many of them worked as gardeners or cleaners without declaring the payment to the Corporation. To do so would risk their welfare and they could not live on either income alone. Not for the first time, Ruth was thankful that she could always ask her parents for money if she was struggling to make ends meet, even if she had not had to do so since she had met Peter and found her own employment. The money he sent home to her was enough to supplement her income and she could keep her and George relatively well with that.

'Have you checked with Robert or John? Knowing them, they've probably pinched it back off your desk to make their own edits.'

He grunted and dropped the paperwork back onto the adjacent desk, before putting his cigarette out in a metal ashtray. He squashed it until it was only a lump of off-white paper. Shoulders hunched, he made off in the direction of his office at the end of their floor.

'Rupert?'

He stopped in his tracks and turned back to face her. This time those green eyes seemed uninterested.

'Can I ask you for something?'

He grunted, which was his way of replying, and patted the pockets of his jacket looking for a packet of Player's before he jammed another cigarette between his lips.

'I want to write about the bombings,' she said, without looking at him. It wasn't so much that she didn't expect any disagreement, but that she hoped if she just appeared to be getting on with it that she wouldn't need to make much of an argument.

'You can't,' he replied.

So much for that then. She let her ballpoint pen drop to the desk, and looked up. She hoped that she was giving her best cross mother expression, but knew that it probably wouldn't work too well on her editor. He had seen it all before and, having had three daughters, knew exactly how to deal with petulant young women, as he had often put it.

'Rupert, listen,' she started, but he cut her off.

'Must we have this argument again, Mrs Holt?' Under normal circumstances, Rupert had no qualms about using her first name, but he reserved her surname for when he really wasn't in the mood for argument. She wasn't to be deterred today. She had had quite enough of writing meaningless articles, ten best foods to take into a shelter, and so on. She wanted, no, needed to get to grips with something more meaningful, and the bombing would give her an opportunity to really examine how the people of Liverpool were feeling.

'I'm afraid we must, *Rupert*,' she replied. Emphasising his first name was more than a little childish, but it felt good to be at least a little rebellious. 'If you keep refusing to give me something more appropriate to get my teeth into, then I'm afraid I will have to keep forcing the issue. I believe it to be only quite reasonable.'

Rupert actually harrumphed when she finished speaking, but she didn't let her smile falter, or become a laugh. He was a patient man, but he wouldn't like to be laughed at. She knew it wasn't his fault, but who else could she go to?

'And I suppose you believe that you deserve a fast track to the top, where others must work for their responsibilities? Is that it?'

It was an unfair comment, she would never dream of using her background to pursue opportunities that others did not have, but she let it go. Knowing Rupert, it might even have been an attempt at humour.

'I've been at this newspaper for several years now, I think I've worked hard towards what I'm asking. I have written every measly article you have ever asked me to write, and only complained about half of them. Besides, there are those working on front-page stories who have been here a much shorter period of time than I have. All of them men.'

She locked eyes with him and did not relent until his cheeks reddened and he looked away chastised. It was the way of the world, but that didn't stop her fighting it.

'You don't have a degree,' he said, his voice now lower. 'You're lucky you've got a job here at all. If the owner didn't have a soft spot for you—'

'Now, that's not fair, Rupert. I work just as hard as the others, harder than some.' She nodded in the direction of a small group of journalists who were sat around their desks, sipping tea and gossiping like old women. 'Qualifications or not, you know I can write.'

The group looked over as they spotted Rupert's gaze on them, then redoubled their efforts to look like they were working hard, as if it wasn't obvious they had been slacking off.

'I can do this,' she said, pulling Rupert's attention back to her. 'I'm a member of the Women's Voluntary Services, which means

I'm there on the ground, seeing everything going on first-hand. I can talk to people, hear their struggles, tell their stories.'

He nodded along, but it was clear from his expression that he wasn't entirely convinced.

'If we don't do it, then the *Echo* or the *Post* will get there first. Don't think they will think it's beneath them to really pry into people's lives. We can do it with a little more . . . decorum, respect, whatever you want to call it. Write stories that show we actually care, inform people about what's going on in the city, offer them information that will help them, hold the Corporation to account.'

'You will have to fight with the censors, and the city won't like it. They've been strict since the war started proper. We have to maintain morale,' he said. It was the first sign of his capitulation and she grabbed it metaphorically with both hands.

'That's fine. I've been dealing with censorship my entire life.' She smiled, but perhaps humour wasn't the best course of action. 'I'll work within what they want. Believe in me, Rupert. I can do this. I can write the best damned articles you've ever seen me write.'

He winced at her swearing then pursed his lips and stroked his chin, the cigarette wobbling between his lips as he thought.

'As a matter of fact,' he said, 'I do have something you can do for me.'

'Oh?' She was interested now, as he knew she would be. Had he been playing her all along?

'Yes.' He lit up the cigarette. 'That chap I had here yesterday, from the Ministry. Didn't like him much, truth be told, but he's also asked us to report on the morale of people in the city. Apparently making sure people don't lose the plot is their primary focus. What do you say?'

'You want me to write about how people are faring in the city?'

'Something like that. He said they'll be back for reports and give more details. I wasn't really paying attention, we're not usually in for working with government offices. He could have gone to the press club to find someone for that sort of thing, but it strikes me that it'll give you the opportunity you're after.'

'Perfect. That's just the sort of thing.'

'Just don't get into any trouble,' he huffed before trudging off to his office, the trail of smoke following in his wake.

# Chapter 6

**Saturday, 31 August 1940**

The chief warden had forced Anthony to take a rare night off and he would rather be sitting at home reading a good book, but John Steele had popped by and insisted that Anthony join them in The Cracke. It was still light as he walked along Hope Street. The lowering sun reflected from the windows, throwing the piles of sandbags into relief. The Anglican cathedral, still unfinished, towered at one end of the street, its sandstone in contrast to the houses that surrounded it.

It was a few minutes before seven, according to his wristwatch. Typically he would arrive early for fear of being late, but when it came to the pub he didn't want that sinking feeling of walking in and finding there was yet no one there.

The pub was so familiar to him that he could find it even in the blackout. He had spent years there as a student, and that was how he had met his friends. He pushed open the door and ducked under the lintel. The pub felt far older than it was, the ceilings built for shorter people in a different time, and Anthony often had to stoop, but it was part of the charm of the place. There was the ever-present odour of sweat and stale ale that he was sure would still be just as strong even if the premises were completely empty, mingling with the tarry vapour of smoke from cigarettes.

The landlord had tried to black out the windows with a tarry black paint, but one or two of the panes allowed thin light through. Anthony let it go. He was in no mood for an argument with the proprietor. Experience told him it wouldn't make a difference. At times Anthony felt like giving up. He was here to relax, if such a thing was even possible.

The patrons represented every echelon from Liverpool's working class to middle class, where Anthony assumed many would place him if they were to have that conversation. He tried his best to understand others, but even he had to admit he had little to no knowledge of the trials of working at the docks, and at the factories and breweries that employed most of the city. If he tried to find out more, they would treat him as an outsider, suspicious and wary. His university education was clear to even those who didn't know him. He had lost his accent a long time ago, and neither sounded like he was from Liverpool, nor surrounding Lancashire. At a push he would say his accent was closer to that of a Midlander. At first he had wanted to get rid of his accent, but then it had become a burden trying to absorb himself into everyday city life.

He pushed his way further into the room, nodding at those he passed as if they were acquaintances. The bar was along the near wall and one had to make their way past it to the secluded seating areas that were like compartments of a train carriage. There were a few old fellas by the bar, but most of the patrons were off duty and in excluded professions like his, or soldiers. Anthony used to come here with some of his fellow teachers, but since Julie had died, he had little time for them. He wanted to spend as much as possible of his time alone, even if it meant being left with his thoughts. Every now and then his conscience would get the better of him and he would make some kind of effort to see people, like now.

His friends were already there, as he knew they would be. It was inevitable, like the rising and setting of the sun. He could almost set his watch by them, such was their frequency. As he worked his way through the pub, he saw them towards the far wall in their usual spot, sat about a round wooden table. It pitched on an uneven leg as Williams leant forward to tell one of his usual stories. Anthony chuckled to himself and then waved as John spotted him. John said something about him being late, but Anthony didn't rise to the bait as John pushed Williams aside with his elbow to make room. How Anthony had come to be friends with these men was a long tale: they were not old university pals, nor were they teachers, each of them had grown together over their time living in the city and drinking in The Cracke. John insisted they call him by his first name, even though Anthony was far more used to using surnames. Ste Baker, who sat opposite him, was about as far from Anthony as one man could possibly get. His muscular frame gave a clue to the fact that he worked down at the docks and he swore with almost every word, but he was a good man, an honest man, and Anthony knew that he would trust him with his life. He nodded his bald head at Anthony as he sat down.

'All right, lad. Haven't seen you in a while,' John said as he clapped Anthony on the shoulder. 'Pint of stout, is it?'

It was a long running joke between them and Anthony, and the glint in John's eyes gave it away. They knew that he hated the thick local brew, preferring something lighter and more palatable, but he let them have their laugh.

'Yeah,' he replied. 'You'd better make it two if you're buying. I'm pretty sure you owe me.'

'See, lads. You were wrong, he does have a sense of humour.' John got up to go to the bar and the table wobbled again.

Williams leant in, arresting it, and continued his story. The mole under his left eye moved up and down as he told that old familiar tale of the time he had rescued some damsel in distress from a fire. Williams's son attended the school and so Anthony knew there was more than a little embellishment to the tale, but as usual he let him tell it. He suspected that for Williams it wasn't so much the story itself, but the telling of it that he lived for. Anthony wondered whether he should ask Ruth about helping Williams to become a writer, but he had no idea whether the man could even read and write. As long as Anthony had known him he had drifted from one job to another, just long enough to put food on the table for his family.

Anthony looked over his shoulder at the bar. John was the only other one of them with what he would call a career. He was a policeman, and Anthony suspected the true source of all of Williams's stories. John winked at Anthony before turning to make his order. John was somewhere between the three of them with broad shoulders that just about gave away the strength there. Anthony knew enough about him to know that he wouldn't fancy getting into a fight with him. Good thing that they were friends, not that he could ever see John spoiling for a fight. Despite his profession he was a gentle man, and probably one of the kindest Anthony had ever met. He just hid it well behind a facade of mocking humour.

Anthony would have offered to help anyone else with the drinks, but he knew John would have nothing of it. Even if Anthony went over there, John would ignore him and carry the drinks himself. Such was the man. He came back only a minute later, somehow carrying four pints in his large hands. A beer sloshed over as he put it down on the wonky table, and the liquid almost splashed over Anthony's hand.

'Sorry, lad,' John said. 'That one's mine.'

'So, why haven't we seen you in ages, Lloyd?' Baker asked, while John settled himself down. 'Given up on your old pals, eh?'

'I've been busy. There's a war on, you know?' He attempted a wink, but felt more of a fool for it. 'I was training to be a warden, then they started bombing the hell out of us and now I'm needed to make sure people like you follow the rules.'

A frown crossed Baker's face for a moment before he broke out into a grin and spoke again. 'So you're enjoying spending time with all the pretty lasses in the Women's Voluntary Services, eh?'

Anthony said nothing. Anything he did say would only confirm Baker's assumption, even if he flat out denied it. That was the way these conversations had always gone, as they tried to set him up with yet another woman. Couldn't they understand that he was happy on his own?

'He is,' Baker continued, slapping a palm on his face and looking to the others for approval. 'He is. He's sweet on one of the women volunteers. I knew it! That's why you've been hiding from us the last month or so.'

John gave Anthony an apologetic look. Even with his sense of humour, there was a line he didn't cross. He hadn't forgotten Julie either.

'Go on, what's her name? Do we know her?' Baker chuckled to himself, not realising that the other three were not joining in. For some reason the image of Ruth flashed through Anthony's head, and he felt himself blush, only making the situation worse. He barely knew the woman, and she was married.

'Come on now, Ste.' John took over. 'We're here for a good time, not to pick on Tony. Leave him alone and let's change the subject. Why don't you two lazy bastards tell us why you haven't signed up for anything yet? We all have to do our part, haven't you seen the posters?'

'Excluded professions, ain't we?'

The three of them returned to good-natured bickering while Anthony sat in silence, weighing up the absence of his wife and the presence of Ruth in his mind. For some reason the image of Ruth's gently mocking smile wouldn't go away. He had only had a few sips of his pint, but maybe that was enough. He knew as soon as he had met Ruth that she would somehow work her way into his thoughts. He didn't trust her as far as he could throw her, yet . . .

'Are we ever gonna get you to the footie, Lloyd?' It wasn't the first time that Williams had asked him.

'You know it's not my thing.' He took another sip of beer, let the tangy liquid slop around in his mouth.

'Aye, but that's 'cause you're a secret red. I know what you're like. You pretend you've got class, but you support the wrong side.'

They had made it a game even after all these years of trying to guess which local team Anthony supported. It didn't matter that he preferred his balls ovoid rather than spherical. He almost stifled a laugh – he was becoming uncouth – but decided to let it pass as a response to Williams's question.

'What does it matter now anyway? The new Northern league isn't worth watching. Liverpool beat Chester six–nil the other week. That can't be fun to watch, where's the challenge? Now, if that was a rugby score, that would have been a pretty spectacular game.'

'How do you score six points in rugby?' Baker asked.

They laughed, and men at other tables looked over as they drowned out the ambient rumble of conversation. None of them were put off by the annoyed glances, it felt good to let go after so long worrying about the threat of German invasion. It had been almost a year of tension, waiting, wondering what was going to happen to them. While the endless training had focused their minds, it had not taken away the worry. Now they had experienced their first raids it was almost as if the fear had gone, now they had action.

Williams was back to telling one of his stories. It was the one about his mother-in-law that Anthony had heard possibly a hundred times before. He had decided the only way to pass the time was to observe which part of the story had changed in this telling, and he was sure by now that it no longer resembled at all the story as he had first heard it. Anthony wondered how much truth there had been in the story in the first place, but he laughed in all the expected places and let Williams have the limelight.

'. . . and then Lord Derby gave her a hundred pound to go away.' He finished to the usual round of chuckles.

'That's not true, though, is it?' It wasn't the first time that Anthony had aired his objection to the story – last time it had been fifty pounds – but he regretted his outburst as soon as the eyes turned towards him.

'What, lad?' Williams almost puffed himself up, and Anthony remembered how much larger the other man was. He shook his head, but Williams wasn't appeased. 'You sit there passing judgement on me, like? Thinking you're better than me, but you're not.'

'At least I don't make up stories.' He didn't know why he was poking the bear, maybe he had hit his head harder than he thought the other week. Or maybe he had just had enough of lies and grandstanding. He opened his mouth to say something but John forestalled him.

'Come on, Tony. We're all friends here.'

'Are we, though?' Williams asked, his voice now coming as a rumble from deep inside his throat. The pub fell silent, and Anthony signalled it was his turn to go to the bar. He tried to push closer, but a pair of older gentlemen blocked his path. They were sitting on stools by the bar, and Anthony would have to squeeze between them to get closer. The barmaid moved away before he could get her attention and he tutted involuntarily at the frustration. One of the men looked back at him and muttered something under his breath.

'Pardon?' Anthony asked, wondering whether he was standing too close to them or had otherwise done something to upset him. It didn't pay to upset the regulars in a pub.

'I said.' He looked up at him, and as he spoke, Anthony could see a few blackened teeth through his straggly grey beard. 'What are you doing here? Why haven't you enlisted?'

Anthony paused for a moment, surprised by the question. Had this man served during the last war? Was that why he was asking? Would Anthony offend him by his response? Had he already offended him?

'They wouldn't take me,' he replied after a few awkward moments, and he regretted immediately how pathetic it sounded.

'That's what they all say. There's always some excuse for being a coward.' He put his pint down firmly on the bar, and had it been fuller, the beer would have spilled over the side.

'Come on now, Fred,' his companion said, placing a liver-spotted hand on the other's sleeve. 'We don't want no trouble here. We're just trying to have a nice quiet drink, right?'

Fred pushed the hand away and stood. Despite his appearance, when standing, he was almost as tall as Anthony, and he stared Anthony right in the eye.

'What makes you think you're so special, eh?' He spat in Anthony's face, and he could smell the beer on his stale breath.

Those words hit Anthony particularly hard. Had he not said

exactly the same to someone else recently? What made him special? Nothing, nothing at all. He wanted to do his bit like everyone else, but no matter how hard he tried, he couldn't.

'You're just a coward, aren't ya?'

Anthony tried to extricate himself from the bar, but realised then that others had stepped up behind him. Was it his imagination, or were they glaring at him as well? Was he really a coward? Trying to remove himself from the situation would only prove them right. Questions flew through his head. He wanted to tell them everything, tell them how he had always wanted to fly, but he knew that it would not appease them. Fred, or whatever his name was, had already made up his mind about Anthony. He pushed in closer, and all Anthony could see was the man's cloudy, drunken eyes. Despite the fogginess, there was emotion in them, something that Anthony couldn't fathom. This man had seen things.

He pushed Anthony in the chest, trying to force him to speak. Even though he was an older man there was still a wiry strength in those arms. Anthony almost moved backwards, but was pinned between the two barstools. He hoped that the others would come to his rescue, but in the press of the bar there was no hope.

'I'm no coward, sir,' he said, directing his words to those pressed around him as if they would stand up for him, but they stayed silent. 'I'm a warden, I stay up all night during the raids making sure people are safe. I've always wanted to do my bit.'

What was he saying? He sounded like a child, a pupil appealing to his teacher for failing to do his prep and coming up with whatever excuse he could think of. It wasn't like him. Maybe he was a coward after all and all it had taken was this man saying it out loud for him to realise it.

'Ooh, a warden, eh? You don't know nothing, lad. That's nothing like fixing a bayonet and staring down the barrel of a machine gun. You sit here drinking this swill while the boys out there are risking their lives so you can live in luxury. What a fucking coward.'

Fred moved back, but as soon as he did his arm swung back and forward. Anthony barely had time to dodge before the fist clipped the side of his jaw. He rocked to the side as his chin stung, but the press of the bodies helped him up. They moved more now as if agitated by the punch, and the noise in the bar rose. Someone near Anthony was shouting, but he didn't hear the words. All he could hear was his own heartbeat.

Fred moved again, like a boxer shifting around the ring, but Anthony didn't wait this time. He just balled his fist and let fly. It connected with Fred's jaw, as his eyes widened. There was a sickening crack, and he fell back onto the bar, scattering his pint glass. It barely had time to shatter before he was up again, and rushing at Anthony. He took Anthony low, like a rugby player. Anthony tried to push back.

'Call me a coward again,' he said, and picked Fred up by his collar. Someone called Anthony's name, but he was too fixated on the whites of Fred's eyes. The older man knew he had underestimated Anthony, but bravado wouldn't let him back down. One of them had to win and the other end up in pieces on the floor. Before he could press his advantage, Fred thrust forward and smashed his forehead against Anthony's nose. There was a crack and his top lip felt wet. Anthony let go and reached for Fred's neck, but a hand grabbed his shoulder from behind. Anthony swung round ready to let loose. The man facing him was the landlord, his ruddy face even redder than usual and his own hands balled in fists. Anthony was running on pure adrenaline and his heart thumped in his chest. He had never been in a fight before in his entire life. Not like this anyway. Maybe a playground scuffle with another boy, but never an actual pub brawl. It wasn't like him at all.

'Out! Out now! Before I call the police.' The landlord took a firm grip of Anthony's jacket.

'I'm sorry. I don't know what happened,' Anthony protested, trying to wriggle free. 'I didn't throw the first punch. It's just a misunderstanding.'

'I don't bloody care. You're out. No one fights in my pub, and if I ever see you back here again, I will get the police. You understand?'

He all but flung Anthony towards the door and he stumbled against a table. The pub had fallen silent again, but the absence of sound was punctuated by a crunch from outside like metal being ripped apart. There was a faint keening, but it was barely audible through the thick walls of the pub.

'What the hell is that noise?' someone asked nearby.

'Fireworks?'

'Don't be sill—'

Anthony wrenched the door open. They had failed to hear the sirens, in the melee. Outside, the evening air was thick with the sound of anti-aircraft guns from around the docks and the battery at Sefton Park. Anthony could just about make out the drone of aircraft in the distance, rising in pitch as they approached.

'Put that light out,' someone from inside the pub shouted then laughed at their own attempt at a joke. Anthony couldn't hear whether the others joined in over the whistling that was now preoccupying him.

'Everyone get down!' he shouted, slamming the door behind him and jumping to the floor. He blacked out as the sound of smashing glass filled his ears.

# Chapter 7

Ruth laid her notebook down on the kitchen table as she heard a bump on wood. At first she didn't recognise it, thinking it was the sound of an empty house, but as it grew louder, more insistent, she realised what it was: a tentative knocking on the door. She wasn't expecting anyone and she paused, wondering who on earth it could be. George was with Harriet for the day, and from a quick glance at the clock, wasn't due back for another few hours. Her family wouldn't come to see her, so who could it be?

She wrenched open the door and her eyes dropped to see a boy hopping from one foot to the other. He could only have been a few years older than George, but she couldn't imagine her son knocking on people's doors like this. The boy had propped his bicycle against a bush and it was snapping back the leaves, but she let it go for now. She shouldn't let things like that bother her. He held out a small orange envelope to her. Ruth stared at it. Peter wrote letters to her, and she couldn't think of anyone who would go to the effort of sending a telegram.

'You'll need to sign for it, ma'am,' he said as he pushed it towards her. He held a form in his other hand, a pen hanging from a length of twine.

She took the envelope, ignoring the form, and ripped it open. It was like removing a plaster, the quickest and most painless way. Her eyes blurred at first, refusing to read that it had come from the War Office, but after a second or two she could focus on the stark black type. She scanned it, murmuring the words out loud.

*Mrs Holt, the War Office regrets to inform you that your husband, Lieutenant Peter Holt, was aboard ... and is presumed to have lost his life ... You will be informed as soon as further information becomes available.*

She read it again, unable to believe. The words blended into one another and all she could focus on was the last sentence.

'What?' It was a stupid question. The message was clear enough, but somehow she couldn't reconcile it. She had questions, as if the boy before her, this *angel of death*, had any answers for her other than what was written on the telegram he had given her. Was this it? Was this how it all ended?

'They've made a mistake. He can't be ...'

A tear dropped onto the paper, smudging some of the words, but what did it matter?

'*Peter*,' she breathed, and she could see the moisture on the cool evening air. It was like his spirit was escaping her, and she almost dropped the paper. Instead, she gripped it more tightly, her knuckles whitening and the sheet crumpling in her grip. She couldn't bring herself to damage it, but then perhaps she might be able to pretend it wasn't real. When his ship had made it through Dunkirk, she had thought he could make it through anything, but she should have known that in this war his days were always numbered. How many had they lost now?

'Ma'am?' The boy's voice somehow seemed younger, reminding her again of George. 'I'm sorry, but could you sign for it, please? Only, I've got others to deliver ...'

She grabbed at the pen, missing it the first time, then scribbled her name, barely taking the time to check whether her signature was legible. Damn them. She didn't care whether they could read it or not. Damn them for informing her like this, through a tiny piece of paper, through those heartless and unfeeling words.

Peter was gone. *Dead*. She felt numb. She would have expected a wave of tears, and an intense burning pain, but instead she simply felt numb. Maybe it was the shock, maybe it was something else. Her thoughts ran away, no longer wanting to be near her, erratic and dark. She slammed the door shut.

Her back hit the wall and she slid down. Within seconds she was a heap on the floor, clutching the telegram sheet in one hand, her vision blurry with tears.

In some way she had always known that Peter was never coming back, but she had never allowed herself to realise it before. Even when they had said goodbye at the docks, a part of her had known it was their final farewell. She hadn't been able to admit it, always pictured him walking through the front door at any moment, a big smile on his face. Now that would never happen.

'What do I do now?' she wailed at the ceiling, thankful that the neighbours were out. 'Why? Why? Why?'

Sometime later the front door opened and a familiar shape appeared in her peripheral vision. She still couldn't focus through the tears, but she knew it was George from the smell of him. Childlike. Pure.

'Mum? What's wrong, Mum?' he asked. She was vaguely aware of him nuzzling into her body in an effort to comfort her. She straightened his fringe and looked him in the eyes. How could they be so like Peter's? She would have to tell him some time, why wait? And yet the words stuck in her throat.

'It's your father,' she said, eventually. 'I promised you he would be home soon. But I was wrong.'

'He's not coming home?' His voice was thinner than even hers felt.

'No, my love.' She looked him directly in the eyes, only just able to make them out through her own tears. 'His ship was sunk in a battle. He died protecting us from the Germans.'

He didn't say anything but pushed his head further into her chest. He was stronger than she gave him credit for. She couldn't say how long they sat there, cheeks wet, but eventually it became dark inside as the sun was lowering in the sky. Her legs became numb, but still she wouldn't stand, couldn't stand.

# SEPTEMBER

# Chapter 8

**Sunday, 1 September 1940**

In the early hours of the morning Ruth's city was on fire and there was nothing she could do to stop it. She had wanted a distraction and she had got it. The Doric edifice of the Custom House, which they had become so used to seeing towering over the docks, had taken a direct bomb hit, but so far its columns had been unaffected. Ruth, volunteering nearby, had felt the shockwave as the windows on the first floor flew out, covering the street in shards of glass. They cracked under her feet as she moved closer. Only a small portion of the building, the largest in the area, was affected, but flames gutted one of the upper-storey offices. Incendiaries had paved the way for the bombs, and there were flames wherever she turned. She knew the building well, had interviewed many of the officials working in there for various articles about city life over the past few years. The fire licked the lintels of the window frames like orange climbing flowers, growing and consuming the roof of the building. If the fire spread it could take the whole building, burning away hundreds of livelihoods in the blaze.

She had been tasked with the mobile catering van, to hand out cups of tea and sandwiches to those men working to clear away the results of the blitz, but she wanted to do so much more. Why should the women be reduced to making cups of tea, when they could help too? She would have to have another word with her section commander and insist on doing something more useful. She didn't doubt that a strong brew helped, especially in this cold, but surely it didn't need all of them to do it? And the sandwiches were truly vile, caught at the bum end of the rationing scale. Most of the men avoided them, especially the second time.

A warden rushed past, the W on his helmet bobbing as he darted over the road, leading the firemen into position. Other volunteers stood around and gaped, but Ruth moved closer to see how she could help. Two men dragged a hosepipe with them, and she could see how heavy it was from the frowns on their faces. They looked like they were trying to win a tug of war, and just then, as if by a poor turn of fate, it caught between a lamp post and the corner of the pavement. The men almost fell as they tugged, but they were too far away now to dislodge it. She wanted to help, but was frozen in place.

The water gushed through. At first the pump was weak but after a moment full pressure took hold and the firemen struggled to aim the stream at the source of the flames. They were already working hard, sweating under the heat which must have been unbearable.

'We need to call back the fire crews heading to Birkenhead. They're needed here,' one of them shouted. 'Someone run to the incident officer and get it sorted.'

None of the firemen could be spared, so Ruth volunteered. Before she could move away there was a low thrum and one of the men in front of her dropped to the ground. Others ducked as the roar of an aircraft's engine grew louder. Ruth hunched behind a fire engine, the scent of oil suddenly thick. Pinging rattled the other side of the vehicle and she spotted another man drop to the ground, his cry drowned out as the bomber flew overhead.

Ruth pressed her back against the engine, unsure whether it was safe to break out into the open again. This was a new threat. Not only was it bad enough that the bombers were dropping high explosives indiscriminately upon them, but they were now turning their machine guns against those tireless civil defenders. It was her first taste of what fighting might be like for those on the front line, but she was no soldier, she had no training for this. She pushed herself down again as more rattling filled the air, but this time it was the sound of the fire engine's motor turning over and then failing to start. Whoever was in the driver's seat tried to start it again, and it roared into life with a shudder.

Already two men were seeing to the shot fireman, turning him over to inspect his wounds. They had either decided it was safe, or they were far braver than she could ever be. From where she cowered she could see him cough bright red blood from his mouth as he fought for air. One of the men was trying to stem the bleeding, but was having no luck as his forearms, with sleeves rolled up, were covered in vital fluid. The fact that she felt she had come to know him in some small way was significant. He thrashed on the ground and then fell still.

The man who had been trying to save him rocked back on his haunches and let his arms drop by his sides. The whites of his eyes met with Ruth's and she could see the defeat in them. If the Germans would even attack the defence volunteers on the ground, then how could they fight back? It was futile. The best they could do would be to survive, but Ruth didn't want to simply survive, she wanted to help as many people as she could.

She reached for the camera she had secreted in her overalls, then hesitated. She had borrowed the camera from the office. Strictly speaking, no one knew she had it, but they would understand when they saw the pictures she had taken. No one else would be able to get as close to the bombing as she could, given her volunteer's uniform. People needed to see what was happening while they were safe in the shelters, or worse refusing to shelter in anywhere but their homes. But taking a picture of that poor man seemed wrong, as if she was intruding on a private moment. What would his family think if they were to see the photograph of his dead body plastered across a newspaper sheet?

She let go of her pocket just as a warden reached down and proffered a hand coated in grime and oil. His face was similarly dirty as she looked up at him, a faint crack in the line of his lips showing white teeth. She thought it was Anthony at first, but this man was shorter, and the lines on his face suggested he was older. Why had she thought of Anthony?

'Lucky escape,' the warden said as she took his hand and welcomed the assistance.

Standing, she could see the damage the bullets had wrought on the fire engine that was now pulling away, and the pockmarks in the sandbags at the base of the nearest wall. She had been lucky after all. Those bullets must have passed only a few inches from her. Dusting herself down, she was thankful for the overalls, but noticed how the knees had been torn by the rough road. For a second it made her think of George and the number of times she had to repair his trousers, if he hadn't grown out of them first.

'How many casualties?' she asked the warden, who shook his head.

'Too early to tell. But there'll be more if they keep machine-gunning us. Best keep out of the way, lass. Let these men do their work.'

He moved off without further word. The Custom House was still blazing, and the heat washed down on her as the firemen fought to keep it under control. Water shot out of the hosepipes, and a fireman frantically operated the stirrup pump, but she could tell he was flagging as the pressure dropped and the water became a deepening trickle. She moved to take over but another fireman beat her to it, pushing his colleague away and shouting at him over the cacophony to take a break. Ruth supposed she should take him a cup of tea, but instead she pulled out the camera. Placing the viewfinder to her eye she tried to take in the scene as she saw it from the ground. Depressing the shutter button with quick stabs, taking as many photographs as she could and hoping that at least a few of them would be worth using. The warden who had helped her up gave her a wary glance, but said nothing as she passed, moving around the building to get a better view.

Once she had taken as many photographs of the Custom House as she dared, she moved on. First, she took a picture of a lone steel helmet lying in the middle of the street, forgotten when they had taken away the body of the man who had been shot, then she photographed the bullet holes in the walls. She wasn't sure how much film she had left, but she wanted to capture it all.

She passed an anti-aircraft gun, one of the ones Peter had told her about. The thought of him made her stomach rise into her throat, but the thumping of the guns soon drowned everything out and she had to cover her ears. Even still, she didn't think the ringing would stop for days. The men worked furiously, running from the ammunition store to reload. She was supposed to take them cups of tea, but they would be no use to them now, and surely cold by the time they had finished. She wanted to lend a hand, help with one of the big crates of shells, but she would only get in their way. What was she doing here?

That was a question she had asked herself many times since she had signed up to volunteer, but she finally had an answer. She was here to document the war, show everyone what they were going through, and force the city and the government to take better care of the people. That had been her cause since she was little, and all the war had done was to focus it, give her something to shout about. She wouldn't let her city or her people down.

She swung the camera around again, determined to use up the entire film, and looked through the viewfinder at a couple of buildings to the south of the city. The sight made her breath catch and she let the camera drop from her eye. It wasn't just the city centre that was on fire. While the bombers had now moved on they had also hit the other side of the River Mersey, this time missing the docks completely.

The greenish glow must have been several miles away. Thankfully they had missed their targets, but there were houses in that area. Ruth wondered how many people had been hurt. It was the newspaper's responsibility to report casualty numbers, even if they couldn't specify where the people had lost their lives. That said, they got their official numbers from the War Office and no one could be exactly sure how accurate they were. She didn't doubt that before this was over they would all know someone who had lost their life, and would be able to count the number of dead in their own small lives, no matter what the official numbers were supposed to be. She headed towards her home and the shelters. At least she could spend some time with George and Harriet, and maybe there was something she could do to help there.

# Chapter 9

Anthony didn't wait to see whether the others had made it out from the pub. Instead, he headed for the shelter he knew was nearby. He was off duty, and he had been drinking, so it made more sense for him to seek safety and wait for this raid to peter out.

Even in the entranceway to the shelter, the air raid siren was an incessant shrill. As if the smell and the dry air weren't enough to remind them. He thought about reporting on the conditions he had seen to the chief warden: the overturned tram, the shattered glass, but they probably already knew more than he did and he would only get in the way. He had heard rumours of shelters in the West End of London full to the brim with ten thousand people and only a bunch of buckets in which to relieve themselves. Of course the official message never mentioned anything like that, so he put it down to hearsay. They were all scared and some were suffering more than others. Some needed to make up stories.

The shelter was already cramped, making the acoustics different and giving the filled space a feel all of its own. A murmur of voices, all mingling with one. It was as if those in the shelter felt they could drown out the air raid siren and the whistle of falling bombs, but didn't want to raise their voices in case the German bombers could hear them. He was amazed by what he saw. Some had brought quilts made from bright fabrics and pillows of every shape and size in with them. And there were people from almost every background. In one corner a Chinese family, presumably from around the Nelson Street area, hunkered down together, the father whispering a story to a young girl in whichever dialect of Chinese he spoke. On the other side was a Sikh man, his white turban like a beacon of pure light in the gloom. Anthony worked his way through the throng to find a secluded place out of the way, passing a number of families. He knew some of them in passing and nodded a hullo.

As his eyes grew accustomed to the dark he recognised a face. A woman in WVS overalls was sitting on a bench in the corner, a small boy, her son, sat on her lap as another woman chatted to her. Her curly red hair spilled out around her shoulders. At first Ruth appeared confused, but then she smiled.

'You again? What on earth are you doing here?' he asked. Would he ever be free of that woman? He knew she must live somewhere nearby, but if he didn't know better he would think that she had been following him. Apparently, she didn't hear him over the din as her grin stayed plastered to her face. He wasn't sure what it was about Ruth that made him want to be so rude. She had a way of breaking down his defences just by her mere presence. It was as if she were some kind of siren. He blinked away the thought. Sirens had other connotations, and he wasn't willing to explore what that might mean. His reaction was quite unexpected. It was like she was prying into his life, ready to sift through the skeletons in his closet with but a moment's notice. He could feel a frown cross his face, but for once he didn't try and stop it.

'Me again.' She smirked up at him, as if hoping to further wind him up. He didn't respond to it. He cursed his legs for taking him closer.

'You look like you've been in a fight.' She indicated his face, and he felt a blush adding to the already purple bruise. If he was honest, it hurt like hell, but he wasn't about to say so. It must have been bad if she could see it in the dim light.

'You should see the other guy.' He was sure he had heard someone say something like that in a film once, but he cringed inwardly at how awkward it sounded on his lips. He didn't know why he was trying to impress her. She didn't care.

'It looks sore. Here, let me take a look at it.' She stood, handing the boy to the other woman, then reached out towards his face. She stopped, frowning, before he leant closer to let her examine the cut. She sucked her teeth. 'Ooh. You might want to get a professional to look at that, and it would probably be a good idea to stop upsetting people too.'

'I'll try.' He laughed, which only caused his head to sting. She wet a handkerchief and wiped the blood away. He felt like a child again. Perhaps she wasn't so bad after all? Or was this another angle to get stories out of him? She paused, turning away from him to address the other woman.

'Where are my manners? This is Mister . . . erm . . . Anthony. I'm afraid I don't know your surname.' If it was possible her cheeks turned a deeper shade of red than his own.

'Lloyd. Mr Lloyd,' he replied, taking over for her. He didn't know why, but he felt an explanation was in order. 'I'm a local ARP warden. Mrs . . . ?'

'Walters, my husband's name is Walters.'

She nodded towards him and reached out a hand for him to shake. She was a couple of decades older than Ruth, possibly old enough to be her mother, but Anthony didn't think so. There was no resemblance there: where Ruth's face was oval, this other woman had a round face with wide eyes and a smile that seemed to hang there as if she didn't even need to think about it. There was something about her that was familiar, then a thought dawned on him.

'Not Mrs Thomas Walters?'

She broke out into a grin. 'You know my husband?'

'Certainly. What a coincidence. I knew your husband before the war. We may have shared the odd drink.'

'Aye, a big drinker, is my Thomas.'

She drifted off into quiet reflection, and Anthony didn't dare tell her how much of a drinker her husband was. But he was a good man, honourable, and there was no way a friend of Thomas Walters could be as despicable as Anthony had suspected. He glanced back at Ruth. Her green eyes almost twinkled in the lantern light. She appeared as deep in thought as he was.

The shelter shook as a rumble filtered through the ceiling. Everyone fell silent as a child whimpered behind Anthony. A moment later some of the conversation resumed.

'This is my son, George.' Ruth gestured for the boy to come to her, but he stayed firmly on Mrs Walters's lap. 'Say hello, George.'

'Hello, George.'

They laughed. The boy reminded Anthony of Marc when he had been a boy, but George had filled out where Marc was a lanky stick of a child. He didn't meet Anthony's eyes, but looked to his mother. She must have fallen pregnant with him soon after meeting her husband.

'It's all right, George.' Anthony squatted to bring himself down to the boy's height. He was a gentle child and Ruth had clearly done a respectable job in raising him. 'I'm pleased to meet you. I'm a friend of your mother's and she and your father are incredibly proud of you.'

Ruth tensed beside him and it was only then that he noticed the tears in her eyes.

'What's wrong?' He reached out to her then pulled back, unsure whether she wanted comforting or not. Even though he had just described them as friends he had to admit it wasn't exactly true, so what right did he have to presume anything? She didn't answer, but shook her head, looking away from him. Her lips moved silently. He placed a hand on her shoulder – damn etiquette – and turned her to face him. Her eyes were full of tears.

'What's happened?' he asked again, taking her a few steps around a corner, away from the others so that she could speak without being overheard.

'Peter,' she whispered and coughed as if the word caught in her throat. It didn't take Anthony a leap of imagination to work out what she was trying to say.

'Peter,' she said again, in between sobs. She reached into her pocket and then pushed a piece of paper into his hands. 'A telegram. He's been lost at sea.'

'I'm so sorry,' he said. He didn't know what else to say. When Julie had died he hadn't heard any of the words others had used to try and console him; it had just been noise. For Ruth it would be the same. And yet, he couldn't just leave her standing there sobbing on her own. He pulled her into an embrace and wrapped his arms around her. They stood there while people stared, but they didn't care. Anthony stroked her hair as her body wracked against his with the sobs. Gradually they subsided and he felt her shoulders drop.

'He may still be alive out there, you don't know.' He pulled away from her, to give her space. He could see that the hope had gone from her eyes. They were dark, almost lifeless. He scanned the telegram and let out a sigh. 'It doesn't say for sure, and they said they would give you more information when they had it. Don't give up hope yet.'

'You're kind to say that, but I really don't think they would have telegrammed me if there was any doubt.'

'Stranger things have happened.'

She smiled at him, but it was a weak effort and it didn't reach her eyes.

'You're sweet, Anthony. But I have to accept that he's . . .'

She couldn't say it, he knew that, even without her obvious hesitation. He had been the same when Julie had died. Even now it hurt to think that word. It was so final. For a long time he had been unable to reconcile the fact that he would never see her again, never hear her voice, laugh at her jokes. It was too cruel.

'I didn't even get to say goodbye.' A fresh wave of tears spilled forth and he pulled her tighter.

He knew exactly what she was going through. He hadn't had a chance to say goodbye either, and that hurt was too much to bear, even if it had been many years ago now. It would take Ruth a long time to come to terms with what had happened, and she might never do.

'I'm here for you. Whatever you need, whenever you need it. You know where to find me. In fact, I'm going to make sure that I check on you regularly.' He put up a hand to stall her protest. 'I'm a warden, all right? It's the least I can do. I'll pop round and see how you're getting along.'

He didn't know exactly where she lived, but he would find her address from the warden's register or ask around. Someone would know. There was a crunch and the wall nearby rocked as something exploded overhead. They pulled apart again, and for the first time in years he felt the absence of a warm embrace. This woman was making him forget himself. It wasn't proper, and she had just lost her husband.

'That was a close one.' She was still shaking, but her breaths were shallower now. A hint of her habitual smile had returned. 'I needed that. Thank you, Anthony. Now, we must get back. The others will be wondering what's happening.'

It amazed him how things could change so quickly. He still wasn't sure he had got entirely the wrong impression of Ruth, but her being vulnerable in front of him had at least shown him another side of her personality. If she was willing to be that honest with him, then he would be willing to open his mind, a little. She led them back to the bench and he sat with them, in quiet reflection while the others murmured softly to each other.

It wasn't long before the all clear was called, but Anthony dreaded what the city might look like when he returned to the surface and they parted ways. And he knew with utter certainty that it would be far from the last raid. The war wouldn't be over by Christmas, no one believed that nonsense, and the press had stopped printing it, but not knowing when it might be over was part of the problem. At least in the shelter they could be ignorant of what was happening to their city, but he had a life to return to. Now he felt like he had a purpose.

# Chapter 10

Ruth stepped off the bus and a few other people followed her. None of them exchanged glances, staring at their feet like naughty children. None of them wanted to be seen near the camp. A sense of shame hung over them, as if it was some kind of prison. Ruth knew it wasn't supposed to feel like that, but she could think of no way of collecting a group of people together that didn't. These poor people were being held against their will. She had heard of the internment camps in Nazi Germany. Wasn't that the very thing they were fighting against? Hitler's fascism wasn't something they wanted here.

But she had to see him, especially after what had happened. She crossed the road as the bus pulled away, chugging its fumes behind it. Her walk took her away from the new council homes that had been built on one side of the road. Huyton was not a place she had known well before they had decided to place the internment camp here. It was only a short bus ride, too far for her to cycle, but it was like being out in the countryside. The houses were newer than hers, and there was more space between them. A village green separated them, almost out of sight of the main road and more trees. This was somewhere where children could grow up.

That was until the internment camp had arrived. She couldn't shift the weight of oppression it gave to the place. Huyton was like two sides of a coin: the sleepy idyll of suburban residency on one side of the road, and the prison camp the other.

She had expected the camp to be ordered wooden huts, made especially for its purpose, but it was nothing like that. From the buildings no one would be able to tell that it was any form of camp at all. The rot festered underneath that. They had taken houses that had just been finished and placed in them every German, Italian or Austrian citizen they could find. Many of them had never even so much as set foot in their countries of birth since leaving as children, but still the British government were wary. Churchill had told his government to lock them all up, lest one of them pose a danger to the country. It was incredible, and Ruth couldn't forgive the Prime Minister for what he had done.

An eight-foot fence had been erected around the houses. Rings of barbed wire prevented anyone from attempting to climb over, and a further ring of barbed wire inside made sure that they wouldn't get out. Her grandfather was a man of eighty who on a bad day struggled to get out of his chair, let alone climb an eight-foot fence. She couldn't even see George scaling something that high. He had wanted to come with her. 'Please, Mummy, I want to see Great-Grandpa,' he had said at the kitchen table, almost begging, but she wanted to keep him from anything like this. Her grandfather was the only one in the family who treated George like family. He doted on George as he had done when Ruth was a child and George loved him, but he was too young for this.

A pair of guards manned a gate, their rifles slung on their shoulders. They tensed as she approached and one of them stepped to block her path. Ruth reached inside her coat and the guard almost went for his rifle. What did they think she was going to do? Pull out a weapon and gun them all down while freeing the internees? No, her weapon was her words, her articles. Through the newspaper she would encourage the public to put pressure on the government. She had already written a piece about a family's experience of losing their home to the bombing. It was the first of a series she planned, but so far Rupert had only allowed her this one. It was with the censors now, so there was no guarantee it would even see the light of day. The guard was just trying to exert his authority, the authority of a soldier over a civilian. A man over a woman. He scowled at her, the dark brown of his eyebrows almost meeting, but she did not stop.

'My visiting order.' She pushed a piece of paper in his direction. At first they had not been able to visit the camp, such was the government's distrust of the inmates, but they had eventually relaxed their controls. She had used her position as a journalist in the beginning, not that they would let her write anything.

The soldier nodded to his companion, a shorter man who was clearly the sidekick. He jumped to and unbolted the gate, before letting one of its doors drift open. Ruth would have to push her way through. It was almost as if they expected the inmates to rush the gate, but as usual none of them so much as lingered by the way out. Nor did anyone turn to look as she entered. It wasn't just the visitors who kept their heads down.

Despite the number of empty houses that had been turned over to the camp, there was severe overcrowding. Ruth passed canvas tents on her way to where her grandfather was housed. Some had holes in them and many were tied up with fraying rope. There was a general sense of dampness about the whole camp. It smelt like the sea despite being miles from the coast, and Ruth wondered whether there wasn't also a large amount of illness. Even if some of these people were sympathetic to the Nazis, it was no way to treat them. They were still human beings.

When she had first come she had been escorted, but now they just let her walk about the camp. The guards no longer cared who she was. Her shoes sank into the earth by the front step. A pipe leaked nearby and there was no one to fix it. Staring at the front door, which looked so normal in this world of strangeness, she took a deep breath and closed her eyes. Even though she had been before, she never knew what to expect inside. The door opened with a click. It wasn't designed to keep anyone out. There was a faint whiff of boiled cabbage in the hallway, but it was soon taken over by the smell of sweat. Mould had already grown up the stairway wall, and there were no pictures on the walls, no trinkets or heirlooms. This was no home.

There were bits of discarded clothing, wooden food containers and other associated rubbish. When she had last visited there had been twelve men living in the house. One of the younger men had told her that he was moving into one of the tents so her grandfather could have more space. It was no way of living, no matter how well the men knew each other, and she knew that even the army wouldn't expect their soldiers to live in such cramped confines. But these men didn't matter, because they were foreigners.

Her shoe crunched on a box, but she didn't dare look down. She could already guess at the kind of mess that had been left around, especially if the smell was anything to go by. The stairs creaked as she climbed them and the banister wobbled in her grip. The houses might have been new, but they were cheap and made in a hurry. The men had given her grandfather the room at the front of the house, which faced south, so that he could have the best possible view. It buoyed her that even in these circumstances people could be kind. She would have to find some way to thank them for that soon, but she wasn't sure what the guards would allow her to bring into the camp. She took another deep breath before entering, then regretting it because of the smell.

Her grandfather sat hunched over an upturned wooden box stacked to make a makeshift desk. His white hair was curled around his ears, and the collar of his sky-blue shirt was turned up at one side. He was wearing only one slipper.

He didn't look up as she entered the room, but carried on scribbling. The pages were yellow and filled with his scrawling script. Ruth knew better than to disturb him. The box room he was occupying did nothing to dispel the illusion of a prison cell, and the door's lock appeared to be broken. The bed was nothing of the sort, a simple pile of straw with some tattered sheets on top. Her grandfather was far from the kind of man who would live the life of a soldier. The bedsheets didn't look slept in, they were neatly folded back on the makeshift bed, and Ruth wondered whether he had spent all his time writing. She couldn't blame him. Who would be able to sleep in here? She wondered whether she could appeal to the camp officer to bring him in an actual mattress, but she knew the answer already. They would not wish to show any favouritism, and they would expect it to be stolen.

She shuffled her feet, being patient while her grandfather finished whatever he was writing. She had expected him to stop at the sound of her movement, but it was as if she wasn't there. He often became engrossed in his projects, but she had never known him to be this oblivious to the outside world.

She risked a quiet 'Grandpappa', but still the pen flicked across the crumpled sheets. She should have brought him some writing paper, he would have appreciated the gesture. It looked as if he was writing over words that he had already written, all fighting for space on the same sheet. She wanted to take his hand and slow him down, help him find some kind of peace, but knew it would only agitate him further. She kept her voice calm as she called out to him again, louder this time.

'Grandpappa? It's Ruth. Can you stop for a moment?'

The wagging pen slowed and switched directions for a second, but it did not stop. He had heard her, despite his actions. What on earth was occupying his attention so? It could wait.

'Grandpa!'

The pen fell from his grasp, rolling with the stalled motion, and clattered down the wooden box to land on the floor. Ruth knelt to pick it up for him – she knew it was precious to him – and came down to his eye level.

'Ruthie?' His voice was like a scratch in his throat, weak and struggling. She assumed that he hadn't spoken to anyone for days. There was no sign of the accent she remembered from when she was little. 'Is that you? What are you doing here?'

'I've come to visit you, Grandpappa.' She laid a hand on his arm, but he had already returned to his writing. 'To see how you were doing.'

His eyes glazed over as if he were viewing another time and place, and Ruth tried to pull him back. 'What were you writing, Grandpappa?' She took his hands in hers, feeling their coldness and willing them to take some of the heat from her body.

'Hmmm?' He glanced down at her hands enveloping his and smiled. 'Oh, that? Memoirs. Of a sort at least. Trying to remember my home, my country. Austria. You know I was born in Austria? A beautiful country. Beautiful. The green hills over the Attersee, so much greener than England. The air was different, purer. We can't let the Nazis destroy it, sully it with their ambition. I will never forgive them that. I stopped visiting then, although I wish I could see it as it was. I fear it's already gone . . .'

He drifted off, but the brightness had returned to his eyes, fuelled by passion. Of course, Ruth had travelled to Austria when she was younger. Her parents had emigrated from Austria to England when Ruth was only a couple of years old and her sister only a baby. Before the war they had returned to their homeland.

'Can I read it?' It was her grandfather who had fostered her love for reading from an early age, reading to her in both English and German his favourite books from romances to history and philosophy. He was the only one who had truly understood when she had said that she wanted to write, and had given her a pen just like the one he used. It was precious to her too. She wanted to tell him about Peter, but when he was like this there would be no point.

'Oh, not yet, I think. I'm not sure I can even read it.' He flashed her a smile that reminded her of when she was little, him sitting on her bed reading to her. 'You know my handwriting, it's like some kind of code that only I can decipher, if I'm in the right mood.'

He shuffled the papers together, making the place tidy, and rested the pen on top. 'It will take me a while to sort through this mess, I think. I just can't seem to force it into any kind of shape, like my mind is unfocused and fluffy. It's all wrong and I just keep writing.'

She knew exactly what he meant. He had always been protective of his writing, as if it was only for him, a way of getting the thoughts out of a busy head to leave room for others. She could empathise with that, but as far as she was concerned words deserved to be read. Words only found their life through the reader. Before he had left Austria he had published a number of poetry collections and even a novel, but had not published anything since. He had been well known in his small community, but now she expected the Nazis had burned his books, along with many others.

'How have they been treating you?' she asked, dreading the answer. She got up from her knees and crossed to the bed, sitting with her back against the wall.

'The others bring me meals, so that's something.' He flashed a smile again, turning to face her and looking something like the man she had once known. 'And their cooking is far better than your grandmother's ever was, I can tell you that. I loved her dearly, but she could have burned charcoal.'

They laughed. It felt good to let the tension go, if only for a moment. Ruth hadn't realised how much she had been holding in. Her laughter was almost hysterical as if a dam had broken inside her. She missed her grandfather incredibly, and she wished she could take him home, but no matter how much she appealed, the authorities would not let him go. The country had to know what was going on, and while their newspaper didn't have much coverage, she was sure that if it was powerful enough word would spread.

Suddenly his eyes dropped to the floor.

'Have you seen my other slipper?' he asked and Ruth answered, but once again she had lost his attention to the sheet of paper.

Ruth wondered whether he had always been like this, or it was simply age. When she was younger he had seemed so confident and impressive, but had that just been the perspective of a doting granddaughter? If only she could ask her grandma what he had been like when they had met, when he had first come to England.

She knew she couldn't stay much longer. She had to meet Harriet and George and she had work to do. But she would spend the next few minutes watching her grandfather, to remember the man he used to be before this terrible war had come and imprisoned him. She would fight to get him out of here, appeal to whoever she could, make as much noise about it as possible.

Harriet was waiting for her near the Albert Dock, George's hand in hers. They looked far more like mother and child than Ruth and he ever did. Ruth almost stopped. Perhaps they were better together, it was not like Ruth was his flesh and blood. George's small face broke into a wide smile when he saw her, then he pulled out of Harriet's grip and rushed over. That grin was always a relief and it reminded her of Peter, even if their faces were not the same. Couldn't be the same. He must have picked it up from watching his father, like the pattern of his speech.

He almost knocked the wind out of her as he collided into her and hugged her. Should she have let him come and see his great-grandfather? Those wide eyes looked up at her, but Harriet was the first to speak as she came close.

'We've been walking up and down the docks. Been looking at all the boats. Haven't we, Georgie?'

George nodded enthusiastically, without breaking eye contact with Ruth.

'Did you like the ships?' she asked, knowing full well that he and Peter had often gone to the docks to look at the boats before the war. George even had a wooden toy that Peter had carved for him, in the shape of the ship he had been serving on at the time.

'There was a big grey one,' he replied. 'With lots of guns and men all on it.'

'That sounds exciting,' she said. Had she always been terrible at talking to children, or had she just grown out of practice while he had been away?

'Like the one Daddy was on,' he continued, breaking his gaze and looking downcast.

'I know, my love. We all miss Daddy, but he's safe now in heaven, far away from this horrible war.' She had never agreed with dumbing things down to George, much to her family's disappointment. He was a smart boy and lying to him would only create more problems in the future. She had told him the truth he deserved, but he also deserved reassurance. 'He would be very proud of you. I'm sure he's thinking about you right now.'

She hugged him tighter, smelling his hair and remembering how it had smelt when he was a baby.

'I wish I could see Daddy.' His voice came muffled from her chest.

'So do I. So do I.' Her voice almost broke, but she had to be strong for him. She was worried that he was more scared of the bombing than he was letting on. He might have asked more questions of Peter had he been there, but she would have to let him ask when he was ready.

Wires cracked, coming loose, and then barrage balloons rose into the sky like silver bullets. They were a sign of what they were living through and cast an oppressive shadow over the docks. It wasn't long before an air raid siren burst into life. She felt George flinch against her chest, and he pulled away. It was early for a raid, but you could never predict when the Germans would come.

'How do they know when the planes are coming?'

'You know, I have no idea.' She knelt down so that she could look him in the eye and hold him. That was something she would have to find out about. 'Your father would have known. We should find out together.'

He nodded and she saw a tear trickle down his cheek. She brushed it away with her thumb.

'Georgie, can you go with Aunt Harriet for me?' She was needed elsewhere. The Matron had relented and given her an opportunity to drive the van, and she didn't want to waste it. But it broke her every time she had to say goodbye.

'I want to stay with you.'

The words choked in her throat. 'I know, but I have to go and help keep us all safe. I will see you after the raid and we can talk about all the boats you saw today. All right?'

Harriet took a hold of his hand again. Ruth watched them both, unable to peel her eyes away, and hoped it was not the last time she saw him.

# Chapter 11

The shattered houses each had a sign outside with a forwarding address scribbled in clumsy white paint. Anthony wondered what had happened to the families that had lived there, but he hadn't yet had time to check up on them. In a way it was no longer part of his patrol, the end of a ruined street where no one lived, but a sense of melancholy made him walk by whenever he was on duty. It was something to do with wanting to remember the lives that had been a part of this street, but also wondering whether there was more that he could have done. As with a number of streets in the city, it had become abandoned. The blackout and the raids only gave a deeper sense of isolation and loneliness. Sometimes on duty he could walk for twenty minutes without seeing another soul. It was like being out in the countryside, like the valleys he had grown up in, but without the trees. The shadows were deeper, as if they too were manmade. The urban sprawl had been a culture shock when he had first arrived, but seeing it fall into disrepair was even more alarming.

A flash of movement from across the road caught his attention. He stopped dead in his tracks to see if he could spot it again. There shouldn't have been anyone around here, even if there wasn't a raid on. It was too dark for anyone to be checking on their former home. It could have been a stray animal. The government had suggested early in the war that it was in their best interest to dispose of pets, but people had refused and now the city was rife with them. Something about the movement suggested it wasn't a wild animal. It was too precise, as if they were trying not to get caught. After several seconds of watching and waiting, Anthony saw a young boy of about nine or ten come around a corner into the open, shortly followed by a friend.

Anthony observed them from across the road as they entered the house. They acted as if they had every right to be there, and had no idea that he had seen them. He wondered whether they were just looking for somewhere to shelter for the night, but he had an unshakeable feeling he had seen them before and they had been up to no good then too. Besides, a partially bombed building was not the best place to sneak into if there was to be a bomb raid. Maybe they thought that old saying was true, that lightning never struck twice, but he doubted it. They were up to something, and it was down to him to find out what.

He glanced along the street. Even in the darkness you could usually see a silhouette or the shadows of people moving about, but tonight the road was completely empty. Wondering whether he should go and find a police officer, he realised he would need more evidence than seeing three young boys outside during the blackout. Even with his ARP credentials the police would tell him they had better things to do. The wardens had fought with the police on these things before, and he knew they thought of the ARP men as busybodies, too ready to complain about the most minor of infractions.

A light flickered in the upstairs window, and he knew then that he had to act. If breaking into someone else's property wasn't bad enough, exposing a light was also a crime. He would give them a warning; he wasn't a monster, but it was better he got there before anyone else saw them, otherwise he might not be able to be so lenient.

Unsurprisingly, he found the downstairs of the house darker

than the street, as he entered through the hole that had been blown in the wall. He was careful not to trip on the fallen bricks following the route the boys had taken. The sound would surprise them and he didn't want them to know he was after them; let them continue whatever they were up to undisturbed.

The stairway led off the main hall as it did in most of the terraced houses in the city. He wondered if any of the houses had been designed differently, but he had yet to see any evidence. There were a couple of portraits along the wall, their sepia eyes watching him as he invaded their home. Each step creaked as he placed a foot on it, even though he climbed with care. He wondered whether they were still stable enough to hold his weight. The boys had managed to climb them, but they were probably less than half his weight, and lighter footed.

There was a loud groan of wood bending and he stopped, unsure of whether he should go back or plunge forward. The banister snapped and he fell. His leg slipped down the side of the stairway before he managed to catch himself. His trouser leg had ripped and he was sure that he was bleeding from a cut along the length of his calf, but it could have been worse. With a grunt he managed to pull himself back onto the stair and stopped for a moment, breathing a sigh of relief. It wasn't far to the ground floor, but he could have done himself more damage if he'd fallen awkwardly, a broken arm or leg.

'What was that?' one of the boys whispered from upstairs, the high pitch of his voice carrying through the now silent house. One of the others shushed him, and Anthony could hear his heart thumping heavily in his chest.

He flicked on his electric torch and plunged through the living-room doorway. The red filter made everything look as if it was covered in rich blood. Only sparing a second's thought for the people who had lived there he made for the staircase.

'Stop!' The boys looked back at him, wide eyes caught in the beam of his torch. One of them had his hand in the top drawer of a chest of drawers and he didn't move it, as if the shock had paralysed him. The boy to his left bolted towards another doorway, hoping to find a way out, but Anthony knew he was standing between the boys and the stairs, the only way down to the ground floor. The boy clattered through the open doorway, dislodging some bricks that fell down to the ground floor and cracked apart. He stopped, teetering on the threshold.

Anthony wished then that he had gone for a policeman. Close up, the boys were older than he had initially realised, perhaps in their early teens, almost ready for the world of work. One of them was almost as tall as Anthony.

'Who the hell are you?' the one in the middle said, his size and attitude marking him out as the leader. He squared up to Anthony and Anthony might have laughed if he hadn't suddenly felt outnumbered. He wondered how he would have dealt with the situation had it happened in the school, but these boys most definitely weren't from his school, and there was something about them that was rather more desperate.

'Never you mind,' he replied, trying to regain the authority. 'What do you think you're doing? You don't live here.'

He shone the torch in each of their faces, to commit them to memory and show he had the upper hand. It wasn't much of a weapon, like a search light against the oncoming bombers, but it was a slight advantage all the same. They would be blinded by the light of which he had control.

'No one lives here, do they? They're all gone, like. It doesn't matter now, they ain't coming back for this.'

'It's still stealing. Now come on, enough of this. Let's go.'

Sensing their time was up, the boys attempted to rush him to the stairs, but he wasn't going anywhere. He blocked their path like a scrum half, crouching low, ready to tackle. The first boy bounced off him and landed on the floor with a thud, while the second grappled with Anthony, his weak hands failing to land punches. Anthony enveloped him in a bear hug.

'That was stupid,' he said.

*

While it wasn't the first time that Anthony had been to see the Liverpool City Police, it was the first time he had dragged in minors. The sergeant behind the mahogany desk barely looked up as he entered, dismissing Anthony's warden's uniform. Then, when he noticed the two boys, he straightened in his seat.

'What's this then, lad?' he asked, folding the newspaper he had been reading. Anthony caught a glimpse of the *Liverpool Guardian*'s masthead.

'This lot been playing with too many candles, eh? Better throw away the key before they bring the whole German army down on us.' Anthony didn't particularly appreciate the smirk the sergeant gave him, but he let it go. He'd learnt from a young age not to argue with the police. He told the sergeant what he had witnessed and the other man's eyebrows rose with each sentence.

'And they just followed you here? Of their own free will.'

'I impressed upon them what would happen if they didn't.'

Anthony was just as surprised that the boys had come willingly, but perhaps they feared things would be far worse for them if they were to attempt to run away. He wouldn't chase after them, but he knew their faces and it wouldn't take him long to track them down.

'I'm sure their parents would have been just as merciful with them as I was.'

It was amazing sometimes how children could be more scared of their parents than authority. Trouble at home was often what led them to misbehave in the first place.

'I, err, guess I'll take it from here then.' The sergeant disappeared behind a wall, unlocked a door and stepped out into the reception area. 'Ta.'

He gestured for the boys to proceed through the now unlocked door, then stopped as someone else came the other way.

'Ahh, Mrs Holt,' he said. 'All done, are we?'

'Thanks, Bill,' Ruth replied and stopped in her tracks as she spotted Anthony. After a moment, a grin broke out on her shocked face. The sergeant disappeared with the boys in tow.

'You have to stop following me like this,' she said. Again there was that glint in her eye that he was quickly becoming used to. He couldn't help but smile.

'Stop getting into trouble, and I'll stop,' he replied, and caught himself before he gave a wink. There was a line he wasn't yet ready to cross. 'On the lookout for another scandalous story?'

'Unfortunately, these days I don't have to look far.' She shook her head, and Anthony wasn't sure if it was in self-deprecation or at the state of the world they lived in. 'I shouldn't be surprised that war seems to bring out the worst in everyone. Still, I've got hard-working public servants like yourself to keep me on the straight and narrow. What happened?'

Anthony wasn't sure why Ruth was really there, nor did he feel like asking her what she actually did at the newspaper. It wasn't any of his business, so he recounted the story of the boys' looting. He respected the fact that she didn't start taking notes in the notebook she was holding in one hand, but he knew she would store away the information for later use, if she could find some way of getting it into a newspaper column. That was why he didn't trust her, he had to guard himself and think before speaking.

'It's a shame,' he said, and she nodded apparently in sympathy. 'I feel like they're letting the city down, giving it a bad reputation. It'll be in all the papers, understandably. I just wish they were old enough to think of what they were doing to our reputation.'

'They're not the only ones—'

'I know,' he interrupted, feeling unusually chatty. It was as if he was confiding in her, and she was someone who understood what he meant. 'But they're all letting the city down. I bet we already have a reputation in London and the other big cities. Don't go to Liverpool, you'll get mugged!'

'That's not quite what I meant.' She grinned in a knowing way and he found it infectious. 'I meant that in the newspaper we're hearing reports of this sort of thing all over the country. Mostly in London, of course, it's much bigger than anywhere else, but all sorts are using the raids as an opportunity to beg, borrow or steal from those less fortunate.'

'I see.' He didn't know what else to say. He felt a fool for his assumption, and as was becoming a habit Ruth had put him in his place. 'Then morale isn't as good as they're saying it is, if people are getting desperate.'

'You're right there,' she replied. 'The censors are keeping things quiet, but obviously any court case has to be published, otherwise word will get out that they're covering things up. I'll have a word with the censors for you, see if they can't protect the city's failing reputation.'

There was that smile again, this time accompanied by a wink.

He knew that she was playing with him, but there was something in him that liked it, reminded him of being younger. Julie had never spoken to him like that, their relationship had been . . . functional, but he had loved her all the same. He wondered whether Julie would think badly of him for thinking of this woman in the same breath as her. Was it betraying her memory? He wasn't sure, but he couldn't help but compare them.

'Well, it would certainly be better for all of us if we kept the city's reputation intact,' he said, realising straight away what a fool he was.

Her face dropped. 'Is that the time?' she asked, looking up at the clock. 'I've got to go!'

Before he could say another word she was out of the door, and he could almost see the wind in her wake. He could hear her bicycle clattering down the street for a few heartbeats, then she was gone. What could she possibly have needed to leave for in such a hurry? Was it something he said? He looked around himself for any other clue.

On the sergeant's desk lay a familiar notebook. At first glance it might be dismissed as a detective's notebook, but to Anthony the mottled black leather cover had become familiar. He hadn't seen her put it down, but she must have done while they were talking. Without thinking, he reached out and pocketed it before the sergeant could notice and ask questions. Anthony had no doubt that he would see Ruth again and he would be able to return it.

# Chapter 12

**Wednesday, 18 September 1940**

Ruth switched on the wireless with a click. A few seconds later, the warming tones of Bing Crosby filled the room. It was a song that reminded her of Peter, but she knew that if she changed the station there would only be another memory. She set her cup and saucer on the side table and dropped into the armchair with a plate of toast. The tea had gone cold, but she didn't mind. She liked the way the flavour was even stronger when the heat had gone and she let it run around her mouth before swallowing. Once upon a time she might have spat it out in disgust, but now the bitterness spoke to her, felt appropriate. Since rationing had been introduced they had to savour everything they could, appreciate everything that had even the slightest taste.

She balanced the plate on the arm of the chair, but knew straight away that she had made a mistake. As she tried to grab it she forced it to smash against the wall. The breadcrumbs covered the carpet interspersed with bits of broken china. Tears ran down her cheeks, blurring her vision. She wanted to punch the arm of the chair, feel its resistance against her fist, but instead she simply balled her hand and let it drop against her thigh. A sound somewhat close to a moan escaped her mouth, which reminded her of some animal, a fox, stuck in a trap and calling for help. She didn't know who would come to her aid, she didn't even know if anyone could help her, and she was not in control of the sound as it grew louder and her tears grew heavier. She didn't know how she had any tears left, her cheeks were raw and her head foggy.

What was she doing wallowing in self-pity? It wouldn't bring Peter back. She had to do something, only she didn't know what. She had to think about George. She had to hold it all together for George. He was the only thing that mattered now. She became vaguely aware of movement in the room, and as her sight cleared she saw George on his hands and knees cleaning up the broken pieces.

'Leave that, dear,' she said. With shaking arms, she pushed herself up and out of the chair.

'But you're crying, Mummy. I'm just trying to help.'

'It's all right, it's all right.' She pulled him close, savouring the smell of his hair. 'We have to go now anyway.'

The carriage clock on the mantelpiece said that it was after six o'clock in the evening. She would be due on duty soon, and she couldn't allow them to see her like this, they would send her home. It didn't take her long to pull on her overalls, and head out of the house. She had done it so many times now that she didn't even have to think about it. With reluctance she led George to Harriet's doorstep. As an air raid siren burst into life on the nearby docks, she realised it had not been a moment too soon.

It was only when she turned the corner and was cycling down towards the docks that she felt a warm wave wash over her, as if the sun was rising across the landscape. Her face felt flushed and tears pricked at her eyes, but if she looked up she could stifle them, just like snuffing out a sneeze before it threatened to take over. She couldn't let the tears win, not now, not while she was on duty. It was hard enough maintaining her position, a woman out at night, a woman working, without letting that veneer of controlled calm disappear. They would judge her, treat her like she was 'just being a woman' – *come on, dear. Just sit down over here and compose yourself* – like some kind of elderly widow.

That word brought another wave of panic. *Widow.* That was what she was now, what she'd forever be known as. But it was easier to deal with that than to think about Peter. Even *thinking* his name was too much. She needed to work, to push these thoughts from her mind. There was a part of her that almost welcomed the bombing raid, but before that thought fully formed she realised that that would only bring pain for others like her. She wouldn't wish these feelings on anyone.

*

The news office was alive with activity the next day when Ruth arrived. She was late, but she had her reasons. Not that anyone would listen to them. Not that anyone would notice when she came in. As long as the work got done, she was generally free to come and go as she wished. Occasionally Rupert would want to know where she was, would want a meeting with her, but most of the time she could come up with a good excuse for being absent. Excuses such as interviewing criminals in jail cells. It wasn't the most glamorous part of her job, but there was always a story behind the thief or whatever else they were, something that had driven them to do what they had done. Most of the public failed to acknowledge that, believing that many people were just evil, but she was determined to dispel that myth.

She thought back to the jail. She didn't know why she had run out on Anthony like that, but something had made her skin flush. Had he been . . . flirting with her? That was impossible, simply impossible. But either way she had to remove herself from the situation as quickly as possible, give herself time to think.

None of the others even glanced at her as she walked through the door, placed her hat on a stand and calmly hung her coat underneath it. She wrapped her lamb's-wool scarf around the hook as she looked around the office for what was causing such a rush. Being invisible often came in useful. She wanted to cough and see if anyone would stop, but the others were too busy pulling copy and transferring pages from one desk to another. Ruth guessed that a big story must have come in. The only time the office had been like this before was when the government's ultimatum to Germany had expired and war had been formally declared. As was often the case, she would be the last to find out.

Rupert was arguing into a telephone receiver in the main office. He kept trying to get a word in and was cut off by whoever was on the end of the line, his face growing redder with each passing moment. Eventually he slammed the receiver down with a pronounced ring, then massaged his temples with one hand. Ruth could see him trying to find his cigarettes with the other. She took a hold of his arm, with about as much sympathy as she could muster.

'What's wrong?' she asked.

'A civilian ship's been torpedoed,' he replied, pulling away from her grip. She wouldn't let him go, not that easily, not without more information. If the conversation had been that heated then she needed to know more.

'What ship? Torpedoed? Where?' She had more questions, but he didn't look like he was prepared to answer any of them, so she would take as much information as she could get. He pulled his arm again, but realising she wouldn't let him go he stopped and turned to face her properly.

'We don't have much detail at the moment. That was the secretary at the Custom House. Trying to get anything out of him is like getting blood from a stone. It's the SS *City of Benares*,' he said as if she should know what that meant. 'You know the one, the evacuee ship. The bastards got at it.'

She thought of Peter, being sunk and drowning in the cold water. The mental image of him drifting away from her, the life dripping out of his eyes, would not leave her. Sickness welled up within her.

'It only left three days ago. There were women and children on that boat.' She was shocked by her own words. There were men too, but somehow it seemed more unacceptable that it was mainly women and children. No child deserved to die in war. No one deserved to die at all.

'Yes, damn it.' He smacked the telephone receiver again as if it was the thing's fault. 'A terrible tragedy. They were innocents in this bloody war, they shouldn't have been involved.'

'How many survived?'

'We don't know yet. We're still trying to get information from the port authority, but they're claiming they're too busy to speak to us. It would be different if we were the *Echo*. They'd be falling over backwards to tell us all about it.'

'Someone could go down there.' Ruth could only think that it was a perfect opportunity to have a look around, see what other information she could get hold of. What had she become, taking advantage of a tragedy like this? Anthony had been right about her all along.

'Sometimes, Ruth, I feel like you think I don't know how to do my job.' His reprimand was only missing a tut. 'Of course someone is going down there. Sam left . . . about ten minutes ago. He should be there by now.'

Ruth felt her opportunity dissolve in thin air.

'Haven't you got your own work to be getting on with?'

She gave him a stern look, but he was no longer paying her any attention. He had picked up the telephone and was already asking the operator to connect him. She left him to it and went to find a desk to work at; she had reports to write up about the state of the city.

She couldn't help but get annoyed at the things their fellow newspapers were writing about the British war spirit. She had seen first-hand in the city that morale was always hanging on a knife edge. And yet they still had to talk about how Britain would win the war, how much better they were than anyone else. If it was up to her to report the reality to the Ministry of Information then so be it. If they didn't take morale seriously, then she would have to find another way to get the information. After a few minutes of trying to write she put her head in her hands and let out a big sigh.

'What's wrong with you?' Robert asked from across a desk.

She sighed again. 'Just trying to work out how the hell we're supposed to write about all this mess.'

He didn't answer at first, weighing up the answers. She didn't bother looking up; closing her eyes helped her feel like the world was far away, even if her mind continued to operate at a rate of knots.

'Aye, it's a challenge,' was his concession to her point. Eventually she looked up, taking in the thin man sitting opposite her. His lips were pursed in concentration, as if he was trying to think of something more intelligent to say, and his balding head reflected the light of the gas lamps into her eyes. The sickly pallor of his skin gave away his reasons for not signing up.

'I'm struggling too,' he said, when he realised she was paying attention. 'Having to say that it was a North West town that was hit. We can't say where, name the street or anything of the sort. It has to be confidential.'

'But why? People know, they hear about it. The secrecy only makes things worse.'

'They's the rules. Even if it does make the writing boring. What do you expect us to do about it? We'll just get shut down, then we'll all be out of jobs. I don't know about you, but I don't fancy that with a housing crisis going on.'

She sighed again and wondered whether the similar reports about the Germans being war weary and struggling stretched the truth as much as the articles did about their own country. Journalism had just become a mouthpiece for the government, and they had to fight as much with the censors as they did with the Germans. If only they had some way of finding out what life was like in Germany, they could report on it and maybe change the course of the war. Her grandfather had made sure that they had seen as much as they could before it had become too much for him and he had fled back to England with them. Thanks to him there were things she missed about German culture – the food, the pragmatism – but even talking about them now would see her ostracised. Was it fair to blame an entire nation for the actions of a few? She couldn't risk asking the question, or she could end up in the camp herself.

Sam and John entered the room, placed their hats on the stand and continued their loud discussion. Robert rolled his eyes at her.

'There've been rumours of spies operating in the city,' one of them said. She thought it was John.

'What? That's all nonsense, they're probably talking about all those poor foreigners sent off to camps. What are they going to do from there, like? Apart from form a choir.'

'Nah. There's people trying to feed information back to the

Germans. They don't have to be German to sympathise with the Nazis, and a good spy wouldn't be obvious, would they? They'd blend in, like.'

For the first time they both looked over at Ruth and Robert, but almost without breath they carried on. She hadn't even heard women gossip as much as these two.

'The HMS *Prince of Wales* was almost sunk in Cammell Laird's shipyard.'

'Really? She hasn't even launched yet. Didn't the build cost several million?'

'Six, I was told.'

It was amazing the kind of gossip one could come across in a newspaper office. Ruth often thought that she needn't even travel far for a story, if she didn't feel like she wanted to see it with her own eyes. But she couldn't trust anything the others in the office said.

'The Boche are going to get what they deserve.'

'Wait till you hear the casualty figures.'

Now they had Ruth's full attention.

'Aye, apparently around two hundred people have died this month alone, with about three hundred seriously injured. Not to mention the number of houses destroyed.'

Ruth felt sick. That certainly wasn't what the papers were reporting. All those lost lives.

One of the office boys dropped a brown paper folder on her desk without a word and left. It was suspiciously clandestine, but she knew the boy had a crush on her and lost the power of speech whenever she was around.

She laid the folder in front of her and stared at it for a time. She couldn't explain why she was nervous, but for some reason she hesitated. When she had passed the roll of film on to the team in the dark room, she hadn't expected much. In fact, she had almost forgotten about it in the few weeks since the bombing of the Custom House. It wasn't really her field, she was a writer, yet there was still a large part of her that wanted the photos to come out well. If only to prove something to herself, she hoped they showed what she had seen during the raid, the fire in the Custom House. Somehow she wanted the photographs to capture the sound, the intensity, even though she knew that was impossible. At the very least, the photographs could help her to write the words she wanted. Still, she hesitated. There was nothing for it, no point in waiting. It was like writing, you just had to plunge in and hope for the best.

She flipped the brown paper cover over and gasped. There right in front of her was the Custom House in black and white. It was almost more real than the memory in her mind, as if the camera had managed to capture something she hadn't. The flames licking out of the top window were rendered in intense white, as if they were burning the very film itself. Next, the photograph of a lone steel helmet.

She grabbed the folder and almost ran to Rupert's office. The door was open and he was leaning back in his chair chewing on a cigarette. He raised his eyebrows.

'Look at these,' she said, almost throwing the folder down on his desk.

He didn't look impressed. A frown crossed his brow and he pursed his lips.

'What am I supposed to do with these?' he asked, flicking through the photographs.

Ruth took a second to hide her disappointment that Rupert had not seen what she had in them. He often needed leading to the point.

'Print them,' she said as if that was all there was to it. She knew better than that, but as ever she pushed her luck. He regarded her with that cool look.

'Now, Ruth, you know that's not going to happen. The censors won't like them. They're too obvious. Look at them, anyone around here would recognise it.'

'They'll have seen the damage anyway and we don't know until we try. Push them, see how far we can go. People deserve to see what is really happening, not some sanitised version. I watched the Custom House burn and if not for the efforts of the firemen it would have been ablaze. Imagine if that had been someone's house? Print the casualty figures too.'

'So you want to scare people, is that it? That doesn't sound like your kind of thing, Ruth. And it's not what we're about here.'

'No. Not scare them, but wake them up to the reality of the situation.'

'People in the city are scared enough as it is. You hear them everywhere, in the cafés, the pubs. They all fear for their lives. What purpose would this serve?'

'The truth. That's what we're here for. That's what I signed up for.'

'I'm sorry, Mrs Holt, but the answer is no.'

He leant back on his chair again, an indication that the conversation was over. She collected the photographs, determined not to let them end up in a bin somewhere. There would be another way of disseminating, and she just had to find it.

By the time she returned to her desk a copy of the morning's paper had been left on it. She flicked through eagerly looking for her name. The *Liverpool Guardian* wasn't a large paper, but it was a few pages before she found it. That didn't matter to her. Her story had made it through the censors and into print. She held the paper to her chest. Peter would have been so proud, she wished she could have told him.

She scanned the words, feeling a sense of accomplishment with each line. It really wasn't bad. Of course, the censors had had their way with it. There was no photograph of the family, and they had also cut out any names, whether of places or the people. There was no way anyone could work out who Ruth had written about, but at least the message was getting through. This was a start. If only she could convince Rupert to let her write more.

# Chapter 13

Anthony was sure he had found the right house, but the red-painted door was strangely intimidating. He hesitated, aware he was turning up unannounced at the home of a woman. He should have knocked by now, and he sensed blackout curtains twitching as neighbours asked amongst themselves, 'Who is this strange man standing on the doorstep?' He was here for good reason, but that wouldn't stop the gossip. Even on this street people knew he was a warden but were unused to seeing him in daylight.

He raised a hand to the knocker, but stopped. What if she didn't want to see him? He should have gone to the newspaper office instead. This had been a mistake. He was about to turn to leave when the door opened with a shudder and Ruth stood in front of him. By the look on her face she was surprised to see him.

'Anthony,' she said, more statement than question. Even still he felt the need to explain, but she continued before he could speak. 'I thought the kids from down the road were messing around again. They've been terrorising George.'

She looked around the crook of the door to see if she could spot them, and Anthony wondered whether it was simply to hide her embarrassment.

'I thought about knocking on the door and running off,' he said, to try and lighten the mood. 'But then . . .'

He held up the black leather notebook he had been carrying around. It took a moment for recognition to dawn on her face.

'I've been looking for that for days. I thought I'd left it at the office, but couldn't find it. I was this close to retracing my steps through the shelters and the bomb sites to see if I could find it. Come in, come in.' She led him into the house. The blackout curtains were still in place and the interior felt almost humid. 'I wasn't expecting company, so I hope you don't mind. I'm not really a good host, but then I don't expect you imagined I would be anyway, did you?'

He nodded. Sometimes, with the way she spoke and held herself, he expected her to live in a country house with a whole host of staff and acres upon acres of land, but at other times he could imagine her hauling crates down at the docks and swearing with all the others.

'Tea?' she asked from the kitchen as he stood in the hallway wringing his hat in his hands.

'Please. If you can spare any.'

'If I'm honest, I don't drink a lot.' When he didn't reply she carried on. 'I know, terribly un-British of me. Sugar?'

'You have sugar as well?'

A cupboard door squeaked open. He could hear her rummaging around and then it shut again.

'Actually, no. Wishful thinking.'

'Then no sugar, thanks.' He couldn't keep the grin from his voice. There was a scrape of metal as she put the kettle on the gas ring, then the whoosh as the gas lit. He wondered how long it would be until gas was rationed and they could no longer make tea whenever they liked. Surely that would affect the great British morale more than any bombing. If the Germans invaded would they bring coffee with them? They would sap away British culture in little ways like that. Did the Germans even drink tea? He hoped he would never have cause to find out.

'Make yourself at home,' Ruth called. 'If you can find a tidy place to sit. Sorry about the mess.'

The house was comfortable, if untidy. Anthony wasn't sure where to sit, there was a blanket over one armchair, and some wooden toys taking up one seat of the sofa, so he stood, waiting for Ruth to direct him. The faint smells of cooking lingered in the hallway, the starchiness of potatoes and something else he couldn't quite place. Rationing had caused them all to come up with more *interesting* meals than they were perhaps used to. Fortunately Anthony was fond of potatoes and most other vegetables, having grown up in the countryside. Ruth returned a minute or so later and pushed a warm cup of tea into his hands.

'You did say you wanted weak grey tea, didn't you?' She laughed an apology, then dropped herself into the armchair, leaving him with the sofa. 'I'm a terrible hostess.'

He wasn't really sure why he had come, he could have returned her notebook next time he saw her. It was something to do with wanting to clear the air between them, to see how she was doing without Peter. However, he wasn't sure how to say it, he wasn't even sure that there was anything between them. He had been presumptuous in coming here and he almost got up to leave. He had no idea what to say. What could they possibly have in common?

'Manners and etiquette are becoming a thing of the past,' he said. 'The war has only expedited matters. For example, a gentleman meeting a lady alone in her house, with the curtains closed.'

'Oh, so you're a gentleman, are you?' Apparently, she stopped short of sticking out her tongue, but she laughed and shook her head at his silence. 'Who cares what the gossips say, eh? I'm just another one of them, after all. But then, how did you know where I lived?'

'I . . . erm . . .' He had picked up the local vocal hesitation years ago, and had to remember to avoid it when teaching. He settled on vagueness. 'I have my methods.'

They fell silent, and Anthony ran a finger round the collar of his shirt. The humidity inside was making him sweat and he desperately wished he could undo his top button, but dreaded to think what it would suggest. To distract himself, he cast an eye along the spines of the books piled haphazardly by the sofa in the front room. '*Mrs Beeton's Book of Household Management*?' he asked, more of an observation than a question, while stifling a laugh. 'Not something I would have expected you to be reading.'

'Oh, that?' Ruth replied. 'It was a gift. I've never even opened it.'

'That sounds about right. It looks like you've got everything under control here as it is.' He smiled at her to indicate he was joking. 'Is there anything I can do to help? I can be useful, and I'm not too bad with a dustpan and brush.'

'No, no, everything's fine, please. I'm sorry for the mess, it's not always like this. Things have been difficult.' She drifted into a reflective silence.

'You should see my house. It looks like a bomb's hit it.' He cringed at the reference. 'Your home is like a palace in comparison. I'm not sure I can even maintain it on my own, not with work and volunteering. It's not been the same since . . . Well, you know, but I try. I actually enjoy being self-sufficient.'

Ruth picked up one of the wooden toys, a bus, and played it around her hands like a juggling ball. She didn't look at it as it moved from hand to hand.

'Your poor wife. Of course,' she said, looking up and locking eyes with him. 'I'm so sorry, it must be tough.'

Anthony ignored the fact that he was sure he had never told Ruth about Julie. He should have known that a journalist would know everything about him. Perhaps he should have been flattered that she had taken the time to enquire about him. He stifled a smile.

'Thank you. It's a long time ago now. Julie was dear to me, but we married young and we had a few wonderful years together. I've got used to it, and at least she's no longer in pain. I think my son misses her more than I do.'

He coughed, and noticed a tear in Ruth's eye. The way he talked made him feel like he was years older than Ruth, but there could only have been a couple of years between them at most. One never asked a woman her age, but somehow he would have to find out. Perhaps he could do some investigating of his own.

'That's not to say that I don't miss her, of course,' he continued. 'It's just a son needs his mother. I did my best for him.'

'I'm sure you did. He's done well for himself, hasn't he? I'm sure you made him feel loved. I can see you being a good father.'

'Thank you,' he said, genuinely touched by the comment. 'Marc used to take up most of the house, as only young men can.' Once he had gone off to enlist in the army his son had put his belongings away in storage. He didn't want his father messing with them, he had said. 'And Julie and I didn't have long enough together to collect too many trinkets.'

'I'm sorry,' she said, eyes downcast. 'You must be lonely.'

He thought for a moment, wondering how exactly he could answer that. It was something he had thought about a lot for the past few years.

'I don't really even know what that means,' he replied eventually. She frowned at him and he understood why. It wasn't just that it was a good way to stall one's conversation, but that what he had said lacked meaning itself.

'What on earth do you mean?' At that moment he felt like he was being interviewed. It was her natural manner, he supposed. He told himself that she meant nothing of it, and he could tell by the genuine interest on her face, she wasn't grilling him for an article.

'I'm not really sure.' He flashed a smile and her frown lessened. 'I just don't truly understand what the concept of loneliness is. Do I feel alone sometimes? Of course I do. I live in a house by myself, when I wake up in the morning there is no one there to wish me good morning. But do I feel lonely?' He paused partly for effect, to see her reaction, and partly because he wasn't sure how to continue. 'I believe I became used to my own company, and that's all right. In fact there are times when I feel as if other people are a burden and risk disrupting my own peace. Oh . . .'

He realised what he had said and started to apologise. 'I didn't mean present company, of course.'

'It's quite all right,' she interrupted. 'In a strange way, I know exactly what you mean. Although, I didn't know how it felt for you before you tried to explain it, but now that you have it makes a certain kind of sense to me.'

She moved the cup to her lips, but didn't take a sip. The strands of steam floated around her nose and she appeared to breathe them in.

'It was different for me,' she continued, but her voice was breaking with each word. 'At least Peter used to come home on leave, and then the house wouldn't feel so empty. But . . . he never will now.'

She put the cup down on the side table and broke into a fresh wave of sobs. Anthony wanted to cross the room and pull her into an embrace, but now was not the time. It would not help, and he was no replacement for Peter. All he could do was wait and listen when she was ready to talk. She knew he was there.

After a minute or two she looked up through the subsiding tears.

'I'm sorry,' she said. 'You were talking about your own experience and I took over.'

'No, no, enough about me. You don't want to hear about all that.' Ruth looked about to protest, but he continued before he lost his nerve. 'I've come here to talk about getting to know you. I mean, having worked with you recently. Volunteering. With everything that's happened recently. I think we rather got off to a bad start. I'm ashamed to say that I didn't trust you. Not to begin with. However, having seen you work, I think I've been a little unfair.'

'A little?' Ruth covered her mouth as if shocked at her own words and her eyes widened.

'Perhaps more than a little.' He smiled at her, letting her know that he wasn't offended. 'Why don't we start with a clean slate? Would you like to talk about Peter?'

She nodded, but stayed silent.

'How long were you married?' he asked, hoping to lead her.

'Oh, for about six years. It was a whirlwind romance, really. It seems so long ago, but I remember I was just about to leave for Dublin, start a new life, when I met Peter.' She stopped as if trying to gauge his response. 'I suppose you think I'm just another silly woman, swayed by a man, don't you?'

He didn't say anything, but tried to placate her with a wave of his hand.

'The house feels rather quiet these days. Since Peter's been gone I have to admit I've felt a bit alone. It's better since George came home, but really I worry for him. He shouldn't be in the city. I was looking into another evacuee billet for him but I'm afraid I've let that go by the wayside since Peter died. It's not safe for George here, and he needs a father figure. It's not the same without Peter.' Her voice broke. 'I shouldn't be telling you this, I'm sorry. It's too hard.'

'It's all right. Dare I ask about work instead?'

'Oh, don't, please. I'm so fed up.' From her tone, Anthony wouldn't have been surprised if she stamped her feet. 'And it's not just this blasted war. My life has become nothing but work. I wake up, I go to work, I finish work, I have just enough time to see George, then I go and volunteer.'

'The war has made things more difficult for everyone.'

'Yes, of course, and it's definitely playing its part, but I want some fun. I don't know what, but something else. This all seems somewhat futile, and I'm not even getting to write the kinds of stories I want to write.'

'Be careful what you wish for.' He smiled at her, and she laughed back. A month ago he would not have expected to have been in this woman's house gossiping and laughing with her. Perhaps he had hit his head harder than he thought during that raid.

'I had no idea you were capable of this kind of compassion.' It was her turn to smile at him, but it appeared forced, as if she was trying to drive her way through the sorrow to happiness. 'It's fair to say that you didn't particularly like me when first we met.'

He stifled a laugh. 'That's true. I was sceptical of the press. Well, I still am really, but you seem all right.'

She looked downcast again, another thought clouding her eyes. 'So, do you think we might be friends? Friends in our shared grief?'

'I'd like that very much,' he said, realising for the first time just how much he truly meant it.

There was a creak of wood as the front door opened, and a wave of cold air blew into the front room. Anthony shuddered as the chill ran down his spine. Ruth didn't seem to notice as she bolted up from her armchair.

'Hullo,' a woman's voice called from the hallway before they heard the door being closed again with a slight thump. 'Are you there, Ruth?'

Harriet appeared in the doorway to the front room, and he stood immediately.

'Good afternoon,' he said, filling the sudden silence.

'Harriet,' Ruth said as if she had only just noticed the other woman's presence. 'Forgive me. Come on in.'

The woman hung her coat on a hook and walked into the front room, treating it like her own home. George trailed behind her. He looked just as surprised as the rest of them.

'Hello, George.' Anthony gave him a little wave, but he almost hid behind Harriet's legs. Looking up, Anthony greeted Harriet with a smile. 'Mrs Holt and I have been working together, and I came to return a notebook she had dropped during one of the raids.'

Ruth stepped over to her son and led him into the room with her hands on his shoulders.

'Say hello, George,' she said. 'What's wrong?'

She turned back to Anthony and shook her head, her red curls bobbing with the motion.

'I'm sorry. He's not usually this shy. But then we don't get many male visitors around here. He's probably a bit nervous. Aren't you, Georgie?'

The boy dipped his head in a shallow nod.

'Don't worry, George.' Anthony squatted. 'We didn't get much chance to talk last time, but I'm a friend of your mother's and I would like to be your friend too. Your mother never stops talking about how smart and brave you are.'

George finally looked back at Anthony and he spotted an inquisitiveness there, just like his mother. The boy wanted to know what his mother had been saying about him, needed some praise.

'She tells me that you brought yourself home from the countryside. All on your own.'

He nodded again. This time it was deeper. 'I did. I didn't like it there. It smelt funny.'

'That's a shame. Where were you?'

'The countryside.' His voice was faint, but he was growing in confidence. 'A village in Wales. Betsy something.'

'Really? That's quite the coincidence. I once made the same journey myself. That's where I'm from. I grew up not far from where you were staying. Although I haven't been home in a very long time. Truth be told, I didn't like it very much myself. Perhaps we should compare notes some time.'

George opened his mouth and gave a faint murmur.

'What was that, Georgie?' Ruth asked.

'I said . . . I would like that.'

'There's lots we could talk about, George. My father was in the military like yours. Although he was a soldier in the Welsh regiment. I could tell you lots of stories, if you like.'

George nodded then clung onto his mother's legs. Feeling the strain in his knees, Anthony finally stood. Ruth's eyes twinkled as she looked at him, and he thought he saw a tear there.

'Well, we will have to make a date for it, but for now I really must be going. I'm rather afraid I've outstayed my welcome.'

He was either imagining it or Ruth shook her head slightly, but still she led him to the door. George mumbled goodbye as he passed and the next thing Anthony knew he was standing back out on the street in the fading daylight. Ruth smiled and waved as she shut the door with a click. He couldn't say how long he stared at that door before he left; the neighbours would be talking again. Only, this time, he didn't care. He would be back, he was sure of it.

# OCTOBER

# Chapter 14

**Monday, 7 October 1940**

Ruth was getting the washing ready. Even though she had two jobs, the laundry still needed doing, especially now that George was back. The empty line in the yard flicked against the light breeze. The women on the street already had theirs out. Monday was national washing day, when they were all supposed to clean their clothes. She wasn't sure how it made any difference to rationing. It was probably so they were all living the same experience for morale.

Harriet had come into the house, distracting Ruth. Harriet had a way of occupying her attention, even if she wasn't really listening. Harriet crossed her legs again, for maybe the fifth time in the last few minutes, swapping one over the other as she often did. Ruth could tell by the swish of fabric and the slight grumble.

'I bought one of them Webflex anti-concussion bandeaux they were advertising in the paper,' Harriet said.

'You didn't?' Ruth wasn't really surprised. For a woman who had little money and a number of children that even Ruth wasn't sure of, Harriet did have a habit of spending money on needless things. Ruth suspected that for Harriet it was a coping mechanism, a way of adding something more interesting to her life. The only problem was that in no time at all she was looking for the next purchase.

'Yeah. It's filled with Dunlopillo cushioning. Proper fancy stuff. It's not that attractive, but if it saves me head then I'm all for it.'

'They're not worth it.' Ruth tried to counter her friend's incessant talking, while sorting her washing and making sure she didn't mix up the colours. 'Taping the money to your head would have helped just as much.'

'Well, we can't all be as smart as you, missus brainy pants.'

Ruth could feel Harriet's smile, even from behind. This was how it was, Harriet accepting that she would never have the same middle-class upbringing as Ruth, and the pair of them mothering each other. In a way it helped distract them. Harriet seldom talked about her husband Thomas, but when she did it was with the utmost adoration. It was too painful for Harriet to mention him, she missed him so much. Ruth missed Peter too, but that was different now. Any distraction was welcome. The other woman could turn the most mundane thing into a treatise, and Ruth would be glad to hear it, trying to suppress a smile the entire time. She thought of Harriet as a sister, or aunt, and it was strange that she was much closer to this woman than her own family. Of course, her parents had long since gone back to Austria.

'I'm not that smart, Harriet. You know that. I'm just good at pretending.'

'That's true, for sure.'

'I've always been good at pretending. I was probably destined for a life on the stage, but then my family would have completely disowned me. It was bad enough I decided to become a journalist. Marrying Peter was the only decision I ever made that they respected.'

They both fell silent. A few seconds later, George ran into the kitchen, almost barrelling Ruth over.

'Mum, Mum,' he said. 'There's a dog out in the road. Can I go and play? Please can I?'

Harriet smiled at her over his head, and Ruth squatted down to his height. 'We have to go soon. Maybe when we come home.'

She tousled his hair, but he pulled back. 'Oh, please. We don't see any animals around here anymore. Please.'

Ruth couldn't help but laugh. 'Go on then.'

He gave her a big hug and then ran for the door.

'But don't wreck your clothes!' she called after him as the front door slammed.

Harriet also gave Ruth a hug when she stood up.

'Right,' she said. 'Are you sure you don't want me to take the little 'un out for the day? He seems restless.'

Ruth hesitated. 'No, thank you. He should see his aunt.'

Harriet's frown suggested exactly what she thought of that. Without another word, she collected her coat and was followed by the gentle click of the shutting door. Ruth was alone with her thoughts again.

*

Ruth didn't want to visit the house up in the Georgian quarter of the city, but it was an obligation of family. Even if there was no way her sister would visit her. Abigail was too busy for that, Ruth too beneath her, and her sister was desperately ashamed of their secret past. But at a time like this Ruth wanted to reach out and try to build bridges. She had left the bicycle at home, and climbing up the hill with George in tow made her heart thump. It was like going home to see her parents, to be judged for the life she had chosen to lead. She gripped George's hand tightly as they arrived at the house and he tried to pull away. The house was imposing and much larger than the workers' houses closer to the docks. She always made a point of arriving by the front door.

The oak door creaked open a minute or two after Ruth had let go of the large brass knocker and stood back. She had expected the housekeeper to answer, giving Ruth time to compose herself, but she was met with her sister's frowning face.

'Ruth? What are you doing here?'

Ruth would never get used to the surprise her sister showed whenever she saw her. Abigail didn't mean to be unwelcoming, but she could at least pretend that she was pleased to see Ruth.

'I thought I would come and see my sister,' Ruth said as if it was obvious, but maybe her sister had really seen through the conceit of it all. They were not exactly close, but most of the time got on well enough. There were never arguments like with the rest of her family, but their lives had taken them in different directions and had made it difficult for them to spend time together. It was hard not to look down on Abigail, both figuratively and literally. Where Ruth might be described as tall, her younger sister was several inches shorter. Ruth always wondered why they looked so different that no one would know they were related. She would describe her sister as pretty in her own way, but Abigail had a thickness to her that Ruth didn't have. Although, she put this down to the fact that she had borne two children and Ruth had not. Ruth would not dare to call her fat, excepting that last time they'd had an argument, and Ruth deeply regretted it.

'Well, how nice.' Abigail's tone of voice said otherwise. 'And George too. It's been quite a while.'

He smiled up at his aunt, but stayed silent. Ruth could sense what he was thinking and was proud of him keeping it to himself.

'Six months, or thereabouts, I think.' Ruth flashed a smile she wasn't sure she felt. 'Too long.'

'Yes, quite. Well, do come in. Come, come.' Abigail waved a hand passively in the direction of the hallway, although Ruth knew exactly where she was being taken. The housekeeper appeared through a doorway at the end of the hall. Her face was flushed as if she had been running.

'Mrs Hastings, please. It is most inappropriate for you to be answering the front door. Please, do allow me to do my job and see to house guests. You do not know who could be at the door. It could be just anyone, and it is not safe. Especially in wartime.'

Ruth wondered who was actually in charge of the household, and knew with almost certainty that it wasn't her sister. Mrs Kerr had been in service for longer than Abigail had been alive, and knew her place in the world. She was in charge, and she knew it, but she was smart enough to position it under the guise of looking after Abigail, her husband and family. This was how things were done in the upper classes in England. She knew well enough from her parents, before they had returned to Austria. Her father was a wealthy merchant, and her mother came from a respected Austrian family. But they had to keep that a secret now. Ruth had always tried to treat the staff like equals. It was her grandfather's influence.

Abigail looked suitably chastened, and her russet-red face reminded Ruth of the schoolgirl she had once been. Ruth felt a bond with Mrs Kerr for putting her sister in her place, before that perpetual scowl landed on her as well. Ruth swallowed, knowing what was coming next.

'And Mrs Holt, you really should not encourage Mrs Hastings to break with convention. It exists for a reason, and that's for the protection of both Mr and Mrs Hastings and British society! What kind of world would that leave for your children?'

Her gaze brushed across George. Ruth squeezed his hand as she heard him mutter something. Only then did Mrs Kerr take a breath, and Ruth had to suppress a smile.

'Of course, Mrs Kerr,' she said. 'How careless of me. Next time I shall not let my dear sister answer the door.'

Mrs Kerr could not tell whether Ruth was serious, and decided to maintain her scowl. Every time Ruth visited she liked to see how far she could wind up the housekeeper. So far Mrs Kerr had failed to erupt, but one day Ruth hoped she would see behind that steely facade. Perhaps then, they might be able to be friends.

The inside of the house was immaculate and Ruth wondered how her sister had time to maintain it all, cook for the family and look after her children. But then, she did have Mrs Kerr, even if all the other staff had left. Ruth felt inadequate beside her. She hadn't managed to keep her husband safe, and the house was a mess. Abigail would say she should give up one of her jobs, but that wouldn't help. Their family never approved of writing, not even her grandfather's; they considered it too frivolous. The house would be no cleaner if she were stuck in it all day.

Abigail's husband, Edward, was a kinder man. It was thanks to him that the two of them were able to stay living in the country, and she would be forever grateful. He worked for Lord Derby as his secretary, writing speeches and conducting research for the War Office, and as a result had quite a handsome income. It was far more than Ruth could ever expect to earn in her line of work and it was yet another way for the family to look down on her. She may have married a naval lieutenant, but she was still only a lowly reporter, and she hadn't even been able to have children of her own. They were pleased when George came into the family, but why on earth couldn't she have had her own child? Peter had been a calming influence on her in those situations. 'What does it matter who gave birth to George?' he had said. 'He is our son.' And that was one of the many reasons she loved Peter.

Ruth sat in the same place she always sat, the place reserved for guests, with George at her side. He wanted to be there even less than she did, but he sat still and patient. He had changed in the countryside.

It was as if the house was stuck in time, everything in its right and proper place. Ruth suspected that damaging the picturesqueness of the house would only serve to destroy the facade her sister put up, and would lead her to admit that none of this made her happy. But today Ruth was not in the mood. If her sister wanted to talk to her, truthfully, then it would be up to her to reach out. Ruth was tired of doing all the work. She crossed her hands on her lap, as a lady might sit, and waited for conversation.

Her sister looked across at her from the armchair, sitting in exactly the same pose. If her sister was less self-centred, then she might have assumed that Ruth was now trying to mock her in the way that she was sitting. Perhaps that was true, but it was only a semi-conscious thought on Ruth's behalf.

They exchanged pleasantries for a few minutes, discussing the weather, before they eventually drifted into silence. She wanted to talk about Peter, but couldn't begin to think how to approach it with her sister. Abigail thought like the rest of the family.

'Things are becoming more and more difficult at the big house.' Abigail broke the silence. It was the most honest she had been with Ruth in a number of years. She blushed and stopped, almost as if she'd realised her mistake.

'How so? Is it the war?'

Abigail hesitated, then glanced over at a pile of papers on the desk. From there Ruth could see the official letterhead. Her sister mouthed words to herself as if trying to compose what she was going to say. 'Of course, the war is making things difficult for everyone.' There was a pause as if acknowledging Peter. Abigail must have heard.

'A number of the staff have gone into war work, others have enlisted. There aren't many staff left, and they're struggling to recruit others. Some have gone with children to the country.'

She looked at George, who only looked at the floor and said, 'I hated it in the country.'

'Yes. I suppose that explains why you are home.' She didn't so much as engage George in conversation but direct the words at him. 'Edward thinks that they may ask me to step up and do my bit.'

'You sound reluctant. But why? You worked before you had the children.'

A frown crossed her sister's brow, Ruth had stepped on a nerve.

'Yes, but that was quite another life. Need I remind you we're trying to move away from our past? Edward is doing important work now, with the War Office. That was what I was referring to. I could help out in service if they need me, I wouldn't turn my nose up at it.'

'*Das ist doch klar wie Kloßbrühe!*' *That's crystal clear.*

Her sister's eyes shot in her direction.

'Don't you dare use that language in this house,' she said. 'It was hard enough leaving all that behind, without the staff hearing it. You place Edward in danger. Don't forget what he did for us.'

'I'm sorry, dear sister.' She held up a placatory hand, to hide George's chuckling. 'I was just concerned and trying to help. A momentary slip. Ignore me.'

Abigail always seemed to forget they were both in danger. She might not remember Austria, but they had both been born there, no matter what they pretended, and their secret background was dangerous for both of them. If the authorities found out they were using false papers they would throw them in the concentration camp with her grandfather. What made it worse was the suspicion that her family back home had thrown their lot in with Hitler. It was disgraceful. She and Abigail were not Nazis.

'Well, just be careful. If someone knew about the family . . . Lord Derby is spending more and more time at home. Don't listen to what they're saying in the newspapers.' Abigail gave Ruth a sideways glance, but she refused the bait. 'London isn't faring well through the bombing. People are breaking into the underground stations during the raids, and Lord Derby has said that he thinks it's safer for his staff to be up here, in Knowsley Hall. Edward is going mad trying to organise everything for them, especially with the lack of staff. These days he is seldom at home.'

Ruth was only half listening. There was an emerging idea on the edge of her consciousness, but it was struggling to become fully formed. She could interview Lord Derby for the paper.

'I'm sorry about Peter.' Abigail's words pulled Ruth from her thoughts, and set off another round of darker imaginings.

'Thank you, it's been difficult. More so for George.' She ruffled his hair, but he too had drifted off. She had thought about Peter, constantly, round and round, until it was like there was a buzzing in her head. Her family blamed her for everything. It was all her fault. They blamed her for wanting to stay here, for pretending to be English. But had Abigail not wanted to stay too? Was it not her husband who had produced false papers for them both? Ruth had tried to build the bridge between them, but she knew now, with the fear of their secret background between them, they would never be friends. It was just her and George now.

She would do her bit to end this war, to prevent anyone else from losing their loved ones. Only, first she had to extract herself from her sister's house and that always took longer than she hoped.

# Chapter 15

It seemed crass to Anthony to be teaching such frivolous subjects as English and history when there was a war on. Perhaps he should be passing on the skills he had learnt as a volunteer, teaching the children how to make barricades so that they might help defend their homes from the bombs. There were ways to help them survive the bombing that even he had not been aware of before he had started training as a warden: where to shelter, when to run away. Whatever this feeling was, it didn't feel right to be here. Their teaching had become too prescriptive, too formulaic. Teaching purely for teaching's sake. He longed to be outside, rather than being cooped up in the dusty school, with only memories to accompany him. All that was left was the smell of dust and polish. He wondered whether it had always been that way, or whether the cleaners had gone to enlist. In his earlier days as a teacher it had felt quite fresh, but now he wasn't sure whether it was the school or him. He hadn't seen the cleaners in some time. Even now the corridor was empty. Silence reigned as if he was the only person in the building.

He took a deep breath as he always did and turned the corner into the classroom, steeling himself before the teaching day. It often surprised him how much teaching was like acting, walking onto the classroom stage to perform. He stepped through the open door.

The room was empty, apart from the motes of dust that drifted in the sunshine spilling in through the opposite windows. Without the scrape of seats being pushed back by standing children, it felt even more silent.

He paced along the empty desks, noticing the words that had been cut into them, the history the children left behind when they moved on. Had the parents finally taken heed and evacuated their children from the city? Or was it something much worse? Could it be that for whatever reason the children were no longer able to come to school? The Liverpool education authority was now enforcing school attendance, but as far as Anthony knew the boys were only getting a warning. Whether it would amount to anything, only time would tell. He would have to find out in due course, but for the time being he sat behind his desk and shuffled together his notes. Often the teaching day could be almost as frantic as the raids and he seldom had time to tidy what remained of his materials and notes. The desk had been there longer than Anthony had, its varnished wooden surface just as battered, dented and marked as the desks the pupils sat behind. If only it was as organised as his home. He had lost more things in the crevices of this desk than he had ever found. On one such occasion he had accused the students of stealing, helping themselves to his notebooks. He had even involved the police, but the headmaster had taken the side of the pupils and all that had come of it had been a stern telling-off for Anthony.

That was the first time he had begun to question what he was doing, then the war had come and distracted him for a time. Now all those thoughts were surfacing again. He didn't have a purpose. He was meandering through life like a river trying to find its way through an unknown landscape.

His train of thought was broken by the clicking of shoes on the hard floor. Slowly, he looked up from his desk. Two boys almost slid around the corner of the doorway, such was their haste. They squeaked to a stop in front of him and had the forethought to stare at their feet.

'You're late,' he said.

'Sorry, sir.' Jones and Smyth held their caps in their hands and appeared genuinely remorseful, so he waved them to their desks. Jones was a good lad, but like so many of the others he didn't want to be there. Not when so many of his classmates were out in the countryside, living what he imagined to be exciting lives. He was too young to realise the loneliness and homesickness many of them must be feeling. Anthony wondered whether he should talk about it, but didn't know how he would explain. Smyth was far more strait laced, and seldom caused a problem. Anthony had once hoped that Smyth would be a good influence on Jones, but often their friendship seemed to have the opposite effect.

Anthony had already worked himself out of teaching mode, but it would only take him a few minutes to work out where he was and what he had intended to do with the class today. Standing, he ignored the papers strewn across the floor, and paced towards the two boys. They had taken up desks by the window, perhaps hoping they could spend their time observing the view, but it was up to him to gather their attention. He would teach them something that would be useful, whether they realised it now or later in life.

'Today,' he said, projecting his voice even though there were only three of them present, 'we will examine the history of the British Empire and its impact upon the world.'

\*

After work, Anthony had been to St John's Market to collect his weekly rations: bacon and butter for frying. It had been a couple of weeks since the last serious raid, and so he had decided to take his time, braving the queues before heading home. The collection of people still made him feel uneasy, but at least he had recovered from his last set of bruises. He was in no doubt that he would get more as soon as the next raid was underway, but at least he had managed to sleep a little better than usual.

He passed the Playhouse Theatre, noting with sadness the large handwritten sign that read, 'Closed until further notice'. Julie and he had enjoyed a regular trip to the Playhouse, although admittedly he hadn't been since she had died. As much as he liked a show, he didn't much fancy going to the theatre on his own, and Marc had never been interested. The arts were not for his son, he preferred the life of the military. No matter how much Anthony had tried to get him to read and enjoy other pursuits, his son had never taken to any of them. Sports and exercise were his thing.

Maybe he would break his habit and go to the theatre on his own once it reopened. He had enjoyed a play or two in his university days. There were other theatres, of course, but the Playhouse held a special significance for him. That was how he had met Julie after all. She had been working as a ticket clerk in the Playhouse. They were barely adults at that time, but they had got talking about Wagner and the like and they had hit it off. He had gone back every week to see whatever was on just so that he could bump into her before he plucked up the courage to ask her if she would like to go for tea. Maybe that was why he couldn't bring himself to go there. Too many memories. Or was it because it felt too 'normal'? As if he was betraying the very fact that there was a war on. The people who passed him were downcast, their thoughts on anything but the theatre, on how they would feed their families and make it through this. What right did he have to think of entertainment at a time like this? And yet, there was something to be said for its influence on morale. There was a part of them all that naturally wanted life to carry on as if things were normal, but they could not escape the regular warning of the sirens and the deadly attention the Luftwaffe paid them. He had heard of a cinema being bombed during a showing, and he couldn't imagine what it must have been like for those people. They had lost their lives because they had not been in the shelters, lost their lives while trying to find entertainment to cheer themselves up. It seemed too callous. Were they supposed to grin and bear it all? He knew it was deliberate, but even his edges were beginning to fray. He didn't have any more time to think about it, as the air raid sirens burst into life as soon as he stepped through his front door

# Chapter 16

It had gone a quarter past the hour and still Harriet hadn't come. It was unlike her to be more than a few minutes late, and rather than give Ruth more time to think about her work she couldn't help but stare at the clock. For some reason the tick of the second hand felt louder than it had ever done before. Each click growing more intense as if she was drifting further towards its face. It echoed through the silence, and she was drowning in it. Time had become something that they were all aware of.

For her it had become even more noticeable since that telegram had arrived, since she had lost Peter. The urge to make every second count, to do something with her life was stronger than ever, even though time had come to move and shift in unexpected ways.

The door crashed open, bouncing off the hall wall with a bang. It sounded as if a bomb had exploded outside. Ruth rushed into the hallway to see what had happened and found Harriet standing on the threshold, her eyes wide. She was alone.

'Where's George?' She couldn't control the volume of her voice. 'Where's George, Harriet?'

She didn't realise until that moment that she had grabbed hold of the other woman's arms. Harriet shook in her grip and Ruth couldn't tell whether she was trying to break free or whether her anger at the woman was the cause.

'A man,' she said. 'There was a man.'

'What man? Where's my son?'

'He was so convincing. It was only afterwards that I thought, there's no way an official would take a child like that. He must have been following us. He said he was from the evacuation office. I didn't know who he was. He had identification and everything. I had no reason not to believe him.'

Ruth hauled Harriet into the kitchen and almost threw her into a chair. It rocked back like some kind of prop from the Playhouse, but she wasn't laughing. The front door banged in the breeze.

'Tell me what happened, and where this man is now,' she said.

Harriet's mouth dropped open and her eyes widened. 'We were down at the docks again. Under the dockers' umbrella, the overhead railway. This man came over, he had this warming smile. He said hello and showed us his ID. It was all official looking, but I didn't get a proper look.'

'And you just let him take George? My son!' Ruth stormed to the kitchen window and gripped the worktop to stop herself from falling.

'I didn't have a chance to stop him. As soon as he showed me his identification he grabbed George and put him in the back of a car. I tried to follow, I promise I did, but it drove off too quickly and I was left there with no one to help.'

'What did he look like?' Ruth took a hold of Harriet again, staring into her eyes as if looks could kill.

'I don't know,' she replied, shaking her head.

'Think. You must remember something about him.'

'He was tall, maybe six foot, fair. Sounded like a docker, but not local. He wore a long coat. That's all I can remember.'

'What about the car?'

'I didn't get a good look at it. I'm sorry! I didn't recognise the badge, and it was black and battered, all rusted up, like. It's what made me realise he couldn't be who he said he was.'

How could Harriet have been so careless? The scant details she remembered didn't narrow things down at all, but at least it was something. Ruth would head back to the docks and see if anyone had seen anything. She let go of Harriet, but the older woman clawed at her as if trying to embrace her. Ruth pulled away. She didn't want to be touched right now. It was too much.

'How could you give my son to anyone else? I trusted you. You of all people, I trusted. You were like family. Better even. I trusted you where I couldn't trust them.'

Harriet burst into tears. 'I didn't know. Oh god, Ruth. I'm so sorry.'

*

It was no good, Ruth had rushed round and round the dock for hours and no one had seen anything at all. Someone had George. She couldn't believe it. With all the other fears and worries of life during the war, her son being kidnapped was one of the last things she had expected. She had not wanted to come home, but it had grown dark and the chances of finding him had diminished. On her way she had passed the police station. Anyone else would have considered going inside, but she knew they wouldn't help her. As soon as they probed into her background they would find out her secret and throw her in the camp with her grandfather. What good would she be to George then? No one would know he was out there, alone. Ruth was stuck in a trap and the kidnapper knew it. She knew that somehow they had found out about her background. No, the police wouldn't help her.

So she had come home, but she had not been able to sit still. She scrubbed and scrubbed, first at her hands and, when they didn't feel clean, her arms. It felt like cleaning a pan, no matter how hard she tried she could never get them completely clean. It wasn't her skin that was the problem, it was all of her. She was impure, dirty, and she didn't think she would ever feel clean again. She had often helped George to clean himself in this bathtub, especially when he had been a baby, newly arrived in their household. And now she thought she would never get the chance again; she had allowed him to be kidnapped, taken from her. She was a terrible mother, she was a disgrace, she had failed him. What right did she think she had to take care of a child?

She didn't know how long she had been in the bath, the water was long cold, but the shivering helped her to at least feel something. She couldn't even remember dragging the tub into the house and filling it with water. It was almost as if the longer she stayed submerged in the water, the longer she would have before her mind had to consider the possibilities of what had happened, what she had been asked to become. Her grandfather's face hovered in front of her, on the verge of telling her stories of Austria, what the Nazis had done to it, but she wouldn't, couldn't listen. England had become her homeland, hers and George's. But she would do anything to protect him. Except, she hadn't. She had failed and allowed him to be taken.

Those same words went round and round in her head as she scrubbed. Her skin was becoming red and raw. She wondered how long it would take to get down to the muscle underneath, the core of her, her existence, her failure and her sin. Would it even hurt anymore when she had felt the ultimate pain? She didn't think she had it in her to feel pain. She had lost Peter and George in a matter of weeks.

Eventually she hauled herself out of the bathtub, shivering and wet. She threw some clothes on and paced the living room, biting her nails. Going out again would be foolish, but a voice at the back of her mind kept telling her that she needed to, she couldn't just wait. The blackout curtains left her in almost darkness if not for the three candles she had lit on the mantelpiece.

She paced into the hallway, and back again, as if each movement was taking her closer to the door. Wet footprints dotted the carpet, but she didn't care. Her brain was driven into paralysis, unable to make a decision even as she walked and walked. Then she stepped into the hallway and stopped.

There was a slim piece of paper lying on the mat inside the door. It hadn't been there when she had last gone into the hallway, and given that it had no postmark it couldn't have been delivered by the postman. It shouldn't have been there. Had Harriet dropped it off when Ruth had kicked her out? No, she wouldn't have had enough time for that and she knew it was far too soon for an apology. This was something else.

*You have access to certain information which we require. Do this for us and your son will come to no harm. If you refuse, then you will suffer the consequences.*

Ruth read the note again three times before she allowed herself to take a breath. Her lungs burned from holding her breath for so long, but it had been unconscious. The longer she paused, the more time she had to avoid that awkward moment of dread. It was typewritten rather than handwritten and there was no address or postmark on the letter. There was no indication at all of who had sent it, but she would find out as soon as she followed the instructions:

*Meet me in the abandoned house on Colquitt Street tomorrow evening after dark. The police will not help you.*

# Chapter 17

The city was deathly quiet, as if completely abandoned. The absence of the air raid siren should have been a welcome relief, but instead it was stark in absence. The enemy was now within rather than without. Ruth was about to find out exactly what kind of man had taken her son, and it would take all her effort not to kill him.

She clutched the note in one hand, as if it would offer her some kind of protection against the dark. Where once she would have been anxious of the blackout, she had become used to weaving through the night. For all she knew she could be heading to her death, but if she could free George beforehand then she would.

She couldn't believe what was happening, and yet all she could think about were those who had already lost so much in this war. At least she had a home to return to, and her family would rally round her if she really needed them. Only, she couldn't ask them, couldn't tell them about George. They would involve the police, and she didn't want to risk the gallows. She wasn't even sure they would help. No, she would have to make up some story when others asked where he was, say he had been evacuated again.

The house on Colquitt Street was like so many others, with scant signs of the docker family that had lived there. It was now just a pile of rubble and memories. She tensed as she passed the threshold, as if invading someone's property, but no one could live in that ruin anymore. She had expected the man to be waiting for her, but it might have been a cruel trick after all and he would never show.

The pale moonlight flickered through the shattered window as it poked through the clouds. A brick clattered down from the opposite wall and she turned as a cat meowed and ran away. Thumping filled her ears as her heart smashed against her chest. The pressure in her ears was so much she wondered whether she would be able to hear anything at all, until a voice came from the darkness.

'Stop right there, missy,' it said.

She froze then hated herself for doing what she was told. With reluctance, she turned on the spot. A man stood in the shadows.

'That's it,' he said.

She couldn't see his face under the brown flat cap he wore. A short white cigarette hung from the corner of his mouth, which wobbled every time he spoke. Ruth wasn't even sure it was lit.

'Don't come any closer, or I'll have to take it up with young George.'

Heat welled up in her and she had to fight to stay upright. There was a faint accent that she couldn't place. Had she met him before? As a journalist? She didn't recognise him, but he would have blended into any crowd.

'Who are you?' she whispered, not knowing why she couldn't raise her voice.

'Never you mind who I am, that's not important. What's important is who you are, Ruth. And I know all about ya.' His voice was low and she had to lean in to hear. He took a pull on the cigarette and the embers burned bright for a second.

'I know who ya family are too,' he continued. 'They gave me a whole dossier on you and ya family. Upper playing at lower class,

I know your kind. And now I know you, you're gonna do a little something for me.'

'How could you possibly know—'

'*Wir sind weit weg vom Vaterland*, Fräulein Brunner.' *We're a long way from the Fatherland.*

Ruth struggled to stifle a gasp and his smile widened.

'*Sie erinnern sich also zumindest an Deutsch.*' *So you remember German at least.*

'I don't—'

He laughed, and she wanted to punch that grin from his face. 'Don't try to hide it. I know everything about you.'

'You're a German then? That's what you want with me.'

'German? No. But let's just say that they're friends. I scratch their back, they scratch mine. It helps to learn the language of your friends. And you and I are going to become friends as well. Aren't we? I want photographs. Details. Things the censors won't let you print. A list of casualties. The *full* list. Stuff those in Westminster don't want the public or the Germans to find out. The kind of stuff you as a journalist, with certain persuasions, have access to. Like the docks.'

'Why would I do anything for you? You have my son.'

'Exactly *because* I have your son. He and I are becoming friends too, but when my friends are no longer useful to me . . .'

If she could follow him, find out where he lived, she would be able to find George.

'Where is my son?' Her voice cracked as she spoke and her knees wobbled beneath her. 'How do you expect me to do anything if I don't even know that he's safe?'

'Enough questions. You'll do what I ask because I don't ask twice. There's far more at stake here than you would ever understand. Not just you and your family. You're nothing to those who matter.'

'Please.' She almost fell to her knees, tears streaming down her face. 'My son. Please. He's all I have left.'

He scoffed, and came out of the shadows. She was expecting him to be rough-looking, but his face was fair and a faint blond beard lined a strong chin. His eyes were a piercing emerald, and she could see the furious calculation going on behind them. Almost handsome.

'He'll be fine, if you do what I ask. I've no interest in hurting the lad, but my superiors might have other ideas if they don't get the information they want.'

'Your superiors? Who?'

He took a step past her, moving towards the doorway, then turned back. The moonlight cast him in silhouette, framed by the doorway.

'Your countryfolk. But you know, neither you nor your lad mean anything to them. They want you to give them information, as much as you can. You see it all, hear it all, don't you?'

'You're working for the Germans? You're a Nazi?'

'I hate that term, it doesn't do our cause justice. I couldn't care less for King George and his ilk. This country has gone down the drain, and workers like me are taking the brunt. I'll do what it takes to be ready when they come.'

It was her turn to scoff. 'You think they'll care about you?'

'We'll just have to see, won't we? Look, you're better than this. I read ya article in the paper about unemployment, and I liked what ya had to say. Not that I completely agreed with it. Sometimes we have to fight the fight if it's the good fight, even if it's not pleasant and we lose people along the way.'

'So you're a moral philosopher as well as a kidnapper.'

She had never wanted to hurt someone so much in her life, but he kept a decent distance between them.

'And you think throwing your lot in with the enemy is best? What makes you and them so different? Working with Hitler? He'll discard you as soon as you're no longer useful.'

He waved his hands at her and his cigarette almost fell from his lips. 'Shush yaself, lass. What if someone overhears you? We'll both be in trouble. And what you have to understand is in the real world things aren't so black and white as one friend and one enemy. Everyone can become your enemy at the drop of a pin. D'ya want to become my enemy?'

'I don't even know your name,' she said, trying to solidify the image of him in her mind. 'Or where to contact you.'

'Don't be stupid. You don't get to know my real name. If you must call me anything, you can just call me Patrick.' He flashed that grin. 'Now, that's about all you're getting out of me. This isn't a social gathering.'

The cigarette teetered on the edge of his lip as he flashed her a grin that didn't do anything to reassure her. It was how she imagined a fox might smile once it found itself inside the chicken coop. What was she going to do anyway? She had no idea where George was, so she needed the man and had to play along. She nodded shallowly, afraid of any words that may leave her mouth.

'Good, so you'll do what I've asked.' He waited as if wanting confirmation and when she refused the nod, he continued. 'I know where you are and I'll send further instructions. I want you to bring me something, to show that you're going to play along.'

'What?'

'For a start, money. Fifty pounds. And photographs of the bombings. Everything we're not allowed to see. And find out from that brother-in-law of yours where all these ships are going. Ya know, HMS this and that. They must be up to something. Leave it all in this here crack and go. I'll let you know when.'

'Fifty pounds? What for? Where am I supposed to get that kind of money?' she asked, but she knew it wouldn't make any difference. This wasn't really about the money. That wasn't what he wanted, he was just testing her to see what she would do to keep George safe. He had done his research and knew her background. He wanted more than money, he wanted her allegiance.

In response, he grinned. 'To keep your son in house and home.' He took the cigarette from his mouth and dropped it to the floor. He trod it into the ground and left without another word. Her defence had gone up in smoke, and if she wasn't careful she was going to end up on the gallows. She knew all about the Prime Minister's rushed Treachery Act. As far as Churchill was concerned anyone betraying the country in any way would be dealt with. The act carried only one sentence: death. Ruth knew exactly what they would do to her if they found out what she was doing. She would hang.

But George was her number one priority now, and getting him back was all she could think about. She stayed in that house for a while, playing through her next actions in her mind. What would she do if she was caught? She couldn't go to the police; they wouldn't listen, at best would send her to the internment camp to rot with her grandfather. The money would have to come from somewhere, she could borrow it from her family. She would do whatever it took to get George back. Whatever it took.

# Chapter 18

The plateau by St George's Hall was busy with visitors. Children in dusty clothes ran amongst the crowd as their parents shouted to them to slow down and behave, and women and older men in expensive suits paraded around the raised promenade. Anthony had wanted to see for himself what the War Week parade was all about, but for some reason he had not expected it to be quite so busy. He had thought that most would be at work, but then he himself had managed to find time to take in the event. There was something about Liverpool that no matter what happened its residents would find a way to let off steam and relax. They would take part in whatever was happening and yet somehow the work would always get done. It was quite impressive and never failed to give the city a lively feel.

St John's Gardens below them was often as busy as it was on that day, with the statue of Britannia in its centre. He remembered looking up at her stone visage when he had first moved to the city as a younger man, wondering what victories she would bring him and hoping that one day he would be able to join the air force and provide his own.

St George's Plateau ran across the top of the park, at the base of St George's Hall, which was modelled after the National Gallery in

London. He had read about that, but having only seen the National Gallery once from a distance the other side of Trafalgar Square, he would have to take their word for it. It was an impressive building and at times acted more like the town hall than the actual town hall up on Castle Street.

Anthony pushed his way through the crowd and onto the plateau, careful not to bump into anyone and thankful that on his own he could pass through with ease. The crowds were so thick he felt a sense of unease.

Dotted around the plateau were volunteers, holding metal buckets and shaking them occasionally. The tink of coins could almost be heard above the hubbub of the crowd. One of them, a young woman, appeared in front of him now, pushing the bucket in his direction with a smile. He reached into his pocket for some coins, and dropped them into the bucket with a loud clatter. Apparently the bucket was quite empty.

He crossed the plateau, making his way around St George's Hall in the direction of the Waterloo Memorial, Wellington stood atop his column. In peacetime he would have gone to the Walker Art Gallery, but now the paintings and frescoes had been taken down and hidden away in case the building was bombed. He had spent many an hour there, sheltering from the elements be it rain or too much shine. He wondered whether he would ever see the paintings again, or whether they would be kept in storage for years to come. If the Nazis came, what would happen to them then?

The crowds were thickest on the Lime Street side of the hall, but even from there Anthony could make out the gold-chain garbed Lord Mayor of Liverpool. He stood near the cenotaph, flanked on either side by army and navy senior officers as well as a group of men whom Anthony assumed were from the Liverpool National Savings

Committee. A number of them shuffled their feet impatiently while policemen kept the crowds away from them.

Anthony worked his way closer. He wasn't sure why, but he wanted to be nearer, to be a part of the ceremony. The mayor was giving a speech, but Anthony couldn't hear much as his words were swept away by the wind and the general noise of the crowd. He only caught the odd word, but could get the idea. It was about the pride of Liverpool, its contribution to the war effort and how they were all pulling together. Anthony wondered how much of his own streets the Lord Mayor had actually seen. Had he been above ground during a raid? Anthony didn't think so, otherwise the Lord Mayor might have taken a different approach.

At that moment a band struck up, causing Anthony to flinch. He hadn't seen the military band waiting patiently on the street until they had started to play. The steady rhythm rose as each instrument fell into line with the others, drowning out the crowd. They preceded the march as it began to snake its way along Lime Street. Liverpool had a strong connection with the military, a number of its regiments had fought through the last war, at Ypres, Passchendaele and others, but Anthony hadn't quite realised how many of them there were currently stationed in and around the city. There were thousands of them in procession, throwing a salute towards the gathered dignitaries as they passed the cenotaph. First came the soldiers in khaki, displaying various cap badges, then the territorials. Navy personnel followed, from ratings to officers, the detail of their uniforms showing their hierarchy. A group of Wrens passed, eliciting wolf whistles and cheers from a group of men.

The march was taking its time, but still the crowds stood by, soaking up the atmosphere and revelling in the pomp. For a second the uniforms of the navy gave Anthony a recollection of the newsreels they had been shown before the war of German soldiers goose-stepping through Nuremberg. He realised, if not for the efforts of the RAF and the anti-aircraft guns, it could quite easily have been the Wehrmacht making their way down Lime Street saluting a newly installed German commander of the city. The thought made him shudder and he took a step away from the masses, feeling the intense pressure of it pushing in on him.

He tripped on the edge of the pavement and dropped. Even as he grappled for some kind of support the ground rushed up at him. It took longer than he imagined, but eventually the road wiped the air from his lungs as his splayed arms were crushed underneath his body. He lay for a moment, collecting his thoughts. The roar of the crowd poked through his dizziness, filtering through like the start of a film reel warming up. He pushed himself to his knees, but buckled again to lie on his side. Looking up, two wide nostrils of a horse filled his view as it reared up in surprise. The officer in its saddle cursed at him as he tried to bring the horse back under control and dodge around Anthony. He offered his apology but it was lost in the roar. Before he could attempt to rise again, a policeman grasped him by the collar of his shirt and hauled him out of the way. The starched linen cut into his throat, stilling any protest he may have had.

'Bloody fool,' the policeman said, giving Anthony a kick in the ribs for his trouble. Then it was over. The policeman left him lying on the ground as the sounds of the military bands disappeared into the distance. Members of the crowd gave him pitying glances as they moved away, pointedly avoiding him. The cobbles were beginning to cut into him and the muscles in his back tensed. With a struggle he hauled himself to his feet. He had become too used to wallowing in self-pity and the only way to fight it was to occupy his mind with something else. His legs ached as he stumbled away, but he had been lucky not to have been trampled by the horse. A few Union flags had been dropped on the ground and he glanced at them as he passed. How quickly national fervour could be forgotten when there was nothing left to see.

He crossed to where the Lord Mayor had stood, taking in the memorial to those lost in the first war. It was designed to look like soldiers fighting in the trenches and though he had no realistic idea of what that had been like, to him it captured the mutual struggle involved in fighting that war. The cenotaph was a block of stone, but that made it no less impressive. He touched a hand to the surface, feeling the cold grey. It might have felt disrespectful, but he wanted to feel it, to connect with those who had perished during the last war. They had given so much to protect them, yet here they were at war with Germany again. A tear rolled down his cheek and he wiped it away.

# Chapter 19

Ruth didn't like department stores at the best of times, but the fact she was constantly looking over her shoulder didn't help. There was something about the way all the goods were laid out, the decadence of the whole thing that was somehow gratuitous and obscene, especially when most people couldn't afford any of the items on show. However, Lewis's did provide something for the local community and its owners tried to make some show of being economical, even if their adverts in the *Post* were always trying to sell the next variety of fur coat.

She preferred to get what she needed from the smaller local shops near her house. Every now and then she made an exception, and over the weekend she had heard on the grapevine, both through her work colleagues and from the neighbouring women, that a shortage of cloth was coming. If it had been one and not the other, she might not have believed it, but hearing from two independent sources was too much of a coincidence to ignore. She had already decided that she needed to make herself some more suitable clothes if she was going to be sneaking around the streets at night, and a cushion for the tea van driving seat. All she needed were the right materials and some time. She had never been a particularly good seamstress, but she could make do. On her way into work she had spotted a notice that was to be printed that prices were due to increase over winter, and she had made her excuses to leave.

Besides, she needed to make a waterproof bundle to store the photographs in. George was never far from her mind, even if she needed to act like life was going on as normal. Harriet was the only other person, besides Patrick, who knew what had happened and Ruth wasn't sure she could ever speak to her again. Harriet would tell her to go to the police or her family. But if the police found out the truth, George might never be freed. Her family wouldn't be much more help, and her sister would likely faint if Ruth were to tell her what happened. Her thoughts and her heart raced, but still she could find no solution than to do what they asked.

Lewis's department store was only a short walk down the hill, and she could be back before anyone had missed her. If they enquired what she was doing with a roll of cloth, then she was sure she could think of a good reason on the spot. They probably wouldn't think twice about a woman doing what they considered to be women's work.

One of the wooden, framed double doors opened and a woman marched out and past Ruth without so much as an 'excuse me'. Fabric was draped over her shoulders and it looked as if she was wearing some kind of hassock. Ruth wondered how many others were hoarding cloth and yarn. Early on in the war, Harriet had shown her the boxes and boxes of yarn she had hidden under the bed. It was like she was confiding in Ruth, saying that should anything happen to her then someone must look after her wool. Of course, that was ridiculous, but it did make Ruth wonder what people truly valued in wartime. For her, it was other people, even if she cherished her own company. Now Ruth had her own secrets that Harriet had to protect for her. It was the least she could do to give Ruth any possibility of forgiving the woman.

Ruth wondered how long it would be before they were all buying up everything in a panic, taking what they could get to look after themselves without thinking about others. She liked to think she was better than that, but deep down she knew she would do whatever she could to protect herself and her family. That thought brought on a wave of nausea and she almost doubled over. Tears pricked at the corners of her eyes, but she blinked them away. She had to stay strong, for George.

Inside, the heat was stifling and she wanted to unbutton the neck of her shirt, but to do so would draw attention. There was a queue of women leading up to the stairs to the haberdashery floor, and without checking to see if it was the queue she was after Ruth rushed towards it before anyone could beat her to it. She had to be out as quickly as possible, and if rationing queues were anything to go by this could take its time. Whether it was negotiating with the butcher for an extra cut of liver, or trying to get the best cloth, people had a way of taking their time.

Ruth turned the corner around a clothes rail with the latest autumn dresses, and stopped dead. Next to the woman at the back of the queue was a young boy. His dusty brown hair was faintly familiar and he held the woman's hand in a loose fashion that suggested he wasn't overly comfortable with the action. Ruth breathed, wanting desperately to say his name. She took a step further hoping the boy would turn around, smile at her in that familiar way and run into her arms. Words caught in her throat and she mumbled an apology as she bumped into a shop clerk.

The woman turned and frowned at Ruth, but it was not anyone

Ruth recognised. The woman pulled the boy closer and as he turned to the side Ruth caught a glimpse of a crooked nose and a lopsided smile. It was not George. It could not have been George, everything about the child was wrong, and she had convinced herself that she was seeing what she had wanted to see.

The queue took another half an hour to snake its way up to the till where she requested and paid for her cloth. She would be late back from her lunch break, but she didn't expect anyone except for Rupert to notice, and even he was too busy these days to pay much attention. As long as the work got done, everything was fine. Not that she felt much like working at the moment, but she had to. She would have to leave her bicycle at work and carry the cloth home. She left Lewis's and the queue behind, now out of the door, and went to work. She would have to hunt for George by night, under the guise of her volunteering uniform.

*

A few days later in the evening, she pushed the bundle into a hole in the brickwork, the brown fabric blending in with the wall. To make sure, she picked up half a brick from the floor and wedged it into the gap. It looked like it was only jutting out from the wall, a slight miscalculation during the building work, rather than a hiding hole. Patrick would know exactly where to look. She was to leave the bundle here, go away, and then he would collect it for passing on to his contacts. That was what they had agreed, but she wasn't going to fall in line so easily. She had taken the money from a savings account, set aside for emergencies. What was this if not an emergency? But she hadn't given him the full amount. If she fell into line that easily then he would ask for more, and he was only testing her. It was still a lot of money to leave around for anyone to find.

The money wasn't the only thing she left for Patrick. Wrapped inside the money was a reel of negatives from the Custom House bombing. Rupert refused to print them, but people needed to see what was happening to their city. She had tried to convince herself that she was doing the right thing giving them to Patrick, but she knew it was a lie. If they printed those photos then someone would trace them straight back to her and she'd be in more trouble than she was in now. Then she would never save George. But what choice did she have? They had her son and she would give Patrick what he wanted until he returned George.

There was an alley down the back of the houses, so overgrown with weeds that no one would have used it to access the houses, even had they not been left unattended, no longer fit for residence after the bombing. If she was seen then there would be questions as to what she was doing there, but she would not be seen. Her green-grey coat would blend in with the weeds and the autumn twilight would play its part. She crouched down, then thought better of it. If she had to wait some time then it would become painful. Instead she pushed herself back into the shadows, hoping to blend in with her surroundings.

She waited and waited, not daring to look at her watch in case the movement drew attention and he spotted her. Could he have seen her already? Perhaps that was why he hadn't come. The wall was damp against her back and her legs were starting to cramp. She wasn't sure how much longer she could stay there, and what if there was a raid? Would she hide waiting while the bombs dropped around her, neglecting her volunteer duty to the city? It was unlikely she would be able to bring herself to ignore a raid.

She was just about ready to pull herself away from the wall and leave, when she heard the click of a brick being kicked by a boot. She pushed herself further into the wall. She would have to wait until she could follow him.

The footfalls stopped. In the silence she could just make out the rustle of the cloth bundle as someone took it from the crevice. She waited long enough for them to make a head start, before she detached herself from the shadows and gave chase. She could hear the steps of boots around the corner, so she followed them, first round one corner, then onto another street and onto a back street. When she turned again, she crashed into someone, winding her. She was just about to apologise when she caught sight of those emerald eyes.

'You've been following me, lassie.' There was no grin on his face this time. She opened her mouth, but no words came out. 'Why'd you go and do a thing like that for?'

'Where's my son?' She grabbed his arm, but he pulled away.

'Now don't go being silly. You're in no position to make demands of me, or of our friends. Your son is fine. He just thinks I'm looking after him because you're too busy. Just like that daft neighbour of yours did. Want him back? You just have to do what we ask.'

'What if I don't? What if I can't? I have no training for this. I'll get caught, and then what? You'll not get what you want either.'

'You'll find a way. If you don't, then, well I don't have to spell it out to ya, now do I?'

'You can't hurt him. If you do then you won't get what you need from me.'

He reached out towards her, but she pushed him away. A squealing sounded like the screech of a stray cat, and as Ruth turned she realised it was an air raid siren. It started faint, but rose to its warning crescendo. She turned back to the street, but Patrick was gone, lost amongst the crowd of people who were now leaving their homes to head for the shelter. Next time she wouldn't let him slip away.

NOVEMBER

# Chapter 20

*Wednesday, 6 November 1940*

The all clear had been called and the sunrise was visible on the horizon, casting a warm glow across the edge of the city, but still Anthony worked. He didn't dare look at his wristwatch, it was beyond the time he should have gone home, grabbed a few hours' kip, then gone to work. But none of that mattered now. There could be people alive under these buildings, and the warden station would also need his report.

'Warden, come quick.'

Anthony was used to being summoned and he no longer waited to see what they wanted. If they were desperate enough to ask for his help, then hesitating would only cost more lives. Stan, a young warden, had become an apprentice of sorts to Anthony over the past few months.

'What's the problem?' Anthony asked as he fell into step with the other man. They had all developed a way of asking questions as they marched along. Every single one of them, the wardens, the rescue men, the women volunteers and residents had come to rush about the place, as if their time was precious. And it was.

'They think they saw a bomb land through the roof of a house, but it hasn't exploded yet. Might have been a dud, might have been imagining it. Thought it best to get you anyway.'

His step only faltered for a second, but it was up to him to keep calm in the face of danger. If he did not, then how would the civilians in his area respond? They looked to him to be a community leader of sorts.

'Right, let's see,' he said. Their speech had become a sort of shorthand, as if their language was evolving to become more efficient. He suspected they had already talked this way in London for years, that city that never stops, but up here in Liverpool, a city of stories, the docks, and music, the work was longer and the speech more deliberate.

'Here.' Stan gestured towards a doorframe at the end of a ruined terrace of houses that was still standing despite the fact one wall had disintegrated. He ducked under the lintel.

Stan led Anthony into the terrace, where a group of heavy rescue men were already on the scene, traipsing over the hillocks of rubble to assess what could be moved and what could be salvaged. Some of them were leaning against a wall, tin mugs clutched in their hands as they chatted amongst themselves. Anthony could hear snippets of conversation, and he had become adept at eavesdropping. These men had Irish accents. They were some of the group of navvies that had been brought in to help with the rescue work. Their experience working on the railways and canals was indispensable. Even though there were almost as many Irish in the city as Liverpudlian, he didn't recognise any of them. They must have been brought in from another station. A couple of them eyed him warily as he passed. He knew the wardens were not thought of fondly by some of the other volunteers, as if there was a class system within the service.

The walls had collapsed to make one larger open space, but the third house along was still in almost one piece except for an internal doorway, which had once connected the ground floors. They hurried through as quickly as they could, but the rubble and bricks under foot could be dislodged in a second. It was like trying to walk over large blocks of sand, and Anthony wobbled with almost every footstep. He almost fell as he crossed the next threshold into the third house and the ground dropped down in front of him. His foot knocked a brick which bounced and clicked down the slope agonisingly slowly to rest less than an inch from an elliptical grey shape at the centre of the crater.

'Yep, that's a bomb all right,' he whispered, almost to himself as if to confirm it in his own mind and to avoid disturbing the bomb. There could be many reasons it hadn't gone off, whether it was a dud or was on some kind of time delay. It could explode at any moment, and yet Anthony was stuck to the spot. If he moved, he might dislodge another brick. If that hit the bomb then he was doomed. If not, then even the sound might disturb the bomb enough to set it off.

'Stan,' he whispered. 'Don't come any closer.'

'What is it? Is it a dud or is it dangerous?' Stan's voice was like a deafening rumble in the abandoned house, echoing off the walls. Anthony wished he would stop talking.

'Shhhh,' he tried, but the whisper was just as reverberant. 'Go and report to the incident officer right away. We need a bomb disposal team here now. That's a parachute mine and it could go off at any moment.'

He felt like he was shouting into a void even though he kept his voice low, but apparently Stan heard him. Anthony listened as Stan made his way over the ruined bricks. It should only take him five minutes to get to the ARP station and five to get back again. Anthony didn't know how long he stood there, keeping as still as possible. He didn't even dare look at his wristwatch. With each passing moment his heartbeat thumped louder and louder and he was sure it would set off the bomb. There was a tickle at the back of his throat and he wanted to cough. The more he thought about it, the worse the sensation became. He tried swallowing, but that only made him choke. A bead of sweat rolled down his temple, and he wanted to scratch it away. At least it distracted him from the need to cough.

After an incredibly long time there was a clattering of footsteps behind him, but he didn't turn to look. Anyone could sneak up on him now and he would be none the wiser.

'They're calling in a disposal team. They'll be here soon.'

It was Stan and while he had been gone Anthony had come up with a plan.

'Can you reach down and hold onto these two bricks by my right foot?' He almost indicated them with a nod, but stopped himself.

Stan prostrated himself on the floor and wrapped his arms around the bricks as if he was giving them a hug.

'I've got them,' he said.

'All right.' Anthony leant down and cupped the bricks as if they were precious to him. 'Ready?'

'Ready,' Stan whispered.

'Run!' Anthony shouted and grabbed Stan's jacket, pulling him afterwards. They left the clattering of bricks in their wake. Running from the building they jumped behind a wall, half expecting a cloud of flame and dust to cover them. Anthony's helmet cut into the back of his neck as he landed. He made himself into the smallest shape he could, pulling his arms and legs close to his body, like a ball.

Nothing happened.

'Is that it?' Stan asked, a few seconds later.

Anthony didn't dare answer. He unravelled himself and looked back over his shoulder, still careful in case he needed to duck again.

The road looked exactly as it had done moments before, the house still the same ruin it had been. The bomb had not gone off as he had expected, but that didn't mean it couldn't still explode.

While they were lying there a group of men in naval uniform arrived on the scene. One of them smirked. 'Don't worry, lads. We've got this now,' he said, following the others into the ruined house.

Anthony heard one of them whistle in surprise, but didn't catch the conversation that followed. He picked himself up, helped Stan to his feet and dusted down his overalls before anyone else saw the state of him. Once again someone else had come along and taken over. He was left impotent, unable to offer any help at all. Stan drifted off without further word, and the rescue men all went on to different tasks, but Anthony could not drag himself from the scene. It had been his chance to make a difference and he had failed, but he also wanted to know what happened, to know the street was safe again and that some life could return to it. He sat down on a low wall and tried to write his report, but his fingers could not clutch the pencil. They shook and ached as he attempted to bend them and he was left staring at his hand. Now his own body was letting him down.

The naval bomb team worked for hours, but from where Anthony sat he could hear nothing. It reminded him of when he was waiting for Marc to be born, unable to do anything, but having to stay put in fear just in case. It struck him that on that occasion his fears had been founded. This time, it would not prove so. He was sure of it. They knew what they were doing.

He stood up and paced across the street, vaguely conscious that he could be anywhere else at that moment. He wanted to see Ruth, to do something with their precious time together, but he was already taking too many liberties with their relationship.

There was a click, and then someone shouted. It was cut off

abruptly as a wave hit Anthony, pushing him from his feet. Time itself slowed. He could see the rubble floating through the air as if it were as light as a feather, a coffee table spinning in midair, and a wall tumbling down one brick at a time, saying to him, 'You could have stopped this.' The smell of cordite was a rich burning in his nostrils like food with too much pepper. All he could hear was the sound of the fire engine bells jingling as they cut through the ringing in his ears.

He landed on his back just as flames erupted from the empty windows of the house. Somehow they washed over him as he put an arm up to shield his face, and then he was rocked again by another shockwave. Everything collapsed. His head hurt from the deafening pressure. Minutes later he was lying on his back struggling to breathe as the burning building gently cooked in front of him.

He had been lucky, but those inside had not. As he stumbled back towards the building he realised that there was nothing left except a hole in the ground. The man who had smirked at him was gone, along with all his fellows. Anthony had let them die.

He stood there a long time looking down at their remains before another volunteer pulled him gently away from the crater towards a refreshment van. Anthony hoped to see Ruth there – he needed to see that warm smile – but was disappointed. There was no one there he recognised.

'Name's Sid.' A man pushed a cup of tea into Anthony's hand without asking whether he wanted one. 'Drink this. I'd get something a bit stronger, but they frown on us drinking on the job. And I wasn't sure whether you was a whisky or a brandy kind o' man.'

The scant light reflected a twinkle in Sid's eye, but Anthony barely acknowledged it.

'Thanks.' He put the cup to his lips, but it was too warm. Instead of drinking he closed his eyes and breathed in the sweet-smelling steam.

'Ahhh, whisky man it is.'

Anthony laughed, despite himself. 'How could you tell?'

'Oh, I can always tell, like.' He tapped a gloved index finger to his nose. 'But if I told you how, I'd only give away my secret, right? And where's the fun in that. Next time I'll get you a dram of the good stuff, and if you can get me drunk enough, I might just tell you how it was I knew.'

He grabbed another cup of tea and swapped it for the now cold one in Anthony's hands.

'That said, no one has ever managed to get me drunk enough yet. Reckon you're up to the task?'

'I'll give it a go.'

'There. That's better. Gotta laugh, ain't ya? Otherwise, we'd all just sit around in a heap crying. That might be good enough for some Greek poets, but we're made of sterner stuff.'

Anthony had been surprised by this big man several times in a few minutes, not least by his aptitude for compassion, but talking about literature and philosophy? That was something he hadn't expected.

'I'll be all right. Thanks again.'

Sid gave him a big pat on the back with a hand that was more like a shovel. At least they could find friendship in their mutual despair.

# Chapter 21

If Ruth had thought her grandfather's living conditions were bad before, they had deteriorated, and she was now worried that his health had worsened. She thought that he required constant care given his age, but she couldn't provide for him in the way he needed, not with everything that was going on. Even still, she felt the need to talk to him. He was the only person in her family whom she could truly rely on, even if he was no longer able to remember all the details. In actual fact, for that very reason, it made it easier to talk to him about what was going on in her life. She knew he wouldn't judge her, and then he would lose most of what she told him anyway.

Ruth knew that she was the only member of her family who came to see her grandfather. Her parents had returned to Austria and her sister would claim she had too busy a life, even though Ruth knew that Abigail didn't want to visit because she was worried it would bring out her secret and damage her husband's reputation. But Abigail wasn't mourning a killed husband and a missing child. Ruth almost choked at the thought. How she wished to tell them, but there was no way she could let them know she had lost George. It would not bring her closer to her family, they were too self-absorbed and they would only blame her. She had enough blame for herself.

She knew that well enough, for what had been done to her, she was close to becoming a traitor herself, and she wanted to know what her grandfather thought about it. He would know what to do, but they couldn't talk about it here, it was too open. Others might hear her confession.

She put her hand on his shoulder, noticing how thin it was. There was hardly any muscle left, only skin and bones. Unusually, he was not writing away, but staring into the middle distance. He was conscious of her presence, but she was sure that he had only pretended to know who she was.

He coughed, turning away from her to save her the view. Even if he couldn't remember everything he still had his manners. So many things they did were based on habit and instinct. Was that all her grandfather had left? He coughed again into a handkerchief, which Ruth didn't get a good look at before he ferreted it away into a threadbare pocket. She could have sworn a pink stain coated the cloth, but she could not be completely sure, the dim light played tricks on her eyes. She would find someone to speak to, they had to know what was going on with her grandfather. There was no point hanging around here watching him deteriorating. She gave him a final hug, careful not to exert too much pressure, and left the house. Before she had taken two steps out onto the dry earth a soldier marched towards her.

'The commandant has asked to see you,' he said without preamble.

'Good.'

She marched across the open grass in the direction of the house she knew they had set up as an office. She had been asking to see the captain of the camp since her grandfather had been rounded up with the others over six months earlier. If it had taken this long for her letters to reach him then she would be damned. It had been so long that she had almost given up on speaking to him, her visitor's rights her only consolation. A pair of soldiers guarding the door let her pass, apparently expecting her. That or her confident stride didn't give them time to even think about stalling her.

The interior of the building was just as spartan as the other houses, and the soldiers had taken no time to make their office feel homelier. She suspected that none of them truly wanted to be there any more than the inmates did. There were wooden crates, but she doubted they were for anything more than show. She took a note of every detail in case any of it would be useful to Patrick, as she was led up a narrow stairway and into an office by a young soldier who looked barely old enough to have left school.

A markedly older man was hunched over a writing desk arranged in the middle of the room, a number of medals pinned to his chest. He must have fought in the last war, she thought, or at least he wanted people to think he had.

'Ah,' he said as he looked up at her and gestured for her to sit with an upturned palm. 'Thank you for coming so promptly. I had expected you might spend more time with your grandfather.'

She chose tact.

'Thank you for agreeing to see me, Captain,' she said. 'I've seen my grandfather and I must say he's not doing well.'

'Yes.' He cut her off. 'A terrible business, all around.'

She opened her mouth to agree, but he did not let her.

'Mrs Holt, I shall cut to the chase. I want you to write about the camp, what the conditions are like here and how these people are living.'

She couldn't still her gasp, but the captain continued as if he hadn't noticed.

'Naturally, you do not have my official authority to do any such thing and if anyone asks whether I compelled you to write an article about the camp I will of course deny it.'

He stood up and came around the desk as he talked, before sitting on the edge of the desk facing her. She supposed it was his way of being more familiar and comforting, but it did not have the desired effect. He had worked with soldiers for years, and his uniform and manner were as off-putting as the barbed wire surrounding the camp, but even still she was surprised by his words.

'I—' she started, but was stalled by her own hesitation and the captain's upturned palm.

'You want to know why I'm asking this of you? I am not as ignorant of the state of the camp as some would have you believe. However, neither do I take absolute responsibility. We must work within a set of restrictions set by His Majesty's government and the resources allocated by the War Office for housing these priso— detainees here. It was not a thought-out process and well, to be quite frank with you, Mrs Holt, we have had to make do with what we have. I have written a number of letters to the War Office requesting greater resources, but they have fallen on deaf ears. My powers are limited in that regard, but I think that you might have more power at your fingertips.'

There was a hope in his eyes that Ruth found both intriguing and horrifying. If only he knew her secret, what power her fingertips had, as he had put it. She worried for them all if the military had as little power as the captain was making out, but then perhaps he was a man at the end of his career, shifted off to some backwater concentration camp where he could no longer be a problem. She could see it in his eyes, and the crow's feet that pulled at them as he smiled at her.

'I will do everything I can.'

*

'Is Mrs Hastings at home?'

'I'll check for you, Mrs Holt. I'll make sure that she is receiving guests.'

The housekeeper shut the door in Ruth's face, without another word. *Guests* indeed. Who did she think she was? Ruth and Abigail were family. If Abigail wouldn't bloody well see her, then she would break the door down and admit herself. A moment later Ruth could just about hear an angry mumbling from the other side of the door, but couldn't make out the words. As she leant forward to get closer the door was wrenched open as if it had offended its own hinges. She almost fell through the doorway, but managed to catch herself.

'Sister?' Abigail asked. She almost managed to hide the frown, but Ruth knew her too well to not notice. 'I wasn't expecting you again. What brings you here?'

'Can I . . . May I come in please, Abigail? It's cold out here, and well, I thought we might be able to talk?'

'Of course, of course. Where are my manners? Come in, come in!'

Ruth was sure that Abigail hadn't spoken like this when they were children, putting on airs and graces as some would call it, but she must have picked it up from their parents. Ruth had always been the rebellious one. She didn't know why, but if her parents had spoken like that then she would make sure that she dropped as many consonants from her speech as possible. They would get angry, but it was always worth it.

'It's all right,' she said, biting her tongue for once.

As before, Abigail led Ruth into the house, past their many photographs, paintings and other evidence of the family's happiness. It was like a museum of their experiences, as if Abigail was trying to show off to Ruth. She couldn't help but feel that there was another, quicker way to get to the living room. They went through the usual procedure of seeing that the other was comfortable in the assigned seat and waiting for the other to sit before doing so themselves. It always amused Ruth that everything the upper classes did was wrapped in tradition and formality. It was a wonder they ever got anything done. But then, it wasn't them that got things done.

'What was it you wanted to discuss, dear sister?' Abigail was staring directly at Ruth from her sofa on the other side of the room, making sure that Ruth knew she was paying her due attention.

'What?' Ruth asked, distracted by the housekeeper and the crackling of the fire.

'You said, on the doorstep, that you "thought we might be able to talk".'

Yes, she had said exactly those words, hadn't she? In reply, she looked at Abigail and smiled, hoping to give herself more time. Abigail and she had not talked in a long time, not about anything serious any way, and when they had it had always resulted in an argument. This time, Ruth wanted to make sure that they could keep things civil. Ruth wanted to tell her sister all about what had happened over the last few weeks, the loss of her husband, her son, how she was not coping at all, but she knew that she would get no sympathy from her sister, not real sympathy. But that wasn't why she had come. She decided to stick to the main purpose of her visit.

'Yes, I did. I thought we should talk about Grandpappa.'

Abigail blinked, but otherwise stayed perfectly still. Ruth thought that perhaps a normal person might ask the question that immediately came to mind – 'is he all right?' – but not Abigail. It would be easy to think that she didn't care about their grandfather, but Ruth knew that couldn't be true, she just had a different way to deal with her emotions. Abigail had always been a quiet child, and she was waiting for Ruth to continue now.

'He's not well. We need to do something about him.'

'Aren't they looking after him?'

'It's an internment camp, Abigail, not a hotel. They don't have the resources to look after him, even if they cared to. They're all forgotten in there, and we need to do something.'

'What could we possibly do? They're interned there because it's the law. We cannot break the law, sister.'

'No,' Ruth said slowly. 'No, we cannot. But you could go and see him. I know he would appreciate it.'

Abigail gave her a look that could have killed. 'And what do you think people would think if they found out I had visited an internment camp for enemy traitors? No, I couldn't do that to poor Edward. It would ruin his prospects. It was difficult enough for him having to help hide our . . . background.'

Ruth opened her mouth to protest, but realised there was no point. Abigail had made up her mind. Perhaps there was nothing they could do for their grandfather after all, but she wouldn't be defeated that easily. She would write the article the commandant had asked her to, and make sure that Rupert printed it. That was her way of fighting the powers that be. With luck it would take attention away from her . . . other activities. Sneaking around trying to find information about the military presence in the city was becoming dangerous, even for a journalist.

She daren't raise the issue again with Abigail, as they sat there for another hour sipping tea from the fine china tea set. Ruth wanted so desperately to tell her sister about George, but she could not bring herself to. Not even when some time later, Abigail said goodbye to her on the doorstep with a kiss to the cheek. Ruth stood there, silent, before slipping off into the darkness.

# Chapter 22

'Here, we need some help down here.'

The morning light after a raid always brought a stark view of the city. It had been a busy night, but then it always was when there was a raid on. All they could do was respond to the fires, or sit back and watch, but the morning brought new light. On his rounds Anthony got to see which parts of Liverpool no longer existed, which homes had been destroyed. Sometimes there were fires still smouldering under the piles of bricks and masonry. Far too often there were those who had become trapped.

The rescue men working in the area were miners brought in from Wales. He relished the accent, reminding him of a simpler time. They didn't know the city as well as he did, but they were hard workers, and at times he had heard them singing songs as they worked. This morning was too solemn for such an occasion.

'Grab some timber, will you? Anything strong that'll hold some weight.'

'Warden?'

That was Sid, asking for his help. Anthony nodded to himself, then crossed the road to one of the ruined houses. Its first floor had caved in, like the ruins of some kind of castle. The floorboards had burned away, but some of the thick beams that held the floor up were still there. He tried to pick one up, but the splinters cut at his hands, even through his gloves, and it wouldn't budge. Towards the corner of the room a table had fallen over, one of its legs missing from the blast. It would have to do.

He pushed it over, and with a kick removed the remaining two and a half legs. The board was as sturdy as any piece of timber he would be able to find. When he couldn't lift it, Sid appeared and helped him drag it over to the miners. With a grateful nod they took it and started placing bricks around it to form some kind of lintel. They were digging into the building, and it was only then that Anthony recognised where he was.

He could just about make out the varnished wood panelling, buried beneath the stone work. This was the place he came to work, every day. The school had been destroyed.

His knees almost buckled beneath him, but he held on to Sid for a moment.

'You all right, lad?' Sid asked, and Anthony could only nod in reply.

He had known others to lose their homes or their places of work, but this was the first time the war had directly affected him. What would he do now? He could appeal to one of the other schools in the area, but it was unlikely they were looking for any staff. There was money put aside in his bank account, but it probably wouldn't last the war. He would have to see if he could get permanent work as a warden.

'There's someone down here,' one of the miners called back over his shoulder. 'There's definitely someone down here, there is!'

Everyone around visibly tensed, but the miners redoubled their efforts, digging even faster than they had been before. Anthony desperately wanted to help, but he would only get in the way. He must have mumbled something to Sid, who had a similar response.

'Keep calm? Yeah, bloody right. Who's keeping calm with all this mess going on?'

Sid was never one to guard his words, and it was one of the things that Anthony appreciated about him. Anthony himself had never found he could simply say what was on his mind, especially as a teacher with young children around. It made him laugh, but Sid didn't look like laughing.

'I heard those posters were unauthorised,' he continued. 'Too bloody right. Rather than keeping my morale up, they make me want to grab a gun and shoot whoever was stupid enough to come up with that slogan in the first place. Next they'll be telling us we're all in this together and we just have to pull together. What, while they sit in their palaces and make us do all the work? Makes me blood boil, that.'

Anthony heard a gasp, but it had not been Sid. It was as if the miners, having completed their dig, had collectively released a sigh of tension. Instinctively, Anthony stepped closer.

There was a shape trapped down there, only visible because it was different to the straight edges of the fallen masonry, more organic, more *alive*. Only, it no longer appeared alive. It wasn't moving. As he scrabbled down the loose bricks, almost losing his footing more than once, he realised that the shape was smaller than those he was used to seeing in the rubble. It was a boy, maybe ten or eleven years old going by the size of the boys in his class. He half expected the boy to be wearing a uniform, but instead he was dressed in tattered rags that had once been a smart brown waistcoat and trousers. Anthony might have worn something very much like that himself.

It was Jones.

What had the boy been doing in the school during a raid? Anthony stumbled over the broken building, drawn by impulse alone. He had not expected to lose the school, but it was even worse to see one of his pupils buried amongst the wreckage.

'Jones?' he asked the still shape.

One of the miners put an arm across Anthony. At first he thought it was to stop him falling, but then he saw the man shake his head.

'He's gone, he is,' the miner said, soft and lyrical. 'There was no helping him.'

# Chapter 23

When things were at their most fraught words filled Ruth's mind. She flicked through her notebook looking for a blank page, one clear of her frantic scribblings. Pages were covered in manic thoughts, like a book of poetry written by a busy mind. Many of those words never made it to an article, but it helped her to compose her thoughts. There were scribblings about Peter, George, and even Anthony, her grandfather and all sorts of things. She had details of those she had met volunteering, their day jobs and some of the things the Ministry of Information had made her privy to. What it didn't contain was the details she had been asked to procure for Patrick: navy movements, number of ships, casualty figures and other things. They were in another notebook she kept at home safely hidden away, where no one would find it.

Giving up on the notebook, she pulled out a folder of items she had been compiling on her desk. Rupert had allowed her to write a number of articles now. At first they had caused some consternation with the other journalists, but the more she had leant into subjects they wouldn't touch, the more they left her alone. It was what she had wanted all along, the freedom as a journalist to pursue the kind of stories she wanted to, to make a difference. That was especially important now, given what Patrick was making her do. So she had started to collect her own articles and writings together, as something she could look at when she needed motivation, and took a moment now and then to look through them.

Of course, there was the first of her recent articles, about the family that had lost their home. It had been heavily censored, keeping only a few quotes about how they were struggling, but that they 'would pull together as a family and do their bit as was the British way'. It wasn't exactly what they had said, but it was all she had been allowed to print. She flipped that sheet over on the desk, revealing another article with her name attached. It still filled her with warmth, seeing her own name in print, and she hoped she would never grow tired of it. This piece had been about the living conditions of people in the city, after her various trips to the shelters. Rupert and the censors had allowed her more room to write what she wanted this time. Not only had they printed some quotes from people in the shelters, they had also allowed her to write a run-down of what it was like in the shelter. As long as it was asking for the Corporation to do better, not as an attack on what they had.

'Many families have to share metal pallet beds with thin mattresses that need replacing. Some have taken to bringing their own sheets and bedding into the shelter to make it into an impromptu home,' she had written. 'But it does not replace the comfort of their own houses. Some of the shelters may be safer, but greater provisions are needed to make sure that families do make use of the shelters.'

She was surprised they had let her get away with that last line, but wondered whether the criticism was perhaps too subtle, or whether it had been read by a more empathetic censor. She would never know. Rupert had even conceded and put forward her photographs for printing, but as she looked at the originals and compared them to what was printed she couldn't help but notice how much had been cut. There was no way to tell where the photographs had been taken, the focus was on the standing buildings, emphasising the point that Liverpool still stood. She might not have agreed with propaganda, but she could see the reasoning here. If they didn't keep their hopes up, then they would fall apart.

Her most recent article was one of her proudest. When she had gone to Rupert telling him that the camp commander had asked her to write about the conditions she had expected him to refuse, but his eyes had lit up. He was clearly aware that they had access to a story that no other paper in the city had. Once again, she compared her copy to that of the final version. Of course, the censors had cut out most of what she had written, but what was left still filled her with pride. There was no way that the government was going to allow her to write about the worst of the camp: the twelve to a house, the poor food and lack of actual beds, but they couldn't avoid the fact that the camp existed. It was clear for anyone who lived nearby to see, and now it would be part of the city's more general consciousness. They wanted it to stand as a warning, and she was more acutely aware of that than anyone, but the newspaper had already received letters asking for more information and what they could do to help. In some small way she had fulfilled her promise to the captain, and for that she was grateful. She had done some good to counterbalance the secret life she was living, the information she was passing to Patrick.

Putting the cuttings away again, she pulled a pad of paper from the desk. It was Samuel's desk, but he wouldn't mind. The top page contained notes about the various things being produced in Liverpool and what was coming through the docks. She took care to remove it from the sheaf and place it on top of his work, making a mental note of the details. It was something she could pass on to Patrick. Let them decide whether it was useful.

Earlier that day she had gone to see Lord Woolton's visit. The Minister of Food was being shown around a new meal kitchen set-up in a shop under a block of Corporation flats. It had been so busy that Ruth had not been able to ask him any questions, but she had overheard him saying where he was touring next.

If they knew what Ruth was up to, then she would no doubt be arrested. In truth, she had been there to report for the paper. She longed for a time when she could just be a journalist, without Patrick's demands in the back of her mind.

She started writing the article she had been planning about Lord Woolton's visit, how he had failed to see the entirety of what the city had to offer. As always she wasn't sure what she would get past the censors, but she had learnt to write anyway and let them decide. She was providing a public service and they needed to know the sorts of things happening in the city. There was one thing she wouldn't get past the censors. She had to pass on details about the Lord's visit and his next location to Patrick. She knew he would want to know that and it pained her that she had even considered it. It was as if she was completely complicit now, passing on information he hadn't even asked for.

The pen dropped from her hand. What was she doing? She was going to be labelled a traitor and hanged. She put her head in her hands and stifled a sob. Why her? she thought. Why had Patrick chosen to pick on her and poor George? Her son had done nothing to deserve this, he hadn't even been born into her family, he had no link to Austria. They had tried to do something good by saving him from a life of foster families, but they had brought him into this.

Her earlier optimism was suddenly shattered. The longer the war drew on, the more difficult it became to muster any kind of motivation and positivity. What was she going to do? She had to fight Patrick somehow.

*

'I'm not who you think I am.' She tried to say it with conviction, but it sounded like an apology. She couldn't look Patrick in the eye. He stared back at her, a frown crossing his brow, before sitting on a pile of rubble, facing her.

She found him in the abandoned house in which he'd asked to meet. There were still signs of the family that had lived here before they'd had their home taken. A few broken trinkets lay around the base of a shattered fireplace, a torn and singed photograph poked out from between scattered bricks. She wanted to reach down and take that photo, see who the family had been, but she became more and more conscious of Patrick's stare. He was waiting for her to speak.

'I can't get the information you need. It's too difficult. I'm not the person you think I am.' She didn't know why she'd decided to try to appeal to his compassion. The kind of man who could kidnap a child surely had nothing she would recognise as compassion. She wasn't capable of doing the things he demanded of her. Unlike him, she was no Nazi. 'I can't get close to the dock house. The navy officials are starting to get suspicious.'

He had asked for casualty figures and details of army and naval movements through the city. Sneaking around the docks wasn't easy, even with her volunteer uniform, but he clearly couldn't get in at all, or he'd never have asked her to risk it. That was why she had given them false information about ship movements. It was a big risk, but how would they know?

'You know what happens if you don't?' They were the first words he had uttered and they boomed as if they were standing in some kind of cavern.

'As far as I know you've already killed . . .' She couldn't finish the thought and a tear ran down her cheek. 'How am I supposed to trust you?'

'Jesus, we can't keep having these conversations, can we? This is a war. Even before France, before Czechoslovakia. Since the last war proved there's only one way to finish a war. Kill those who oppress you.'

'Please. Just tell me how my son is, give me some kind of hope. You know I can't just keep doing this for you on promises alone. I need to know he's safe, I need proof.'

'What kind of proof do you think we can give you?'

'Show me where he is. Let me talk to him.'

'No way. You're not doing that. You'll only make things worse for all of us. No, it's better if you let him think he's being looked after and we're just waiting for the war to be over before we return him to you. That is what we're waiting for, isn't it? And you're going to help them end this bloody war so we can get back to our lives. Aren't ya?'

'Yes,' she said, her eyes dropping to look at the floor in front of her, the cracked tiles. 'Yes, I'll help end this war.'

She didn't have to say she would make sure that it wasn't the Germans who won. She would feed them false information if that was all they wanted. She'd already made up details about ships that had left the dock. She didn't dare say another word. There was no other way out of this than do what he wanted. Apparently selling your soul to the devil was simple, but she would keep on tricking them. If they could get the information themselves then they didn't need her.

'Here.' He passed her a handwritten note. She expected another list of demands, but it was in George's handwriting. *Hi Mummy, enjoying my stay with Patrick. Love you.*

'You bastard.'

Patrick gripped her chin, putting pressure on her jaw like a vice. She couldn't talk. He held her still like that for a long moment, staring deep into her eyes. She couldn't see the colours of his eyes in the gloom, but she suspected they resembled the fires of hell.

'If you follow me again, lassie,' he growled. 'I will kill you. So don't you dare think about it.'

As he left, he failed to notice the hand that lifted the wallet from his coat pocket. She waited until she was home before rifling through its contents. There were all sorts of papers, but little money. The first thing she noticed was a selection of cards. One gave the name of Thomas Connor, gardening services, and another Philip McAllister, painter decorator, and a Patrick Ward. There were a number more, each with a different name and details, but they were all printed in the same style as if they were aliases. Patrick was a man of many talents and professions. Each of them had a different address, but none that she immediately recognised. Was he moving George around? That confused things, but at least it was a start. She would check the details with the phone book and records in the office. There were a couple of handwritten notes, including one that simply said 'Knowsley Hall', the home of the Earl of Derby and where her brother-in-law worked. Butterflies fluttered in her stomach. Did Patrick have a connection with the Earl or her brother-in-law? Had that been how he found out about her? She was planning to go to the house anyway, and she would see whether she could find any connection to him there. But with these details she could start to fight back.

# Chapter 24

*Thursday, 28 November 1940*

A woman in a tweed skirt ran towards Anthony. She must have been cold in the November chill, but like all the others they had been told not to stop if the alarm was sounded. The bombers could arrive at any moment, and Anthony was sure that he could already hear the faint drone on the horizon. They had all become so used to the sound in only a few months. It seemed to be the only thing that forced him into action now.

'Come on, madam. Get to a shelter as quickly as possible.'

'I'm not sure where to go.' She was crippled by indecision. Maybe she was not familiar with this part of the city, perhaps she was not from Liverpool at all. 'I'm visiting family, but they were out when the alarm was sounded.'

He stopped. This was precisely the reason he had signed up as a warden, now it was all he had.

'You've got two choices from here. Schools,' he said. Perhaps one of them would offer him work.

'Which way? Which is the nearest?'

'This way,' he said, deciding it would be quicker to show her. Stepping into a brisk pace, he hoped that she would follow. He could sense the bombers in the air, they would arrive at any moment. Too many had been caught in the open, or trying to shelter within their homes when the bombers had arrived. He had failed them all.

They reached the school door when the first bombs landed. The woman gave her thanks and rushed inside, leaving Anthony alone in the darkness. He was unlikely to see her again, but he was glad to have helped. He hoped that she saw it through the war, could return to wherever it was she had come from.

*

There were hundreds of aircraft in the sky. Every time the moon flashed between clouds Anthony could see more and more. He wouldn't be surprised if the entire Luftwaffe was up there. Guns coughed in response, but even they wouldn't be able to stave off this raid. No matter how much flak they pumped into the sky, bombers would make it through. Bombs dropped down in clusters and on the ground Anthony was powerless to stop them. All he could do was stand and stare, like a child. It was a curious thing being a warden; at the beginning of a raid he was always busy, rushing around making sure that everyone was where they were supposed to be, then picking up the pieces, sometimes literally, after the bombers had gone. But in between he was left to stop and stare, see the city pounded and set alight, wondering what on earth he could do to help. Not for the first time recently he felt without purpose.

A bomber flew low, breaking his reverie as he flinched. It disappeared overhead, its engine noise merging into the cacophony. Even in the gloom he could see the white flower of the parachute as it dropped frustratingly towards the ground. It was not the parachute of an escaped airman, but attached to a mine. Anthony tried to orientate where it was going to land. It was up to him to direct the recovery teams as quickly as possible.

Keeping his eyes on the fluttering white of the parachute, he ran towards it. If not for practice he would have tumbled over the debris on the ground. Every now and then he had to glance down to make sure that he didn't run into a lamppost, or wall. All he could do was follow it and hope that he could direct the teams quickly enough to limit the damage it might cause. It disappeared behind the chimney stack of a building and Anthony quickened his pace to get it back into his line of sight. As he turned a corner he saw it land with a sickening finality. It hit the roof of a school, smashing through the slate tiles with a crash that was audible even over the drone of the bombers and the bark of the guns. The parachute lodged itself on the jagged beams that remained of the roof and flapped in the wind, like some kind of white flag signalling the school's surrender.

He stopped as he expected an explosion to burst from the upper-storey windows, but nothing happened. He had time to think it was a dud, before he heard a dull crump. A second later, the foundations of the building collapsed in a flash. The building didn't so much topple as fly outwards. The shockwave hit him before he heard it, throwing him back against a wall. It forced the air from his lungs, and he gasped, struggling to take in air.

The bomb had penetrated the basement into the shelter under the school. It was the only way the explosion made sense, seeming to come from below the very building and throwing it upwards. The building burned from inside and shattered glass lay across the road. He had been lucky to avoid any cuts, luckier than those inside.

His exhausted brain questioned everything he had seen. The out-of-towner had been in that shelter, the woman he had led to safety. And it had all been his fault. If only he had advised her to go somewhere else then she would not have lost her life. When would it end? He had wanted to go to war, to do his bit, but these people didn't deserve this. They were civilians, just trying to live their lives. Bringing the war to them was callous and cowardly. The Germans wanted to demoralise the people of Britain, and Anthony suspected it was starting to work.

He rushed to the doorway where he had left her, but the flames pushed him back. There was no way of getting inside. Already he could hear the jingle of the fire engine's bell. Maybe they could save the school, but Anthony doubted there was anyone still alive under there.

*

Bricks tumbled down as if someone was playing a game. Anthony could feel the warmth of the explosion through the soles of his boots, having warmed the bricks to almost breaking point. They warped and cracked under his footsteps. It was a scene he was becoming all too familiar with, but this was his own neighbourhood. He knew these people well, thought of himself as a part of their lives. He had decided to continue on his patrol, after seeing the school go up in flames, and a group of incendiaries had led him to his own street. He couldn't process what he was seeing, in the space of an hour it had become a ruin.

His neighbour knelt upon the ruin of his house. Anthony rushed over to him. He didn't know the man well, and his hands were bloody from clawing at the bricks. Anthony pulled him away but he pushed back, fighting like a caged animal. Together they rolled down the mound, before Anthony pulled him up and held him still.

'Stop,' Anthony said. He didn't dare say it would be all right. 'Shhhh.'

'You're lucky,' his neighbour replied, tears streaming down his dirtied face. Anthony suddenly knew what he meant. Having to recover the bodies of his own family from a wreckage was a feeling he could only imagine. A fate worse than death, because Anthony knew that he would rather have died than lost his Julie when she had given birth to Marc. 'You're lucky you had no one.'

'I'm sorry,' Anthony muttered. The words had lost all meaning now. How could anyone be sorry in this disaster? They were all experiencing grief, they had all suffered from the bombing. Some more than others, of course, but saying sorry no longer made any difference. People were no longer comforted by the word. The only way they could make a difference was by helping each other, supporting each other, but that was easier said than done. His neighbour had lost his entire family and there were no words of comfort nor any actions that would be able to help him now. It would be a long journey of recovery for him, if he even made it that far.

Anthony put his arms around the sobbing man and pulled him gently away. He needed to get warm to help the shock.

'There, there.' He hoped that the softness of his voice would do something at least. He led the man over to the WVS team that had just arrived on the scene and a woman took him away from Anthony, wrapped him in a blanket. Another came to Anthony.

'Bad one this one, I'm afraid,' he said to her, noticing that none of them appeared shocked anymore. He pointed over his shoulder. 'His whole family was in that house. Wife and three kids.'

'We'll take care of him,' she said as if it was the most natural thing in the world. 'Anyone else?'

'I haven't checked yet, but at the moment it looks like it was only his house and the one next door.'

She blew her lips out in a huffing sound. 'And which poor soul did that house belong to?'

'Me,' he replied, watching for her reaction. 'That used to be my home.'

He walked away from the street. It seemed he had made up his mind, he was going to see the chief warden and apply to join as a full-time warden. Only, he had to survive this raid first.

# Chapter 25

It was a quiet time for Ruth to visit the office. The next edition was in the print room and the writers were out finding stories, or missed sleep. It was a time she often liked to work, when there were fewer distractions. When they hadn't needed her to drive the van that night, she had thought that she could have some time to herself, but as soon as she was left alone the thoughts all came flooding back. Where was George? How was she going to get him back?

She flicked through her notepad trying to form the words in her mind. She needed to work, but all she could think about was George. The words were slow today, dropping onto the page in an irregular drip. Clever words, if only she could work them into her article. Her thoughts wandered and she thought about writing fiction. Anthony would like that. One day she would write the story of her life, tell everyone what had happened to her. She only hoped that she wouldn't have to do it from a prison cell, forcing the stream of words as she waited for the gallows noose.

She pushed the notepad away and her pen clattered to the floor. She didn't stoop to pick it up, but dropped her head to the table to rest on her crossed arms. She closed her eyes, breathing in the woody, ink-stained scent of the desk. She was going to have to do the unthinkable, against every fibre of her body. But it was all for

George. She had made a choice to be responsible for his life; his was more important than hers. She fingered the cards she kept in her handbag. She had memorised the addresses written on them.

Pushing herself up from the table, she took a deep breath. She knew exactly what she needed to do. She would go to each of those addresses until she found her son. It wouldn't be easy, but then nothing ever was.

*

It was the penultimate address from the ones she had snatched from Patrick's wallet, but she hoped it would be the last. She stood outside the supposed home of Philip McAllister, or Patrick, or whatever his name was, on Bailey Street and took a deep breath. It was remarkable how unremarkable the houses were, just row upon row of terraces. But this one could contain her son. She didn't know what she was going to do if she found him, but she had to go in and try. The front door hung loose on the hinges, moving slightly in the breeze. It wasn't a good sign, but at least she didn't have to break in.

Inside, she felt like calling out George's name, but knew it was ridiculous. She moved through the hallway, searching for any clues. It reminded her of the house her grandfather lived in at the camp. There were bits of litter strewn everywhere and an overpowering stench of damp. There was nothing in the kitchen, where part of the rear wall was missing, nor in the living room, so she made her way upstairs. She winced with each creak of the wooden steps, but no one came. It was the only sound in the house.

From the landing she rushed into a bedroom hoping to surprise anyone who was there, but it was just as empty as the downstairs. There was only a simple bed in the corner, missing a mattress. Yet there were signs that someone had been living there recently: discarded bits of clothing, and a newspaper dated from the first week of the month. She moved on to the other room, but was disappointed not to find George. That last room was in the same state of disrepair as the rest of the house, but amongst the discarded items she spotted one piece of clothing she recognised. It was the shirt George had been wearing when he had been kidnapped. She rushed to it and picked it up, wrapping herself in it as if it were her son. It still smelt faintly of him and she breathed deeply, but it was tinged with the smell of damp. She put it in her overall pocket and moved to a bedside table.

She rifled through the pieces of paper that lay on it, but there was nothing of use. The only name on them was the alias that Patrick was using at this address. Philip McAllister. It could have been his real name, but she had found no further records of him existing outside this house. He didn't officially exist.

The house was not what she was expecting. There was nothing there, it was just yet another house abandoned after a raid. That was the only reason she could think that Patrick was using it. It had brought her no closer to her son. He must be moving George from one abandoned house to the next. She mentally checked the list of addresses she had found in his wallet. As she thought, there was only one more address left to try. George would have to be there, or she was lost.

### Saturday, 30 November 1940

It wasn't straightforward to get to Knowsley Hall from the city centre. Ruth had to get the train to Knowsley station, then the bus, and walk the rest of the way along a country lane and up the secluded path to the big house. Train travel was discouraged unless it was essential or for the war effort, but as a journalist she would be able to make an argument for it. She had taken the bicycle just in case, but the muddy paths soon had her regretting it.

They had been expecting her. It was like gaining access to an exclusive club, forbidden to her as both a common worker and a woman. She had been led into a library by Mrs Reed the house-keeper, in which thick leather-bound tomes lined the walls. While she waited Ruth took a look around. The books looked as if they had never been read, if the dust was anything to go by. One must appear well read, even if one wasn't. But as she had heard from her sister, they had found it difficult to retain staff at the house. A writing desk was arranged at an angle to the seating area, so that whoever sat there could engage in conversation with those by the fire. She took a closer look. There were locked drawers in the top section, but swathes of paper were left on the writing panel. Glancing over her shoulder to check she was unobserved, she flicked over the first sheets.

She wondered whether she should make a mental note of where everything lay on the desk, but she didn't have the time. Besides, the desk was disorganised and cluttered and there was no way Lord Derby would be able to remember where things had been. She flicked over another piece of paper. She didn't know exactly what she was looking for, but there had to be something she could pass on to Patrick. Her stomach lurched as her conscience screamed at her from somewhere in the back of her mind.

Most were notes about the running of the household, things to be fixed in the gardens, who was responsible for the wall and the end of the estate, that sort of thing. Her pace quickened as she looked for anything to make sure this was not a wasted trip. Even should her interview with the Lord prove fruitless, she was sure she could find something here. She read and read, speeding up as she sensed her time was short. There were so many scribblings she didn't know what she was reading and she was about to give up when something more formal caught her eye.

There was a typewritten note from the War Office. They were moving the North Atlantic Command to Liverpool. There it was. That was something she could pass on to Patrick. His handlers would want to know. The other sheets detailed naval movements in and out of the city, and she started scribbling notes in her notebook. Her stomach dropped again. Was she betraying other seamen like Peter? Surely the Nazis would find out someway if not from her. What choice did she have? She had to do something.

'Mrs Holt! What on earth are you doing?'

Ruth spun on the spot and dropped her notepad to the floor. It landed with a thump then slid a few inches on the freshly polished wood. She was forced mute, and the housekeeper repeated her question.

'I beg your pardon, Mrs Holt, but this *is* a private residence. May I ask what you thought you were doing by that writing desk?'

The housekeeper had crossed her arms under her chest, and looked down her spectacles at Ruth like a school mistress. Ruth could imagine Anthony looking at a pupil in the very same way, and she almost smiled before she shook the thought away.

'My sincerest apologies, Mrs Reed. I didn't mean to be impertinent. However, while I was waiting I took it upon myself to find some writing paper. For the interview.'

It wasn't much of a lie, but she hoped that it would pass. There was no way that the housekeeper could have any suspicions of what she was truly up to.

'I see,' Mrs Reed said after a pause. 'Did you not think perhaps

208

to bring some with you? I would rather expect writing paper to be one of the tools of your profession.'

'Of course, Mrs Reed. Only, I forgot to bring my bag from the office, and when I realised it was far too late to go back. . . I would have missed the appointment and kept Lord Derby waiting. I rather thought that was a worse crime than borrowing some writing paper.'

'Yes, quite. Well, let me see whether I can find you some before Lord Derby comes down. Only, you won't be able to borrow it, I'm afraid.' She smiled a wicked smile, the creases on her face highlighting her many years. 'You shall have to keep it!'

'Thank you,' Ruth replied, giving the short laugh that she was sure was expected of her. 'I would be grateful.'

'Wait here. And do not touch anything else. In fact, make yourself comfortable on the Chesterfield. Lord Derby will have the armchair. He prefers to sit closer to the fire.'

Ruth moved away from the writing desk, picking up her notebook. She was thankful that Mrs Reed hadn't pointed out the obvious fact that she could write in her notebook, but perhaps she had not noticed Ruth drop it. A minute later Mrs Reed came back into the library with a young man in tow. He was dressed in a suit which had clearly been tailored in Savile Row. It fitted him well, the lines of its dark navy cotton emphasising his height. Ruth was so flustered she simply curtseyed and waited to be introduced. Lord Derby simply smiled in response and held out his hand to shake hers.

'What would you like to know, Mrs Holt?' he asked as he took a seat. 'I don't often get journalists here, and I certainly don't often allow them in, but let us just say that I was intrigued by your letter. And I hear you are sister to my assistant's wife. You say you would like to know about the running of the house? I suppose I'm the last person you should be asking about the day to day, but perhaps I may be of some, minor, assistance.'

She had expected an older man, but it was only then that she realised that the son had taken over the estate from his father. He too had links to the War Office, but how much he knew, she would have to find out.

'I'd be obliged if you would tell me everything,' she said. 'I'm sure our readers would be fascinated to hear about all the works of a Lord such as yourself and the great house of Knowsley Hall.'

He beamed at her, and she knew then that he would literally tell her everything. All she needed to do was write it down and work out the significance later. Not just because of the interview, but the letters she had found, she finally felt as if she were getting somewhere.

\*

She was surprised that Anthony was waiting for her at home when she returned after that evening's raid.

'It occurred to me that we hadn't seen each other in a week or two,' he said. 'And I did promise that I would keep an eye on you.'

Ruth smiled at the pretence, unlocked the door and showed him in. It would be a few hours before the sun came up, and she wondered why he had decided to come so early rather than going home first to get some sleep. But she didn't ask. It was genuinely nice to see him. He sat on the sofa as she lit a candle and placed it on the small table in the middle of the room.

'I realised I hadn't seen George in some time,' he said. 'So, I've brought something for him. Has Harriet already put him to bed?'

'He's gone,' she said, then caught herself. No, she couldn't tell him. Not yet. Probably not ever. Still, the words spilled out like a confession. 'I had to send him away again. I couldn't bear him being here in the city, when we're all in danger. It's safer for him as far away from the war and all the bombs as possible.'

She didn't like lying to Anthony, he didn't deserve that. This was her life now, lies wrapped in more lies.

'You kept that quiet. I would have liked to say goodbye to him before he left.'

'I'm sorry, it was a spur-of-the-moment thing. I was getting worried for his safety. But well, we all hope he'll be back soon, don't we? It breaks my heart thinking of him out in the countryside without me.'

Her voice broke as the emotion hit her and Anthony almost came to her but appeared to think better of it.

'I thought you had decided to keep him here? Where you could keep an eye on him?'

'I had decided that, yes,' she replied, emphasising the words as if they were stupid. 'But things change.'

'Oh well, it's nothing much. Maybe you can post it to him out in the countryside. It might help him pass the time more quickly. Call it an early Christmas present.'

He took out a small item and placed it on the table next to the candle. The silver reflected the scant light.

'What is it?' she asked.

'It's my father's cap badge. The Welsh regiment from the last war. I thought he might like it. I used to keep it on my dresser, but I no longer have a dresser.'

She looked up at him sharply. Whatever could he mean? As if sensing her question, he continued.

'I no longer have a house for that matter. It was bombed last night.'

She couldn't contain the gasp. No wonder he had come to see her so early in the morning. He had nowhere else to go. Realising even a man like Anthony could find himself homeless was quite a shock; it could happen to any of them.

'What are you going to do?' she asked, pushing away the mental image of him lying down to sleep on the sofa.

'I still own the bricks, but I'm no builder. I wouldn't know where to start with putting the house back together. And besides, most of them are damaged. I may be able to sell them and make some money back, but never anything like what the house was worth. I'm afraid I've rather lost everything.'

As she had come to know him Anthony's softness had become more and more obvious, but this was the first time she had seen him openly upset about something, unless it was expressed in anger. His melancholy was in some way endearing, evidence there was a depth to him that she had always suspected was there but had never experienced before.

'That wasn't quite what I meant,' she said, smiling inwardly at his naivety. 'Where are you going to live now?'

He paused, as if he hadn't considered the question himself, then his head dropped.

'You know, I don't really know,' he said. 'I'll think of something.'

He took a few breaths, and she could tell he was thinking.

'Say,' he said. 'Would you like to go to a concert at the Phil? There's Elgar at the moment.'

She hesitated, stuck somewhere between not wanting to disappoint him and wishing dearly that she could go. He noticed her pause and carried on.

'Sorry, it was a silly idea. I don't know why I asked, we're both too busy and it was presumptuous of me. Forget it.'

'No, no.' She laid a hand on his arm. 'It was a lovely suggestion. I'm just not sure about it. You know, with everything going on.

Firstly, it just seems a little privileged to go to a concert when there are people, real people, struggling and dying in the city. Why should we be so lucky?'

He opened his mouth to stop her, but she continued anyway. She knew what he would say. 'And I'm just not sure I would be able to relax and enjoy myself. It wouldn't be fair on you, I wouldn't be good company.'

He closed his mouth again and nodded, lost for words, his eyes downcast. Gripping his arm tighter, she wanted to weep for all the things she couldn't tell him.

'Why don't you move in with me?' She filled the silence, then almost put a hand over her mouth, surprised at her own words. His eyes widened and his lips pursed.

'I—' he started. 'Thank you. I would appreciate that.'

It was settled then. She was reluctant to let anyone into her world, but Anthony was different. He had become a friend, and even though she was trying to convince herself she was simply doing the right thing, she had to admit she liked him. He was a good, caring man. Things would be different about the house, but it would be nice to have some company. The only problem was, it was going to be even more difficult to keep her secret. She couldn't tell him that yet, possibly not ever. She would still be on her own.

# DECEMBER

# Chapter 26

*Thursday, 5 December 1940*

What was left of his belongings were arranged in neat lines on the table in Ruth's living room, and Anthony wondered where they could go in this new house. In his study at the school his books had been in alphabetical order. Others had commented on his fastidiousness before, saying he was too rigid, too inflexible. It only occurred to him now, stood on his own in this unfamiliar house, that it wasn't that everything needed to be in its proper place. He didn't really care about those kinds of details. It was that he was leaving places tidy for those who came after him, the only thing he could really control in his life, as if it was the only way to bring order to a chaotic world. At least he had a full-time job again, now that he had been approved as a full-time warden.

He picked up a hairbrush and moved it to the other end of the line, just because he could. It was made of brown painted wood, which was now blackened round the edges as if it had been thrown on a fire. His other belongings were in just as poor a condition, but at least he had managed to salvage something from the ruin of his house. He picked up one of the two books he had salvaged, a copy of *A Christmas Carol*, and played it in his hands, feeling the roughness of the paper cover. He thought about the fact that now even the book itself was accumulating stories. Not just the stories he attributed to it, but the stories it was living itself. Like him, it had survived a bombing. For all he knew, the book would probably outlive him. Someone would find it next to his corpse, a final testament to the man he had been in life. It wasn't as chilling a thought as he might have expected.

The other was H. G. Wells's *The War of the Worlds*. Both had been gifts from Julie, expressing their shared love of books and reading. Back then he had always begun discussions on what he thought Wells had been trying to tell them, but now his story seemed even more significant. An enemy they couldn't fight. Ruth had told Anthony that Wells had helped to found the Workers' Birth Control Group, and Anthony realised he knew very little about the man. Anthony liked the idea of writing a scientific romance once the war was over. He placed both books back on the table, they had become even more precious than they had been before.

'What have you got there?' Ruth asked as she walked into the room, pointing at the floor.

There was another item, which he hadn't organised with his collection of keepsakes. When he had entered the house he had dropped a floral canvas bag by the leg of the table. Until now he had almost forgotten about it. It wasn't that he was keeping it a secret, but the bag itself had a special significance for him and it wasn't something which he had ever talked about.

'It belonged to Julie,' he said. 'I suppose it's the last thing I have of hers.'

He picked it up by the long handles and dangled it over the table before placing it carefully next to his things. Ruth watched silently.

'Well, she didn't have much in the house, but this was precious to her. It contained her knitting, and knitting was the only thing she could really manage when she was pregnant with Marc.' He didn't know why he was telling Ruth all of this, but that was where they were in their lives now. It was strangely comforting to be able to talk about these things which he had kept locked up inside for so long. It was a relief that he knew Ruth would not judge him, not really. She was capable of turning the journalist inside her off when it came to personal matters. He trusted her, and yet he was still uneasy. 'I suppose Julie was too young to get pregnant. We were barely old enough to be married, and she didn't respond well.'

Ruth put a hand on his arm; she had sensed where his story was going.

'I didn't expect to gain Marc and lose her at the same time. I should have done more to take care of her.' He could feel the tears pricking at the corners of his eyes, but he blinked them away. It didn't pay to cry, he was supposed to be a man. It wouldn't do at all. He returned to the bag. 'I kept this because it reminded me of those times we spent together, and it smells of her.'

He closed his eyes, recalling the memory of her loving face. Sometimes she faded from view, blurred around the edges, but in this moment the memory was strong. Still Ruth had not said anything, only faintly murmuring in sympathy while he talked. He supposed that she had never heard him speak like this before and was unsure how to respond. He decided to change the subject.

'You'll never guess what's inside,' he said, picking up the bag again and forcing a smile onto his face.

'Oh, what?' Ruth replied, playing along.

'Knitting!' He chuckled to himself and felt the weight lift from his shoulders.

'I would have thought so, but what specifically? Are you playing games with me, Mr Lloyd? Show me.'

With another chuckle he did as he was told. Opening the clasp, he pulled out a bundle of black wool and handed it to Ruth.

'What's this?' she asked, unfurling it. 'Oh, it's a balaclava. Why was your wife knitting balaclavas? Were you planning to rob banks? Oh!'

'You remember the "If You Can Knit You Can Do Your Bit" campaign? Well, after Julie died I couldn't stand her unfinished projects, and I thought that knitting might bring me closer to her, might help me better understand her. We had such little time together. Well, recently, in my spare time, I have taken to knitting these for the services. They're not very good.'

He handed her a few other items he had assembled, including the start of a pullover on which he had recently been working.

'They're better than I could do,' she said. 'A few dropped stitches here and there, but I've never seen a man do anything like this before. Peter never would, and I'm sure that the servicemen would be grateful, even if they're not perfect. You're a man of surprises, Anthony.'

She handed him back the balaclavas, and he almost didn't notice it, but her expression dropped.

'And when exactly does a man like you have spare time?' she asked.

He thought for a moment. Circumstances had been strange recently. Yes, he was a teacher, but now the school was gone. His home had gone, but he was still a volunteer.

'I err . . . I have never slept particularly well. Especially since Julie died. I suppose that's why volunteering works so well for me, it keeps me busy at night, but when there are no raids then I need something else to occupy my mind. Stop it from wandering, if you understand what I mean?'

'I do. Honestly. I think you and I are very similar in that regard.' She moved towards the living-room door.

'Some Ovaltine before bed?' she asked. He hadn't had any in years and he was struck by the domesticity of it. How quickly they settled into their roles.

'No, thank you. I don't think it will help much.'

She smiled at him and left the room. A few seconds later he heard her footsteps on the stairs. He would wait a few minutes before following. Looking at the bag, he realised how much he wanted to follow her to her own room, but he couldn't. It had been a long time since he had felt that impulse and he quickly extinguished it. That wasn't why he was here, he was a guest and he had his own room to go to, an unfamiliar bed in an unfamiliar room. He would get no comfort tonight, other than the comfort of having a roof over his head and a place to sleep, and he supposed that was a lot more than many people in this city had. He was grateful and, as he walked up the stairs to that unfamiliar room, for the first time in years he wasn't lonely.

*

The blade flicked a drop of water over the side of the bowl as he waved it back and forth. It had been several days since he had been able to find the time to shave. Time had been filled with raids and the fallout of losing his home. Stubble rubbed at the crook of his neck. He had never liked that sensation, and was eager to get rid of the growing beard. At first it had felt strange to ask Ruth for a place to shave, but after a few days he had become desperate. The metal bowl was already flecked with shaving cream as he worked away at one side of his jaw.

She had already left for work, and he was thankful that she was not a witness to this act. Something about shaving felt intimate. It was something that could not be shared, an act of changing his appearance and changing how he wanted the world to see him. Even now that he was sharing a house with Ruth he didn't want her to see behind the front that he presented, the front he had spent years cultivating. He wasn't ready for that.

He flinched as the old blade cut his skin, which only made it worse. Blood dripped down into the now cooling water. It was the closest he had ever come to wielding a dangerous weapon, but the most he had done was cut himself. He had never wanted to kill another man, even if he did want to enlist. That was different; it was like joining a service, 'doing your bit' as everyone said. He had once been halfway through a shave when an air raid siren had been sounded and he had gone on duty with half a face of stubble. Thankfully in the blackout no one had noticed, but he made sure now not to shave too late in the evening. The Germans couldn't keep him from a clean face.

He looked at himself in the battered mirror, bloodied but cleanly shaved. In many ways today was a new beginning and it gave him hope as he cleaned up and went to work out what he was going to do with his day.

# Chapter 27

*Friday, 20 December 1940*

The postbox squeaked as the postman pushed letters through it. A small breeze followed, blowing in the autumnal air. Ever since the telegram about Peter, Ruth had met the post with trepidation. The world could be pushed through that thin hole, in all its fiery hell. She often waited until she had the mental fortitude to see what had been delivered. Most were junk, circulars detailing Christmas gifts in the department stores. Others notices raising money for the Corporation's Spitfire fund, as if the people around here had any extra to spare. They might want to defend their homes, but they'd sooner put food on their families' plates. She had been apprehensive even before Patrick had pushed a handwritten note through the door. Since then things had been different. At first, she had just been off food, snacking when her stomach allowed, but the feeling of nausea had not disappeared. Now, she took a deep breath every time before reading. If she didn't she was sure she would be sick. With Anthony in the house, it had become more difficult to hide it.

He took one look at her, stood still at the bottom of the stairs, and went to get the post himself. They had fallen into an easy routine. Sorting through the letters, he went back into the living room as she followed him. He dropped the pile on the table and turned over a white envelope in his hands.

'One for me.' He tore into it, ripping up the envelope as if it were wrapping paper. He took a moment scanning the words, then his eyes widened.

'This is ridiculous.' He waved the letter in the air like a white flag. 'Quite ridiculous.'

'What is? What have you got there?' She couldn't help the feeling in her stomach. Her mind raced; someone had told Anthony everything. She should have told him already, she couldn't stand the guilt anymore, but worse was the prospect of losing him, him no longer trusting her. She bit her tongue, hoping against the worst.

'It's from the Corporation,' he said, slowly reading through the words again as if they would be different the second time. She had done the same thing before. 'They're saying I still owe them land rent for my house. The house that no longer exists.'

She took the letter from him, but rather than reading it she looked up into his eyes. His frustration reminded her of the first time they had met. The passion.

'What are you going to do?' She placed a hand on his arm. He didn't seem to notice.

'I'll have to go and speak to them.'

She wasn't listening; she had something else on her mind. Their eyes met, the brown of his deepening as they got closer. She hadn't realised how close they were until she could smell his breath, sense that lavender scent again.

An air raid siren broke the tension and they pulled apart. Thinking they had been left in peace was a mistake. They didn't dare to hope, even if it had been three weeks since the last bombs.

The Germans had been lulling them into a false sense of security. She stormed into the kitchen.

The worst part was that they could never plan ahead. Many took themselves down to the shelters every night just in case. Some had even made them a second home. It hadn't helped those who had already lost their homes. There wasn't enough room in the shelters.

'We need to get out of here,' Anthony shouted from the front room.

'I think you might be right.' She let go of the blackout curtain. The view of the night sky burning a vibrant orange would stay with her for the rest of her days.

*

It had been an intense raid, with bombers attacking the city for just over nine hours. The city burned a deep orange, and the roar of flames could be heard from streets away. Ruth was exhausted, having worked all through it. Once upon a time she would have returned home to a fitful sleep, but since George had been kidnapped she had lost the ability to sleep at all. Her dreams were waking nightmares of her son calling out her name. As soon as the all clear was called she excused herself. She had decided to go to the last address she had. Patrick and George would either be there or returning after being in a shelter. Anthony wouldn't be home for a while yet, this was her only chance.

She felt her way through the dark streets, occasionally illuminated by the red glow of flames. She felt a presence behind her, but when she turned there was no one there. She knew she was being paranoid. The lack of sleep gave her hallucinations, and even the daytime provided a purple-orange tint to the edge of her vision. With only a few more stops she arrived at the address. This house just off the back of London Road looked only slightly better than the last one she had been to. Once again the door was open, but it was more solid than the last. She steeled herself in case there was anyone the other side, but her heart only thumped harder when she was not approached.

The smell inside was pungent, like in the shelters. It was urine mixed with something else she couldn't quite put her finger on. Once inside, she could tell that the entire upper storey was missing from the back of the house and the staircase led to nothing. What passed for a bedroom was in the living room. There were two wooden pallets on either side of the room, once again reminding her of the internment camp. Her head dropped again. She had so much hope that they would be here that she had almost convinced herself this would be it. It was exactly the same as the last house: empty, but with signs that someone had lived here. Just like before there were bits of discarded clothing and refuse. Once again, they had missed something of George's. It was a simple toy, a wooden ship, but George had loved it. She didn't realise he'd had it with him when Patrick had taken him. He would miss it sorely. She looked around for other signs of when they had last been here. There was a *Telegraph* newspaper dated from two days before. She had missed them by only a couple of days at most. Tears pricked at the corners of her eyes, blurring her vision. She couldn't bear to think of her son, trapped, scared and calling out for her. She swayed where she stood, exhaustion taking over.

They were long gone. Where they were now, she had no idea. This was the last house on her list. She collapsed onto a pallet. The nausea rose up in her stomach and she pitched into the corner where she was sick. It did nothing to improve the smell in the house. She had no idea what she was going to do next. Her only lead had dried up. She could check the houses again, but she didn't think they were likely to return to where they had already been. She would have to take matters into her own hands, no more hoping that fate would help her. She had to find another way.

*

Ruth knew the docks well, had spent most of her life living nearby, playing along them when no one was looking and as an adult walking along them with Peter while he talked about the various ships and how they worked. It had been a constant part of her life, so much so that she could almost describe the layout of every dock from the Stanley Dock to the Brunswick Dock from memory. But it was completely different in the dark, as she crossed under the dockers' umbrella, the overhead railway that ran the length of the river. Even though the all clear had been signalled the docks felt abandoned. They had become a warren of shadows and obscured spaces, filled with tripping hazards and dangerous drops into icy cold water. It was a wonder there weren't more accidents as the dockers unloaded and loaded the ships, but then, she supposed, if there were then the general public would not hear of them. It would be too damaging to morale, and that wouldn't do. It smelt of brine and the iron of rusting ships.

She worked her way around one of the brick warehouses, uncertain exactly what she was looking for. Anthony had spoken of his policeman friend – John, she thought his name was – having to keep a lookout on the docks for illicit activity. The last thing she needed was to be arrested for loitering, or worse. She knew what she was looking for, but didn't know where she would find it. It was a case of wandering around until she had a better idea of where she was going. If she saw anyone who looked like police then she would get out of there as quickly as looked natural.

'All right there, love?' The voice came out of the darkness. She turned to see a sailor lounging by a gangway. 'What brings a beautiful woman like you down to a dump like this?'

She didn't answer, leaving the sailor to think about his question, but it didn't stop him.

'Can I interest you in some fancy nylons for sale? Won't find these in Blacklers or Lewis's.'

'No, thank you.' She made to walk away again. He could have been the kind of man she was looking for, but she wasn't sure. Let him appeal to her needs, she wasn't going to beg. She was fairly sure that wasn't how these things worked.

'Hold on,' he called after her again and she stopped. 'What about some lippy? It won't break the bank.'

Was he inexperienced, or was that part of the bit? His eagerness to sell her something only played into her hands. But was that to lure her in and then he would up the prices? She was alone on the dock with only these men. They could mug her and take her money anyway, but if they had wanted to do that they would have done it already.

'No, thanks. Not what I'm looking for.'

'You looking for a man, then?' He cackled and then coughed, his lungs thick with smoke.

She hoped the steely look she gave him said everything she needed to say about that question.

'What else have you got?'

'That depends what you're looking for.'

Standing closer, she could see how young the sailor was. He was barely out of his teens and what she had mistaken for a beard in the darkness was nothing more than a bit of tentative fluff growing in patches on his chin. She stepped closer, smiling away, now knowing that it would unsettle him and give her the advantage.

'I want something for protection,' she said. When he looked blankly at her she wondered whether she had seen too many films at the Futurist before the war, but then his eyes widened and she could almost hear the penny dropping. Was she asking for the right thing? Or was this sailor just selling knockoff clothes?

'Ooh, that's serious stuff.' He whistled through his teeth. 'You'll be wanting the boss then.'

He turned and called over his shoulder, but the words were lost in a sudden gust of wind.

'Joe?' he called again as a shape appeared by the rail.

'Don't use my name, stupid.'

The newcomer's American accent was obvious, shouting as he came down the gangway. He also didn't look like a sailor: his suit and trilby hat made him look like he had dressed for a night on the town, ready to visit one of the dancing halls and then take some poor lovestruck young woman home. He took the sailor in his arm and scruffed up his hair in an apparent show of camaraderie. Ruth wasn't swayed; there was something dangerous about the man that he was trying to hide behind his slick look.

'We don't get many ladies down the dock,' he said, squaring up in front of her even though he was about the same height, and looking her up and down as if she was a piece of merchandise.

'I'm no lady,' she replied, for some reason riled by this arrogant American.

'Let me be the judge of that.' His smile was wide and one hand played with the pocket of his jacket. 'So what can I do you for?'

She hesitated, unsure what to ask. This was so far outside her comfort zone and everything seemed so wrapped up in euphemisms that she wanted to get it right. Still his grin didn't shift, and he played a hand round the rim of his hat before taking a look back over his shoulder.

'Come on, lady,' he said. 'I ain't got all day.'

'Protection. I want protection.'

'What kinda protection? Got a man who won't leave you alone?'

'Something like that,' she replied, trying to get to the point. 'I want a handgun. Surely an American like you has something like that.'

'Woooee,' he whistled, and rocked back on his feet. 'Not my everyday business, but maybe there's something I can do for you. It'll cost ya.'

She wanted to tell him to keep his voice down, but if he was not concerned then there couldn't be police nearby. Had he done something like this before? She had no way of knowing.

'I've got money,' she said. She would use every last penny she had left on her mission.

'You'd better do,' he said before turning to the side and shouting. 'Sammy, bring me up a piece. Make it snappy.'

The sailor, Sammy apparently, ran up the gangway and disappeared from view. The American's grin dropped from his face as he looked over his shoulder.

'Quick,' he said. 'Over here.'

Before she could resist, he pulled her behind a stack of crates. They were barely tall enough to obscure either of them. He pushed her against the crate and closed in on her as if he was about to kiss her. She resisted, grabbing at his arms.

'What the hell are you doing?'

'Shhh, you'll get us both busted. Just shush.'

He hugged her, putting his head on her shoulder. She could feel him breathing deeply in her ear and wanted to be sick, but she held her breath. Clearly he had been spotted by someone and was trying to hide them both.

'Joe? Hey, Joe? That you?' They both tensed, but a second later Sammy appeared around the corner. 'What are you doing behind there?'

Joe let go of Ruth, with a nod, then clipped the sailor around the ear like a naughty child.

'Idiot. Now gimme that.' He took a brown parcel from the boy and held it out in front of Ruth. She went to take it, but he pulled it back.

'Uh, uh, uh,' he said. 'Money first. That'll be fifty of your English pounds. And make it quick. That cop will be back around in a few minutes.'

Undoing the clasp on her handbag, she pulled out a brown paper envelope and handed it to him. She didn't know how much was in there, but it was at least fifty. Joe handed it to Sammy, who with glee started counting the notes. Without a word, he nodded at Joe and pocketed the cash.

'Here,' the American said, handing her the packet. 'Now get outta here quick, and I don't ever want to see you again. If I do, then I've got more like that and I'll have to make use of them. If anyone asks, you've never heard of me, right?'

She nodded, dropping the packet into her pocket. It almost didn't fit.

'Good,' he said, and nudged Sammy with his elbow.

Ruth didn't watch as they disappeared. She was too concerned with getting away from the docks and getting home as quickly as possible. She still wasn't safe from being spotted, but she could disappear into the warren of streets as soon as she'd crossed the dock road and no one would pay any attention to her, nor the illegal item now in her possession.

It was for self-defence, she reminded herself. It was heavy in the pocket of her coat, but it would do exactly what she needed it to do. It would allow her to threaten him, to turn the tables and finally take back control.

# Chapter 28

Across the water a dockside warehouse was hit and burst into flames. Ruth could only just make out the destruction of the building. The orange flames reflected off the water, making the conflagration seem twice as large. If not for the constant noise of the raid the view would be almost picturesque. The water rippled as the current went out making the flames look like jewels on the churning waves. Ruth hoped there had been no one in that warehouse. A few seconds later another warehouse caught a glancing blow. Even still more fires caught, adding to the light show. They had had three weeks of respite, now the Germans were back with even greater ferocity. Birkenhead was already on fire, while the fire crews still doused the flames of the previous night's bombing of Liverpool.

She had come here to make a list of the naval ships in dock, but she was done; George was somewhere in the city. He wasn't safe. If it meant her going out in the middle of the raid to try to find him then so be it. She went out every night she could, under the pretence of volunteering. So far Anthony had not asked any questions, but she knew he was starting to wonder just how many shifts she was taking. Of course she would put George's life before hers, but there was the paradox. If she got herself killed in a raid then there would be no one to save George. No one else knew he had been taken, except Harriet, and Ruth couldn't bring herself to speak to her. Harriet may have worked out Ruth's secret, and she couldn't take the risk. She had to keep Harriet out of this, to keep them both safe.

She wrestled with the thought of telling Anthony, but she couldn't bring him into this. It wasn't fair. Besides, what would he think of her, working for the enemy? He had enough on his plate, with losing his home. He was also worried about his son. Ruth wasn't sure if she would ever meet him, but she hoped she did.

Ruth had been to a meeting at the town hall earlier that day, when residents had raised their concerns at the state of housing in the city. Their words still haunted her.

'Where will we live? Our homes are gone, our possessions dust. What shall we do?' Many others had called out their assent, adding to the cries. The hall was full of people, some holding their remaining possessions in their hands. Some called on them to calm themselves, but those voices were masked by those of desperation and unhappiness.

'Please, someone help us,' a mother called out, a baby wrapped in dirtied swaddling in her arms. 'Please.'

The note of desperation in her voice pulled at Ruth. The authorities should be doing more to help those in need, and those who had lost their homes. She stopped herself from offering. Having Anthony there was already a big enough risk, but she had not been able to refuse him. He was a good man, but if he ever found out her secret, she had no idea how he would react. She hoped it would never come to that, but the more evenings she spent searching for George, the greater the risk.

She took one last look at the glow of burning buildings across the river, the copper dome of Birkenhead's town hall just visible, then turned back to the city.

The Women's Voluntary Service had set up a rest centre in a church hall. Ruth had been asked to come and lend a hand. Refusing would have suggested that she thought she had better things to do. She couldn't help but look around her, as if somehow through this she would find George. There had to be a link to her son somewhere she could follow. Maybe someone here had seen something, knew something. Not that she could ask them.

The hall was about the size of a double-decker bus laid on its side, and they had managed to get some pallet beds from an old military billet or prison cell. Orange rust covered them and no one had taken care to clean it off. The mattresses and sheets were threadbare and thin, and Ruth didn't dare question where they had come from.

She had heard that they had been ordered to make the rest centres as basic as possible. The government was concerned that if the conditions were too comfortable people would want to stay. Ruth couldn't imagine anyone wanting to live communally like this, even if conditions were better. They just assumed the working class were always trying to take advantage of the situation, that they were all thieves and beggars. All desperate people did desperate things, regardless of their background. She knew that as well as anyone.

On the other side of the hall she spotted Sarah Cavanagh, who beckoned her over. Ruth hesitated; she wasn't there to see friends or neighbours, she was there as a reporter, but maybe talking to someone she knew would help her to better gauge the kind of responses she was given. Maybe Sarah had seen George. Ruth worked her way through the beds. She was in a precarious position, her dual worlds colliding. Sarah's home had apparently been bombed and she was living here until they could find somewhere else for her. Who knew how long that would take?

'Sarah,' she said when she was stood by the bed, and she didn't know what else to say. Let Sarah talk, she was the one who had called her over. She was a few years older that Ruth, crow's feet pulled at her eyes and she wore an uneasy smile that spoke of her headlong journey to spinsterhood. Ruth empathised with her, it must not have been easy to find a husband with a war on, even in a city. Ruth wondered whether in actual fact she didn't even want a husband. Why should she?

'Ruth. I'm so pleased to see you.' She stood up, and the folds of her dress stayed rumpled up around her midriff, revealing the white socks around her ankles and giving the impression of a much younger woman, a girl even. 'I wondered whether I wouldn't in fact be left here all on my own.'

Sarah must have thought Ruth had need of rehoming herself.

'How's your family?' Sarah asked. They had met at a suffragette meeting, Sarah finding a kindred spirit in Ruth, but she didn't remember ever having really talked about her family.

'They're fine.' How easy lies came to her now. She simply didn't have the emotional energy to discuss them.

'I can't understand ya.' Sarah shook her head as if to emphasise her point.

'Oh, I'm sorry, I have a habit of mumbling. Please do ask me to repeat myself, I won't be offended.'

'Nah, it's not that. I can hear ya just fine. But I can't understand you. Fine young lady like you. What are you doing slumming it around here? You should be up at some big country house taking some foolish young lord for all his money.' She cackled. 'It's frustrating, ain't it? Being down here on the bread line. You deserve much better, lass.'

Ruth wasn't sure that she did. If only Sarah knew the truth about her, she wouldn't be speaking like this. Could the other woman know about her family and their links to the 'big house' as she had put it. She couldn't do. No one did, not even her colleagues. She hadn't even told Anthony, but then he had never asked about her family, perhaps he didn't think it was proper.

'I'm just having a look around, Sarah. But if there's anything I can get you, let me know.'

'You don't happen to know of a good house going, do you?'

Once again Ruth felt guilt at keeping her home life private, but it would be better for Sarah if the rehoming service found her some-where to live. Going by the smile on her face, she didn't really expect Ruth to help her out, she was just trying to keep the conversation going.

'I have to go,' Ruth said, turning away from the gurney. Sarah's arm shot out and grabbed the fold of Ruth's skirt. 'What are you doing?'

'Don't let them forget about us, will ya, lass? Don't worry about little old me. I'll make do, I always have, but others round 'ere.' She looked out of the corner of her eye first to one side, then the other, as if the two of them were conspiring together. 'Others are not so lucky, no? There's kids to think about, the elderly too. Hell, we'll all pull together, but if the authorities forget about us all, then some of them won't last that long, ya know?'

Ruth nodded, thinking only of George. What could she say that she hadn't already thought herself? The situation was growing dif-ficult. More houses were being destroyed during every raid. People were dying and those who survived were struggling. It was a far cry from the image of the raids the newspapers were trying to portray. The stories were sanitised, the housing problem glossed over. Morale was important, but at what cost?

'I'll do what I can,' she whispered. 'I promise.'

*

Ruth couldn't stop staring at the clock as it steadily approached half past six. Many would already be making their way inside the shelters, what was left of them after the previous night, but she couldn't drag herself away from that clock, even if she had become numb to time itself. She flicked through a notebook, looking for something, anything she could give to Patrick. The bombing had been relentless and she had felt more trapped than ever.

The sirens sounded and she rose immediately. It was almost as if she had been waiting for it, waiting for the call to head out into the night and look for George again. She had already changed into her overalls, and she grabbed her steel helmet from the peg by the door before opening it.

She stopped. A boy was stood on her doorstep, looking up and down the road as if hoping he was not seen. But she realised that he was wondering what to do now that the sirens had sounded. It was the same boy who had delivered the telegram about Peter. She almost shut the door in his face, but part of her hoped it was good news. The back of her mind told her that she was trying to convince herself, that somehow positive thinking would make the telegram into something good, but she knew that these telegrams were never such.

She stared at the boy, who was becoming increasingly agitated. It seemed that he too remembered the last time he had darkened this doorstep and could not count on Ruth to sign the form quickly. She didn't dare reach out and take the yellow envelope. Could it be for Anthony instead? Had something happened to Marc? She was still lying to herself.

At that moment Anthony appeared on the pavement. He looked as if he had been running, but stopped as soon as he saw the boy and looked over at Ruth.

'What is it?' he asked, frowning.

There was no choice but to take the telegram and sign for it. Seeing her scribble and apparently satisfied, the boy mounted his bicycle and rushed away as if he had been called back for dinner. She hoped he got to wherever he was going before the bombs started falling.

Anthony had stepped closer to her, and she realised that he was waiting for her answer. Ever patient, she could feel his breath on her neck as he stood, unspeaking. It was addressed to her after all, but there was no point in prolonging it. She ripped open the envelope and began reading. It was from the commandant at the internment camp.

'Oh, no,' she whispered, and Anthony didn't wait in putting a reassuring arm around her. She could sense the question in his thoughts. 'It's about my grandfather. His illness progressed and he passed away two days ago.'

Her lip trembled at the words and before she could stop them tears burst from her eyes. Anthony pulled her closer, and she buried her head in his chest. Her grandfather had been the only member of her family whom she had trusted, whom she had felt she could truly be herself with, and his loss would be keenly felt. She couldn't imagine never hearing one of his stories again. She had lost everything.

'I'm so, so sorry,' Anthony said, somewhere through her darkening thoughts. 'It seems like we always come together in tragedy.'

She attempted to nod, but the press of his body and her numbness prevented her.

'I'm here, I'm here,' he continued. 'Through all this, there's something that draws us together. Some kind of hope, I'm sure of it. Our meeting was serendipitous, a light in the darkness.'

She pulled back from him and looked into his eyes. His arms were still around her. The sirens still blaring. Others rushed past and cast a glance in their direction, but kept moving. Ruth was not going anywhere in a hurry.

'Have you always been such a poet?' she asked.

Anthony let out a small chuckle.

'My mother always said I should have been a writer, but Father wouldn't approve. He wasn't keen on me going to university either. It wasn't a man's job, being a fusty academic. I still think I would like to write, at times. But it seems frivolous in the current situation.'

'You should.'

'How's this for poetry?' He looked deep into her eyes, and even through her tears she was fixed in his gaze. 'I feel like my whole life has been leading me to you. I know how ridiculous that sounds, but I don't know how else to say it. I'm not equipped with the vocabulary for this.' He gave her what she thought was an apologetic look. 'Now I know why writers always fall back on cliché. They don't know how else to express these feelings, because there are no words for them.'

'Anthony,' she started, her voice barely above a whisper, before he stalled her.

'I know. I know,' he said, his grip slackening.

He didn't. He didn't know at all how much she wanted him to pull her into him, to wrap himself around her and comfort her, to look after her and tell her everything would be all right. It went against everything she believed in, but she knew in that moment that she needed him. She hadn't broken eye contact as if she could implore him with her look.

He didn't pull back as she had initially expected, but reached out and placed his palm against her cheek. It was warm there, comforting and strangely familiar. He leant ever so slightly into it, eyelids lowered. Their lips brushed together, nervous at first, and then they pressed together as if hungry for each other. He tasted warm, like a spice she couldn't place, and she wanted more, but he pulled back, smiling at her.

'I can't tell you how long I've wanted you to reach out like this,' she said, in the pause. 'It feels good.'

She fully closed her eyes then and took a deep breath. A smile turned the corner of her lips, and she leant further into his hand. He took hold of her then, letting his hands slip to her waist and pulling her into an embrace. He closed his eyes and laid his head on hers. The smell of him was almost overwhelming, but she could have stood there breathing it in for days on end.

'I'm glad you're here,' she said, voice muffled in the crook of his shoulder.

'Me too.'

# Chapter 29

*Tuesday, 24 December 1940*

Anthony always looked forward to breakfast. It was the one moment he could pause and think before the day got away from him. He didn't particularly care what the breakfast was, as long as it was more than a mouthful. If he could, he would drag it out for as long as possible before having to resign himself to the working day. It wasn't that he often had much to think about when it came to food and where it was coming from, not like some of his pupils, but rationing had made things difficult for everyone. It was absolutely the right thing to do, even if some complained that their usual lifestyles were disrupted. They all had to pull together to get through the war, and God knew Anthony was doing his bit.

However, today was Christmas Eve and he was going to enjoy the breakfast he had been saving for himself. He had put some aside for Ruth as well, but she hadn't been sure whether she would be able to join him or not. The life of a journalist was unpredictable at best. All their lives were at the moment. Since her grandfather had died, she had taken to going for a walk every day. In her words it was to 'get me out of the house', but he couldn't help but wonder whether she had just wanted to be alone or away from him. Since they had kissed he had felt a little bit awkward, and while he had thought it may bring them closer together, she had become more distant. But he was putting that down to grief.

He had another bowl of porridge, to push those thoughts away. It tasted earthy and not really like what he would describe as food. He longed for some sugar to add to it, to make it palatable. At least it made him glad that Ruth was not there, he would be embarrassed if she had to experience this poor excuse for a breakfast. He didn't even want to eat it himself. He pushed it away and treated himself to another piece of bread with a thin layer of butter, the treat he had been saving, but that wasn't particularly better. Even between the two of them they were struggling with rations. He knew it was designed to make the food go further, but what good was it if volunteers like them were perpetually hungry? More people would suffer.

His stomach rumbled and he stood up. It would be better to be out of the kitchen. In the living room he ran a finger along the spines of books, wondering what to do with himself. He had already tidied the house twice, putting all of Ruth's disordered books into alphabetical order by author on the shelves, placing his two remaining amongst them. It was an act of consolidation, but he wasn't sure Ruth noticed the symbolism.

Anthony carefully placed the copy of *A Christmas Carol* he had been flicking through back on the bookshelf. He was not particularly fond of most of Dickens's work, there was an uneasiness to the man that came through his writing that Anthony couldn't place, but there was something about that book that had come to mean something to him. The sentiment he attached to it had many layers and the book had become one of his most treasured possessions. It had been years since he had received a Christmas gift from anyone, and it meant a lot to him.

Marc was usually quite attentive at Christmas, making sure that his father was all right, but as a young man he didn't think much about gifts, and even if he did they weren't particularly well thought out. Anthony didn't know where his son was, he hadn't written in a month or so, but he hoped that wherever he was he was warm and sheltered, and perhaps thinking of his father. Although he never expected that of Marc, he was his own man and had his own life to lead, even if Anthony wished he was out there with him. Anthony wondered what Marc would make of Ruth. Knowing his son, he would probably have liked her too. He was a good judge of character, his son, a far better man than he was.

He had left a forwarding address with the post office and had hoped to receive something from his son, but so far the postman had not brought Anthony any letters. For months he had thought he would be alone this Christmas, with Marc being away and no other living relatives nearby. He had come to terms with it, in fact, months ago, as he often liked to think of Christmas in advance. After Julie had died they had been difficult, but there was something about the time of year that he always enjoyed. He was almost the opposite of Dickens's Scrooge and he had annoyed Marc with his Christmas traditions many a time before. In fact, he suspected that Marc would not even come back for Christmas if he was able, anything to avoid the old man's incessant joy. Anthony had already sent him two Christmas cards, just in case the first one didn't arrive. Julie would have made them all go to church at midnight, but that was something Anthony didn't go in for. Especially now that he was living with an unmarried woman. Maybe he should go to church after all and confess his sins, but they didn't do that sort of thing in his church anyway, and was he really a sinner? He didn't think so. He had always tried his best to help others, becoming a teacher, a warden.

He liked Christmas because everyone needed the celebration. When the winter was cold and dark and the typical Mersey winds came in to rock their windows in their frames, everyone needed the warmth of the ceremony, the love and joy. It was the only time of year he allowed himself to be that sentimental, again for those others around him. So when he thought that he might be alone, it had not sat easily with him. Now he would get to spend it with Ruth and George, and he hoped he could infect them with his enthusiastic traditions. He'd go easy on them first, it was their house after all, but who knew? Maybe Ruth enjoyed Christmas as much as he did?

He caught himself then. He was being stupid. Of course Ruth wouldn't enjoy Christmas. It would be her first since her husband Peter and her grandfather had died, and with George out in the countryside. Anthony collapsed into a chair. It wasn't that he was disappointed, in himself perhaps, but it was that he realised now he would have to be careful. He had no wish to upset Ruth and he would do everything he could to make sure that he respected the situation. He could ask her what she wanted to do, but he was worried that would bring up painful memories for her. Anthony would focus on George, make sure it was a wonderful Christmas for him, wherever he was.

A few minutes later he heard the front door click and Ruth walked into the hallway. She placed her hat and coat on the hook and came and sat down in the living room. She didn't say anything but leant back and closed her eyes. She was exhausted, they all were.

'I was wondering,' he said, looking at her as her eyes opened and she smiled back at him. 'Are you sending anything to George? Only, I have a present for him as well.'

Her eyes closed again, and he realised he had been insensitive.

'Sorry. You must miss him. I'm the same with Marc.'

'I miss him terribly,' she replied, standing and walking over to the barely alive fire. They had all had enough of fires the past few months, and even though this one was meant to keep them warm, there was a part of him that wished he didn't have to look at it. It was a relief and a curse that fuel was hard to come by.

Ruth lit another candle with the wick of the one she was holding and it flickered into life with a crackle. She placed the series of white candles on a candelabra on the mantelpiece and carried on lighting more.

'Don't you think we should save candles for the winter?' Anthony asked. 'We don't know how long rationing will last.'

Ruth turned to look at him, her face thrown into shadow by the candle flickering in her hand, like some kind of pantomime villain. The grin she flashed at him didn't make her look any less so.

'I like candles,' she said as if that was the final say on the matter. Then with a sigh she realised that he wanted her to say more. 'This time of year, when it's so dark we need light. Even if it's artificial. I've always liked the calming flickering of the wicks, and the smell when they go out. It's a pity they can't manufacture a candle that smells like that all the time.'

Her eyes were full of sadness and he so desperately wanted her to talk to him, to tell him everything that was going on behind those eyes.

'You know what happened with the chocolate scarcity last month. Next people might be having arguments about and hoarding candles. How will we find our way to shelters then?'

'Then we'll still have electric lamps and torches. They're more common than you might think these days. Don't be a stick in the mud. We've got to have *some* fun.'

She was right, and he would do anything to take her mind off

Peter and George. He stood up from the seat and crossed the room before taking her hand holding the candle in his. His hand almost enveloped hers and he gently pushed it across to light another candle.

'How's this for fun?' he asked. He closed his eyes, leant in and kissed her. She held the kiss for a long moment, the warmth of her strong against his lips, before wax dripped on her hand and she cursed. Far from damaging the mood, Anthony laughed with her. He had known since he met her there was something about her free and easy attitude that appealed to him and brought him out of himself.

'That was *quite* fun, I suppose,' she said. 'But I think we can do better.'

She touched his arm gently with the pads of her fingers and looked up into his eyes. Her lips were pursed, almost curling into a smirk. Until then he hadn't realised how heady, how soporific her scent was. He wanted to drown himself in her, smell every part of her body, taste her. He put his hands on her waist, enjoying the comforting curve in his palm and pulled her closer until they were pushed so close together there was almost no air between them. Her body was pressed tightly against his and he could feel the warmth of her, feel her heart beating in her chest. She wanted him as much as he wanted her. She pushed her hips against him as if they could get any closer and her lips pressed against his. They were wet and smooth and he revelled in the sensation of being that close to her, breathing her in between kisses.

*

He was gentle, but passionate. For some reason Ruth hadn't expected that. She had thought that underneath that calm facade was a raging inferno of pent-up aggression, that he kept all of his frustrations at the world locked up inside. But he was controlled as he was in everything. He took a hold of her, making sure to grip her as firmly as possible, but never exerting enough pressure to cause pain. His lips pressed against hers, hot and wet. The smell of lavender was stronger than it had ever been, soporific and tantalising. She wanted all of him in that moment. At first, they had made the living room their nest, Anthony pressing himself against her on the sofa, the warmth of their bodies intertwining, becoming one. Then they had made it to the bed before once again wrapping themselves together. That time Ruth had pushed him down on her bed so that she could see the deep browns of his eyes as she straddled him. She had never experienced anything like it. Heat tickled her body, lighting up all of her nerve endings and she never wanted that feeling to stop.

Some time later they lay together on the bed, sweating as their hearts beat almost in rhythm. She had never had another man in her bed and she had a sudden moment of guilt before he rolled over and ran the tips of his fingers down the side of her waist. The smell of lavender was now mixed with something else, something more masculine and raw and she breathed in every breath, feeling that tingling sensation again. She realised then that she would never have enough of him.

Eventually he pulled himself away from her and she let her hands drop as she traced the lines of his stomach. He grinned at her, kissed her on the nose and then went to wash himself. Ever the fastidious one, but she could grow used to it, especially given the reason for his needing to clean up.

She rolled over and pulled a box from under the bed and sat up on the edge of the mattress. No one else knew that the box existed, but it held a collection of prized possessions: a cinema ticket stub, a box of matches and a sheaf of letters she had been looking for.

She had collected all the letters that George had written to Father Christmas since he had been old enough to hold a pencil. The writing at the top of the pile was all lines and firm touch, indecipherable from a drawing, but as she flicked through she could see the letters start to form, his demands becoming clearer. It brought a smile to her lips as she thought of her son trying to find the right words to ask for what he wanted, but as soon as it came it was gone. Now all she could think of was George trapped and alone somewhere, with no one to listen to what he needed.

She dropped the letters back into the box, losing control of her hands, as there was a sound outside the room. Anthony poked his head through the threshold and his beaming smile dropped as soon as he read the expression on her face.

'What's wrong?' he asked, a frown crossing his brow as he took a step further into the room. 'What have you got there?'

He didn't sit down on the bed, but stood over her, still too awkward to relax in her presence, let down his guard of formality. She wondered if he would ever let himself be vulnerable in front of her, but then she had not intended him to see her like this.

'Just a box of memories,' she replied. 'I'm thinking of adding you to it.'

Smiling up at him, she realised she would have to tell him the truth one day, but today was not that day. Let them enjoy their time together before the war ripped out her heart again.

# Chapter 30

Anthony clicked the wireless on and tuned it to the BBC. He felt strange manipulating someone else's wireless, but Ruth didn't seem to mind. She sat with her feet tucked under her, worrying at a piece of thread on her cardigan. She looked up as she noticed his gaze fall on her and smiled. How quickly they had reached that point of unspoken conversation, where they seemed in synchronisation with each other's thoughts, but didn't need to ask. It warmed his heart and he couldn't help but smile back. If all they did was sit there exchanging smiles then he would be a happy man indeed. Despite rationing they were still in a lull after the Christmas fare they had managed to throw together, chicken and potatoes making up most of the meal, but what more did a person need?

One of the BBC news reporters on the wireless droned on in that style of theirs, both completely clear and alienating all at the same time. Anthony didn't hear what he was saying, being too distracted by Ruth. It was only when the national anthem started up that it caught his attention. He jumped up from the seat before the wireless had finished broadcasting the first bar, and tucked his hands behind his back. Ruth chuckled once before joining him in standing, mimicking his stance. A few months ago it would have riled him up to be so mocked, but there was something he knew now about her manner that encouraged him and let him know that she only joshed from a position of care. She wouldn't even notice if she had no interest in him. It was just the way she was. At least she hadn't saluted.

The national anthem abruptly faded out to be replaced by a long moment of silence, punctuated by the faint clonk of footsteps on a wooden floor in a large room. They sat down next each other, this time arm in arm on the sofa, awaiting the broadcast.

'In days of peace the Christmas feast is a time when we all gather together in our homes . . .' His Majesty King George VI began, speaking slowly and carefully. His voice only just cut through the hum of the wireless and Anthony had to crane his head to hear. He dared not stand and turn the volume up, for he would have to leave Ruth's side.

'. . . the young and the old to enjoy the happy festivity and goodwill which the Christmas message brings. It is, above all, the children's day, and I am sure that we shall all do our best to make it a happy one for them, wherever they may be.'

Ruth wriggled on the sofa, and her elbow bumped into his side as she stood. He couldn't see her face, but he could sense that she was crying. While the King's words were well meant, it could not be easy to hear for those who had young children who had been evacuated. Even though Marc was a young man, Anthony still felt a pang of sorrow for his son, wherever he may be.

'Are you all right?' he asked, voice blending with the slow words of His Majesty.

Ruth nodded, rubbing her nose with her right index finger as if distracted.

'I need a moment,' she said. 'You stay and listen.'

Anthony listened to the rest of the broadcast, almost mesmerised by the King's slow and graceful speech, and when Ruth came back downstairs he was ready for her. He stood up and picked up Julie's canvas bag.

'I got you something,' he said and her eyes widened. 'I didn't think you would appreciate my wasting paper on wrapping it.'

He opened the bag and handed her the item he had been working on the past month.

'It's wonderful,' she said, playing it about in her hands. 'You made this?'

'I did. All that knitting came in handy, and I thought it better to make you something than to buy something. The wool was spares from the rest, but I wasn't sure what to make.'

It was true, he had agonised for hours, trying to think what pattern he could make for her, what special significance a certain item might hold, then he had settled on it.

'There's always a need for warmer gloves,' he said as she tried on the single glove for size. He'd had to guess, but he had a fairly good idea. 'I'm already working on the second one.'

She laughed and hugged him. Before he could kiss her there was a scraping noise from outside, like a piece of timber being pulled along stone. He tensed, expecting an air raid siren, and Ruth pulled away, apparently expecting the same.

'What was that?' she asked, lifting up the blackout curtain and stealing a peek outside. Now there were more noises, some of which sounded like a church congregation muttering to themselves.

'There's only one way to find out.'

'The neighbours are leaving their homes, but I didn't hear an alarm.'

He took hold of her hand.

'Come, on,' he said. 'Let's go and have a look.'

They all filtered out onto the road following the noise. One of Ruth's neighbours put out a candle as soon as they spotted Anthony, and then the only light they had on the road was provided by the obscured moon. Yet, they had all become used to navigating the streets in the darkness, could sense the presence of others, even if they couldn't easily see facial expressions or gauge manner. There had become an almost unspoken relationship between them all, that they respected each other in the dark and could communicate almost telepathically whether they were in distress. There were so many on the streets now that it felt crowded, like one of the shelters. Everyone had been drawn from their homes by the sound of carols, the haunting music coming from somewhere in the distance, a stark contrast to the drone of German bombers they had become used to. To Anthony it felt dangerous, so many people standing outside under the moonlight with nothing to protect them from the bombs that could fall. But he would let them have their respite after the recent bombings. No doubt if the sirens whirred into life everyone would bolt for safety, but for now let them enjoy this time of joy.

As they progressed around the corner of the terraced houses the sound of music became clearer. Somehow a pianist had dragged an upright piano from out of their home and across to sit amongst a pile of rubble. Some of the keys were slightly out of tune, which only added to the haunting nature of the sound as it reverberated from the brick around them. The pianist himself was singing.

'Hark! The herald angels sing,' he began in a deep bass that barely carried over the discordant tones of the piano. As the neighbours came closer, some too began to sing, joining in with the words as they knew them. Someone to Anthony's right joined in, so quietly at first that Anthony thought he was out of time, before he realised that the man was starting a round. Ruth sang too, and it occurred to him that he had never heard her sing before. It was one of the most beautiful sounds he had ever heard. Surprisingly for her, she didn't sing with confidence, but her calm soprano was clearly audible by his shoulder, an almost-lullaby. He was not confident about singing himself, but caught up in the moment he mouthed the words under his breath. He didn't want to be seen to be refusing to join in, even if the others couldn't see him well in the dark. The moonlight flickered off belt buckles, badges and steel helmets and Anthony thought that the only way the scene could be improved would be by the addition of candles. If not for the blackout which would see them all on a charge.

He had no idea that this many people lived on Ruth's street. They filed in filling up every available corner between the ruins and the still standing houses, many singing along at the top of their voices. They must have come from the surrounding streets, drawn, like them, by the sound. The pianist went through a couple of other Christmas carols, some people accompanying while others barely knew the words, before starting the opening melody of 'Silent Night'. In some kind of telepathic union everyone stopped singing to allow the pianist his own solo, the drop in volume strangely appropriate.

Ruth interlaced her hand with Anthony's, and even through their gloves he could feel every curve and line of her fingers. He realised then that she was crying. She was not making any noise, but tears rolled down her cheeks, reflecting the moonlight, before she used her other glove to wipe them away. He wanted to ask her what was wrong, but he already had all the answers. Instead, he gave her hand a squeeze, letting her know that he was there.

He wasn't going anywhere, not if he could help it.

1941

JANUARY

# Chapter 31

***Wednesday, 1 January 1941***

Ruth stepped out onto Victoria Street. It was raining heavily, like a scene from some pulp novel. If it wasn't for her waxed raincoat she would be soaked to the bone. It may have been early, but the winter sun was setting, throwing the road into shadow. Soon the darkness of blackout would descend upon the city and getting home would be treacherous. A car rumbled past and with its lights out she would not have noticed it if not for the sound of its engine. She had stopped using her bicycle for these expeditions. The last thing she needed was an accident.

She moved through the dark alleys as if she was hunting something, or someone, but it was she who felt like she was being hunted. Through letters they had arranged to meet under cover of darkness, but she couldn't shake that feeling that someone was following her.

Only a few months ago she would have resisted such a command, but now, what choice did she have? Back then she would have jumped at the shadows expecting someone to attack her, but now she was used to them. The shadows had become a part of her life, and she was determined to make sure that she was the one in charge of her fate, not anyone else. George's fate too. After all, this was all for him. Somehow she would get him back and make those who had taken him pay. She hadn't exactly been truthful about all the detail she had given Patrick, giving the wrong name of a ship or saying they were still in dock when they weren't. What was one more lie? If they could clarify her information then they wouldn't need her.

Tonight the streets were silent, no siren, nor constant drone of bombers. These days she could even tell apart the slight differences in pitch of the various aircraft used by the Germans. She caught herself whenever she thought of them as *the Germans*, as if she was any different. Despite the fact that she had lived in England for most of her life, they would only see the traitor. If they found out she had been born in Austria and was living here under false pretences, then they would think of her as one of them. She was now one of *the Germans*.

Her identity as a Brit had been important to her ever since she was little, even if originally it had been a lie, and she couldn't cope with anyone thinking that she sympathised with the Nazis. She was doing what she had to, just as so many others were doing what they had to in order to survive. She was no different, she had family to think about too.

She stood alone in the abandoned house, wondering whether she had made a mistake. Anyone could have followed her, even Anthony. He was a good man, but she wouldn't put it past him worrying about her, sneaking after her to make sure that she was safe. George was her priority. She had to think about him above all else. Anthony was a distraction, a welcome distraction, but all the same he was in the way. She had exhausted the list of addresses she had stolen from Patrick. She had no choice but to meet him.

A shape moved across the ruined doorway. It may have just been a passer-by. The road was quiet, and she couldn't even hear the distant rumble of a tram over the force of the rain. Ruth's hair stood on end as if she was being watched, but no matter which way she turned she could see no one. The pouring rain played tricks on her eyes, reflecting the light in strange ways. She was about to give up and go home when she heard a noise.

'Hullo, lassie.'

She turned, tracking the voice, but it bounced back from the bare walls, muffled by the rain. After a second her gaze landed on what looked like a piece of discarded tarpaulin between this room and the next. The rain spattered from its still, black surface, but Ruth couldn't be sure it had been there before.

'Lovely weather for it,' Patrick said, and the tarpaulin moved just enough to confirm Ruth's suspicions. He was remarkably calm, in his weather-beaten raincoat, from his years of experience of working undetected.

She handed him a brown envelope she had bundled under her coat. Thankfully it had managed to keep off the rain and there were only a few darkened patches around the edges.

'What's this?' he asked, pocketing the bundle without looking at it.

'The casualty figures and other things you asked for. Some photos I took of the raids. Things we can't print. Do what you like with it.'

'Interesting.' He patted his pocket, and the frown on his face indicated it was anything but. He found the cigarette packet he was looking for and lit a stub he had put out before. Ruth would have taken one right then had he offered, but he didn't. He just let it hang there as he looked at her, the patter of the rain falling around the building, only just obscured by the remains of the roof they were standing underneath.

'It'll do, but I think you'll have to start doing better than that. This isn't an opinion piece, it's serious. Time to dig up the real dirt.'

'I can't do it,' she said, not knowing what 'it' was, but hoping that somehow Patrick would relent this time. 'I just can't.'

'You don't have a choice, lassie.' He dropped his cigarette on the floor, but didn't bother to stamp it out. He placed another in his mouth, lighting it before he continued. 'You know what happens if you stop. Your son had a nice Christmas, by the way.'

'You bastard.' Her words only intensified his serpentine grin. 'That's not exactly what I mean. I know I have no choice, but I can't do this anymore. It's not working.'

'All right.' He took a step towards her. She couldn't help but flinch, yet it only made him laugh. 'How are we going to do this then? What do you have in mind?'

'You're sick and twisted, you know? Not to mention completely self-absorbed.'

'Now hold on just a minute, lassie. You don't know me. I love this country, unlike some people, and I will do whatever it takes to make it great again. If that means doing unpleasant things, then so be it, it's the price I'll pay, but I'm certainly not doing this for myself. So don't you dare preach at me. The Germans know what they're about and I'll gladly do my bit until they get here.'

'What's this got to do with me though?'

'I've told you before. You're connected, lassie. You go all the way back to the fatherland. Your family. You know the reasons.'

'It's about that. I can't get you what you want.'

'Oh, why? You said that before, and yet here we are.' He patted his pocket again.

'No, not that. My brother-in-law. I can't use his name anymore.'

'What, don't they want to know you anymore? Sick of having a traitor in their midst, eh?'

'They know nothing. They don't know I'm here. They don't

know you have George. And most importantly my brother-in-law doesn't know anything about what's going on in the war. He's only a secretary and they're cutting down on loose tongues. I can't do it.'

She was bending the truth, but it wasn't the first time.

'I see.' He turned and paced back to the other wall. It was the first time Ruth had seen him do anything that seemed like thinking. He stopped dead. 'There is another way. You have family back in the fatherland, yes?'

Ruth's stomach sank.

'In Austria,' she corrected him. 'Although I'm not in contact with them. I haven't been for years.'

'That doesn't matter. What you got from your brother-in-law's house was good. It'll do for now. But now I'd like you to make contact with your family for me. I'll send you further instructions about what we want next.'

'They won't work for you if that's what you think.' In truth, she had no idea where their sentiments lay. They had gone back to Austria years ago and broken off contact. Now Patrick had designs on them, as if he could work his way into their sympathies. If the Germans invaded then they would do away with him as quickly as they would her. She glared at him, willing him to challenge her. She felt the bulge in her overall pocket. She couldn't bring herself to use it; she had no idea where George was.

'We'll see. Now get out of here. I've got work to do and so have you.'

'Wait. I need more proof George is alive, otherwise I'm not doing this.'

He sighed, then rooted around in his pocket and produced another scrap of paper. 'No more demands.'

This time she waited for him to go, too anxious of causing another argument if she followed too closely behind. She hadn't given up hope of tracking him, but the weather would not help. A few seconds later a battered car drove past. In the back she could just about make out the face of a boy. George? She took a step towards it, but it was gone. In the gloom she couldn't make out the numberplate.

She glanced at the note. *Dear Mum, Went to see the ships like Daddy's. Miss you.* She stood there for a few minutes, letting the cold rain run down her face to hide the tears, before pulling her coat tight around her and setting off into the darkness again.

# Chapter 32

Anthony kicked a stone as he climbed onto the wreckage of the house and it clattered down onto the road. The street had been bombed almost four days ago and the wreckage was still unsafe. Things had become so desperate that they had asked for volunteers. He had decided that he needed a distraction. It was backbreaking work at times, but rewarding to see the wreckage start to disappear and something like normality return. The houses may have been ruins, but when the rubble was cleared, it at least looked like progress was being made. They could rebuild over time, if the Luftwaffe gave them the chance.

One of the men called out and made Anthony jump. He was waiting to catch a brick from another and drop it into the wheelbarrow at the bottom of the pile. Then they would haul it off to somewhere to see what could be reused and what needed to be broken down. Ruth had told him that much of the rubble was being dumped in parks and even the beaches, but he didn't dare think about it. Instead he picked up one of the rough red bricks, playing it around in his hands. He wondered what kinds of things that brick had seen before it had been dislodged from its home: children growing up, adults going to work, lives all passing by this brick without even thinking about how it was keeping them safe.

'Come on, Ant.' Sid's voice sounded beside him. He hadn't noticed him climb up the slope. 'The sooner we get this lot shifted the sooner we can get back to our homes.'

He rubbed his hands together. *Yeah, home,* Anthony thought. He handed the brick to Sid and gave him a grin. *Give me a hand then,* it said. He reached down for another brick and stopped. There was a faint sound that wasn't the clattering of dislodged bricks. It was high pitched, but not a burst pipe.

'Did you hear that?' he asked Sid, kneeling down closer.

'Hear what?' Sid's voice was playful. 'This is one way to get out of work, for sure, but I don't think it will work for long.'

'Shut up and listen for a moment, Sid. I'm not joking.'

There was the sound again, like a sort of hissing cry, muffled by the layers of brick.

'Was that . . . a cat?' Sid was suddenly at his shoulder.

'I think so. Here, over here,' he shouted. 'I think we've found something.'

Without waiting they both started pulling bricks and rubble apart, throwing the rubble back down the pile behind them not caring where they fell. More men joined as they desperately tried to dig out the cat. Its small frame had probably allowed it to survive the collapse, but who knew how much longer it would live if they didn't get it to safety. Any sign that something could survive this would give them hope. Anthony could almost feel the adrenaline coursing through his body, spurring him on.

'There's too much rubble, there can't be any air down there.'

He wouldn't give up, even though his hands were being torn to shreds by the shards of brick. He needed the hope, to know that he had made a difference, that he had saved something. Eventually they had removed enough that a burrow was visible through the wreckage. The bricks were smaller as if they had been compressed by the weight above. The cry was louder though intermittent and sounding less like a cat now that the rubble was no longer muffling it. A small shape was protected by a tomb of bricks that had fallen to leave a crawl space underneath, propped up like a bridge.

It was a baby, covered in dust, but unmistakable. A little bundle surrounded by the splintered wooden joists of a crib that had miraculously fallen to the side. He told the others to stop, not wanting them to accidentally crush the child.

'Blimey,' Sid said, leaning in. 'It must have been under there for at least three days. Poor thing. Where are its parents?'

Anthony picked up the baby, ignoring Sid and taking care not to dislodge it from its swaddling cloth. He had once held Marc like this and it brought a flash of memory. Where was his son now? The child scrunched its face and cried as Anthony held it. The bricks that had been sheltering the child clattered together, filling the hole where it had lain.

He licked a thumb and then gently rubbed the dust from its cheeks and forehead. The crying abated and bright blue eyes looked up at him. A smile curved on that tiny mouth and Anthony couldn't help but smile too.

'Is there anyone else down there?' Sid asked of no one in particular. They couldn't be sure until they dug the entire place out. With reluctance Anthony handed the baby over to one of the rescue men, who would take it to be checked over, and try to find out to whom the child belonged.

They carried on digging. There were no more cries from under the rubble and with each layer they removed, the closer they got to the ground. Anthony knew what he was seeing, but it took him some time to admit it to himself. There could not possibly be anyone else left under the ruin of the house. He kept going, even though his hands were now bleeding. Next time, and there would be a next time, he would have to wear gloves. For now, he simply didn't care; there were worse things in this world than cutting your hands – growing up without parents for one.

A hand grabbed his shoulder. 'Stop,' Sid whispered. He'd never known the big man to talk so quietly, but its contrast affected Anthony. 'There's no one else, Anthony. Save your energy. You'll need it.'

Anthony looked up and realised he was the only man still digging. The others were standing nearby, some already had tin cups of tea and the baby had been taken away to be checked over by a medic. One of the other men, Clive, had stooped to poke at an object amongst the rubble.

'What's that?' Anthony asked.

The object was shiny against the dull grey and brown of the rubble. All the paint on its outside had been burned away by the flames leaving only the metal exposed to the elements.

'It's a tin,' Clive said. 'Still warm to the touch.'

He moved it around in his hands from corner to corner like a hot potato. Wedging one side under his arm he used his fingers to yank open the opposite end. It opened with the scrape of metal on metal and its contents almost bucked out. Clive's eyes widened.

'Bugger,' he said, quite unaware of the others staring at him. 'There's hundreds of pounds in here.'

He rifled through the notes and then suddenly noticed the others. He looked at each of them in turn, as if weighing up their thoughts, and then slowly closed the lid.

'I found it,' he said, staring directly at Anthony. His low voice like a child's who had been caught misbehaving. Anthony had heard it many times before and there was only one way to deal with it.

'It doesn't belong to you, Clive,' he said. 'Now hand it over.'

Clive looked between him and the tin twice, before he clutched it to his chest. 'I don't see why I should. It's not like they're going to miss it.'

He nodded towards the centre of the wreckage and there was an intake of breath from behind.

'It's not yours, lad.' That time he was sure that it was Sid who had spoken. 'We'd all like a share, but it's theft, whichever way you look at it.'

Clive's head dropped and he stared at the tin he held. Even from several feet away Anthony could see the look in his eyes, the verge of tears pulling at the corner of them as if he felt like he had no choice. Still he wouldn't let the tin go. Anthony wouldn't have been surprised if Clive started stroking it. Sid moved to pass Anthony and go up the mound, but Anthony held an arm out to stop him. It wouldn't help things.

'Perhaps they will appreciate you returning it and give you some as a reward for your kindness,' Anthony proffered and Clive's expression brightened. With a big sigh he took one last look at the tin and then passed it over to Anthony.

He hadn't expected Clive to give it up, and now he had the responsibility of what to do with the money. He could feel all their eyes on him, and knew he had to say something.

'Thank you. I'll make sure this gets to the civil defence station. I can count the contents if you'd like me to, and then you'll know that it has all been returned.'

The others shook their heads and went back to work leaving Sid and Anthony perched on the mound. Clive still stared at his feet, apparently in thought. Anthony wasn't sure how the wreckage of this home had affected him, but it had affected him somehow, and he wasn't sure there was any way of getting through to the man.

'The others trust you,' Sid said, his voice back to its usual joviality and bringing Anthony's attention back to his surroundings.

'Think it's time to knock off yet?' he asked. 'I think we've had enough for one day.'

'Could be, could be.'

Another warden came past, from the direction of the section office, and Anthony seized on an idea.

'Hey, you,' he shouted as he ran towards the man. 'Any news on the family of the baby we found?'

'Oh, that was you?' He turned to face Anthony, taking the steel hat from his head and holding it in his hand. 'We've been checking, but according to their neighbours they were in the house when the raid started. They didn't see them in the shelter, but that wasn't unusual. They preferred to sleep under the staircase instead. Madness.'

Neither of them could look at each other.

'You know what that means then?' Anthony asked, passing the tin to the other warden. He hated himself for stating the obvious, but he felt that it needed to be said. 'She's on her own then.'

*

What right did they have to judge him? They couldn't help but stare at Anthony on his way to what he now thought of as home. What was he doing that was any worse than what they were getting up to? He had seen enough during the raids to know that promiscuity was no longer kept to brothels and dark alleys. He had caught his own neighbours in a tryst during a raid, one of them a married man whose wife was volunteering. At least he had behaved as a gentleman, when so many he knew had become like animals, falling together through the fear and worry. He didn't blame them, not one bit, but when they judged him for his honest emotions then they had gone too far. He couldn't abide hypocrites.

Harriet was the only person on the street who didn't frown at him as he passed. He felt a kinship with her at that moment. The others were welcome to judge, he didn't really care. He had come to care about Ruth and she was more important to him than what any of them thought. Let them gossip and scoff. Their relationship was not harming anyone. She had filled a void in his life left by Julie that he had never thought could be filled again. He hadn't forgotten his late wife. He smiled, thinking how happy she would be for him, and noticed as a neighbour frowned. He threw them a wave and a hullo and carried on down the street. Let them talk.

As soon as he was inside he locked the door, leaning against it with a heavy sigh and sliding to the floor. He took in air as quickly as he could. At least he hadn't let them see him like this. Ruth's coat was not on the hook and the building was silent.

The sound of the crying baby played over and over in his mind, alone in this world. Would they find parents for her? Would they take good care of her? He would never know, but he was haunted by the doubt. When he had calmed himself he headed to the kitchen. He hoped a glass of water would fix whatever was wrong with him. Water splashed across the front of his overalls as he turned on the tap and he cursed. It would dry, but the blood stains would stay. He heard the scrape of a key in the lock and froze. A moment later the door opened with a gust of cool, wintry air.

'Where have you been?' He marched into the hallway. These days she seemed to spend more time outside the house than in it and they hadn't talked for days. 'I was worried.'

She shrugged off her coat and let it fall to the floor, apparently already forgotten.

'You shouldn't worry about me, Anthony. I'm not worth it.'

'Of course I worry about you. Not because you're not capable, but simply because if there's anything I can do to help I will. But I need to know, I need to know what I can do.'

'Nothing. This whole thing, the war, everything else, has just broken me. I want to lock myself in a room without windows and just scream and scream until I have no energy left but to sleep for a thousand days. Can you imagine what that feels like?'

'I have some idea.'

'Do you?'

'Yes, I do actually. When Julie died and I was left with a baby to look after I wanted to run away from it all too. There may not have been a war on, but there was a war in my heart and my mind. Even now, I have no idea how I coped with what happened. It was all a blur.'

'I'm sorry, I don't know why I'm arguing with you. With you of all people. I'm sorry.'

He didn't respond, but pulled her into an embrace. The last thing he wanted to do was argue. He simply wanted to feel her, to be comforted by her closeness and to know that he had something in this world to live for. If he could stay there with her in his arms for the rest of his days he would, but he knew that would not be enough for her. Regardless, he closed his eyes and held her, living in the moment for as long as possible.

# Chapter 33

Ruth wouldn't have come to the meeting, but she was getting desperate. George could be anywhere in the city, and she was sure that Anthony was beginning to grow suspicious. She had meant to meet the conscientious objectors earlier to write an article, to hear their side of the story. Now she wondered if they were not just the people who could help her. They opposed the war in the first place, wouldn't they sympathise with her? Not that she could tell them exactly why she was here. There was also the note she had found in Patrick's wallet that read, '*Miles – Lewis's*', and Ruth knew that the organiser of the conscientious objectors, a Miles Landry, also worked as a clerk at Lewis's department store.

They met in a Quaker hall on Hunter Street. Some of the conchies were Quakers, but not all of them objected on religious grounds. Members of the Peace Pledge Union also attended. A man in a scruffy suit carried an urn of water through the front door. It reminded her of the WVS tea vans she had been allowed to drive.

Pushing open the heavy wooden door after him, she stopped to adjust to the change in light. It was dark inside the hall, as if the meeting was clandestine. There were lit candles in sconces on the walls and they cast shadows across the floor. The smell of over-brewed tea was strong in the air, masking a faint hint of something she couldn't put her finger on.

She smiled as she saw the organiser, and he gave a shallow nod to acknowledge her as he started his speech.

'We have not just a religious objection to this war, but a moral one as well.' His voice carried well across the hall. He was used to projecting his voice. Ruth guessed that he had a lot of practice. 'It is, for many, too easy to forget the lessons of the last war. The number of lives lost, the amount of damage done to our lives, our society. But we must not let them forget.'

There were grumbles of assent from around the room and more than one or two nods. Ruth felt herself getting caught up in the speech.

'It may also be too easy to treat this war the same as the last one, and we shall not win any arguments by doing so.'

He took a breath and regarded them all, making sure to show that he acknowledged each of them one by one with a look in the eye.

'We have to understand the nuance and sentiment of this war in a way that we have not done before. The fight against fascism is an important one, but we must also fight the fascism in our own government. We cannot be seen to be like the Nazis.' Ruth thought he glanced in her direction. 'We do not sympathise.'

'Hear, hear,' said one of the men in the front row, on the edge of his seat.

'Forcing men to fight against their will is a withdrawal of man's basic freedoms. Religious objection is almost always readily accepted, but moral and able objection is treated with derision and mistrust. Are we not patriotic enough?' He banged his fist against the lectern. 'Do we not love our country? they ask. And how do we respond?'

One of the men next to Ruth stood up. 'Yes, we love our country,' he shouted.

'But we do not love entering into a war that is not our war. Look around you at the streets of this fair city. Look at the suffering and fear that is being caused. Your neighbours, family and friends did not ask to be a part of this war, and yet the war has come to them.

'Smith.' He pointed at one of the men in the front row, who was slouched but sat up when he heard his name. He ruffled his cap in his hands as Landry spoke. 'You came to us because your family lost their lives during a raid. A tragic accident some might say, but we know better. It could have been avoided.'

Ruth felt the urge to speak. The temperature in the room was rising. But now was not the time. She didn't want to draw any more attention to herself. She was here to meet Landry, under the pretence of writing an article. He continued for a few more minutes.

'We must remain strong in our conviction that to help the war effort would only prolong it. It may not be easy at times, but life is not easy, and it is made less so by war. If we were to aid in winning this war then who knows what may happen once we have defeated Germany? Must we then take wars to other nations that do not fall in line with our definition of democracy? When will it all end? Not in conspiring with the enemy.'

Ruth almost fell from her chair. Had he seen through her? Had she made a mistake coming here? A moment later there was applause and the assembled men shook hands and began conversations. Miles Landry was talking to a man in army uniform. Ruth's heart skipped a beat. She wondered what he was doing here. He had his hat under one arm and was talking quietly to Miles. The soldier's presence spelt danger and she was tempted to turn and leave, when Miles came to welcome her.

'Mr Landry, a pleasure to meet you again.' She held out a hand and he shook it gently.

'Mrs Holt, a pleasure as always to see you, though I must admit I did not expect to see you here.' Miles was all charm and it was easy to see why these men followed him. 'Of course, all are welcome, regardless which side of the debate they may lie. Journalists as well, someone must hear our voice.'

'Thank you, Mr Landry. I must also admit, I didn't expect to see a member of His Majesty's armed forces in attendance. Are you tempted to switch allegiances?'

His manner was so natural it brought out the humour in her, but there was still an undercurrent of anxiety. She knew she was being paranoid, but a soldier being involved complicated matters.

'Miles, please. You mean Sergeant Major Abbott?' He nodded towards the leaving soldier. 'It's too complex to say that he is a supporter of our objection to the war, but let's just say he has a certain sympathy towards our cause. Of course, he never says explicitly and I fear I'm rather telling a journalist too much of a story which isn't mine to tell.'

There was that smile again, with an added hint of self-deprecation. He had realised that she had allowed him to go on without interruption. He laughed. 'You would make a good priest in confession. No wonder you became a journalist. Does everyone open up so easily to you?'

'Not everyone,' she murmured. 'But enough. I hope I haven't made anyone feel uncomfortable.' Was she being paranoid again, or were there a few nervous glances in her direction?

'Not at all. Not at all. But was there something else I could help you with? I was sorry to hear about your husband.'

Ruth started. She had no idea he knew. It seemed news travelled fast around the local community.

'Actually, I'm looking for a man.' Miles smiled again and Ruth could feel her cheeks flush. 'What I mean to say is, I'm looking for a Patrick Ward. I believe he did some work for you.'

The smile fell from Miles's face as soon as Ruth mentioned Patrick's name, and something else entered his eyes. She couldn't be sure, but she thought it was anger. Mentioning Patrick's name was a mistake.

'That man . . .' he whispered. 'You won't find him here. I employed him to do some work at the department store. He didn't strike me as the sort of person you would be interested in working with, Mrs Holt, but then I don't know what you're working on.'

'I—' she started.

He shook his head. 'I don't wish to know. Ignorance is better where that man is concerned. If you really want him, he's booked to come back and fix some of the damage he did in early May. After hours, of course, lest he cause any trouble again.'

It was a fresh lead, but she couldn't wait that long.

'Do you know where he lives? Where I can find him?' Desperation entered her voice and he appeared to notice.

'Absolutely not, Mrs Holt. And if I were you I would stay well away from him. Now I must be getting on.' He turned and walked away leaving Ruth with scant hope. She couldn't wait months to find George, she needed to find him as soon as possible. She left quickly, feeling the prying eyes on her back. She was no longer welcome.

# Chapter 34

Peter's memorial service had taken a long time to arrange, in part because there was no body to recover, but also because Ruth and the family couldn't agree on anything. As he had had a simple military funeral shortly after he passed, his family had insisted on holding a memorial for him and had invited Ruth out of obligation. It was the most contact she had had with his family in years, and the stress of it all made her want to break down. Now, after the service, the fake smiles and sympathies, she wanted only to lock herself in a dark, quiet room and forget about the world. The way home was the slowest she had ever walked, trailing her mourning dress. She took a deep breath on the front step before entering.

'Come, I've got a surprise for you.' Anthony took hold of Ruth's hand as soon as she had come in the front door.

'Where are we going?' Ruth half expected him to produce a blind-fold from his pocket, but he led her through the house and into the kitchen.

'You'll see,' he replied, a faint smile on his lips. He didn't stop in the kitchen, but opened the back door with his free hand and almost pulled her outside. She hadn't seen him like this before, his childlike enthusiasm showing through. It made her think of George, bringing a fresh wave of grief. As soon as they were outside, back in the cold of the open air, his face dropped, became more sullen and there was a look in his eyes that reminded her of when they had first met. It made her want to hug him, but before she could get a chance, he pulled her around to face the side wall of the little yard at the back of the house.

'What do you think?' he asked, his voice low, as if he would disturb the neighbours, but she knew it wasn't because of that. He pointed when she wouldn't take her eyes off his face.

He had moved Peter's bicycle, and in the corner there was a small wooden cross, painted white, with two small flower pots either side to keep it upright. One pot was filled with sprigs of lavender and the other lilies, her favourite flowers. How had he known?

'Where did you get them from?' she asked.

'I have my contacts, just like you.' She could hear the smile in his voice. 'Take a closer look.'

She leant down and noticed that he had worked on the cross. It was tied on the crossbeam with lengths of brown string. There was a name etched into the wood. 'Peter,' she breathed.

He laid a comforting hand on her shoulder and she covered her mouth with her hands. Tears threatened to prick at the corners of her eyes, and she blinked them away. 'You did this . . . for me?'

'It felt like the right thing to do.' He shrugged and looked away. 'As you didn't get to have a proper burial, I thought this might help. I'm sorry if I overstepped the mark.'

She could barely see his face through the tears that streamed from her eyes, nor could she get any sound to escape her mouth that wasn't a faint murmuring. She wasn't sure she knew what to say anyway. Instead, she pushed herself into Anthony's chest and let the tears come. At first he hesitated, then he put his arms around her and rested his lips on her hair. Anthony didn't say anything more;

he simply held her, squeezing her with a control that made sure that the air wasn't pushed out of her lungs, but that she felt reassured all the same. She closed her eyes and breathed him in, slowing her breaths with each wracking sob.

In that moment she couldn't help but think about Peter. Had he been scared when he died? Had he thought of her? But she was glad that Anthony was there. She couldn't do anything now to bring Peter back, but it was right that she should think of him, and she couldn't imagine anyone other than Anthony making this kind of gesture. She thought that Peter would have appreciated it too. He may even have liked Anthony, though you could never be sure where men were concerned. They had a lot of similarities, but they were also very different men. Anthony simply stroked her hair, allowing her to cry.

She didn't really know him all that well, but she felt like she did. She couldn't explain that. It wasn't as if he had told her everything about himself and there was nothing left to learn, it was more like she *knew* him, knew his character, the kind of man he was, and that he was above all else caring and good. But really, she had come to know him these past few months. They had been through things together that people wouldn't go through during peacetime. She knew him now almost as long as she had known Peter when they were courting before he had proposed to her. It had seemed a long time back then, but now, with everything going on in their world it seemed both like no time at all and forever. War had a strange way of disrupting her perception of time.

She wiped the tears away with her hand and looked up at him. There was a look in his eye, something she had only seen on one occasion before, when she had told him about Peter. The only way she could think to describe it was a deep compassion, as if he felt her pain intensely, as if he lived it himself. Despite that there was a strength she hadn't realised. More than just physical strength, Anthony had an emotional strength she didn't think was possible for a man to have.

'Thank you,' she said. 'I don't know what to say.'

'You don't need to thank me. I just wanted to do something for you.'

She nodded and pushed herself into his arms, letting him envelop her in a warm embrace. She closed her eyes almost on the verge of sleep, reassured by the comfort of him. If only she could truly confide in him, let him know her innermost thoughts and ask for his help. But she could not ask for anyone else's help, least of all in finding George.

'How many more will die before this is over?' she asked instead.

He was silent for a few moments, before he spoke softly. 'I don't know. Too many. I don't see this thing being over any time soon, do you? We need to take the fight to Hitler before this will be over. We're on the defensive, covering ourselves, making sure we can last another day. I don't know when the tide will turn, but it must. Perhaps if the United States enters the war?'

It was her turn to nod against his chest. Anthony was right, but here she was being forced into doing their bidding. Somehow, some way, she would turn this against them too. She had to. She couldn't help them, not really. For George's sake she would give them the impression that she was giving them what they wanted. She would have to stay one step ahead of them all the way. If only she could tell Anthony, bring him into her confidence, but she wasn't ready for that yet. He was too kind, too pure for what she had to do, and she wouldn't tarnish him like that. She would protect him as she protected everyone else. At all costs.

# FEBRUARY

# Chapter 35

*Monday, 3 February 1941*

Across the road the Womack's greengrocer's stand was bare except for a few browning apples and a couple of heads of lettuce that looked as if someone had been slowly picking away at the leaves. Anything that was useful had already been taken away. The metal beams smelted down for the war effort, and what was left was stacked haphazardly. It wasn't the greengrocer's fault. Some were luckier than others, their supplies coming from larger farms, but rationing had affected them all. Ruth would have planted her own vegetable patch at the back of her house, if only she had the time to maintain it, or the green fingers. Her family would probably have their own farm by now, or would tell everyone they did. Perhaps that was more of Anthony's kind of thing, she would have to ask him.

Ruth was too busy stalking the streets, using her volunteer's uniform as a free pass. She told herself she was looking out for others, but she wondered if really she was not just trying to make some sense of their situation. As she suspected many others were. Although not all of them had the problems she had, some had worse.

As she watched, a girl snuck out of an alley and onto the main road. She had no idea that she was being watched, but Ruth had seen her before and knew where to look for her. The little girl, in her baby blue dress, was always somewhere near the greengrocer's, but every time Ruth saw her, the girl's dress became more and more marked by the grime of the city's streets. Now she looked bedraggled, her hair was loose from its pigtails and the hem of her dress had a thick brown stain that would take many washes to get out. In spite of it all there was still a life about her. Her cheeks were red, as if embarrassed, or as if they had been pinched by a mother frustrated at her daughter. Ruth, however, wondered if this little girl even had a mother to return to, if she even had someone who would wash that dress and pinch her cheeks. That was why Ruth watched. She couldn't tear herself away from the sight of the girl, her concern taking over. Peter would once have told her there was nothing she could do, but she knew better. There was always something you could do for those in need, always some way of helping, even if the idea didn't present itself at first. Even if you had to give something of yourself.

A man in a smartly pressed brown suit left the greengrocer's and noticed the girl, but she was not perturbed. At first she stood there as if she were working the stand, happy to fill a bag for any who came past. Only, there were no bags, and precious little in the way of produce to fill them. She smiled sweetly at him as he touched the brim of his hat and walked on down the street. Alone again the girl reached a delicate hand up and over the edge of the nearest wooden box, and with a quick jerk pulled an apple into her sleeve, like a bird pecking at feed.

Ruth resisted the urge to call out, but even still the girl spotted her as she turned back to the road. She froze. Ruth tried to flash a smile that was more reassurance than knowing criticism, but she knew already that it hadn't come across that way. The girl's face flushed red, and Ruth felt as if she was almost going to spit at her like an angry cat. She even hunched and pulled one leg back as if preparing to strike, her skinny arms raised in front of her as if they would be any kind of defence.

Ruth flashed a smile again and raised her palms, before walking past the girl and down the alley from which she had appeared. She hoped that the girl would follow, but would Ruth have followed if she had been in that situation? Or would she have run as fast as she could without looking back? Probably the latter, but then Ruth had absolutely no reason to trust anyone. She took each step carefully, allowing the child room to not feel intimidated. She noticed that the girl was shaking, but she did not run. It was cold outside, but Ruth didn't think her shivering was caused by the breeze.

'It's all right, sweetheart.' Ruth crouched down so that she was less intimidating to the girl. She couldn't imagine what it felt like to be lost and lonely in a city like this as a child. It was severe enough as an adult. 'I'm here to help. There's no need to be frightened anymore.'

Ruth crouched there for what felt like a few minutes, before the girl took a few tentative steps back towards her. Ruth noticed that her shoes were damaged as she stepped. One had a loose sole and on the other, the buckle was broken. It gave the child a disjointed, fragmented gait, as she tried to adapt to them. Ruth stayed still, hoping that her smell and the calmness she was trying to exude would put the child at ease. They faced each other for a little while, like two gunmen in some kind of standoff, before the child came closer again. She reached out one arm, plucked the apple from her sleeve and held it out to Ruth.

'For me?' Ruth asked, wiping away a tear that blossomed on her cheek. 'Oh, sweetheart. Thank you, but it's yours. You look after it.'

Ruth would forgive her the theft, even if the greengrocer wouldn't. People, even children, did bad things when they were desperate. She thought for a moment as the apple disappeared up that sleeve again. 'Why don't we go and find some more apples just like that? Some nice shiny, juicy ones. Does that sound like something you'd like to do?'

Ruth stood up, slowly, and held out her hand for the child to grasp.

'I will look after you.'

The girl took her hand and hugged Ruth close, as if she was frightened that she would leave her on her own again. There was no choice for it but to take her home and see what was what.

*

'Who's this?' Anthony asked, later on, when he had returned to the house after another day of trying to find work.

'Anna!' the girl shouted before Ruth could even open her mouth. She was dressed in some of George's old clothes and had it not been for her ringlets, would have looked like a boy.

'Oh, well. Hello, Anna. Pleased to meet you.'

Anna flashed him a smile, but he could see there was a wariness in her eyes.

'At first I couldn't get her to say much,' Ruth said. 'But it seems she is happier to talk to you.'

'Well, then I am most flattered,' he said, bowing towards Anna.

'Why don't you go upstairs, Anna, and play with those toys I showed you?'

Anna got down from the chair and rushed up the stairs with barely a moment's hesitation. Both of them looked at the ceiling as her footsteps softened into the bedroom.

'What's going on?' Anthony asked. 'Who is she?'

Ruth passed him a cup of tea, then sat down at the kitchen table in the chair Anna had left and held her own mug. There wasn't much she could tell him. Anna had been steadfastly quiet since Ruth had brought her back to the house.

'I found her on the streets. She was all alone and in a terrible state. I've given her a wash, but I've only managed to get some of the dirt out.'

He took a sip of the tea, winced, then placed it back on the counter.

'That's good of you, but who is she?'

'I don't know. Other than her first name she wouldn't tell me anything else. She stole an apple from the greengrocer's, and I knew then that she was on her own.'

'She stole? To feed a family?' Anthony joined her at the table and pulled her hand into his. He clasped his knuckles around her hand and closed his eyes.

'No, I don't think so. She only took the one, not even enough to feed herself. I can only think her family passed in one of the raids, but of course she wouldn't be able to articulate that. It's not easy for a child to understand.'

'Why on earth didn't the warden for that section find her and find a place for her in the rest centres?'

'They're not as good as you might think, Anthony, and perhaps their warden was not a nice man. Perhaps she ran away from him too. You may ask her some time if you like, but I think for now that we should just do what we can to care for her. At least until we've spoken to the authorities to see if she has any family.'

He nodded, showing he knew he was defeated. There were many things they disagreed about, but it was clear this was not one of them. She couldn't exactly explain to him, but looking after Anna, even for this short time, made her feel like she was at least doing some good.

'Well, we'll have to look after her for the time being, won't we?'

he said, and for the first time in months Ruth felt a warmness in her heart that she couldn't describe. They would find out what had happened to her family, but it would be nice to have a child in the house again. Ruth knew exactly how little the authorities cared about adoption legislation as long as you could provide a home for the child. If only she could find George and they could all live happily together. Her heart sank again as she thought of him. Was she neglecting him by not expending every effort to find him? Was bringing Anna into the house betraying him as if she had forgotten about him? She hadn't given up yet. She would find him, and she would make sure Patrick paid for his crimes.

# Chapter 36

The office was as dark as Anthony had expected when he had imagined it after finding the address in the newspaper. He had been shown in by an elderly secretary, who had trouble climbing the stairs to the first-floor office in her heels. There were blinds on the windows that tilted down, directing the sunlight towards the floor, as if to divert prying eyes. Anthony understood why; he had made sure that no one had seen him between the house and this office, he didn't want anyone to know he was here in a private investigator's office. Especially Ruth, as it was because of her that he was here. God knows what she would make of it if she found out, but the idea wouldn't leave him after he had seen the advert in one of her newspapers that she had left on the kitchen table.

'Please sit, mister . . . ?' A plump man offered Anthony a hand and he shook it. The thought of using a false name flashed through Anthony's head, but if this man was really worth the money then he would find out Anthony's real name in no time anyway. What difference did it make?

'Lloyd. Thank you.' He took the seat on the opposite side of the desk as Mr Crane slumped into his own high-backed chair. It dwarfed the man and made him look wider than he was tall. His beady eyes never stopped searching the room, never quite resting on Anthony but taking in everything around him. Anthony wondered whether Crane had taken something, but he put it down to his inquisitive manner. The man was an investigator after all.

'How can I help you?' He leant forward and steepled his fingers in front of his face. It was supposed to give the impression of curiosity, but the piles of papers on the desk's surface gave him a lopsided appearance, which was more comical than careful. Anthony stifled a smile. Crane had a good reputation, what did it matter if the man was disorganised and frankly a mess? As long as he got the end result, that was all that was important.

'I need help finding . . .' He didn't know why he hesitated. Was it because he felt like he was betraying Ruth's trust by enquiring about her and George? Or did he not really think it was a good idea to go down this route? Crane pulled a crumpled piece of paper towards himself and gripped a pencil between his fingers as one might hold a cigar. 'I need help finding information about a woman and her child. A young boy to be precise.'

Crane scribbled notes furiously as if he was taking dictation.

'An illegitimate child?' he asked, looking up suddenly. 'How discreet do you need me to be? The usual thing, checking to see whether they have any claim to inheritance. I've done that sort of thing many a time before.'

Anthony's temperature rose and he mopped his brow with a handkerchief he pulled from his jacket pocket. How dare Crane? Coming here had been a mistake after all, and Anthony almost stood, but he felt committed now. He couldn't escape what he had chosen to do, otherwise the questions would gnaw at him. What harm could it do to find out more about Ruth? Her background, where George was. He had tried to ask her himself, but she had always changed the subject. He had intended to enquire about Anna too, but Crane had derailed the conversation.

'No, not at all,' he said, biting down his temper. 'Nothing like that. The boy has been evacuated, but I'm not sure where.'

'Evacuated? Hmmm.' Crane was silent for a long moment that seemed to drag on as the sun disappeared behind the blinds, plunging them into further gloom. 'And is the child your son? The mother won't tell you where he is and you wish to find him?'

'It's not that, no. But it's complicated. I'm sorry, it's difficult to explain and would take rather a long time. Longer perhaps than it would for you to find the information. There's also a young girl we rescued from the streets, the only name we have is "Anna".'

'I understand completely, Mr Lloyd. Luckily for you, I deal in complicated. And may I ask, what is your relationship to the woman?'

Anthony wasn't sure how to respond. He didn't know the answer himself. Why had he come? How exactly did he expect this to help things? He should have been more direct with Ruth, asked her what was going on.

'We, err, we live together.'

Crane's beady eyes looked at him. They stayed still for an awkwardly long moment, like he was trying to fully understand Anthony's answer.

'I see,' he said, at length, in the kind of tone someone used when they were judging. 'I don't usually take on domestic cases, but as you say this one is a lot more complex. What's the boy's full name? And what other descriptors can you give me to identify them? Do you know anything about when he was evacuated that may help me? Any details that you can give me, Mr Lloyd, will help to expedite this case.'

Anthony didn't know why he hadn't thought that Crane would want George's full name, but for some reason he was reluctant to give it to him. It was as if he was betraying the boy, giving him up to an enemy. All Anthony wanted was information, he didn't want to lead Crane to Ruth or George and he didn't want the investigator to speak to Ruth about this. He expected the man to be subtle, but Ruth was an intelligent woman and she would notice someone following her. Anthony struggled in his seat, wanting to wipe the sweat from his brow. It was too hot in that room. How could a man like Crane stand it? Anthony's hands balled around the arms of the chair to support him.

'I think this may have been a mistake.' He rose, knocking over a pile of papers at the foot of the desk. 'I apologise.'

'It's quite all right, Mr Lloyd.' Crane stared at him. 'Please do sit down. It's quite ordinary to have doubts about engaging the services of someone such as myself, but we might as well discuss how I can be of help. Take as much time as you need, my next appointment can wait.'

'No, no, no. It's not right. I've said too much. I shouldn't have come here.'

Crane stood as Anthony backed towards the door. He started to move around the desk, but Anthony held up his hands as if he was trying to ward off an attacker.

'Please forget everything I've said.'

'It's clearly been a traumatic experience. When you've had a chance to think about it I would be happy to help. I'll make sure the boy is safe.'

Anthony almost ran out of the door, without saying a further word. He half expected Crane to follow him. There was something about the man, despite his size, that was oppressive. He was used to people taking his word and unused to disagreement, or he made sure that those who disagreed with him would not do so again. Anthony had seldom had dealings with such men before, and he knew then that he wouldn't be back. Despite what Crane thought.

Anthony had made a terrible mistake, but he hoped he had stalled it enough that it didn't come back to bite him. He had come to care about Ruth deeply, and he did not want to hurt her. As he pushed open the front door of the building past the protesting secretary, the daylight hit him like a spear. Blinded, he put his arm above his eyes to shield them and stumbled along the street, trying to regain his composure. He didn't know where he was going, but somehow he would find his path. He had to, for Ruth and George's sake.

# Chapter 37

'She's not well, Anthony.' Ruth was furious, but she couldn't really place her finger on why. Was it simply because she was concerned for Anna? Or was it because all of this was keeping her from her pursuit of Patrick and George? She had still come no closer to finding her son.

'What do you mean?' He came around the kitchen table, and crouched down beside Anna. He tucked a curl of her hair back behind her ear while she scrunched up her shoulders and balanced on the balls of her feet. 'She seems perfectly fine to me.'

Ruth decided not to answer, not while the girl was still in earshot. It wasn't fair to talk about her as if she wasn't there, but Ruth also didn't want to concern the child any more than she already had. Ruth wondered whether she wasn't just looking after Anna because she missed George so much. She needed to do something good, something honest to salve her conscience. If only she could explain that to Anthony, without giving everything away.

'Why don't you run along upstairs and play, sweetheart?' Ruth opened the kitchen door for Anna. She only hesitated for a moment, looking for a shallow nod from Anthony before she ran out of the room with a giggle. She had become more joyful the past week or so, but Ruth was still concerned she wasn't coping with what had happened to her.

'I don't think she has been eating and she's been living out on the streets. There's something wrong with her.'

'I see.' Anthony leant against the worktop and regarded her with those deep eyes, in the way he always did when he wanted her to carry on talking, as if he was eager to take it all in and didn't want to interrupt her train of thought.

'I don't just mean the stress of being left on her own, having to fend for herself at that age. I think something medical as well. We should take her to a doctor.'

'First things first.' He held up a hand. 'We need to establish who she really is, whether she has any family left in the city. Next of kin, that sort of thing. We can't just take her in like a stray pet and think that'll do. There may be someone looking for her.'

She fixed him with a stare. How could he be so blind? Anna was suffering and her health was far more important than anything else at this stage.

'I can check the registers,' he continued. 'If she knows her full name then there will be some kind of paper trail.'

'I think we should take her to the doctor first.'

'You do, do you?' He smiled and shrugged his shoulders.

'Yes.'

'Then I suppose I'm defeated.' Sometimes it could be infuriating how easily he gave in to her. She wanted him to fight sometimes, to come out of his shell, but he always let her win. 'Should I take her, or do you want to?'

'I'll go,' she said. 'She feels safer with me.'

He grumbled, but nodded all the same. She hadn't meant it as a criticism. Like him she was trying to be kind, but her words always came out wrong unless she wrote them down.

'This is the address of the doctor I went to regarding my heart,' he said, jotting down an address on a scrap of paper from one of her notebooks on the kitchen table. 'He's thorough and less expensive than some of the others.'

'That's good.'

'Of course, I'll help with the costs. Don't let him fob you off.'

She stroked his cheek, trying to open up to him. Wanting so desperately to embrace him.

'You don't have to, I brought her into this house. She's my responsibility.'

He grabbed her wrist, not unkindly.

'She's our responsibility,' he replied, the browns of his eyes blazing, then hugged her. 'As we are each other's.'

*

'She has shingles, amongst other things, Mrs Lloyd. Really, she's in quite a poor way, but she's strong at least. A lesser child would be stuck in bed, but she's resilient, for sure. I can give you some idea of the kind of remedies she needs, but I'm afraid it will cost you a pretty penny.'

'Actually, it's Mrs Holt.' She looked down at her ring finger, remembering she still wore the ring that bound her to Peter. Anna was distracted by some of the doctor's charts and was busily trying to read them. The surgery on Hope Street was larger than she had been expecting, and she was worried that Anna would run off to play in its halls. Surprisingly Ruth herself had never had reason to visit such a place.

'I do apologise, Mrs Holt. I had presumed as Mr Lloyd sent you, but my mistake.' He was tidying up his tools and washing his hands in a small sink in the corner before coming back to the expansive desk, which he kept his paperwork on. 'About the payment?'

'I have money,' she replied, stalling any further discussion. She wanted Anna to get better, that was the most important thing. She knew she was fortunate that she could afford to make such decisions, when so many in this city wouldn't have had the opportunity, but at least it allowed her to do some good for a child who had no one else. 'Whatever you need, I will find the money.'

*

Ruth put the letters back into the box and covered it up with the little black notebook. She had come upstairs, leaving Anna to play with Anthony so that she could find the money they needed for the doctor. She would ask Anthony to take it around and get the medicine, then she could work out what else she was going to do. Then the letters had distracted her. They had been arriving more regularly. Some were brief with nothing she could discern as any kind of usable detail or instructions, whereas others had clear messages. The former, she had guessed, were designated as part of the disguise. If anyone were to read them, then they would see them as the innocuous, meaningless letters they were. Each time she read one, her appetite disappeared and she had a feeling in her stomach as if she needed to be sick. Every time the letterbox creaked and another envelope fell onto the carpet, her heart thumped in her chest. It was even more fraught now that Anthony was living with her, now that they were acting like a couple. She had been stupid to let him get too close to her, but then one didn't decide these things, they simply happened.

It was a strange feeling, and she didn't think she would ever get used to the fear of not feeling completely in control of her own life. She was under no illusions that as a woman she had never really had much in the way of control, but as the days drew on, she felt her grip lessening and lessening. She was but a puppet now, in the control of her German masters. She hated them for it, and they didn't even know her.

But she had made her decision. It was now or never, and her son was more important than anything else. She pushed the box back into its hiding place. It was a risk keeping it under the floorboards in the bedroom they often shared, but she could think of no other place less likely that Anthony would spot it. She climbed down the stairs, wincing at every angry thump. Anna was sitting at the kitchen table sketching on a piece of scrap paper. She was surprisingly good for her age, and Ruth was sure that given the opportunity she would develop into an incredible artist, if that was who she wanted to be. Anthony was watching her, apparently deep in thought.

'I've been down to the record office,' he whispered to Ruth. 'Anna's parents are reportedly dead in a raid. She was listed as missing, and there's no next of kin. The poor thing's alone.'

'That's settled then. She's not alone, she has us, and I'm not volunteering anymore.' Ruth didn't even look at him as she spoke. She moved things around the kitchen that didn't need to be moved, as if making space, but really it was just something to occupy her while they had this conversation.

'What do you mean?' He didn't raise his voice, but the concern was clear for all to hear. 'I thought volunteering meant a lot to you? What's changed?'

He sat down at the kitchen table, next to Anna, waiting for Ruth's response.

Still, she wouldn't look at him. She knew she didn't owe him an explanation, but he wanted to know, to try to understand why she had made this decision. She knew that he felt it was through volunteering that they had met, that it meant something to both of them, and it did. But how could she explain that wasn't why she was quitting?

'Why?' he asked again. 'Although I have to admit, there is a part of me that's happy that you'll be safer at home, or in a shelter. It's become a constant worry, when a raid's on, that you're out there somewhere risking your life for others.'

'Oh, but I suppose it's okay for you?'

'I didn't mean that.'

She waved him away, she wasn't angry with him, not exactly.

'I just don't have the time anymore,' she said, dropping some plates into a bowl of water with a clatter. Apparently, she had decided to clean everything, even though Anthony had accepted that as one of his roles around the house. It was a welcome distraction, and a way to focus her thoughts. She could tell him everything, but then what would he think? She would lose him for good, she was sure of it. No, she had to have another reason. Eventually she looked at him, as she had run out of plates to throw into the bowl.

'Anna needs someone to look after her, we can't just leave her on her own. Not again. Work at the newspaper is taking its toll, we have so much to do.'

He nodded, and she could tell he still didn't really understand how that could have changed, but thinking better of asking. She frowned at him. What was he thinking, truly?

'Look,' she said. 'I know you want to help out and your work as a warden is very important, but we women don't really do much. It's not like making tea and handing out sandwiches really helps anyone, does it?'

Now she was full on lying, but she couldn't help it. She was trying to protect him, wasn't she?

'It keeps spirits up—'

'I just felt like it was a waste of all our time,' she interrupted him. 'And now we've got Anna to think about. She doesn't have a family, for goodness' sake. She's made a home here and is starting to settle. Losing another family would absolutely destroy that poor girl. No, that's all there is to it, it's not up for debate. I've made up my mind.'

'I agree. But Harriet can look after Anna.'

She ignored his last comment, knowing she couldn't explain it.

'I wasn't asking you to agree, but good. You should do after all. We have to look after our own through all this.'

He looked as surprised as she was at her own words, but it had been one of those days. At least she had made her decision and she was going to stick by it whatever he thought.

# Chapter 38

The postman had been and it had become a challenge to see which of them could get there first. In the early days it had been a bit of fun, but now it seemed as if desperation had crept in on Ruth's part. Today, he had got there first and picking up the pile, he noticed a letter had come for him. He still wasn't used to receiving letters to this address, and when he did it was invariably bad news, so this time he turned it over and looked at the return address. He almost dropped the letter; it was from Crane.

Anthony wasn't expecting the man to get in touch, but he had to admit, things weren't getting better. Ruth was acting strangely, and it wasn't just that she was out at all hours, they both were, but he felt like she wasn't telling him the truth. He didn't know everything about her family, had decided it was better not to ask. There were times when he felt he should have done, but he wasn't sure that it would get rid of the sick feeling in his stomach every time he thought of her life before they had met. She hadn't stopped volunteering yet, but he was sure that it was only an excuse for whatever else she was up to.

For a second he thought about simply burning the letter, but he wouldn't be able to do it without Ruth or Anna noticing. They had such little fuel for a fire, and anywhere else they would see. Should he simply take it out into the street and discard it some other way?

No, some kind neighbour would return it to him without realising what they were doing. He had no choice but to read it. He took it into the living room where he would be alone for a few minutes, and deposited the other letters on the table.

He ripped open the letter and read the contents, his heart sinking with every word. Most of it he knew, but there was one line that surprised him when he got to it.

*She has missed many of her volunteering shifts, as reported by the section chief, with no explanation given.*

It didn't make sense. Ruth had told him that she was giving up volunteering. Unless, she still wanted the uniform to sneak around for her journalism, or something else. He read it two more times to make sure that he had got it right, then crumpled it into his jacket pocket. It barely took him four strides to march into the kitchen.

'Are you sleeping with another man?' he asked. 'I know we're not married and well, things are complicated, but I didn't think you would swan off with some other chap, like some kind of . . . some kind of . . . I don't know.'

'What on earth, Anthony? What's brought this on? And how dare you!' She threw a tea towel to the counter and turned to him, her eyes wide with what he presumed was anger. Thankfully Anna was upstairs, but there was no doubt she would be able to hear their raised voices.

'Of course I'm not sleeping with anyone else. Is that truly what you think of me? That because I'm a socialist I just fuck whoever I want? Really, Anthony. I thought better of you. I've trusted you more than anyone this last year, more than my own family, and this is how easily you can think I would go off with some other man? Is that the kind of woman you think I am?'

'No, I mean, I didn't think so, no. But I . . . I don't understand what you've been up to.' He couldn't tell her about Crane, that was too much of a betrayal. 'You're not volunteering anymore. None of this makes any sense.'

'But what does that have to do with you? It's my choice, and I wasn't doing any good. I told you all this.'

'What about everything else? Where is George?'

She hesitated and he thought he had caught her out. Not that he wanted to, he wanted her to tell him that he was wrong and that he was being stupid, but she didn't.

'What do you mean everything else? There is no everything else, and George is safe away from the bombs living with another family. I miss him dearly of course, but it's for the best.' Her voice broke then and he knew she was being genuine.

'I'm sorry,' he said. 'I guess that even after everything we don't really know each other that well.'

'No, and I suppose that's all my fault as well, isn't it?'

'No. No, it's not. This damned war.'

'Listen, I don't want to argue with you. We're both exhausted. Why don't you go and calm down somewhere? Go upstairs and see to Anna. And we can talk later.'

He didn't say another word, but took her advice. The letter was burning a hole in his pocket and he needed to dispose of it. He had no wish to read it again, it would only cause harm and he should have never read it in the first instance. Instead of going to Anna, he trudged up the stairs and went into the bedroom he had recently started sharing with Ruth. Anna was best left on her own when he was in this mood, and even though her laughter would make him feel better he felt as if he would only traumatise the child. A lie-down would be the best option. Already the scant winter light was disappearing from the room.

He sat down on the bed and undid his shoes. As he leant down to remove the first shoe the floorboard wobbled and tipped to the side. Something in the cavity glittered and he reached down with both hands to pull at the floorboard. It came away with a wrench and he almost pitched back onto the bed. The object was a small wooden box, poorly painted with a black metallic lacquer and a lid that only fit at an angle. He lifted it out and wondered whether it had been misplaced. He placed it on the bed next to him and the lid slid off as the box tilted on the quilt, revealing its contents. A few of the items were keepsakes, but there were other things, sheets of paper bundled together. He went to replace the lid, but caught himself. He picked up one of the bundles, knowing already that he was breaking some kind of code, but unable to stop.

There were a number of letters addressed to Ruth. At first he thought they were from Peter, but the postmark was not what he had expected, and they had all been sent since he had had been lost. He wanted to read the letters, but that would be a betrayal of her trust. He had already gone too far by looking in the box. She wasn't aware that she knew of its existence, and he had only meant to have a quick peek and see what was so important. He turned the letters over and back again, thinking, then let them drop into the box.

A small, leather-bound black book spilled out of the box as he tipped it. With careful hands he set the box back down on the bed. He wasn't sure what he was doing, but curiosity compelled him. The book had fallen onto the floor between his shoes, and he bent down to pick it up. There was a separate piece of paper sticking out from between the pages and from its bent end he wasn't sure whether it had been like that before the book had fallen, or whether his actions had dislodged it. He dropped the notebook back in the box and stared at it.

It was as if it was calling to him, begging him to look inside. The first few pages were blank, and then the pages were filled with scribbling as he flicked through them. None of the symbols on the page made any sense; it was like no book he had ever seen before. It was some kind of codebook, but there was also an occasional word in some other language than English. There were marks and corresponding symbols. It was exactly the kind of thing someone might use to send hidden messages. Perhaps it belonged to George, a childhood toy, or Peter, but he doubted it.

He heard footsteps on the landing, but rather than pushing it back into the box and hiding it quickly under the bed, he held it up.

'What's this?' he asked Ruth as she walked into the bedroom, knowing the answer already, but wanting to fill the silence. Even still, he dreaded her response, hoping that whatever she said would still his beating heart and soothe his burning imagination. For a long moment she just stared at him, as if weighing up her thoughts. He could feel his heartbeat grow louder in his ears. Her hands jumped to her mouth and her eyes widened again.

'It's not what you think,' she said, but she had lost the conviction of earlier. Her voice had broken. Those five words were not exactly what he had been expecting, but then what did he expect her to say? She had been keeping secrets from him. She had no obligation to tell him everything, but he had hoped that he meant more to her than that. It was a silly thought, he knew, but he couldn't help it all the same.

'Well, I don't really have any idea what you must think. But I can explain everything if you give me a chance. I didn't have any choice.'

Anthony shook his head, signalling he wanted her to stop. He wondered where the lies started and where they ended. Was Ruth even capable of telling the truth? He had been right about journalists all along. His first instinct upon meeting her had been correct and he should have listened to it. Journalists couldn't be trusted, they had their own agenda and would betray everything to achieve it, and yet he had fallen for her. He had thought she was different, that despite their reputation she was one of the good ones, the journalists who wanted to try to make a difference. She had changed him too, helped him to become a better version of himself, be more considerate, more compassionate, but all along she had been lying to him, keeping a dark and terrible secret. And it was worse than he could have possibly imagined, telling by the small details he knew, with his imagination filling in the rest. He didn't dare ask her to tell him more, he feared the answer would be even worse than he had imagined, but he did so anyway. He had to know.

'What have you done?' he asked.

'What I had to.' A steely resolve entered her voice, punctuating each of her words. 'They didn't give me much choice.'

'Go on,' he said, forming his lips into a thin line, a gesture he made automatically that signalled to his pupils he was serious.

'I'm sorry, I didn't want to drag you into this.' She took a step closer to him, but he pulled back first one step then another. It didn't feel far enough, but he wanted to hear the rest of her story. It was like watching the flames of a burning building, he couldn't drag himself away. Morbid curiosity fuelled him.

Ruth looked at her feet, her brow wrinkled and her voice dropped to a whisper. 'They have George,' she said, and at first Anthony wasn't sure that he had heard her correctly.

'What? I thought he had been evacuated?'

She looked up at him and there were tears in her eyes. 'I made that up. If I hadn't then I would have had to tell you what had happened. They took him while Harriet was looking after him, I—'

'I don't care about that.' He wasn't sure whether he was more angry at Ruth for her lies, or at them, whoever 'they' were, for kidnapping a small child and using him as a bargaining chip. Right now, he decided, it was the former. 'You've been lying to me for months, probably since we met. How could you? How did you think that I wouldn't find out?'

'I should have told you sooner,' she said, her speech becoming quicker and ragged. Her breaths were as short as the words she forced out. 'I'm sorry.'

'I'm not sure that would have made any difference.' He couldn't even look at her. Instead he stared over her shoulder fixing his gaze on the clock on the wall. 'It doesn't change what you've done. What you are. It's not just that you lied to me, it's that you are a lie yourself.'

He couldn't believe the words that were coming out of his mouth. He had never spoken like this before, but this was what Ruth had brought out in him. It was all her fault, she had created these lies when maybe he could have helped her. What hurt the most was that she didn't seem to trust him. He had come to trust her, despite his better judgement, had come to love her, and yet she couldn't trust him. What had he done to make her doubt him?

'You're not really explaining yourself, Ruth. I've given you a chance.'

'I know,' she replied, holding her head in her hands again and standing still in the doorway. 'I'm sorry. Truth is, I don't really know where to start. It's complicated.'

'Isn't it always? But I realise now that I don't really know you at all. I moved in with you and we became a couple, but I know next to nothing about who you are.' He stood, and pushed past her to the door. 'I should leave.'

Ruth grabbed at his arm, firmer than he had ever felt her grip him before.

'Please, don't. Please,' she said. 'Don't go. I can explain everything.'

# Chapter 39

Ruth let go of his arm, realising that she had made a mistake. She had wanted to feel closer to him, to hold him back, but it would only make him angrier.

'Please, just wait,' she said, hating the pleading in her voice. Everything had happened so suddenly and the careful planning she had done in her mind for this very eventuality was ripped to shreds in seconds. She could explain parts of it, but the whole story would take time, and she wasn't sure it even made sense to her.

She realised that he was waiting. 'Did I ever tell you my grandfather was from Austria? He hated the Nazis, but even still this country treated him like he was one. The government put him in a camp, twelve men to a house and beds of straw. As his mind went, they left him there to die.'

Anthony sighed, the closest she would get to seeing that compassion she knew he was capable of. 'What's this got to do with what you've done?'

'I'm getting to it, but please, I need to start at the beginning.'

He nodded, an acknowledgement of sorts, and she wouldn't waste the opportunity he had given her.

'It made me want to hate the government, but that's not the point. My family are Austrian, that makes them the enemy, whether they are Nazis or not. My brother-in-law works for Lord Derby and the War Office. But I can't tell you all the details. What you need to know is that a man used it against me. He took George away when he was with Harriet. And he made me do it.'

'Made you do what? You're still not making sense.' He pushed past her to the wardrobe and took his suitcase down from on top of it. When he dropped it onto the bed, she knew she was quickly losing her chance to convince him, to ask for his help.

'I was born in Austria, Anthony. He used that against me to make me pass him information.' Surprise marred the edge of her words as she had not expected to say them. She had never told anyone her background before and it had thousands of connotations. Was she also now Anthony's enemy? 'I've lived here almost my entire life. I don't *think* of myself as Austrian. I'm British. But I had no choice. He made me a spy, to get George back.'

She looked at him, pleading with him to say something, to understand what she was going through, but what could he possibly say to her?

Anthony parted his lips to speak, but only a faint murmur came out. He was still between the suitcase and her.

'At least that's what people will call me,' she continued, when he remained silent. 'It's not like I had a choice. I didn't wake up one morning and think, oh today I shall be a spy. It's not like that at all. And I'm not even a particularly good one. I don't want to do it. But he has George and so I have no choice. I've become a sort of messenger for the Nazis and I hate myself as much as you do right now.'

'You have no idea,' he said, and those words cut her more sharply than any knife could have done. She stifled a sob, and plunged on.

'I even thought that maybe I was doing the right thing helping the Germans, that I was somehow making amends for my grandfather's death. But he would have hated it, if he had really known what I was up to. Of course I had told him, but he was too far gone to truly understand. I think he thought it was some kind of story, a book I was writing or something. He needed me too and I failed him. All because of this man, this Patrick who has George. Don't you understand? I'll do anything to get my son back! I lied to them too. I gave them false information. You have to believe me, I was trying to do the right thing.'

'I don't believe you.' She knew he was angry, that he was trying to show her just how angry he was. 'This is some kind of joke, a story you've made up. You're making fun of me and I don't get it. Haha. You've been playing me from the start, since we met. Now tell me what's really going on.'

'I haven't, I swear to you. George was only taken in October, we've known each other longer than that.'

'I can't believe this.' He started taking clothes from the wardrobe. He didn't have much, but each item gave her a stab of pain as he threw them on the bed. 'George has been missing for four months, and you haven't told me? Why didn't you ask for my help? You may be a traitor, but I would have listened!'

'I didn't want to hurt you. I couldn't bring you into this. They made me break everything I believed in, but I couldn't do that to you. You didn't deserve that.'

He scoffed, and pushed the wardrobe shut with a bang.

'What I deserved,' he said, 'was the truth. You didn't trust me enough to confide in me, and now you're trying to pretend that it was all for my own good. It doesn't hold water.'

'I know it sounds crazy, but what would you have done if they'd taken Marc?'

'How dare you bring my son into this? I'm going,' he said, pushing a pair of crinkled trousers into the suitcase and tying it up. He snatched it up as he stomped over to the doorway. Ruth stood by, her mouth hanging open but no words coming out. She expected him to turn around, but he wouldn't look at her, he refused to look at her. She understood completely. She had got everything wrong. What could he possibly say? She wished he wouldn't but he had no choice. She had betrayed everything he believed in, betrayed his country, and he had to leave. She was not who he thought she was. He couldn't be associated with her anymore.

'I'm sorry,' she called after him, but he didn't reply. A second or so later the front door slammed shut. Ruth stood there, her body shaking, trying to will the tears away, before she fell to the bed and wrapped herself in darkness. He was gone. They were all gone now.

# MARCH

# Chapter 40

*Monday, 10 March, 1941*

Ruth was so tired. It went beyond physical exhaustion, she was tired in her brain as if it no longer worked. Her skull felt numb and her eyes were foggy, and no matter what she did she couldn't clear them. Turning on the tap in the kitchen sink, she splashed water on her face. She worried that it was a waste, but she had to do something to shake this feeling. It was like she had gone to sleep and had not woken up properly. Anna was playing upstairs and the thumps as she jumped around sent jolts of pain into Ruth's head like a migraine.

She wanted to just go to sleep and never wake up again. Maybe if she did, the world would right itself and people could get on with their lives. She wouldn't be able to hurt anyone again, or let them down. She would have had a bath, but wasting water was selfish, and she had run out of washing-up liquid with which to wash her hair. She had grown used to the chemical smell that it gave, but now the matted strands of her hair smelt like sweat and dust.

Harriet took a hold of Ruth's hands as she reached for the tap again, stopping her with a gentle tug. Ruth couldn't remember when the woman had come back into her life, but a distant part of her was grateful she had. It had been in one of the first few days after Anthony had left. She had walked in without knocking on the door and taken over where Ruth couldn't. Without her, Ruth would not have been able to function at all, let alone take care of Anna, that poor sweet girl.

'Come on now, love,' Harriet said as she led Ruth to the table. She couldn't remember whether she had thanked Harriet or not, but something in the back of her mind told her it was time to forgive and rebuild that bridge.

'Thank you,' she said as she sat down and let her hands fall onto the table. They were red raw from scratching, and the ache came vaguely into her mind for the first time since she had caused the damage to herself.

'You know,' Harriet said, putting the kettle onto the gas ring, 'they're the first words you've said to me in months.'

She rooted through the cupboards, looking for tea, then finding a tin at the back, put what was left in the pot.

'Have to make do with what we've got,' she said, in between humming a tune to herself. It was one of the show tunes, but Ruth couldn't remember which. She knew vaguely that she should reply, but couldn't find the words.

'Got any milk?'

'I think there's some on the cold slab,' she replied, wanting to get up and help, but pinned to her seat with fatigue.

'Nah. I checked there. And all I could find in the pantry was an empty tin of that Carnation evaporated stuff. It must have done what it said on the tin.'

She cackled, but when Ruth didn't return the laugh, she turned to look at her.

'Come on,' she continued. 'You can't go on like this. It's not you. You were always a woman of action. You were always the one telling me not to let things stand and fight for what's right. A cup of nice . . . erm . . . weak tea will fix ya up no end.'

She poured the now hot water into the pot and let it steep. Somewhere in the distance an air raid siren burst into life. Ruth had almost forgotten that sound, but now she rose to attention like a stray dog hearing a tin of food being opened.

'Damn it all,' Harriet said, raising her voice. 'Will we ever have peace?'

She marched over to the table and helped Ruth to her feet.

'Anna?' Ruth asked.

'Don't worry, love. I'll look after her. You do what you've got to do.'

Ruth hadn't told Harriet that she had stopped volunteering, but seconds later they were all out of the door, Harriet holding Anna in her arms. The girl was scrunched up into a ball, and Ruth wanted to hold her to her, reassure her, but something had awakened in her, finally. Harriet took off in the direction of her own home to round up her family, but Ruth went back inside to change into her overalls. She hadn't returned them yet, in the hope they would still get her where she needed to go.

# Chapter 41

Everywhere Anthony looked people stared back at him through the pouring rain. Even if they had been facing away from him their bodies turned as if on a pivot, following his path as he walked past. At least he had thought he was walking, but as he felt the pressure of their gaze on him he realised he had almost been running. No wonder they were looking at him. They were like marionettes on strings, their blank faces turning to him, full of judgement. Was this how it felt to be led to the gallows? The dismissal, the blankness that they had already made up their minds? If you were not a patriot, then you were a traitor. That was what they all thought.

He screwed his eyes shut, so hard that it was almost painful. It was the least he deserved. He tried to control his breathing, but it came in ragged jerks. He could still see their blank stares behind his eyelids, feel them pressing in, ready to destroy him at any moment. Slowly his breathing slowed and returned to a regular rhythm.

When he opened his eyes again he was alone on the road. The figures had been a part of his imagination, something within himself that had broken down. He had heard of soldiers experiencing traumatic situations and suffering from shell-shock, but he had never thought anything like that could happen in civilian life. Was he sick?

His skin felt warm to the touch, but he had never really been sick in his entire adult life. Maybe once or twice as a child, the usual growing adaptations of childhood, but he had never experienced anything like this.

The figures had been real. He had felt as if he could have reached out and touched them, felt the resistance of their bodies. Somehow, his mind had become broken.

The weather was appalling, the rain was falling sideways as the typical Merseyside wind blew against it, but it matched his mood. Everything had taken a turn for the worst. He had thought that his life was improving, but it had been a lie.

As he stepped under the arch, Lime Street station was surprisingly busy given that it was wartime. Anthony himself had little cause to catch a train in the last couple of years, and other than those going to see evacuated family members, he couldn't think of many reasons for these people to be travelling. Visiting London to go to the West End and watch a play seemed like a ridiculous idea, and they had perfectly good theatres here in Liverpool. Of course, they had been advised that they were to travel only if it was absolutely necessary.

Some might complain about feeling trapped in their city as if it were some kind of island in the North West, yet he couldn't help but remind them there was a war on. For the most part they were safer at home, and any unregistered absences only made the rescue work more difficult. If someone was down in London visiting family and their warden didn't know, then they may have to send rescue men into their building to look for them, putting the men at risk for no reason.

There were only two trains in the platforms. He didn't know whether services had been cut due to the war, or whether he had just missed them. Everything had been a last-minute affair and after hastily packing his only belongings into a bag, he had found himself at the station without a plan, with little more thought than returning to Wales to see his family. He hadn't seen them in years, and there was a large part of him that just wanted to go, to forget everything about this city he had come to call his home, to return to his real home. Yet, as soon as he had stepped under the large brick arch that formed the entranceway to the station and provided a place for taxis to drop off their fares, he had stopped in his tracks. A taxi driver tooted his horn at Anthony and poked his head out of the window to shout something. Anthony didn't hear what he said, his attention was fixated on the locomotive in front of him. Its steam billowed around the platform, like fog on the Mersey, and it reminded him of the aftermath of the bombings. He could almost imagine the flames licking up to engulf the engine.

In the past he had enjoyed train journeys, but now a fear welled up inside him that he hadn't imagined he could feel. It wasn't fear of the train, it was a fear of leaving Liverpool, of leaving his life behind. Leaving Ruth behind.

'Damn!' he shouted to no one in particular and didn't apologise as more heads turned his way. An elderly woman tutted and shook her head, then walked away, a nervous young man carrying her suitcases in her wake. He couldn't do this. He had been so sure before, had finally found conviction in his actions, which had drawn him out of his own self-pity, but now he was here in the station it was nothing but a bad idea. He couldn't move. Fear gnawed at his stomach; he had made a mistake that night. When he had left Ruth he had not been saving himself from her lies, but damning them both.

The cabbie swore at Anthony and drove his taxi up on the kerb to pass him. He only caught a glimpse of the driver's shaking fist as the black shape passed. Anthony almost swore back, but the taxi was gone before he could think of what to say. He found himself back out on the street. His legs apparently had a will of their own.

'Oh, God. What have I done?' he asked the heavens as the rain fell, running in streams down his cheeks. He was one step away from shaking his fists at the sky, but that was too dramatic even for him. Besides, people were watching and he didn't want them to ask any questions he wouldn't have been able to answer. The less people noticed him the better.

He had thought Ruth was an honest woman, a good woman, but she had been lying to him since he had met her. His first impressions about her had been right, but still there had been something else, some instinct that had driven him closer to her, into her embrace. Even given what had happened, that could not have been wrong. It was clear that he didn't yet have the full picture. He needed to give her a chance to tell him her story, the full story, not leaving out any detail. Only then could he be absolutely sure. When he had sorted himself, he would have to go and speak to her. He had to give her a chance, otherwise what was it all for?

APRIL

# Chapter 42

*Thursday, 3 April 1941*

Anthony had to go back, there was no other choice. As he ran towards her house, all the thoughts of the last few months ran through his mind, and he realised that leaving would be one of the biggest mistakes he had ever made.

He needed to see her, not just wanted to. It was a physical need like hunger, a need like no other he had experienced before. He felt that if he didn't see her soon then he would suffocate, as if he couldn't breathe. He needed to breathe her in, smell her perfume, her warmth and compassion. It had all been a terrible mistake, and while he was still angry, he knew that he could overcome it, if only he could see her, if only they could talk. He would listen and he would understand, he was sure of it. His pace quickened as he thought about seeing her. If only he could bend space itself and be with her now. His dear Julie would have said he read too many novels, but for the first time since he had met Ruth he didn't feel guilty at the thought of his late wife. He knew deep down that she would be urging him on now, driving him back towards Ruth. 'It's for your own good,' she would have said. 'You can't live without her.'

He had built it up in his head. All that nonsense about her not being able to trust him, not caring enough about him to confide in him, had been a mistake. She hadn't told him precisely because she did care about him, she had said that she hadn't wanted to drag him into it and that had been true, yet he had been a bullheaded idiot. Julie would have scolded him for being such a fool. Ruth was dealing with one of the worst periods of her life, and he was too stupid to see it. If anything happened to her then he would never forgive himself.

He ran across the road, knocking over an empty can with a rattle, and didn't even stop to compose himself before knocking on the door. It took a long time before it opened.

'We need to talk,' he said as Ruth stared him from the narrow opening. Her skin was paler than he remembered, but there was still the light behind those eyes that made his heart race.

'Yes,' she replied, opening the door a little wider.

He tried not to show that he had expected her to say more than that, and realised that his own words were caught in his mouth. He took two deep breaths.

'Here?' she asked, apparently trying to fill his silence.

'Anywhere,' he replied, with more certainty. 'It doesn't matter to me, as long as I'm talking to you.'

She led him into the house. It was almost exactly the way it had been when he had first found it and there was barely a mark of his having lived there. The blackout curtains were across the windows, and Ruth stood with her arms crossed facing him across the narrow living room. She was waiting for him to talk, when he wanted to hear what she had to say. Things weren't going how he had imagined they would, but then things never did where Ruth was concerned and that was part of what he enjoyed.

'I don't understand this world,' he said, breaking the stalemate. 'Not one bit.' He moved around the living room, closer to the sofa, so that he wasn't stood in the doorway and he could see her more clearly in the faint light. 'Every time a piece of the puzzle seems to fall into place something comes along and shatters the illusion again. It just doesn't make sense. There's no rhyme, no reason to it.'

'I know what you mean.' Her voice was a whisper. 'I can't seem to take control of my life at the moment, everything keeps going wrong.' She winced, then looked up at him, those familiar eyes wide and open.

'But you were something good,' he continued. 'Something worth fighting for. I want to know what happened. I want to understand, truly I do.'

'I don't know what to say,' she said. 'After last time . . . I spoke and you left, and I thought you would never come back.'

He thought he could see a tear roll down her cheek. 'I came back, I'm here now. This is me, you know me. I'm here and I want to listen. I wasn't listening before, but it was a mistake.'

She uncrossed and crossed her arms again, this time swapping arms. He wanted her to sit down, to ease some of the pressure on them both, but it was probably better this way.

'When Peter was killed, I felt like everything was falling apart. Then you came along and made me smile. But things weren't that easy, I didn't want to drag you into this. Enough people have been hurt already. Keeping it from you was the only way to protect you.'

He could have crossed to her, consoled her, but now wasn't the time. 'But I was a part of it,' he said. 'Whether you wanted to drag me in or not, I was your partner, I was living here and I was a part of your world. Tell me what happened, so I can understand, so that I can work out how to fix it.'

'When we met George was at home. He wasn't supposed to be, we had sent him out to the countryside in Cheshire. He was supposed to be safe there. But he didn't like it. He missed me and the family whom he was living with were not keen on having him there. So he decided to come home. If he hadn't then this would never have happened, but I can't blame him for that.'

'They would have found another way to get at you, I suspect. This was never about George.'

'Yes, you're probably right, but that doesn't make it any easier. I did think about having him evacuated again, but when that ship was sunk with all those women and children on, I couldn't risk it. I wish I had now. He might be safe somewhere else. I might even know where he was.

'That's the worst thing about all this for me. I have absolutely no idea where my son is.'

Anthony could empathise, he wasn't entirely sure where Marc was even if his son wrote to him from time to time. He couldn't really say where he was, and even though Marc was an adult he imagined it was similar to how Ruth was feeling. He didn't want to say anything, though, or it might feel like he was trying to diminish her emotions. He simply said, 'I understand.'

Ruth carried on. 'I had Harriet look after him when I was working, and as you know I was probably working too much. I wanted to do my bit to help the homeless, try and get the authorities to acknowledge the problem, but we had bigger problems with the censors. And well, the volunteering, I just had to, didn't I? You know what I mean, you're the same. I couldn't help myself. I couldn't hide in a shelter and wait for someone else to make sure people were all right. I had to do it myself. I always have to do it myself.'

Tears rolled down her cheeks again and she scrunched her eyes closed, as if trying to force them back inside.

'You could have come to me,' he said, knowing truly that she couldn't have. It would never have worked that way.

'What could I have said? Help, Anthony, I'm a spy? You would have run quicker than you did when you found out, and I would not have blamed you. I couldn't even go to my family.'

He didn't know what to say to that. She was right and he knew it. He didn't realise that he had moved closer to her when he had seen her cry.

'I've missed you,' he said.

She nodded and swallowed deeply, and he knew that she felt the same way. But things were not back to normal yet, if they could ever return to normal. All he knew was that he couldn't stop staring at her, he was mesmerised. Just like the time when he had first seen her.

'We can keep talking and talking,' he said, 'saying these words over and over again, but what really matters is our actions. You lied to me, and I don't know if I can trust you.'

'I know.'

'The problem is, I really, really want to trust you.'

'Then I need to tell you something else. No more secrets.'

He nodded, bracing himself.

'George isn't my son. At least, not biologically. I still love him just as much as I would any of my own children.' She reeled off the words as if defending herself in front of a jury. 'Peter and I adopted him. We wanted to do something good, rather than bringing another life into this world.'

He laughed. It was deep in his stomach, but not mocking or ridiculing her, an honest laugh.

'I know,' he said. 'I expected a secret far worse than that.'

'You do?' Her eyes widened. 'How could you know? George doesn't know.'

'Well, I suspected. He doesn't look anything like you or the photographs of Peter. And well, don't blame her, but Harriet rather confirmed it for me.'

She hit him on the arm and he just laughed again. 'How could you not say anything? I was so worried about telling you!'

'I didn't think it mattered. George is your son as far as we're all concerned, and that's all that matters. We just need to work out how to get him back, and then we can put all this behind us.'

'I don't think putting this all behind us will ever be possible, but I'm willing to try. I've been trying to get him back, but I don't know how.'

They were only standing a breath apart now, he could smell the faint floral perfume she used. He closed his eyes, taking a deep breath.

'I'm a complete idiot.' He paused, wondering how to go on. He knew that no words could accurately describe what was going through his mind. 'I always have been.'

It was pathetic and he knew it, but Ruth just looked at him, waiting in that manner of hers. She had come to know that he took his time to say what he really meant and he appreciated that she would wait. He had become familiar with the considered, patient look she gave him.

'My Julie always used to laugh at me.' He noticed Ruth wince as he mentioned Julie's name, and regretted bringing her up immediately.

'I'm sorry.' He paused again. 'At the time I thought Julie and I were good together, but in truth we were growing apart towards the end. I don't want to grow apart from you. Not ever.'

There was a long moment before Ruth said, 'You don't need to apologise for anything. And if it helps, I don't think you're an idiot.'

'Oh, but I am.' He knew he was labouring the point, but he couldn't help himself. 'I always used to rush into things without thinking. Then I became too cautious. It's hard to find balance.'

Ruth nodded, as if she knew what he meant.

'I cared too much about things, and people. Then I stopped caring at all. Somehow it felt safer that way, like I was protecting myself.'

Not only was Anthony an idiot, he was also weak. A man shouldn't be airing his thoughts like this. But Ruth had changed him, helped him to open up, and he was all the better for it.

'I shouldn't have let myself fall for you. It was my responsibility, and my fault. I shouldn't have been so stupid, and I should have known better. It would have been better for both of us.'

'Anthony,' Ruth tried to interject.

'No, I'm sorry. I'm an idiot, and I've put too much pressure on you. It's not fair.'

She placed the palms of her hands on his cheeks and pulled him towards her. They kissed, pushing against each other as if it could make up for the gap that had arisen between them. Wrapping his arms around her waist, he held onto her as their lips pressed together. As always, she tasted sweet and warm, a taste that couldn't be recreated in anything else. After too short a time she pulled back and glittering green eyes looked up at him.

'I like the beard,' she said, rubbing the palm of her hand around the new growth.

'Thanks.' If he was honest, he had come to like it too, but he had never thought of himself as a beard wearer. He wondered whether it made him look older. His hand joined hers, feeling the texture of her skin.

'I'm sorry for everything,' she said, caressing his face with her thumb. 'I wanted to tell you for so long, but I didn't want you to think badly of me. I realise how silly that was, but I wasn't thinking straight.'

'I can't imagine having to make those decisions, to feel so alone. But I'm here now, to lessen the burden.'

'So what are we going to do?' She pulled back in his arms and he let go of her. He wanted to reach out and pull her closer to him again, but he knew that now wasn't the time for that.

'What can we possibly do? We have to go to the police, or the army or someone. Tell them that George has been kidnapped and you're being forced to procure information for them.'

She pulled back further, mouth open. 'We can't. I can't. They'll arrest me, Anthony. They won't stop to understand, they'll just treat me like a traitor. I'll hang.'

'There are compassionate grounds.'

'No. Don't you remember what they did to my grandfather? Do you think they'll be even that compassionate with me? We can't trust them. We can't trust anyone.'

'Then we take matters into our own hands. There're people who can help.'

'Who else can we trust not to turn me in?'

'Harriet came to see me. She worked out that I had found out what happened. She wanted to make amends and help you find George.'

Ruth frowned. 'What did you tell her?' she asked.

'I said she would have to speak to you, that it wasn't my decision whether to involve her or not. I didn't think you trusted her anymore.'

'She's been helping me while you were gone, but I don't know. She has a family of her own, I can't expect her to risk everything for me and George.'

He pulled her closer again. 'Look,' he said. 'I love you.'

He kissed her again, wanting to feel as close to her as possible.

'I will do anything I can to protect you, to help you, I promise you that. I can't lose you again. I'm not sure that it'll work, but I'll do my best as a warden to track down George. I'll ask my friends for their help.' For a long time he had come to terms with the thought that nothing in this world could have a happy ending, but perhaps he had been wrong. Maybe he just needed to rethink what happiness really meant for him and not focus on the ending, but the journey itself. Given everything that had happened, that thought was difficult, but it also gave him a sense of hope he hadn't experienced in a number of years. 'Together, we'll get George back.'

# Chapter 43

**Wednesday, 16 April 1941**

A newspaper slid across the desk where it was thrown. Ruth didn't look up from the words that now lay at a crooked angle in front of her. 'What's this?' she asked, wondering what she had missed; it wasn't today's issue.

'Oh, I think you know.' She recognised the man's voice immediately. Sam, one of the other reporters. It didn't take her long to look up to his face. His grey and dark green outdoor clothing would have helped him blend into a crowd, if only he wasn't the only one in the room. There was absolutely nothing remarkable about his features, except for a frown above his eyes that looked as if they intended murder. 'The Treachery Act, have *you* read it?'

'I think you'd better explain, Sam. I'm at a loss.' She spoke quickly to cover her shock.

She had barely had any dealings with Sam, maybe the occasional hullo, but she couldn't remember having anything approaching a conversation. He preferred to be called Samuel, but she wasn't able to break the habit. Nor could she recollect any of her colleagues mentioning him more than in passing terms. She had no idea whether he was married, had a family, where he lived, or any of the other things that one expected co-workers might know.

She slowly pulled the wad of papers she had been writing on towards her, straightening it. The paper came with it, its bold head-line making her stomach sink. She had forgotten she had helped Roger to write the article when the act had been introduced. Her vision swam. She coughed, hoping that Sam hadn't noticed her reaction.

'If you've got an issue with my writing, then you should probably take it up with Rupert.' She pushed the paper aside.

'Bitch.' His nostrils flared and she could feel his breath on her face as he stood over her. 'Don't try and play games with me. I'm not as stupid as the rest of these idiots. I won't let you get away with it.'

'Bugger off, Sam, and wash your mouth out. I've got no idea what you're talking about and I don't really care. If you're annoyed that Rupert has been giving me more articles than you, then take it up with him.'

She returned to her work, but still the shadow over her wouldn't leave.

'I followed you. I've always been suspicious of your motivations, but I followed you and you're working with some German.' He whacked the rolled-up newspaper into his hand with each word as if it was some kind of truncheon. 'Giving him messages. You stole shipping information from my desk. Calling you a spy would be giving you too much credit, you're sloppy.'

The pen fell from her hand, an annoyingly inconvenient admis-sion of guilt. She didn't dare let him see her face, but she had no choice.

'Leave me alone. You're mad.'

'You're one of those fifth columnists, aren't you? A British Nazi.'

'Nothing of the sort. You have no idea what you're talking about.'

'Yeah, I've heard about your lot. I thought they'd locked all of you up last year. I never trusted you. That's why I've been following you for months. What is it, you want German rule over here? You want us all to be speaking your language? Is that it? Never really thought of yourself as being British? Well you can go back there, you know. Never wanted you here anyway.'

Before she knew what she was doing she stood and grabbed hold of Sam's shirt. She pulled him closer and balled her other fist. How did he know?

'Shut up,' she said. 'You have absolutely no idea what you're talking about. I'm no Nazi. I'm as socialist as the rest of you, and I would never throw my lot in with those fascists. If you don't understand something then don't jump to conclusions. Ask the person in a rational fashion.'

He grinned at her and looked down at her fist.

'I knew you were as guilty as sin. And if you don't tell Rupert what you're up to, then I'll tell him for you.'

\*

'Anthony, he knows.' She burst into the house, having barely stopped since running out of the office. He was in the kitchen cleaning some plates, which he put down as soon as he took one look at her, then came over.

'Who knows?' he asked.

She was glad he was perceptive enough not to ask what she was talking about. Her mind raced. He took a gentle hold of her arms and led her to a chair by the table. She didn't feel like sitting, but he was probably right. She was too worked up and needed to relax.

'Sam. He's a reporter at the paper.'

'And? Did he react as badly as me?' He attempted a smile, but she wasn't in the mood.

'Worse. I don't really know him at all. It's the first conversation I've ever had with him, but he knows. He knows that I've been passing on messages. He followed me.'

'Does he know what they're about? Anything like that? Or does he just suspect?'

'I don't know. We didn't exactly discuss the details. He said I had to tell the editor or he would.'

'Well, that's something.'

How could he be so positive?

'If he's only thinking about the newspaper, he's not thinking about the police. It makes things easier.'

How quickly Anthony had begun to talk like a co-conspirator, like he was a seasoned spy. She loved him for it; he had come this far, all for her. Deep down, she knew he still had some doubts, but he was determined to show that he cared about her.

'But what if the editor goes to the police? They'll hang me. Didn't you hear about that woman in London who was writing letters to some German lord? They didn't even give her a chance to deny it before . . .'

She ran a finger across her neck. Anthony paced the room, one hand on his chin and the other on his waist.

'We need time to think, to work out what we're going to do.'

'We don't have time. We need to make a decision now.' She took a hold of his arm, pulling him towards her so that he would stop pacing. 'I could tell Patrick what happened. Let him deal with it? If they want me to keep working for them then they'll need to protect me too.'

Anthony ran a hand down her cheek and stared deep into her eyes as if he had not seen her in months.

'They'll kill him. They're not going to play games. They're not

337

above kidnap. If they can coerce you into doing what they want then they won't just go, have a nice talk with him and ask him to forget it. They'll make sure he never speaks again.'

'Then maybe that's what we have to do.' She pulled away from his grasp. This wasn't a time for being intimate. Their lives were at risk.

'No, Ruth. No. You don't mean that. This isn't Sam's fault. He's now mixed up in this and the best thing we can do is leave no trail for him to follow.' He went to fill the kettle. 'No, we have to come up with a better plan, one that means Sam can't prove anything and we can get to Patrick.'

'Then we have to turn this against the Nazis. Capture Patrick somehow and clear my name. We have to get George back above all.'

'I've been thinking about that.' He lit the gas hob and placed the kettle on top. He was giving himself time to think, but she wished he would just get to it. 'You see to destroying all the evidence, I mean all of it. Codebooks, letters, whatever you have.'

'But what do I do if Patrick demands I do something for him?'

He took a hold of her again. 'You no longer need them. We're going to find him, we're going to put an end to this, but first we need to make sure no one can trace it back to us. We *will* find George, and the kidnapper will never bother you again.'

# MAY

# Chapter 44

*Friday, 2 May 1941*

Anthony didn't know how much breath he had left, but if he stopped to think about it he would surely collapse. It was incredible how used to running he had become as a warden, how fit he had become, and yet due to the lack of food he had become weaker. He was as broken as the buildings around him, and even without the inferno raging across the city he would still feel as if his lungs were burning. At the beginning of all this, he had thought that the regular exercise would help, make him fitter, but like so many other things that had been a lie. They had all been through too much since then and he wasn't sure their bodies would ever recover.

As he crossed the road there was a shape like a carpet rug, a brown furry mass that warped and twisted on the ground, and it took him a long moment to realise that it was a plague of vermin, swarming together. He had never seen so many rats together in one place, in fact he couldn't even remember seeing more than one at a time. He ran towards them, determined that they wouldn't get in his way. They were escaping the flames, while he was running headlong towards them. For the first time in his life he realised that even rats were probably smarter than him. He longed to reverse his run, to return to Ruth and get her out of this, but the number of bombers in the sky suggested it was going to be a heavy raid and they would need his help. He had left her with Anna, with a promise they would make good on their plan to find Patrick. He had asked his fellow wardens to keep an eye out for anything suspicious involving a small boy, but he couldn't say much more than that.

The warden station was housed in an old shop. The windows had been blown out during a previous raid, and rather than replacing them, they had simply boarded them up with strips of cardboard and tape. No one needed to see into the station, but it gave the interior a gloomy brown hue. Anthony flicked an electric torch on, no longer caring whether the light could be seen or not. If the Luftwaffe couldn't spot the city with the fires they had started then they never would. One torch was little more than a pinprick of a star in a sky of burning suns.

Inside, the control station was empty. Anthony had never seen it without at least one person manning it, but such was the situation they found themselves in. There were too many fire incidents and not enough volunteers. He had overheard someone calling for fire engines to move up to Bootle, but they couldn't spare them from the city centre. He had been dispatched to call them back, or call in more fire engines, or whatever he could do. The commands by the chief warden had been so frantic that all Anthony had understood was they needed help. He'd come as quickly as he could to the station, the only telephone he knew of in the area.

'Hullo? Hullo?' He whacked the receiver against the wall a couple of times, but when he placed it back to his ear there was still no hum to signify a connection. He didn't know what he had expected, but it was worth a try. Sometimes things just worked if you gave them a gentle push.

Another warden ran into the station, Justin, he thought. He was just as out of breath as Anthony and he took a few deep breaths before he could say anything.

'It's not good,' he said. 'The lines are dead. I saw one of the exchanges on fire. The others are probably in the fire zone too.'

'Then we need to send someone over to the fire station and send a message.'

The other warden came over to the table and picked up a dispatch pad and pencil. He waved them at Anthony. 'It'll have to be either you or me.'

'Where's everyone else?'

Justin gave Anthony a look that had become too familiar. 'We've lost most of the shift in one way or another. Most of the firewatchers were lost in explosions and collapses, and those of us that are left are, well, as exhausted as the two of us.'

Anthony walked back over to the doorway, and poked his head outside. The sky was an orange glow, and the steady rumble of explosions suggested it wasn't going to go away any time soon. He turned back to the other man. 'They need as much water as they can get. The whole city is on fire.'

'You're not wrong there.' Justin was panting like a dog.

'Then, I'll go,' Anthony said, heading back out into the flames again to risk his life for others.

*

'Ruth, Ruth, wake up.' Anna squirmed beside her. 'It's daylight.'

Ruth pulled herself out from underneath the stairs. Ruth and Anna had taken to hiding under the stairs when a raid was on. They had pulled blankets down there and made a little cubby hole to hide in. The two of them had decided it after Anna had refused to go into a shelter, and Ruth had agreed. The shelters were no safer anyway. Too many had taken direct hits, losing everyone inside. Ruth had taken the blankets in when, during a thunderstorm, she had found Anna hiding under there. The rocking of the nearby streets had almost shaken them to sleep.

She had had to pull back the blackout curtain to get a proper look. An orange glow framed the curtains, giving the impression that it was indeed daylight. Only it wasn't. Liverpool was on fire, as far as Ruth could see. The skyline resembled a gigantic coal fireplace, roaring in the hearth. It looked as if there couldn't be a building left that wasn't on fire. She pulled Anna close to her. There was no way the child could fully comprehend what she was seeing, but Ruth knew how bad this was. George was out there somewhere.

She turned, vomit erupting from her mouth without warning. Specks of yellow liquid covered the floorboards and the room was filled with the smell of burning sulphur. She only had a chance to let go of Anna before being sick again. This time her stomach was empty and it became a dry retch that scratched at the back of her throat.

'What's wrong? What's wrong?' Anna asked, but Ruth couldn't answer. She wanted to hug Anna closer, reassure her, but she was covered in the contents of her own stomach and wasn't sure whether she would feel the need to be sick again. It was as if all the worry, pain and fear had been building up behind a dam that had suddenly burst. She heaved again, her throat becoming raw. George was out there somewhere, afraid, and she was here doing nothing. Had she subconsciously given up on trying to find him? Had Anna filled the void that he had left?

She needed a glass of water, then she would work out what she was going to do. Grabbing a glass from the sideboard, she turned on the tap, but only a faint trickle dripped into the sink. An explosion must have burst a pipe. She screwed her eyes shut, and made a decision in that moment. There was only one place that she thought Patrick could be. Lewis's department store. Her stomach almost heaved again, but she was determined. She had to try, George needed her. She marched back to the front room, took one look at Anna and heaved her up into her arms. Anna was getting heavier. Good, she was eating more and recovering.

Out on the street the noise was louder, something like a never-ending firework display. Just when you thought there was a moment of quiet, another crack sounded followed by a rumble. Most of them were far away, but the crackling of flames made Ruth feel like she was in the middle of a raging fire.

A few minutes later, she was knocking heavily on the door of an Anderson shelter. It took time for it to open, the owners likely surprised at what they were hearing, then a familiar face appeared through the crack. 'Harriet, I need you to take Anna,' Ruth said, handing Anna over to her friend. As soon as she let go, the sirens gave out a loud wail, a single continuous note. It was the all clear. Ruth cursed to the surprise of both Harriet and Anna.

It was too late. She would try again tomorrow.

# Chapter 45

'Ruth! Ruth? Where are you?'

Anthony rushed into the house, fearing the worst. The city was ablaze and he had left Ruth and Anna alone. They had been all right the previous night, but he couldn't leave them again. He should have known better. They were all he could think about. In the kitchen he found Harriet sipping a cup of tea while Anna played with a toy on the surface of the dining table. Ruth was nowhere to be seen.

'Where is she?'

'I couldn't stop her.' The teacup shook in her grasp as she drifted into silence.

'Harriet.' He seldom raised his voice, but all he could think about was Ruth.

'Lewis's. She's gone to Lewis's. To find *him*.'

He felt sick in a way that he couldn't explain. It wasn't in the pit of his stomach, but higher up as if he had trapped wind, but as he hadn't eaten in a few hours it couldn't be that. Nor was it hunger. Typically he could go for hours without a bite to eat and not even feel the slightest pang. No, this was another kind of sickness. What was she thinking? There was no way he would be there. Her lack of sleep and desperation must have taken over.

He turned away from Harriet. He couldn't stay in the house any longer, he had to get to Ruth. He had to find her. Sweat broke out on his brow in spite of the cool evening air. The windows of the house rattled in their frames as a bomb landed somewhere to the south of the city. It wasn't close enough yet to see, but it was close enough to feel. The glassware and photo frames left out in the house shook as the bombardment drifted closer. He stepped out into it, pulling the door shut behind him.

To the south of the city the Wirral burned. It was as he imaged an active volcano might look. Bright orange flames licked at the sky, buildings burning, shells of lives and livelihoods. He felt for the people of the Wirral, they had all suffered so much. Still the shrill air raid siren wailed through the night sky. The Germans were on their way, and he should be on his.

He felt like he was always running of late, only these days he was running towards something rather than away. He followed the stream of people. They didn't acknowledge him either, all wrapped up in their own private anxiety.

The city centre had become a mess of red and blackened-grey masonry, thrown around as if by some giant child, unhappy with their toys. Once proud buildings were now nothing but ruins, a stark reminder of what the city had suffered. How many people had lost their homes due to the bombing, he wondered as he passed former shops and houses. How many had lost everything?

He couldn't bear to think about it all. Even though he knew it wasn't his responsibility he couldn't think about losing his family, not again, he had to do something to save them. Anthony wondered whether he was going to find her in time. He would follow her anyway, even if that meant putting himself in danger. He would do anything. Anthony didn't have much in this world, but would fight every step of the way for what he did. He couldn't lose his family, not again.

He didn't think he had seen so many aircraft before. The sky was filled with the silhouettes of German bombers, backlit by the waxing moon. He was transfixed by the image, before the whistle of dropping bombs brought him back to the present. The Germans had decided they were going to wipe out his city, pummel Liverpool from existence, and he was caught in the middle of it.

He dropped his eyes from the sky, he didn't want to see his own death coming for him, and ran. If the Germans were dropping that many bombs, then even the shelters wouldn't be safe, he thought. None of them were safe. Still, he had to find her, somehow get her away before she made a mistake. The kidnapper wasn't even in the building. He couldn't be. Not in this. He had to stop her, before she got hurt, find George and then get them all out of the city. Maybe he could steal a car and drive them out. Somehow he had to get them all out. They couldn't stay here amongst the bombs and the ruins of their lives.

It wasn't just the Germans that were killing them, the city was too. It was like a prison, its terraced houses the walls, the River Mersey a deadly wet barrier at its heart. During the last year, he had felt as if it was closing in on him, threatening to crush him, and it was only getting worse. He had felt trapped, under constant pressure that their time was short, that the next raid could be their end. They needed to escape the city. The sickness rose up in his stomach again, almost doubling him over.

The crump of bombs exploding drifted through the night, somewhere off in the distance across the river. Far enough away, for now. His ears were sore from the cacophony, and he knew it wouldn't let up any time soon. He ran down Myrtle Street, noticing how different it had become. A shop from which he used to buy sweets for Marc when he was a child was an empty shell, its owners gone. There was a single abandoned car pulled up outside as if its driver had stopped for something, but the street itself was empty. He didn't see another soul, not even a volunteer. He was utterly alone, with only the flames and smoke to keep him company. He turned another corner and all of a sudden the sky was as bright as daylight.

There was a crash and he was flung to the ground. It took a few seconds before his hearing came back with a piercing ring. The bomb had landed on the roof of a nearby shop, levelling its upper floor. He pressed a finger to his temple to push away a headache. It came back damp, but he didn't have time to think about that now. With a groan he hauled himself back up from the rubble and was running again. He was lucky to still be breathing, he realised. He was covered in brick dust and his last good clothes were tattered and torn. His body ached, but he wouldn't give up now.

Anthony turned left onto Renshaw Street. As he ran further into the centre of town, the sky grew brighter with flames. He followed the light like some kind of moth, knowing that it would bring him closer to what he sought. Finally he spotted a group of people at the other end of the road outside the Adelphi Hotel. Some of them came and went in a hurry, but others simply stood and stared, illuminated by the fire at the opposite side of the square. As Anthony ran closer he could see the terrible inferno, but it wasn't coming from the hotel. There was a chain of people passing water between them.

Across the road Lewis's department store was on fire. Flames licked at broken glass windows as the pressure of the heat broke its way out of the building. It must have taken a direct hit as the building was already engulfed. The volunteers worked to fight the flames, but they were already losing the battle. He marvelled at the damage, feeling an unexpected sense of sorrow as something so familiar, a building no less, literally went up in flames. Its Portland stone facade might survive the flames, but the business was gone. They all knew several people who worked within the building, either serving its many customers, or helping with stock and cleaning. The building itself was a bustling landmark on the way into the city. You knew you were in Liverpool when you saw it.

He thought he heard cries from inside the building, like people in great pain, but he couldn't be sure over the roar of the flames. He pushed through the other volunteers. Their eyes didn't follow him, too intent on the burning edifice in front of them. He wanted to avoid awkward questions, but he couldn't stop now. It wouldn't make sense to them, even though they risked their lives nightly to protect others. It wasn't the city he was trying to protect now – it was too late for that – but those who were close to him, those who meant the world to him.

A shape caught his eye. At first there was nothing that separated them from everyone else, but somehow he recognised them. There was something familiar even in the dark night filled with flickering light. He couldn't say whether it was the outline that was familiar or the way that they moved, but it was unmistakable. Instinct drove him after that shape as they disappeared into the building. He followed, stepping into a run again. But he only got a few feet before strong hands held him, almost pinning his arms behind his back as if he had been arrested.

'No,' said a voice near his ear. Not loud, but commanding all the same. 'No, lad, it's too late. You don't want to go in there.'

Anthony realised then that a moan had escaped his lips, the sound of longing, pure animal fear at the sense of abandonment the world had dealt him. He didn't know if he could control himself, if not for the man holding him back. He didn't know what he was going to do, his entire life had disappeared within that burning building. With a struggle, he pulled himself out of the arms that held him and ran into the flames after the woman he loved.

# Chapter 46

The flames ripped up out of the now open roof of the building, licking at the sky like angry tongues. Where the windows had been there were now bright orange and red patches, which hurt the eye to look directly at. Ruth could feel the heat, but it wasn't the pleasant comforting warmth of a nice fire, but the searing heat of pain. Going inside the building had been a bad idea, but Patrick was in there somewhere. He had to be. She couldn't take any more.

The fire had started while she had been looking inside, sneaking around under the cover of darkness. She had seen the glow through section doors, but hadn't realised at first that it came from inside the building. She had been surprised how quickly it had spread. At first it had taken over the department, then the way out had disappeared in a wall of flame. She coughed as smoke blocked her throat.

The fire service would be along at any minute, alerted by someone no doubt. That was, unless they were already tackling another conflagration in a different part of the city. Ruth edged through the first floor, but a burst of fire pushed her back. Everything was a wall of noise, and she couldn't hear the people outside. There shouldn't have been anything dangerous in the department store, but something was causing the flames to erupt and spit at the onlookers. Perhaps there was more than one unexploded bomb lying inside those walls.

She was thankful that no one had been working inside the store at this time, but now many more people would lose their livelihoods, many of whom couldn't afford to do so. As if the city hadn't already suffered enough.

The flames licked at the walls. There was no way out. The heat was intense and increasing by the second. Ruth kept turning, expecting some way out to present itself, but the smoke got into her eyes, blinding her. She had to wipe the back of her overall sleeve across her face to clear the tears. She pushed closer to where she thought the door was, her arm still raised ahead of her as if it would stave off the flames. A jet of flame pushed her back into the middle of the room and her sleeve caught fire. She attacked it with her other hand, trying to extinguish it. The pain in her palm was fleeting, but nothing compared to the melting of her sleeve against her forearm. If she didn't get out of there soon, it wouldn't matter anyway.

A lintel beam fell from above a doorway, bouncing before its flames joined with those of the wall. The inferno burned brighter for a moment with its added fuel, before the two melded together. Ruth thought about making a run for it through the gap, in a minute the wall would come down and there would be no escape.

She thought she heard a voice in the distance, calling out. Was she that close to death? She remembered the pistol in her pocket and realised that she might be able to use it as a hammer to break down the wood that had fallen across her exit. It was hot to the touch.

Orange flames played around the doorway, like some kind of fiery portal beckoning her on to the underworld. Where she belonged. A shape appeared through the flames.

'Help,' she croaked. 'Help!'

'Ruth?' The replying voice was distorted by the cracking of the flames. A second later the shape was pushing its way through the burning door, kicking planks of wood out of its way. It called to her again, that avatar of her fate, before it resolved into a familiar figure.

'You again?' She attempted to smile, but she was too weak.

'Where did you get a gun? Never mind, it doesn't matter.'

Anthony took the gun then lifted her in his arms, like a mother cradling a baby. Together they stumbled down the stairwell one step at a time. Bits of burning timber fell around them as they descended into hell. A final sheet of flame burst out at them, the inferno's last attempt to keep them within its grasp before they fell from the building out into the cool evening air.

Anthony fell on top of her as they collapsed to the street. It reminded her of that first time they had met, but this time she was glad. She had never been happier to see him than she was now. It was all she could think about as she passed out.

## Tuesday, 6 May 1941

St Luke's Church burned, the flames reaching up and out of the roof. There was nothing they could do for it now as the wooden joists had been consumed by the fire, and the stained-glass windows had begun to melt under the heat. In parts the glass had shattered and lay on the grass around the building, but there would not be enough pieces left to repair them when this was done.

Anthony had left Ruth at home to recover, after she had refused to go to hospital, and even with his own wounds he could not sit still. As soon as he'd shown up on duty, a fireman he knew had called to him for help. As if the last two nights had not been bad enough, the Germans were attacking again.

'Here we go again!' The fireman jumped up onto the running

board of their engine and thumped on the wheel arch to indicate they were ready to go, but the vehicle didn't move. Its engine idled as those around looked on confused. Anthony knew that the man had once been a taxi driver, and was sure that he had given him a lift across town before the war, but neither man truly knew each other. Even after all their shared experiences there were many strangers in this city.

'There's no way we're getting through there, lad. It's chocker.'

The driver pointed along the road at where a row of houses had collapsed during the previous night's bombing. It had been so intense, there had been no way to clear it all yet. Anthony had heard that the rescue men hoped the bombing would relent tonight so that they could use the time, but early signs were not encouraging.

'Back up and go around the back street.'

'No chance, lad. The whole area's a wreck. If we burst a tyre then we'll never get this thing going.'

Anthony moved closer, but before he could say anything the fireman turned to him.

'Here, what about your lot?'

Anthony looked around him; there was a group of rescue men collecting tea from the mobile WVS van, along with Sid and two or three other wardens dotted about, waiting for the call. He nodded at the fireman.

'We're on it. Two ticks,' he said, walking back to the station, shouting as marched. 'Come on, you lot, we've got a road to clear. Grab your shovels and pickaxes and let's get going.'

Despite the dropping of their shoulders and their downcast looks not a man grumbled at his order, nor did they rebel at being told what to do by a warden. They had all come along together in this, and roles and ranks had become a thing of the past as far as the work was concerned. Anthony would throw his lot in with them any time they needed it, and they all knew that.

Sid gave Anthony a shovel-like pat on the back, and he almost pitched forward, but managed to regain his balance. 'No rest for the wicked, eh?' Sid smiled down at him. He was always a reassuring presence in these situations.

'Oh, that reminds me.' He stopped for a second. 'Almost forgot, idiot that I am. You know you were asking after that illegitimate child?'

Anthony stopped dead in his tracks. That wasn't exactly what he had said, but he had allowed the others to come to their own conclusions.

'Well, I saw the strangest thing earlier today. I was up by the women's hospital and there was this boy being taken out of a car. I couldn't get a proper look, but the whole thing looked off. He was calling out for his mummy, and I'm sure he said the name Ruth. Sure of it.'

Anthony couldn't breathe. 'The women's hospital?'

'Aye.' Sid nodded. 'Only a couple of hours ago.'

Anthony could have kissed him. 'I'm sorry, lad! I've gotta go,' he called over his shoulder. He ran, as Sid and the others called after him in shock. It didn't matter what they said, he only had one thing on his mind. He passed the bombed bank on Bold Street and around the corner. The city was still alight, but he made his way easier on foot than he would have done if he'd had a vehicle. In minutes he was back at the house, rushing in to find Ruth.

She'd covered up the dressing on her arms with a long blouse, and was apparently waiting for him when he arrived.

'Women's hospital.' He could barely get the words out, he was so exhausted. 'Sid saw him, by the hospital. Today.'

Her eyes widened. 'Wait a second.' She ran up the stairs and returned a minute later clutching the box of letters and notes. She hadn't been able to destroy it as he had suggested and he could understand, even if it was a risk. She pushed a scrap of paper into his hand.

'Look at this I took from Patrick's wallet. I thought it was the name of one of his women, or something.'

It simply read, *41 Catharine S.*

'How could I have been so stupid? Don't you see? It's incomplete.' She looked up at him, those green eyes still wide. Her lips pursed.

'It's an address,' he whispered. He knew exactly where it was: on the same road as the hospital.

'This is the last house.' She smiled. 'He has to be here.'

# Chapter 47

The building wasn't at all how Ruth had imagined it. In her mind she had seen a broken-down house, one of the ruins left by the bombing, with refuse and other bent household items discarded on the ground around it. She had expected young men loitering outside, looking for trouble and intimidating any who dared to walk past. Ruth had allowed that picture to grow in her mind's eye, becoming an impenetrable castle and the thought had made her heart race. Was that the kind of place they were keeping her son? Not for the first time since the start of the war she wondered just what on earth she was doing. Had the stress of the raids and the bombing, the constant threat of death, caused her to lose her mind completely? But this house looked little different from her own, and she could imagine finding a family living there peacefully.

The bombing still roared across the city, but they had managed to avoid any prying eyes as they ducked down the back streets they had come to know so well when volunteering. Anthony held her hand as they crossed the road, crouching down like soldiers attacking a target. They were almost unrecognisable in their plain clothes and balaclavas, and Ruth could well imagine someone thinking they were being invaded should they be seen.

Anthony turned to her as they stopped at the corner of the house, only the whites of his eyes were visible through the balaclava.

'You go find George,' he whispered. 'I'll deal with the kidnapper.'

'Anthony—'

'Go.' He pushed her away, not allowing any argument.

She was to skirt around the back of the house, while he let himself in through the front door. It was all part of their plan, and it had to go exactly as they had discussed otherwise they would risk being caught. She tried the handle of the back door and it was unlocked as she had expected. It was dark inside the house, but silent. The blackout curtains covered the windows and there were remains of a simple meal on two plates on the kitchen table. She tiptoed, too frightened to make a sound, and worked her way towards the stairs. Her heart thumped in her chest and she was worried it would betray her, so she took a couple of deep breaths before continuing upstairs.

'George?' Ruth tried to whisper, but her voice wavered every time she said his name and came out as a shout. She couldn't help herself, feeling so close to him now that she could almost touch him. And yet, she couldn't find him. She had thought that the maternal instinct women talked about only applied to biological mothers, but even though George wasn't her own flesh and blood she could sense him. He was somewhere in these ruined houses, somewhere close by. Upstairs it looked almost like her own house; there was a door at the top of the stairs and two leading off the other way from the landing. It struck her that if she was to kidnap and imprison a child she would keep them in the room farthest from the stairs. She tried that door first and it was locked. As expected.

'George?' she tried again and heard a shuffling inside. That settled it. She leant back and then forced all her weight against the door. She tried again and this time the door flew open, the lock splintering.

'Mum?' George asked, wide-eyed from his position leaning against the bed.

'Georgie!' She rushed towards him, kicking a stack of wooden toys out of the way, and hugged him tight. He had grown in the last few months, and might have lost weight, but he was alive and well. There was a pile of ration books on the bedside table. They had different names, Stephen Smith, Albert Rogers, but it was clear they all belonged to George. Patrick had been moving him around, and that was why she hadn't been able to find him, until now. It didn't matter, her son was returned to her; he was George Holt again.

*

Anthony carefully climbed down into the basement space that had been knocked between the two houses, and turned the corner. The basement was full of old furniture and luggage, a hoard of pilfered goods.

'Who the fuck are you?' A man was sitting in an old armchair, and he started as he saw Anthony.

Anthony wasn't going to be drawn in, he was done being stupid. 'Names aren't important,' he said. 'You know that as well as I do. You see, I know all about you, and what you do, but I don't know your name, Patrick, but that really doesn't matter, does it?'

'All right.'

The man made to stand up, but Anthony raised the pistol he'd taken from Ruth and tilted his head to show he wasn't going to let the man do what he wanted.

'What do you want then?' Patrick asked.

Anthony moved around the room away from the stairs, all the while keeping his gaze and the gun on the kidnapper. He hadn't expected it to be like this. The other man was almost calm, as if he was used to having a weapon pointed at him, whereas Anthony's palms were sweating and he was sure that if he moved too much the gun would simply fall from his hands.

'You seem to know me, but I don't know you. So what d'ya fucking want, laddie? You come into my house and point that thing at me. If you're going to shoot me then get on and do it, will ye? Cause if you don't, I'm gonna find you and make sure you bleed for this.'

'Where's the boy?' Keep things simple, that was the only way Anthony was going to get through this. For all he knew Ruth may have found him already, but he had to make sure. If he could provide enough of a distraction then he might even buy her more time. That was the most important thing now, that Ruth and George got out of this. It didn't matter what happened to him.

'Oh, so that's what this is about?' He smiled his serpentine grin. 'The lassie has finally sent someone to task for her, eh? Got ye wrapped around her little finger, does she?' He made to stand up again, but Anthony halted him.

'Don't,' he said, simply.

There was a scrambling sound from the stairs. It drew Anthony's attention, but it was a mistake. He felt a blow as Patrick launched himself and tackled Anthony. The gun fell from his grip as he was forced back against the wall, clattering across the floor. They grappled as Anthony tried to force him away. Anthony could smell the beer on the his breath. He was a wiry man, but Anthony was stronger. He managed to push him back into the middle of the room, just in time to see Ruth step in. She took one look at him, then picked up the gun, a grimace crossing her face.

She raised it at the kidnapper.

'Ruth, no.' His voice echoed around the basement.

'It's too late.'

The pistol bucked in her grip, deafening in the enclosed space.

'Kill those who oppress you,' she whispered.

# Chapter 48

'What are we going to do with him?' Ruth couldn't bring herself to use the word 'body', as if it would force her to acknowledge she had killed him. She wouldn't even look in his direction. Anthony had a hold of her and he almost shook her to get her to look him in the eyes, but obviously thought better of it. She didn't want to look at him, didn't want to tarnish his soul with what she had done. Ruth had to bear that guilt on her own.

Anthony stared at her, then shook his head. What choice had she had? Patrick would have come after them. Anthony crossed over to her and took the gun out of her unresisting hand.

'Well, there is something,' he said, his voice seeming so quiet after the crack of the gunshot. 'The rescue men are still working through the ruins.'

He pocketed the gun as she crossed to where Patrick lay. The man smelt of alcohol and the iron-tang of blood. She couldn't bring herself to look at the wound she had inflicted as she tried to move him. 'He's too heavy.' She let his leg drop and looked to Anthony.

'There's enough wood here to go up.' He paused, letting the significance of his words settle. 'No one would tell the difference of one fire from another.'

'We'll have to get out pretty quickly. What if someone sees the flames?'

There was another sound from the stairwell. She had told George to stay upstairs and run away if he heard anything. He came down the stairs now, wide-eyed, and she ushered him back towards the ground floor before he could see what had become of Patrick.

She looked back over her shoulder and Anthony nodded. They both knew what needed to be done. She led George upstairs, through the kitchen and out into the alley behind the house. At some point she would hear his story of what happened here, but now was not the time. They hid in the shadows, while they waited for Anthony to join them.

It was a long few minutes before the dark, hunched shape of Anthony left the house. He reached out for them, trying to find them in the darkness, and when his fingers landed on Ruth's arm, he whispered to her.

'The basement's lit. When they find the house, there won't be much left. There was petrol down there and all sorts. We'd better move away quickly.'

She didn't reply. There was nothing to be said. She grabbed his arm, not wanting to let go of either him or George. From the main road they could see over the rest of Liverpool, down towards the river. The flames burned all along the dock, making the Mersey resemble a river of flame. The conflagration reflected back from the surface of the water, making any navigation from the harbour treacherous. Not that anyone would be foolish enough to try to escape this in a ship. She hoped that all the crew were on land and in a shelter, but she had no idea whether the navy even allowed their sailors such protection. Once upon a time she would have asked Peter, but that thought only brought about a pang of sorrow.

The Custom House was fully ablaze now, its roof entirely gone. The orange glow that erupted from it was like a beacon, lighting up the night-time sky. People would be able to see the inferno for miles, and the Luftwaffe would have a target to focus their efforts on.

Behind them the orange glow of flames wrapped itself around the house on Catharine Street, obscuring the marks of crimes committed in its fiery embrace. Patrick would never cause anyone to suffer again.

# Epilogue

**Summer 1945**

The sand covered the tops of his brogues as he crossed the beach. From here he could already hear the sounds of George and Anna playing, the sounds of children enjoying themselves without a care in the world. His children. It was an odd thought, but they had become a family and he was grateful.

They would laugh at him for not wearing suitable footwear, but these days he would laugh too. He hadn't had time to really think about it. Ruth had taken them off to New Brighton and told him they would be back later. They had left him to have some time alone to work on the new house, but rather than doing that – it could always wait until another day – he had decided to surprise them at the beach.

Before he had met up with them he had stopped at the ice cream man, joining the queue by his little white cart that he wheeled up and down the promenade. 'Two mint chocolate chip, please.' Their favourite.

The cream was already dripping down his hands and he was sure that the breeze was blowing sand into them, but today it didn't matter; today they were free. He would lick the ice cream from his hands after surprising them with the treats.

George was already building a sandcastle, his small body

obscured by the hole he had dug himself, meanwhile Anna was busy throwing tiny handfuls of sand back into the hole, accompanied by bouts of high-pitched giggling.

Anthony was sorely tempted to stand there and just watch them for a while, to take in their joy, but then they would never get their ice creams. He struggled across the sand, the uneven rise and fall of his feet reminding him of stumbling across the rubble after a raid. They could have gone to Crosby Beach, but the sands there were still stained by the wreckage that had been carted out of the city and dumped. It brought back too many memories, memories that none of them wished to recall.

'Anthony!' Ruth looked up at him and smiled as he drew nearer. The surprise written on her face was welcome these days, especially as the pain he had once seen there so often seemed to be waning. Gone was the gaunt, pale face that had taken over early in the war. The man they knew as Patrick had taken an incredible risk by kidnapping George and trying to extort information from Ruth. Anthony wondered whether it had all been worth it, but they had all done crazy things during wartime. And not all of them had ended badly. They had lost too many, but they had found each other.

Ruth looked genuinely happy to see him as she scrambled to stand up from the sand and rushed towards him. Lifting the ice creams gently from his hands she passed them over to the children.

'I had no idea you were coming,' she said. 'I'm glad you did.'

They embraced and he breathed in that now familiar scent of her, reluctant to let go. He felt a splatter on his trousers and looked down, fearing one of the ice creams had ended up there. As he did so he caught sight of Anna, another fistful of sand being raised above her shoulder. She giggled again and let fly. The sand hit his waist and she ran off in the direction of the water.

'Sorry,' he whispered to Ruth as he let go and ran after Anna. The sand made it even more difficult to run, but then, wasn't that part of the fun? If he caught Anna easily then it would be too short, and they couldn't have that.

'Oi!' he shouted after her, but that only encouraged her giggling further. She crouched down and picked up another handful of wet sand, but as he got too close she ran off again, keeping a steady distance between them even though her little legs couldn't take her at any great speed. In truth, Anthony wasn't putting as much energy into running as he might, he preferred to see her excited at the chase. This beaming child was a far cry from the lost, lonely and ill child Ruth had found down a backstreet of Liverpool. Even though she had suffered that terrible tragedy of losing her parents, she was growing, glowing, and he would do everything he could to foster that.

The war might have come to an end, but there was still a lot for them to do. The psychological burden of the bombings had never quite left them, even after the Luftwaffe had turned their attentions elsewhere. What Ruth and he had got up to during the blitz was known only to them. The journalist who had accused Ruth had kept his secret until the end. They had later found out that he had been injured during the May blitz and had other things to worry about. He had moved abroad and they had no idea what had happened to him.

One day Anthony would write a novel about his experiences. He would have to leave out some of the details, but maybe he could subvert them and write obliquely as his hero Wells had done. No one would ever know.

Now that Ruth and he were due to be married, and the war was over, she would never have to worry about her background again. Perhaps one day they would visit Austria as a family, visit her parents, but for now they would work on rebuilding their lives.

George had never spoken of his experiences of being a captive, and they both hoped that his age would allow him to forget that time, but they would never stop watching him carefully, watching and waiting for realisation of what had really happened to dawn. They had all been through a lot, even on the home front, so far from the actual fighting. Anthony looked around at the three of them, taking in each of their smiling faces, etching them into his memory, lest the world fall apart again. If they could stay together, support each other, their unconventional family, then they were going to be all right.

# Historical Note

Liverpool and the Merseyside area was the most bombed area outside London during 1940 and into 1941. Indeed, there are still, over eighty years later, parts of the city where the bomb damage is clear to see: as buildings left standing alone, street-level car parks built on the cleared rubble, or as the bricks and stones still visible on Crosby Beach where they were abandoned.

*The German Messenger* is a work of fiction, but I have tried where I can to show the horrors of the blitz for the people of Merseyside and be as accurate as possible in representing their story. When the first bombs started to fall in August 1940 many children had returned to the city, often called back by their parents who thought that as nothing had yet happened they were now as safe as they were going to be. They were not to know how devastating the Luftwaffe's bombing of the city would be, and this culminated in May 1941 with several consecutive days of bombing that flattened parts of the city.

During the course of the blitz, over 3,800 people were killed in the area, with at least a further 3,400 seriously injured. Many thousands of people lost their homes, as Anthony did, with nowhere else to go. The volunteers worked incredibly hard to keep the city going, and there are many stories of bravery and sacrifice throughout the area. The blitz spirit itself is open to discussion with much of our present-day perspective being influenced by the propaganda that was necessary at the time to keep morale up and prevent, as much as possible, the Luftwaffe's terror tactics having their desired effect. However, people did not always pull together. There are a number of reports in local newspapers of people ignoring the blackout and other rules designed to protect each other, most likely through being paralysed by their own fear or through acts of self-preservation.

The internment camp at Huyton existed, and many German, Austrian, and Italian nationals were kept there in awful conditions, with other similar camps around the country. Many died in these places, with others becoming seriously ill. Only later in the war were they released when the government realised they were no longer a threat to national security.

The blitz was a horrible time for the people of Merseyside, and I hope to have shown you that throughout the novel. Whether it was the lack of appropriate shelter or rationing, everyone faced struggles. Each of the bombing raids in the story is based on an actual raid, with many of the situations being fictionalised versions of true events. But I also hope to have shown that through kindness and love, many people managed to make it through together.

I hope you enjoyed reading.

M.J. Hollows – October 2022

# The German Nurse

**Her past could kill you.**

Guernsey, 1940. As war storms through Europe, Churchill orders the evacuation of all military personnel from the island. Boats ferry soldiers and vulnerable young children to England, leaving their parents and loved ones behind to face the invading German army on their own.

**Her love could save you.**

One of the few remaining policemen on the island, Jack must protect not only his friends and family, but also the woman he loves: Johanna, a Jewish nurse from Germany, whose secret faith could prove fatal to them both.

**Her fate is in your hands.**

When the Nazis arrive, everything changes. Jack is forced to come to terms with the pain and loss of a world re-making itself around him. And then a list of Jews on the island is drawn up, and he must make an awful choice: write down Johanna's name and condemn her, or resist and put his family in immediate danger…

# Goodbye For Now

**As Europe is on the brink of war, two brothers fight very different battles, and both could lose everything...**

While George has always been the brother to rush towards the action, fast becoming a boy-soldier when war breaks out, Joe thinks differently. Refusing to fight, Joe stays behind as a conscientious objector battling against the propaganda.

On the Western front, George soon discovers that war is not the great adventure he was led to believe. Surrounded by mud, blood and horror his mindset begins to shift as he questions everything he was once sure of.

At home in Liverpool, Joe has his own war to win. Judged and imprisoned for his cowardice, he is determined to stand by his convictions, no matter the cost.

Dear Reader,

We hope you enjoyed reading this book. If you did, we'd be so appreciative if you left a review. It really helps us and the author to bring more books like this to you.

Here at HQ Digital we are dedicated to publishing fiction that will keep you turning the pages into the early hours. Don't want to miss a thing? To find out more about our books, promotions, discover exclusive content and enter competitions you can keep in touch in the following ways:

JOIN OUR COMMUNITY:

Sign up to our new email newsletter: http://smarturl.it/SignUpHQ

Read our new blog www.hqstories.co.uk

🐦 https://twitter.com/HQStories

f www.facebook.com/HQStories

BUDDING WRITER?

We're also looking for authors to join the HQ Digital family! Find out more here:

https://www.hqstories.co.uk/want-to-write-for-us/

Thanks for reading, from the HQ Digital team

## About the Publisher

### Australia
HarperCollins Publishers (Australia) Pty. Ltd.
Level 13, 201 Elizabeth Street
Sydney, NSW 2000, Australia
http://www.harpercollins.com.au

### Canada
HarperCollins Canada
2 Bloor Street East - 20th Floor
Toronto, ON, M4W, 1A8, Canada
http://www.harpercollins.ca

### India
HarperCollins India
A 75, Sector 57
Noida, Uttar Pradesh 201 301, India
https://harpercollins.co.in/

### New Zealand
HarperCollins Publishers (New Zealand) Limited
P.O. Box 1
Auckland, New Zealand
http://www.harpercollins.co.nz

### United Kingdom
HarperCollins Publishers Ltd.
1 London Bridge Street
London SE1 9GF
http://www.harpercollins.co.uk

### United States
HarperCollins Publishers Inc.
195 Broadway
New York, NY 10007

http://www.harpercollins.com